D0058958

ONCE MORE WITH FEELING

How dare Brandon Carstairs walk into Raven Williams's life after all these years! The mesmerizing musician had broken her heart; now he was back with a passionate proposition. Were the benefits of a collaboration worth the risk that a reunion could entail? Raven had graduated from the school of hard knocks—but would she ever be able to forget Brandon's lessons in loving?

SONG OF THE WEST

Rugged rancher Jake Tanner was the most irascible and bossy man Samantha Evans had ever met! Though he frustrated her with his demands, she couldn't ignore the electricity in his touch. Samantha had traveled to the majestic mountains of Wyoming in order to help her very pregnant sister. She never expected the long, lean cowboy next door to rustle up dreams of a family of her own.

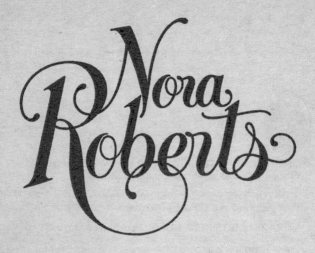

Nora Roberts

ONCE MORE WITH FEELING

SONG OF THE WEST

Silhouette Books®

Published by Silhouette Books New York

America's Publisher of Contemporary Romance

SILHOUETTE BOOKS
300 East 42nd St., New York, N.Y. 10017

ONCE MORE WITH FEELING © 1983 Nora Roberts
First published as a Silhouette Intimate Moments

SONG OF THE WEST © 1982 Nora Roberts
First published as a Silhouette Romance

NORA ROBERTS REISSUE edition published May 1991

ISBN: 0-373-48238-8

CONTENTS

Books by Nora Roberts

Silhouette Romance

Irish Thoroughbred #81
Blithe Images #127
Song of the West #143
Search for Love #163
Island of Flowers #180
From this Day #199
Her Mother's Keeper #215
Untamed #252
Storm Warning #274
Sullivan's Woman #280
Less of a Stranger #299
Temptation #529

Silhouette Intimate Moments

Once More With Feeling #2
Tonight and Always #12
This Magic Moment #25
Endings and Beginnings #33
A Matter of Choice #49
Rules of the Game #70
The Right Path #85
Partners #94
Boundary Lines #114
Dual Image #123
The Art of Deception #131
†Affaire Royale #142
Treasures Lost,
Treasures Found #150
Risky Business #160
Mind Over Matter #185
†Command Performance #198
†The Playboy Prince #212
Irish Rose #232
The Name of the Game #264
Gabriel's Angel #300
Time Was #313
Times Change #317
Night Shift #365
Night Shadow #373

†Cordina's Royal Family

Silhouette Special Edition

The Heart's Victory #59
Reflections #100
Dance of Dreams #116
First Impressions #162
The Law Is a Lady #175
Opposites Attract #199
*Playing the Odds #225
*Tempting Fate #235
*All the Possibilities #247
*One Man's Art #259
Summer Desserts #271
Second Nature #288
One Summer #306
Lessons Learned #318
A Will and a Way #345
*For Now, Forever #361
Local Hero #427
°The Last Honest Woman #451
°Dance to the Piper #463
°Skin Deep #475
Loving Jack #499
Best Laid Plans #511
The Welcoming #553
Taming Natasha #583
°Without a Trace #625

*MacGregor Series

°The O'Hurleys!

Silhouette Books

Silhouette Christmas Stories 1986
''Home for Christmas''
Silhouette Summer Sizzlers 1989
''Impulse''
Nora Roberts Reissue 1991
Once More With Feeling
Song of the West

Dear Reader,

Thinking back, I realize that I began writing romance novels because relationships fascinated me—their variety, their potency, their continuity. After a decade of writing, I've come to understand a few basic truths. Love is timeless. The world needs heroes. And men and women, no matter how much they might squabble, will always seek out that one person who lights the spark.

From my first book to my last, I've tried to tell stories that celebrate those basic truths. It's an enormous pleasure for me that Silhouette Books is reissuing two of my early romances in this volume. I certainly hope it's yours, as well.

Song of the West, a Silhouette Romance first published in 1982, offers you both the rugged and tender as a devoted sister travels to Wyoming to care for her pregnant twin and runs headlong into the cowboy next door. *Once More With Feeling,* my first Intimate Moments book, is a story of two songwriters given a second chance to love as they struggle to make music and heal old wounds.

While I'm delighted to see old friends reach new readers, I'm equally pleased to announce the upcoming publication of The Calhoun Women. In this series, I wanted to try something a little different, with the hope that my readers would appreciate the twist. The Calhoun Women is the story of four sisters and the star-crossed romance from the past that affects all of their lives. The series will be published in all four of Silhouette's lines, beginning with *Courting Catherine* for Silhouette Romance in June. *A Man For Amanda*— my first Desire—follows in July, with *For the Love of Lilah,* a Special Edition, in August. To complete the series, *Suzanna's Surrender,* for Intimate Moments, will be published in September.

I had a wonderful time writing this series, just as I did writing *Song of the West* and *Once More With Feeling.* I very much hope you'll settle down, take a few hours for yourself and enjoy the romance.

All the best,

Nora

ONCE MORE WITH FEELING

NORA ROBERTS

Chapter 1

He stood out of view as he watched her. His first thought was how little she had changed in five years. Time, it seemed, hadn't rushed or dragged but had merely hung suspended.

Raven Williams was a small, slender woman who moved quickly, with a thin, underlying nervousness that was unaccountably appealing. She was tanned deep gold from the California sun, but at twenty-five her skin was as smooth and dewy soft as a child's. She pampered it when she remembered and ignored it when she forgot. It never seemed to make any difference. Her long hair was thick and straight and true black. She wore it simply, parted in the center. The ends brushed her hips and it swirled and floated as she walked.

Her face was pixielike, with its cheekbones well-defined and the chin slightly pointed. Her mouth smiled easily, but her eyes reflected her emotions. They were smoky gray and round. Whatever Raven felt would be reflected there. She had an over-whelming need to love and be loved. Her own need was one of the reasons for her tremendous success. The other was her voice—the rich, dark, velvet voice that had catapulted her to fame.

Raven always felt a little strange in a recording studio: insulated, sealed off from the rest of the world by the glass and the soundproofing. It had been more than six years since she had cut her first record, but she was still never completely comfortable in a studio. Raven was made for the stage, for the live audience that pumped the blood and heat into the music. She considered the studio too tame, too mechanical. When she worked in the studio, as she did now, she thought of it exclusively as a job. And she worked hard.

The recording session was going well. Raven listened to a playback with a single-mindedness that blocked out her surroundings. There was only the music. It was good, she decided, but it could be better. She'd missed something in the last song, left something out. Without knowing precisely what it was, Raven was certain she could find it. She signaled the engineers to stop the playback.

"Marc?"

A sandy-haired man with the solid frame of a lightweight wrestler entered the booth. "Problem?" he said simply, touching her shoulder.

"The last number, it's a little..." Raven searched for the word. "Empty," she decided at length. "What do you think?" She respected Marc Ridgely as a musician and depended on him as a friend. He was a man of few words who had a passion for old westerns and Jordan almonds. He was also one of the finest guitarists in the country.

Marc reached up to stroke his beard, a gesture, Raven had always thought, that took the place of several sentences. "Do it again," he advised. "The instrumental's fine."

She laughed, producing a sound as warm and rich as her singing voice. "Cruel but true," she murmured, slipping the headset back on. She went back to the microphone. "Another vocal on 'Love and Lose,' please," she instructed the engineers. "I have it on the best authority that it's the singer, not the musicians." She saw Marc grin before she turned to the mike. Then the music washed over her.

Raven closed her eyes and poured herself into the song. It was a slow, aching ballad suited to the smoky depths of her voice. The lyrics were hers, ones she had written long before. It had only been recently that she had felt strong enough to sing them publicly. There was only the music in her head now, an arrangement of notes she herself had produced. And as she added her voice, she knew that what had been missing before had been her emotions. She had restricted them on the other recordings, afraid to risk them. Now she let them out. Her voice flowed with them.

An ache passed through her, a shadow of pain buried for years. She sang as though the words would bring her relief. The hurt was there, still with her when the song was finished.

For a moment there was silence, but Raven was too dazed to note the admiration of her colleagues. She pulled off the headset, suddenly sharply conscious of its weight.

"Okay?" Marc entered the booth and slipped his arm around her. He felt her tremble lightly.

"Yes." Raven pressed her fingers to her temple a moment and gave a surprised laugh. "Yes, of course. I got a bit wrapped up in that one."

He tilted her face to his, and in a rare show of public affection for a shy man, kissed her. "You were fantastic."

Her eyes warmed, and the tears that had threatened were banished. "I needed that."

"The kiss or the compliment?"

"Both." She laughed and tossed her hair behind her back. "Stars need constant admiration, you know."

"Where's the star?" a backup vocalist wanted to know.

Raven tried for a haughty look as she glanced over. "You," she said ominously, "can be replaced." The vocalist grinned in return, too used to Raven's lack of pretentions to be intimidated.

"Who'd carry you through the session?"

Raven turned to Marc. "Take that one out and shoot him," she requested mildly, then looked up at the booth. "That's a wrap," she called out before her eyes locked on the man now standing in full view behind the glass.

The blood drained from her face. The remnants of emotion from the song surged back in full force. She nearly swayed from the power of it. "Brandon." It was a thought to be spoken aloud but only in a whisper. It was a dream she thought had finally run its course. Then his eyes were on hers, and Raven knew it was real. He'd come back.

Years of performing had taught her to act. It was always an effort for her to slip a mask into place, but by the time Brand Carstairs had come down from the booth, Raven wore a professionally untroubled face. She'd deal with the storm inside later.

"Brandon, it's wonderful to see you again." She held out both hands and tilted her face up to his for the expected, meaningless kiss of strangers who happen to be in the same business.

Her composure startled him. He'd seen her pale, seen the shock in her eyes. Now she wore a façade she'd never had before. It was slick, bright and practiced. Brand realized he'd been wrong; she *had* changed.

"Raven." He kissed her lightly and took both her hands. "You're more beautiful than anyone has a right to be." There was the lightest touch of brogue in his speech, a mist of Ireland over the more formal British. Raven allowed herself a moment to look at him, really look at him.

He was tall and now, as always, seemed a bit too thin. His hair was as dark as her own but waved where hers was needle straight. It was thick and full over his ears and down to the collar of his shirt. His face hadn't changed; it was still the same face that drove girls and women to scream and swoon at his concerts. It was raw-boned and tanned, more intriguing than handsome, as the features were not altogether even. There was something of the dreamer there, from his mother's Irish half. Perhaps that was what drew women to him, though they were just as fascinated by the occasional British reserve. And the eyes. Even now Raven felt the pull of his large, heavy-lidded aquamarine eyes. They were unsettling eyes for as easy-going a man as Brand Carstairs. The blue and green seemed constantly at odds. But it was the charm he wore so easily that tilted the scales, Raven realized. Charm and blatant sex appeal were an irresistible combination.

"You haven't changed, have you, Brandon?" The question was quiet, the first and only sign of Raven's distress.

"Funny." He smiled, not the quick, flashing grin he was capable of, but a slow, considering smile. "I thought the same of you when I first saw you. I don't suppose it's true of either of us."

"No." God, how she wished he would release her hands. "What brings you to L.A., Brandon?"

"Business, love," he answered carelessly, though his eyes were taking in every inch of her face. "And, of course, the chance to see you again."

"Of course." Her voice was coldly polite, and the smile never reached her eyes.

The sarcasm surprised him. The Raven he remembered hadn't known the meaning of the word. She saw his brow lift into consideration. "I do want to see you, Raven," Brand told her with his sudden, disarming sincerity. "Very much. Can we have dinner?"

Her pulse had accelerated at his change of tone. Just reflex, just an old habit, she told herself and struggled to keep her hands passive in his. "I'm sorry, Brandon," she answered with perfect calm. "I'm booked." Her eyes slipped past him in search of Marc, whose head was bent over his guitar as he

jammed with another musician. Raven could have
sworn with frustration. Brand followed the direction of her gaze. Briefly his eyes narrowed.

"Tomorrow, then," he said. His tone was still light
and casual. "I want to talk to you." He smiled as to
an old friend. "I'll just drop by the house awhile."

"Brandon," Raven began and tugged on her
hands.

"You still have Julie, don't you?" Brand smiled
and held on to her hands, unaware of—or ignoring—her resistance.

"Yes, I . . ."

"I'd like to see her again. I'll come by around
four. I know the way." He grinned, then kissed her
again, a quick, friendly brushing of lips before he
released her hands, turned and walked away.

"Yes," she murmured to herself. "You know the
way."

An hour later Raven drove through the electric
gates that led to her house. The one thing she hadn't
allowed Julie or her agent to thrust on her was a
chauffeur. Raven enjoyed driving, having control of
the low, sleek foreign car and indulging from time to
time in an excess of speed. She claimed it cleared her
head. It obviously hadn't done the job, she thought
as she pulled up in front of the house with a short,
peevish squeal of the brakes. Distracted, she left her
purse sitting on the seat beside her as she sprang from

the car and jogged up the three stone steps that led to the front door. It was locked. Her frustration only mounted when she was forced to go back and rip the keys from the ignition.

Slamming into the house, Raven went directly to the music room. She flung herself down on the silk-covered Victorian sofa and stared straight ahead without seeing anything. A gleaming mahogany grand piano dominated the room. It was played often and at odd hours. There were Tiffany lamps and Persian rugs and a dime-store flowerpot with a struggling African violet. An old, scarred music cabinet was filled to overflowing. Sheet music spilled onto the floor. A priceless Fabergé box sat next to the brass unicorn she had found in a thrift shop and had fallen in love with. One wall was crowded with awards: Grammys, gold and platinum records, plaques and statues and the keys to a few cities. On another was the framed sheet music from the first song she had written and a breathtaking Picasso. The sofa on which she sat had a bad spring.

It was a strange hodgepodge of cultures and tastes and uniquely Raven's own. She would have thought *eclectic* a pretentious word. She had allowed Julie her exacting taste everywhere else in the house, but here she had expressed herself. Raven needed the room the same way she needed to drive her own car. It kept her sane and helped her remember exactly who Raven Williams was. But the room, like the drive, hadn't calmed her nerves. She walked to the piano.

She pounded out Mozart fiercely. Like her eyes, her music reflected her moods. Now it was tormented, volatile. Even when she'd finished, anger seemed to hover in the air.

"Well, I see you're home." Julie's voice, mild and unruffled, came from the doorway. Julie walked into the room as she had walked into Raven's life: poised and confident. When Raven had met her nearly six years before, Julie had been rich and bored, a partygoer born into old money. Their relationship had given them both something of importance: friendship and a dual dependence. Julie handled the myriad details attached to Raven's career. Raven gave Julie a purpose that the glittery world of wealth had lacked.

"Didn't the recording go well?" Julie was tall and blond, with an elegant body and that exquisitely casual California chic.

Raven lifted her head, and the smile fled from Julie's face. It had been a long time since she'd seen that helpless, ravaged look. "What happened?"

Raven let out a long breath. "He's back."

"Where did you see him?" There was no need for Julie to ask for names. In all the years of their association only two things had had the power to put that look on Raven's face. One of them was a man.

"At the studio." Raven combed her fingers through her hair. "He was up in the booth. I don't know how long he'd been there before I saw him."

Julie pursed her lightly tinted lips. "I wonder what Brand Carstairs is doing in California."

"I don't know." Raven shook her head. "He said business. Maybe he's going to tour again." In an effort to release the tension, she rubbed her hand over the back of her neck. "He's coming here tomorrow."

Julie's brows rose. "I see."

"Don't turn secretary on me, Julie," Raven pleaded. She shut her eyes. "Help me."

"Do you want to see him?" The question was practical. Julie, Raven knew, was practical. She was organized, logical and a stickler for details—all the things Raven wasn't. They needed each other.

"No," Raven began almost fiercely. "Yes..." She swore then and pressed both hands to her temples. "I don't know." Now her tone was quiet and weary. "You know what he's like, Julie. Oh, God, I thought it was over. I thought it was finished!"

With something like a moan, she jumped from the stool to pace around the room. She didn't look like a star in jeans and a simple linen blouse. Her closet held everything from bib overalls to sables. The sables were for the performer; the overalls were for her.

"I'd buried all the hurts. I was so sure." Her voice was low and a little desperate. It was still impossible for her to believe that she had remained this vulnerable after five years. She had only to see him again, and she felt it once more. "I knew sooner or later that I'd run into him somewhere." She ran her fingers through her hair as she roamed the room. "I think I'd always pictured it would be in Europe—London—probably at a party or a benefit. I'd have expected him there; maybe that would have been easier. But today I just looked up and there he was. It all came back. I didn't have any time to stop it. I'd been singing that damn song that I'd written right after he'd left." Raven laughed and shook her head. "Isn't that wild?" She took a deep breath and repeated softly, wonderingly, "Isn't that wild?"

The room was silent for nearly a full minute before Julie spoke. "What are you going to do?"

"Do?" Raven spun back to her. Her hair flew out to follow the sudden movement. "I'm not going to *do* anything. I'm not a child looking for happy-ever-after any more." Her eyes were still dark with emotion, but her voice had grown gradually steadier. "I was barely twenty when I met Brandon, and I was blindly in love with his talent. He was kind to me at a time when I badly needed kindness. I was overwhelmed by him and with my own success."

She lifted a hand to her hair and carefully pushed it behind her shoulders. "I couldn't cope with what he wanted from me. I wasn't ready for a physical relationship." She walked to the brass unicorn and ran a fingertip down its withers. "So he left," she said softly. "And I was hurt. All I could see—maybe all I wanted to see—was that he didn't understand, didn't care enough to want to know why I said no. But that was unrealistic." She turned to Julie then with a frustrated sigh. "Why don't you say something?"

"You're doing fine without me."

"All right, then." Raven thrust her hands in her pockets and stalked to the window. "One of the things I've learned is that if you don't want to get hurt, you don't get too close. You're the only person I've never applied that rule to, and you're the only one who hasn't let me down." She took a deep breath.

"I was infatuated with Brandon years ago. Perhaps it was a kind of love, but a girl's love, easily brushed aside. It was a shock seeing him today, especially right after I finished that song. The coincidence was..." Raven pushed the feelings away and turned back from the window. "Brandon will come over tomorrow, and he'll say whatever it is that he has to say, then he'll go. That'll be the end of it."

Julie studied Raven's face. "Will it?"

"Oh, yes." Raven smiled. She was a bit weary after the emotional outburst but more confident. She had regained her control. "I like my life just as it is, Julie. He's not going to change it. No one is, not this time."

Chapter 2

Raven had dressed carefully, telling herself it was because of the fittings she had scheduled and the luncheon meeting with her agent. She knew it was a lie, but the smart, sophisticated clothes made her feel confident. Who could feel vulnerable dressed in a St. Laurent?

Her coat was white silk and full cut with batwing sleeves that made it seem almost like a cape. She wore it over matching pants with an orchid cowl-neck blouse and a thick, gold belt. With the flat-brimmed hat and the carefully selected earrings, she felt invulnerable. You've come a long way, she had thought as she had studied herself in the bedroom mirror.

Now, standing in Wayne Metcalf's elaborate fitting room, she thought the same thing again—about both of them. Wayne and Raven had started the rise to fame together, she scratching out a living singing in seamy clubs and smoky piano bars and he waiting tables and sketching designs no one had the time to look at. But Raven had looked and admired and remembered.

Wayne had just begun to eke out a living in his trade when plans had begun for Raven's first concert tour. The first professional decision she made without advice was the choice of her costume designer. She had never regretted it. Like Julie, Wayne was a friend close enough to know something about Raven's early personal life. And like Julie, he was fiercely, unquestionably loyal.

Raven wandered around the room, a much plusher room, she mused, than the first offices of Metcalf Designs. There'd been no carpet on that floor, no signed lithographs on laquered walls, no panoramic view of Beverly Hills. It had been a cramped, airless little room above a Greek restaurant. Raven could still remember the strange, heavy aromas that would seep through the walls. She could still hear the exotic music that had vibrated through the bare wood floor.

Raven's star had not risen with that first concert tour, it had rocketed. The initial taste of fame had been so heady and so quick, she had hardly had the time to savor it all: tours, rehearsals, hotel rooms, reporters, mobs of fans, unbelievable amounts of money and impossible demands. She had loved it, although the traveling had sometimes left her weak and disoriented and the fans could be as frightening as they were wonderful. Still she had loved it.

Wayne, deluged with offers after the publicity of that first tour, had soon moved out of the one-room office above the *mousaka* and *souvlaki*. He'd been Raven's designer for six years, and although he now had a large staff and a huge workload, he still saw to every detail of her designs himself.

While she waited for him, Raven wandered to the bar and poured herself a ginger ale. Through all the years of luncheon meetings, elegant brunches and recording sessions, she had never taken more than an occasional drink. In this respect, at least, she would control her life.

The past, she mused, was never very far away, at least not while she still had to worry about her mother. Raven shut her eyes and wished that she could shut off her thoughts as easily. How long had it been that she had lived with that constant anxiety? She could never remember a life without it. She had been very young when she had first discovered that her mother wasn't like other mothers. Even as a little girl, she had hated the oddly sweet smell of the liquor on her mother's breath that no mints could disguise, and she had dreaded the flushed face, the first slurred, affectionate, then angry tones that had drawn mocking stares or sympathetic glances from friends and neighbors.

Raven pressed her fingers against her brow. So many years. So much waste. And now her mother had disappeared again. Where was she? In what sordid hotel room had she holed herself up in to drink away what was left of her life? Raven made a determined effort to push her mother out of her mind, but the terrible images, the frightful scenes, played on in her mind.

It's my life! I have to get on with it, Raven told herself, but she could feel the bitter taste of sorrow and guilt rise in her throat. She started when the door across swung open and Wayne walked in.

He leaned against the knob. "Beautiful!" he said admiringly, surveying her. "Did you wear that for me?"

She made a sound that was somewhere between a laugh and a sob as she moved across the room to hug him. "Of course. Bless you!"

"If you were going to dress up for me, you might at least have worn something of mine," he complained but returned the embrace. He was tall, a thin reed of a man who had to bend over to give her the quick kiss. Not yet thirty, he had a scholarly, attractive face with hair and eyes the same rich shade of brown. A small white scar marred his left eyebrow and gave him, he preferred to think, a rakish profile.

"Jealous?" Raven grinned and drew away from him. "I thought you were too big for that."

"You're never too big for that." He released her, then made his way across to the bar. "Well, at least take off your hat and coat."

Raven obliged, tossing them aside with a carelessness that made Wayne wince. He gazed at her for a long moment as he poured out a Perrier. She grinned again and did a slow model's turn. "How am I holding up?" she demanded.

"I should have seduced you when you were eighteen." He sighed and drank the sparkling water. "Then I wouldn't be constantly regretting that you slipped through my fingers."

She came back for her ginger ale. "You had your chance, fella."

"I was too exhausted in those days." He lifted his scarred brow in a practiced gesture that always amused her. "I get more rest now."

"Too late," she told him and touched her glass to his. "And you're much too busy with the model-of-the-week contest."

"I only date all those skinny girls for the publicity." He reached for a cigarette and lit it elegantly. "I'm basically a very retiring man."

"The brilliance of the pun I could make is terrifying, but I'll pass."

"Wise," he concluded, then blew out a delicate trail of smoke. "I hear Brand Carstairs is in town."

Raven's smile fled, then returned. "He never could keep a low profile."

"Are you okay?"

She shrugged her shoulders. "A minute ago I was beautiful, now you have to ask if I'm okay?"

"Raven." Wayne laid a hand on top of hers. "You folded up when he left. I was there, remember?"

"Of course I remember." The teasing note left her voice. "You were very good to me, Wayne. I don't think I would have made it without you and Julie."

"That's not what I'm talking about, Raven. I want to know how you feel now." He turned her hand over and laced his fingers through hers. "I could renew my offer to go try to break all his bones, if you like."

Touched and amused, she laughed. "I'm sure you're a real killer, Wayne, but it isn't necessary." The straightening of her shoulders was unconscious, a gesture of pride that made Wayne smile. "I'm not going to fold this time."

"Are you still in love with him?"

She hadn't expected such a direct question. Dropping her gaze, she took a moment to answer. "A better question is, Did I ever love him?"

"We both know the answer to that one," Wayne countered. He took her hand when she would have turned away. "We've been friends a long time. What happens to you matters to me."

"Nothing's going to happen to me." Her eyes were back on his, and she smiled. "Absolutely nothing. Brandon is the past. Who knows better than I that you can't run away from the past, and who knows better how to cope with it?" She squeezed his hand. "Come on, show me the costumes that are going to make me look sensational."

After a quick, final glance at her face, Wayne walked over to a gleaming Chippendale table and pushed the button on an intercom. "Bring in Ms. Williams's designs."

Raven had approved the sketches, of course, and the fabrics, but still the completed designs took her by surprise. They had been created for the spot-lights. She knew she'd sparkle on stage. It felt odd wearing blood red and silver sequins in Wayne's brightly lit, elegant room with mirrors tossing her image back at her from all angles. But then, she re-membered, it was an odd business.

Raven stared at the woman in the mirrors and lis-tened with half an ear to Wayne's mumbling as he tucked and adjusted. Her mind could not help but wander. Six years before, she'd been a terrified kid with an album shooting off the top of the charts and a whirlwind concert tour to face. It had all hap-pened so fast: the typical overnight success—not counting the years she had struggled in smoke-choked dives. Still, she'd been young to make a name for herself and determined to prove she wasn't a one-shot fluke. The romance with Brand Carstairs, while she had still been fresh, hot news, hadn't hurt her career. For a brief time it had made her the crown princess of popular music. For more than six months their faces appeared on every magazine cover, dominating the newsstands. They'd laughed about it, Raven remembered, laughed at the silly, predictable headlines: "Raven and Brand Plan Love Nest"; "Williams and Carstairs Make Their Own Music."

Brand had complained about his billing. They had ignored the constant flare and flash of cameras because they had been happy and saw little else but each other. Then, when he had gone, the pictures and headlines had continued for a long time—the cold, cruel words that flashed the intimacies of private hurts for the public eye. Raven no longer looked at them.

Over the months and years, she had grown from the crown princess to a respected performer and celebrity in her own right. That's what's important, she reminded herself. Her career, her life. She'd learned about priorities the hard way.

Raven slipped into the glistening black jumpsuit and found it fit like a second skin. Even her quiet breathing sent sequins flashing. Light streaked out from it at the slightest movement. It was, she decided after a critical survey, blisteringly sexy.

"I'd better not gain a quarter of an ounce before the tour," she remarked, turning to view her slim, sleek profile. Thoughtfully, she gathered her hair in her hand and tossed it behind her back. "Wayne..." He was kneeling at her feet, adjusting the hem. His answer was a grunt. "Wayne, I don't know if I have the nerve to wear this thing."

"This thing," he said mildly as he rose to pluck at the sleeve, "is fantastic."

"No artistic snub intended," she returned and smiled as he stepped back to survey her up and down in his concentrated, professional gaze. "But it's a bit..." She glanced at herself again. "Basic, isn't it?"

"You've got a nice little body, Raven." Wayne examined his creation from the rear. "Not all my clients could wear this without a bit of help here and there. Okay, take it off. It's perfect just as it is."

"I always feel like I've been to the doctor when I've finished here," she commented as she slipped back into her white slacks and orchid blouse. "Who knows more about our bodies' secrets than our dressmakers?"

"Who else knows more about *your* secrets, darling?" he corrected absently as he made notes on each one of the costumes. "Women tend to get chatty when they're half-dressed."

"Oh, what lovely gossip do you know?" Fastening her belt, Raven walked to him, then leaned companionably on his shoulder. "Tell me something wonderfully indiscreet and shocking, Wayne."

"Babs Curtain has a new lover," he murmured, still intent on his notes.

"I said shocking," Raven complained. "Not predictable."

"I've sworn an oath of secrecy, written in dressmaker's chalk."

"I'm very disappointed in you." Raven left his side to fetch her coat and hat. "I was certain you had feet of clay."

"Lauren Chase just signed to do the lead in *Fantasy.*"

Raven stopped on her way to the door and whirled. "What?" She dashed back across the room and yanked the notebook from Wayne's hand.

"Somehow I thought that would get your attention," Wayne observed dryly.

"When? Oh, Wayne," she went on before he could answer. "I'd give several years of my young life for a chance to write that score. Lauren Chase...oh, yes, she's so right for it. Who's doing the score, Wayne?" Raven gripped his shoulders and closed her eyes. "Go ahead, tell me, I can take it."

"She doesn't know. You're cutting off the circulation, Raven," he added, disengaging her hands.

"Doesn't know!" she groaned, crushing the hat down on her head in a way that made Wayne swear and adjust it himself. "That's worse, a thousand times worse! Some faceless, nameless songwriter who couldn't possibly know what's right for that fabulous screenplay is even now sitting at a piano making unforgivable mistakes.''

"There's always the remote possibility that whoever's writing it has talent," he suggested and earned a lethal glare.

"Who's side are you on?" she demanded and flung the coat around her shoulders.

He grinned, grabbed her cheeks and gave her a resounding kiss. "Go home and stomp your feet, darling. You'll feel better."

She struggled not to smile. "I'm going next door and buy a Florence DeMille," she threatened him with the name of a leading competitor.

"I'll forgive you for that statement," Wayne said with a hefty sigh. "Because along with my feet of clay I've a heart of gold."

She laughed and left him with her rack of costumes and his notebook.

The house was quiet when Raven returned. The faint scent of lemon oil and pine told her that the house had just been cleaned. As a matter of habit, she peeked into her music room and was satisfied that nothing there had been disturbed. She liked her disorganization just as it was. With the idle thought of making coffee, Raven wandered toward the kitchen.

She had bought the house for its size and rambling openness. It was the antithesis of the small, claustrophobic rooms she had grown up in. And it smelled clean, she decided. Not antiseptic; she would have hated that, but there was no lingering scent of stale cigarettes, no sickly sweet odor of yesterday's bottle. It was her house, as her life was hers. She'd bought them both with her voice.

Raven twirled once around the room, pleased with herself for no specific reason. I'm happy, she thought, just happy to be alive.

Grabbing a rose from a china vase, she began to sing as she walked down the hall. It was the sight of Julie's long, narrow bare feet propped up on the desk in the library that stopped her.

Raven hesitated, seeing Julie was on the phone, but was quickly gestured inside.

"I'm sorry, Mr. Cummings, but Ms. Williams has a strict policy against endorsements. Yes, I'm sure it's a marvelous product." Julie lifted her eyes from her pink-tinted toenails and met Raven's amused grin. She rolled her eyes to the ceiling, and Raven settled cross-legged in an overstuffed leather chair. The library, with its warm, mahogany paneling and stately furnishings, was Julie's domain. And, Raven thought, snuggling down more comfortably, it suited her.

"Of course, I'll see she gets your offer, but I warn you, Ms. Williams takes a firm stand on this." With one last exasperated glance at the ceiling, Julie hung up. "If you didn't insist on being nice to everybody who calls you, I could have thought of a few different words for that one," Julie snapped.

"Trouble?" Raven asked, sniffing her rose and smiling.

"Get smart and I'll tell him you'll be thrilled to endorse his Earth Bubble Shampoo." She laced her fingers behind her head as she made the threat.

"Mercy," Raven pleaded, then kicked off her elegant, orchid-toned shoes. "You look tired," she said, watching Julie stretch her back muscles. "Been busy?"

"Just last-minute nonsense to clear things for the tour." A shrug dismissed the complications she had handled. "I never did ask you how the recording went. It's finished, isn't it?"

"Yeah." Raven took a deep breath and twirled her rose by the stem. "It went perfectly. I haven't been happier with a session since the first one. Something just clicked."

"You worked hard enough on the material," Julie remarked, thinking of the endless nights Raven had spent writing and arranging.

"Sometimes I still can't believe it." She spoke softly, the words hardly more than thoughts. "I listen to a playback, and its all there, the strings, the brass, the rhythm and backups, and I can't believe it's me. I've been so incredibly lucky."

"Talented," Julie corrected.

"Lots of people have talent," Raven reminded her. "But they're not sitting here. They're still in some dreary piano bar, waiting. Without luck, they're never going to be anywhere else."

"There are also things like drive, perseverance, guts." Raven's persistent lack of self-confidence infuriated Julie. She'd been with her almost from the beginning of Raven's start in California six years before. She'd seen the struggles and the disappointments. She knew about the fears, insecurities and work behind the glamour. There was nothing about Raven Williams that Julie didn't know.

The phone interrupted her thoughts on a lecture on self-worth. "It's your private line," she said as she pressed the button. "Hello." Raven tensed but relaxed when she saw Julie smile. "Hi, Henderson. Yes, she's right here, hold on. Your illustrious agent," Julie stated as she rose. She slipped her feet back into her sandals. Raven got up from her chair just as the doorbell chimed.

"I guess that's Brandon." With admirable ease, she flopped into the chair that Julie had just vacated. "Would you tell him I'll be along in a minute?"

"Sure." Julie turned and left as Raven's voice followed her down the hall.

"I left it where? In your office? Henderson, I don't know why I ever bother carrying a purse."

Julie smiled. Raven had a penchant for losing things: her purse, her shoes, her passport. Vital or trivial, it simply didn't matter. Music and people filled Raven's thoughts, and material objects were easily forgotten.

"Hello, Brand," Julie said as she opened the front door. "Nice to see you again." Her eyes were cool, and her mouth formed no smile.

"Hello, Julie."

There was warmth in his greeting. She sensed it and ignored it. "Come in," she invited. "Raven's expecting you; she'll be right out."

"It's good to be here again. I've missed this place."

"Have you?" Her tone was sharp.

His grin turned into a look of appraisal. Julie was a long-stemmed woman with a sleek cap of honey-blond hair and direct brown eyes. She was closer to Brand's age than Raven's and was the sort of woman he was usually attracted to: smart, sophisticated and coolly sexy. Yet, there could never have been anything between them but friendship. She was too fiercely devoted to Raven. Her loyalty, he saw, was unchanged.

"Five years is a long time, Julie."

"I'm not sure it's long enough," she countered. Old resentments came simmering back to the surface. "You hurt her."

"Yes, I know." His gaze didn't falter at the confession, and there was no plea for understanding in his eyes. The lack of it touched off respect in Julie, but she dismissed it. She shook her head as she looked at him.

"So," she said softly, "you've come back."

"I've come back," he agreed, then smiled. "Did you think I wouldn't?"

"She didn't," Julie retorted, annoyed with herself for warming to him. "That's what matters."

"Julie, Henderson's sending over my purse." Raven came down the hall toward them in her quick, nervous stride. "I told him not to bother; I don't think there's anything in it but a comb and an expired credit card. Hello, Brandon." She offered her hands as she had at the recording studio, but now she felt more able to accept his touch.

She hadn't bothered to put her shoes back on or to repaint her mouth. Her smile was freer, more as he remembered it. "Raven." Brand brought her hands to his lips. Instantly she stiffened, and Brand released her. "Can we talk in the music room?" His smile was easy, friendly. "I was always comfortable in there."

"Of course." She turned toward the doorway. "Would you like something to drink?"

"I'd have some tea." He gave Julie his quick, charming grin. "You always made a good cup of tea."

"I'll bring it in." Without responding to the grin, Julie moved down the hall toward the kitchen. Brand followed Raven into the music room.

He touched her shoulder before she could cross to the sofa. It was a gesture that asked her to wait. Turning her head, Raven saw that he was giving the room one of his long, detailed studies. She had seen that look on his face before. It was a curious aspect of what seemed like a casual nature. There was an intensity about him at times that recalled the tough London street kid who'd once fought his way to the top of his profession. The key to his talent seemed to be in his natural gift for observation. He saw every-thing, remembered everything. Then he translated it into lyric and melody.

The fingers on her shoulder caressed once, almost absently, and brought back a flood of memories. Raven would have moved away, but he dropped the hand and turned to her. She had never been able to resist his eyes.

"I remember every detail of this room. I've pic-tured it from time to time when I couldn't do any-thing but think of you." He lifted his hand again to brush the back of it against her cheek.

"Don't." She shook her head and stepped away.

"It's difficult not to touch you, Raven. Especially here. Do you remember the long evenings we spent here? The quiet afternoons?"

He was moving her—with just his voice, just the steady spell of his eyes. "It was a long time ago, Brandon."

"It doesn't seem so long ago at the moment. It could be yesterday; you look the same."

"I'm not," she told him with a slight shake of her head. He saw her eyes darken before she turned away. "If I had known this was why you wanted to see me, I wouldn't have let you come. It's over Brandon. It's been over for a long time."

"Is it?" Raven hadn't realized he was so close behind her. He turned her in his arms and caught her. "Show me, then," he demanded. "Just once."

The moment his mouth touched hers, she was thrown back in time. It was all there—the heat, the need, the loving. His lips were so soft, so warm; hers parted with only the slightest pressure. She knew how he would taste, how he would smell. Her memory was sharper than she had thought. Nothing was forgotten.

He tangled his fingers in the thickness of her hair, tilting her head further back as he deepened the kiss. He wanted to luxuriate in her flavor, in her scent, in her soft yielding response. Her hands were trapped between their bodies, and she curled her fingers into the sweater he wore. The need, the longing, seemed much too fresh to have been dormant for five years. Brand held her close but without urgency. There was a quiet kind of certainty in the way he explored her mouth. Raven responded, giving, accepting, remembering. But when she felt the pleasure drifting toward passion, she resisted. When she struggled, he loosened his hold but didn't release her. Raven stared up at him with a look he well remembered but had never been able to completely decipher.

"It doesn't seem it's altogether finished after all," he murmured.

"You never did play fair, did you?" Raven pushed out of his arms, furious and shaken. "Let me tell you something, Brandon. I won't fall at your feet this time. You hurt me before, but I don't bruise so easily now. I have no intention of letting you back into my life."

"I think you will," he corrected easily. "But perhaps not in the way you mean." He paused and caught her hair with his fingers. "I can apologize for kissing you, Raven, if you'd like me to lie."

"Don't bother. You've always been good at romance. I rather enjoyed it." She sat down on the sofa and smiled brightly up at him.

He lifted a brow. It was hardly the response he had expected. He drew out a cigarette and lit it. "You seem to have grown up in my absence."

"Being an adult has its advantages," Raven observed. The kiss had stirred more than she cared to admit, even to herself.

"I always found your naïveté charming."

"It's difficult to remain naïve, however charming, in this business." She leaned back against the cushion, relaxing deliberately. "I'm not wide-eyed and twenty anymore, Brandon."

"Tough and jaded are you, Raven?"

"Tough enough," she returned. "You gave me my first lesson!"

He took a deep drag on his cigarette, then considered the glowing tip of it. "Maybe I did," he murmured. "Maybe you needed it."

"Maybe you'd like me to thank you," she tossed back, and he looked over at her again.

"Perhaps." He walked over, then dropped down beside her on the sofa. His laugh was sudden and unexpected. "Good God, Raven, you've never had this bloody spring fixed."

The tension in her neck fled as she laughed with him. "I like it that way." She tossed her hair behind her back. "It's more personal."

"To say nothing of uncomfortable."

"I never sit on that spot," she told him.

"You leave it for unsuspecting guests, I imagine." He shifted away from the defective spring.

"That's right. I like people to feel at home."

Julie brought in a tea tray and found them sitting companionably on the sofa. Her quick, practiced glance found no tension on Raven's face. Satisfied, she left them again.

"How've you been, Brandon? Busy, I imagine."
Raven crossed her legs under her and leaned over to
pour the tea. It was a move Brandon had seen many
times. Almost savagely, he crushed out his cigarette.

"Busy enough." He understated the five albums
he had released since she'd last seen him and the
three grueling concert tours. There'd been more than
twenty songs with his name on the copyright in the
past year.

"You've been living in London?"

"Mostly." His brow lifted, and she caught the
gesture as she handed him his tea.

"I read the trades," she said mildly. "Don't we
all?"

"I saw your television special last month." He
sipped his tea and relaxed against the back of the
sofa. His eyes were on her, and she thought them a
bit more green than blue now. "You were marvelous."

"Last month?" She frowned at him, puzzled. "It
wasn't aired in England, was it?"

"I was in New York. Did you write all the songs
for the album you finished up yesterday?"

"All but two." Shrugging, she took up her own
china cup. "Marc wrote 'Right Now' and 'Coming
Back.' He's got the touch."

"Yes." Brand eyed her steadily. "Does he have
you, too?" Raven's head whipped around. "I read
the trades," he said mildly.

"That comes under a more personal heading." Her eyes were dark with anger.

"More bluntly stated, none of my business?" he asked, sipping again.

"You were always bright, Brandon."

"Thanks, love." He set down his cup. "But my question was professional. I need to know if you have any entanglements at the moment."

"Entanglements are usually personal. Ask me about my dancing lessons."

"Later, perhaps. Raven, I need your undivided devotion for the next three months." His smile was engaging. Raven fought his charm.

"Well," she said and set her cup beside his. "That's bluntly stated."

"No indecent proposal at the moment," he assured her. Settling back in the hook of the sofa's arm, he sought her eyes. "I'm doing the score for *Fantasy.* I need a partner."

Chapter 3

To say she was surprised would have been a ridiculous understatement. Brand watched her eyes widen. He thought they were the color of peat smoke. She didn't move but simply stared at him, her hands resting lightly on her knees. Her thoughts had been flung in a thousand different directions, and she was trying to sit calmly and bring them back to order.

Fantasy. The book that had captured America's heart. A novel that had been on the best-seller list for more than fifty weeks. The sale of its paperback rights had broken all records. The film rights had been purchased as well, and Carol Mason, the author, had written the screenplay herself. It was to be a musical; *the* musical of the nineties. Speculation had been buzzing for months on both coasts as to who would write the score. It would be the coup of the decade, the chance of a lifetime. The plot was a dream, and the reigning box-office queen had the lead. And the music...Raven already had half-formed songs in her head. Carefully she reached back and poured more tea. Things like this don't just fall in your lap, she reminded herself. Perhaps he means something entirely different.

"You're going to score *Fantasy*," she said at length, cautiously. Her eyes met his again. His were clear, confident, slightly amused; hers were dark, guarded, a little puzzled. "I just heard that Lauren Chase had been signed. Everywhere I go, people are wondering who's going to play Tessa, who's going to play Joe."

"Jack Ladd," Brand supplied, and the puzzlement in Raven's eyes changed to pure pleasure.

"Perfect!" She reached over to take his hand. "You're going to have a tremendous hit. I'm very happy for you."

And she was. He could see as well as hear the absolute sincerity. It was typical of her to gain genuine pleasure from someone else's good fortune, just as it was typical of her to suffer for someone else's misfortune. Raven's feelings ran deep, and he knew she'd never been afraid to show emotion. Her unaffectedness had always been a great part of her appeal. For the moment, she had forgotten to be cautious with Brand. She smiled at him as she held his hands.

"So that's why you're in California," she said. "Have you already started?"

"No." He seemed to consider something for a moment, then his fingers interlaced with hers. Her hands were narrow-boned and slender, with palms as soft as a child's. "Raven, I meant what I said. I need a partner. I need you."

She started to remove her hands from his, but he tightened his fingers. "I've never known you to need anyone, Brandon," she said, not quite succeeding in making her tone light. "Least of all me."

His grip tightened quickly, causing Raven's eyes to widen at the unexpected pain. Just as quickly, he released her. "This is business, Raven."

She lifted a brow at the temper in his voice. "Business is usually handled through my agent," she said. "You remember Henderson."

He gave her a long, steady look. "I remember everything." He saw the flash of hurt in her eyes, swiftly controlled. "Raven," his tone was gentler now. "I'm sorry."

She shrugged and gave her attention back to her tea. "Old wounds, Brandon. It does seem to me that if there was a legitimate offer, Henderson would have gotten wind of it."

"There's been an offer," Brand told her. "I asked him to let me speak to you first."

"Oh?" Her hair had drifted down, curtaining her face, and she flipped it behind her back. "Why?"

Because I thought that if you knew we'd be working together, you'd turn it down."

"Yes," she agreed. "You're right."

"And that," he said without missing a beat, "would be incredibly soft-headed. Henderson knows that as well as I do."

"Oh, does he?" Raven rose, furious. "Isn't it marvelous the way people determine my life? Did you two decide I was too feeble-brained to make this decision on my own?"

"Not exactly." Brand's voice was cool. "We did agree that left to yourself, you have a tendency to be emotional rather than sensible."

"Terrific. Do I get a leash and collar for Christmas?"

"Don't be an idiot," Brand advised.

"Oh, so now I'm an idiot?" Raven turned away to pace the room. She had the same quicksilver temper he remembered. She was all motion, all energy. "I don't know how I've managed all this time without your pretty compliments, Brandon." She whirled back to him. "Why in the world would you want an emotional idiot as a collaborator?"

"Because," Brandon said and rose, "you're a hell of a writer. Now shut up."

"Of course," she said, seating herself on the piano bench. "Since you asked so nicely."

Deliberately he took out another cigarette, lit it and blew out a stream of smoke, all the while his eyes resting on her face. "This is an important project, Raven," he said. "Let's not blow it. Because we were once very close, I wanted to talk to you face to face, not through a mediator, not through a bloody telephone wire. Can you understand that?"

She waited a long moment before answering. "Maybe."

Brand smiled and moved over to her. "We'll add stubborn to those adjectives later, but I don't want you mad again."

"Then let me ask you something before you say anything I'll have to get mad about." Raven tilted her head and studied his face. "First, why do you want a collaborator on this? Why share the glory?"

"It's also a matter of sharing the work, love. Fifteen songs."

She nodded. "All right, number two, then. Why me, Brandon? Why not someone who's scored a musical before?"

He answered her by walking around her and slipping down on the piano bench beside her. Without speaking, he began to play. The notes flooded the room like ghosts. "Remember this?" he murmured, glancing over and into her eyes.

Raven didn't have to answer. She rose and walked away. It was too difficult to sit beside him at the same piano where they had composed the song he now played. She remembered how they had laughed, how warm his eyes had been, how safe she had felt in his arms. It was the first and only song they had written and recorded together.

Even after he had stopped playing, she continued to prowl the room. "What does 'Clouds and Rain' have to do with anything?" she demanded. He had touched a chord in her; he heard it in the tone of her voice. He felt a pang of guilt at having intentionally peeled away a layer of her defense.

"There's a Grammy over there and a gold record, thanks to that two minutes and forty-three seconds, Raven. We work well together."

She turned back to look at him. "We did once."

"We will again." Brand stood and came to her but this time made no move to touch her. "Raven, you know how important this could be to your career. And you must realize what you'd be bringing to the project. *Fantasy* needs your special talents."

She wanted it. She could hardly believe that something she wanted so badly was being offered to her. But how would it be to work with him again, to be in constant close contact? Would she be able to deal with it? Would she be sacrificing her personal sanity for professional gain? But I don't love him anymore, she reminded herself. Raven caught her bottom lip between her teeth in a gesture of indecision. Brand saw it.

"Raven, think of the music."

"I am," she admitted. "I'm also thinking of you—of us." She gave him a clear, candid look. "I'm not sure it would be healthy for me."

"I can't promise not to touch you." He was annoyed, and his voice reflected it in its crisp, concise tone. "But I can promise not to push myself on you. Is that good enough?"

Raven evaded the question. "If I agreed, when would we start? I've a tour coming up."

"I know, in two weeks. You'll be finished in six, so we could start the first week in May."

"I see." Her mouth turned up a bit as she combed her fingers through her hair. "You've looked into this thoroughly."

"I told you, it's business."

"All right, Brandon," she said, conceding his point. "Where would we work? Not here," she said quickly. There was a sudden pressure in her chest. "I won't work with you here."

"No, I thought not. I have a place," he continued when Raven remained silent. "It's in Cornwall."

"Cornwall?" Raven repeated. "Why Cornwall?"

"Because it's quiet and isolated, and no one, especially the press, knows I have it. They'll be all over us when they hear we're working together, especially on this project. It's too hot an item."

"Couldn't we just rent a small cave on the coast somewhere?"

He laughed and caught her hair in his hand. "You know how poor the acoustics are in a cave. Cornwall's incredible in the spring, Raven. Come with me."

She lifted a hand to his chest to push back, not certain if she was about to agree or decline. He could still draw too much from her too effortlessly. She needed to think, she decided; a few days to put it all in perspective.

"Raven."

She turned to see Julie in the doorway. "Yes?"

"There's a call for you."

Vaguely annoyed, Raven frowned at her. "Can't it wait, Julie? I . . ."

"It's on your private line."

Brand felt her stiffen and looked down curiously. Her eyes were completely blank.

"I see." Her voice was calm, but he detected the faintest of tremors.

"Raven?" Without thinking, he took her by the shoulders and turned her to face him. "What is it?"

"Nothing." She drew out of his arms. There was something remote about her now, something distant that puzzled him. "Have some more tea," she invited and smiled, but her eyes remained blank. "I'll be back in a minute."

She was gone for more than ten, and Brand had begun to pace restlessly through the room. Raven was definitely no longer the malleable young girl she had been five years before; he knew that. He wasn't at all certain she would agree to work with him. He wanted her—for the project and yes, for himself. Holding her, tasting her again, had stirred up much more than memories. She fascinated him and always had. Even when she had been so young, there had been an air of secrecy about her. There still was. It was as if she kept certain parts of herself locked in a closet out of reach. She had held him off five years before in more than a physical sense. It had frustrated him then and continued to frustrate him.

But he was older, too. He'd made mistakes with her before and had no intention of repeating them. Brand knew what he wanted and was determined to get it. Sitting back at the piano, he began to play the song he had written with Raven. He remembered her voice, warm and sultry, in his ear. He was nearly at the end when he sensed her presence.

Glancing up, Brand saw her standing in the doorway. Her eyes were unusually dark and intense. Then he realized it was because she was pale, and the contrast accentuated the gray of her irises. Had the song disturbed her that much? He stopped immediately and rose to go to her.

"Raven..."

"I've decided to do it," she interrupted. Her hands were folded neatly in front of her, her eyes direct.

"Good." He took her hand and found it chilled. "Are you all right?"

"Yes, of course." She removed her hands from his, but her gaze never faltered. "I suppose Henderson will fill me in on all the details."

Something about her calm disturbed him. It was as if she'd set part of herself aside. "Let's have dinner, Raven." The urge to be with her, to pierce her armor, was almost overwhelming. "I'll take you to the Bistro; you always liked it there."

"Not tonight, Brandon, I . . . have some things to do."

"Tomorrow," he insisted, knowing he was pushing but unable to prevent himself. She looked suddenly weary.

"Yes, all right, tomorrow." She gave him a tired smile. "I'm sorry, but I'll have to ask you to leave now, Brandon. I didn't realize how late it was."

"All right." Bending toward her, he gently kissed her. It was an instinctive gesture, one that demanded no response. He felt the need to warm her, protect her. "Seven tomorrow," he told her. "I'm at the Bel-Air; you only have to call me."

Raven waited until she heard the front door shut behind him. She pressed the heel of her hand to her brow and let the tide of emotions rush through her. There were no tears, but a blinding headache raged behind her eyes. She felt Julie's hand on her shoulder.

"They found her?" Julie asked, concerned. Automatically she began kneading the tension from Raven's shoulders.

"Yes, they found her." She let out a long, deep breath. "She's coming back."

Chapter 4

The sanitarium was white and clean. The architect, a good one, had conceived a restful building without medical overtones. The uninformed might have mistaken it for an exclusive hotel snuggled in California's scenic Ojai. It was a proud, elegantly fashioned building with several magnificent views of the countryside. Raven detested it.

Inside, the floors were thickly carpeted, and conversation was always low-key. Raven hated the controlled silence, the padded quiet. The staff members wore street clothes and only small, discreet badges to identify themselves, and they were among the best trained in the country, just as the Fieldmore Clinic was the best detoxification center on the west coast.

Raven had made certain of its reputation before she had brought her mother there for the first time over five years before.

Raven waited in Justin Karter's paneled, book-lined, tasteful office. It received its southern exposure through a wide, thick-paned window. The morning sunlight beamed in on a thriving collection of leafy green plants. Raven wondered idly why her own plants seemed always to put up only a halfhearted struggle for life, one they usually lost. Perhaps she should ask Dr. Karter what his secret was. She laughed a little and rubbed her fingers on the nagging headache between her brows.

How she hated these visits and the leathery, glossy smell of his office. She was cold and cupped her el-bows, hugging her arms across her midriff. Raven was always cold in the Fieldmore Clinic, from the moment she walked through the stately white dou-ble doors until long after she walked out again. It was a penetrating cold that went straight to the bone. Turning away from the window, she paced ner-vously around the room. When she heard the door open, she stopped and turned around slowly.

Karter entered, a small, youthful man with a corn-colored beard and healthy pink cheeks. He had an earnest face, accentuated by tortoise-rimmed glasses and a faint smattering of freckles. Under other cir-cumstances, Raven would have liked his face, even warmed to it.

"Ms. Williams." He held out a hand and took hers in a quick, professional grip. It was cold, he realized, and as fragile as he remembered. Her hair was pinned up at the nape of her neck, and she looked young and pale in the dark tailored suit. This woman was far different from the vibrant, laughing entertainer he had watched on television a few weeks before.

"Hello, Dr. Karter."

It always amazed him that the rich, full-toned voice belonged to such a small, delicate-looking woman. He had thought the same years before when she had been hardly more than a child. He was an ardent fan but had never asked her to sign any of the albums in his collection. It would, he knew, embarrass them both.

"Please sit down, Ms. Williams. Could I get you some coffee?"

"No, please." She swallowed. Her throat was always dry when she spoke to him. "I'd like to see my mother first."

"There are a few things I'd like to discuss with you."

He watched her moisten her lips, the only sign of agitation. "After I've seen her."

"All right." Karter took her by the arm and led her from the room. They walked across the quiet, carpeted hallway to the elevators. "Ms. Williams," he began. He would have liked to have called her Raven. He thought of her as Raven, just as the rest of the world did. But he could never quite break through the film of reserve she slipped on in his presence. It was, Karter knew, because he knew her secrets. She trusted him to keep them but was never comfortable with him. She turned to him now, her great, gray eyes direct and expressionless.

"Yes, doctor?" Only once had Raven ever broken down in his presence, and she had promised herself she would never do so again. She would not be destroyed by her mother's illness, and she would not make a public display of herself.

"I don't want you to be shocked by your mother's appearance." They stepped into the elevator together, and he kept his hand on her arm. "She had made a great deal of progress during her last stay here, but she left prematurely, as you know. Over the past three months, her condition has...deteriorated."

"Please," Raven said wearily, "don't be delicate. I know where she was found and how. You'll dry her out again, and in a couple of months she'll leave and it'll start all over. It never changes."

"Alcoholics fight a continuing battle."

"Don't tell me about alcoholics," she shot back. The reserve cracked and the emotion poured through. "Don't preach to me about battles." She stopped herself, then, shaking her head, pressed her fingers to the concentrated source of her headache.

"I know all about alcoholics," she said more calmly. "I haven't your dedication or your optimism."

"You keep bringing her back," he reminded Raven softly.

"She's my mother." The elevator door slid open, and Raven walked through them.

Her skin grew colder as they moved down the hallway. There were doors on either side, but she refused to think of the people beyond them. The hospital flavor was stronger here. Raven thought she could smell the antiseptic, the hovering medicinal odor that always made a hint of nausea roll in her stomach. When Karter stopped in front of a door and reached for a knob, Raven laid a hand on top of his.

"I'll see her alone, please."

He sensed her rigid control. Her eyes were calm, but he had seen the quick flash of panic in them. Her fingers didn't tremble on his hand but were stiff and icy. "All right. But only a few minutes. There are complications we need to discuss." He took his hand from the knob. "I'll wait for you here."

Raven nodded and twisted the knob herself. She took a moment, struggling to gather every ounce of strength, then walked inside.

The woman lay in a hospital bed on good linen sheets, dozing lightly. There was a tube feeding liquid into her through a needle in her arm. The drapes were drawn, and the room was in shadows. It was a comfortable room painted in soft blue with an ivory carpet and a few good paintings. With her fingers dug into the leather bag she carried, Raven approached the bed.

Raven's first thought was that her mother had lost weight. There were hollows in her cheeks, and her skin had the familiar unhealthy yellow cast. Her dark hair was cropped short and streaked liberally with gray. It had been lovely hair, Raven remembered, glossy and full. Her face was gaunt, with deathly circles under the eyes and a mouth that seemed dry and pulled in. The helplessness stabbed at Raven, and for a minute she closed her eyes against it. The tears were coming, burning to be free. She let them fall while she looked down on the sleeping woman. Without a sound, without moving, the woman in bed opened her eyes. They were dark and gray like her daughter's.

"Mama." Raven let the tears roll freely. "Why?"

By the time Raven got to her front door, she was exhausted. She wanted bed and oblivion. The headache was still with her, but the pain had turned into a dull, sickening throb. Closing the door behind her, she leaned back on it, trying to summon the strength to walk up the stairs.

"Raven?"

She opened her eyes and watched Julie come down the hall toward her. Seeing Raven so pale and beaten,

Julie slipped an arm around her shoulders. Her concern took the form of a scolding. "You should have let me go with you. I should never have let you go alone." She was already guiding Raven up the stairs.

"My mother, my problem," Raven said tiredly.

"That's the only selfish part of you," Julie said in a low, furious voice as they entered Raven's bedroom. "I'm supposed to be your friend. You'd never let me go through something like this alone."

"Please, don't be angry with me." Raven swayed on her feet as Julie stripped off the dark suit jacket. "It's something I feel is my responsibility, just mine. I've felt that way for too long to change now."

"I am angry with you." Julie's voice was tight as she slipped the matching skirt down over Raven's hips. "This is the only thing you do that makes me genuinely angry with you. I can't stand it when you do this to yourself." She looked back at the pale, tired face. "Have you eaten?" Raven shook her head as she stepped out of the skirt. "And you won't," she concluded, brushing Raven's fumbling hands away from the buttons of the white lawn blouse. She undid them herself, then pushed the material from Raven's shoulders. Raven stood, unresisting.

"I'm having dinner with Brandon," Raven murmured, going willingly as Julie guided her toward the bed.

"I'll call him and cancel. I can bring you up something later. You need to sleep."

"No." Raven slipped between the crisp, cool sheets. "I want to go. I need to go," she corrected as she shut her eyes. "I need to get out; I don't want to think for a while. I'll rest now. He won't be here until seven."

Julie walked over to pull the shades. Even before the room was darkened, Raven was asleep.

It was some minutes past seven when Julie opened the door to Brandon. He wore a stone-colored suit with a navy shirt open at the throat. He looked casually elegant, Julie thought. The nosegay of violets was charming rather than silly in his hands. He lifted a brow at the clinging black sheath she wore.

"Hello, Julie. You look terrific." He plucked one of the violets out of the nosegay and handed it to her. "Going out?"

Julie accepted the flower. "In a little while," she answered. "Raven should be down in a minute. Brand..." Hesitating, Julie shook her head, then turned to lead him into the music room. "I'll fix you a drink. Bourbon, isn't it? Neat."

Brand caught her arm. "That isn't what you were going to say."

She took a deep breath. "No." For a moment longer she hesitated, then began, fixing him with her dark brown eyes. "Raven's very important to me. There aren't many like her, especially in this town. She's genuine, and though she thinks she has, she hasn't really developed any hard edges yet. I wouldn't like to see her hurt, especially right now. No, I won't answer any questions," she said, anticipating him. "It's Raven's story, not mine. But I'm going to tell you this: She needs a light touch and a great deal of patience. You'd better have them both."

"How much do you know about what happened between us five years ago, Julie?" Brandon asked.

"I know what Raven told me."

"One day you ought to ask me how I felt and why I left."

"And would you tell me?"

"Yes," he returned without hesitation. "I would."

"I'm sorry!" Raven came dashing down the stairs in a filmy flutter of white. "I hate to be late." Her hair settled in silky confusion over the shoulders of the thin voile dress as she stopped at the foot of the stairs. "I couldn't seem to find my shoes."

There was a becoming blush of color on her cheeks, and her eyes were bright and full of laughter. It passed through Brand's mind quickly, and then was discarded, that she looked a little too bright, a little too vibrant.

"Beautiful as ever." He handed her the flowers. "I've never minded waiting for you."

"Ah, the golden Irish tongue," she murmured as she buried her face in the violets. "I've missed it." Raven held the flowers up to her nose while her eyes laughed at him over them. "And I believe I'll let you spoil me tonight, Brandon. I'm in a mood to be pampered."

He took her free hand in his. "Where do you want to go?"

"Anywhere. Everywhere." She tossed her head. "But dinner first. I'm starving."

"All right, I'll buy you a cheeseburger."

"Some things do stay the same," she commented before she turned to Julie. "You have fun, and don't worry about me." She paused a moment, then smiled and kissed her cheek. "I promise I won't lose my key. And say hello to . . ." She hesitated as she walked toward the door with Brandon. "Who is it tonight?"

"Lorenzo," Julie answered, watching them. "The shoe baron."

"Oh, yes." Raven laughed as they walked into the cool, early spring air. "Amazing." She tucked her arm through Brandon's. "Julie's always having some millionaire fall in love with her. It's a gift."

"Shoe baron?" Brand questioned as he opened the car door for Raven.

"*Mmm*. Italian. He wears beautiful designer suits and looks as though he should be stamped on the head of a coin."

Brand slid in beside her and in an old reflex gesture brushed the hair that lay on her shoulder behind her back. "Serious?"

Raven tried not to be moved by the touch of his fingers. "No more serious than the oil tycoon or the

perfume magnate." The leathery smell of the uphol-
stery reminded her abruptly of Karter's office.
Quickly she pushed away the sensation. "What are
you going to feed me, Brandon?" she asked
brightly—too brightly. "I warn you, I'm starving."

He circled her throat with his hand so that she had
no choice but to meet his eyes directly. "Are you
going to tell me what's wrong?"

He'd always seen too much too quickly, she
thought. It was one of the qualities that had made
him an exceptional songwriter.

Raven placed her hand on top of his. "No questions, Brandon, not now."

She felt his hesitation. Then he turned his hand
over and gripped hers. Slowly, overriding her initial
resistance, he brought her palm to his lips. "Not
now," he agreed, watching her eyes. "I can still move
you," he murmured and smiled as though the
knowledge pleased him. "I can feel it."

Raven felt the tremors racing up her arm. "Yes."
She drew her hand from his but kept her eyes steady.
"You can still move me. But things aren't the same
anymore."

He grinned, a quick flash of white teeth, then
started the engine. "No, things aren't the same anymore."

As he pulled away, she had the uncomfortable
impression that they had said the same words but
meant two different things.

* * *

Dinner was quiet and intimate and perfect. They ate in a tiny old inn they had once discovered by chance. Here, Brand knew, there would be no interruptions for autographs, no greetings and drinks from old acquaintances. Here there would be just the two of them, a man and a woman amidst candlelight, wine, fine food, and an intimate atmosphere.

As the evening wore on, Raven's smile became more spontaneous, less desperate, and the unhappiness he had seen deep in her eyes before, now faded. Though he noticed the transition, Brand made no comment.

"I feel like I haven't eaten in a week," Raven managed between bites of the tender roast beef that was the house specialty.

"Want some of mine?" Brand offered his plate.

Raven scooped up a bit of baked potato; her eyes seemed to laugh at him. "We'll have them wrap it up so I can take it home. I want to leave room for dessert. Did you see that pastry tray?"

"I suppose I could roll you to Cornwall," Brand considered, adding some burgundy to his glass.

Raven laughed, a throaty sound that appealed and aroused. "I'll be a bag of bones by the time we go to Cornwall," she claimed. "You know what those whirlwind tours can do." She shook her head as he offered her more wine.

"One-night stands from San Francisco to New York." Brand lifted his glass as Raven gave him a quizzing look. "I spoke to Henderson." He twirled a strand of her hair around his finger so absently, Raven was certain he was unaware of the gesture. She made no complaint. "If it's agreeable with you, I'll meet you in New York at the end of the tour. We'll fly to England from there."

"All right." She took a deep breath, having finally reached her fill of the roast beef. "You'd better set it up with Julie. I haven't any memory for dates and times. Are you staying in the States until then?"

"I'm doing a couple of weeks in Vegas." He brushed his fingers across her cheek, and when she would have resisted, he laid his hand companionably over hers. "I haven't played there in quite a while. I don't suppose it's changed."

She laughed and shook her head. "No. I played there, oh, about six months ago, I guess. Julie won a bundle at the baccarat table. I was a victim of the slots."

"I read the reviews. Were you as sensational as they said?" He smiled at her while one finger played with the thin gold bracelet at her wrist.

"Oh, I was much more sensational than they said," she assured him.

"I'd like to have seen you." His finger drifted lazily to her pulse. He felt it jump at his touch. "It's been much too long since I've heard you sing."

"You heard me just the other day in the studio," she pointed out. She took her hand from his to reach for her wine. He easily took her other one. "Brandon," she began, half-amused.

"I've heard you over the radio as well," he continued, "but it's not the same as watching you come alive at a concert. Or—" he smiled as his voice took on that soft, intimate note she remembered "—listening to you when you sing just for me."

His tone was as smooth as the burgundy she drank. Knowing how easily he could cloud her brain, she vowed to keep their conversation light. "Do you know what I want right now?" She lowered her own voice as she leaned toward him, but he recognized the laughter in her eyes.

"Dessert," he answered.

"You know me so well, Brandon." She smiled.

She wanted to go dancing. By mutual consent, when they left the restaurant they avoided the popular, trendy spots in town and found a crowded, smoky hole-in-the-wall club with a good band, much like the dozens they had both played in at the beginnings of their respective careers. They thought they wouldn't be recognized there. For almost twenty minutes they were right.

"Excuse me, aren't you Brand Carstairs?" The toothy young blond stared up at Brand in admiration. Then she glanced at Raven. "And Raven Williams."

"Bob Muldoon," Brand returned in a passable Texas drawl. "And my wife Sheila. Say howdy, Sheila," he instructed as he held her close and swayed on the postage-stamp-sized dance floor.

"Howdy," Raven said obligingly.

"Oh, Mr. Carstairs." She giggled and thrust out a cocktail napkin and a pencil. "Please, I'm Debbie. Could you write, 'To my good friend Debbie'?"

"Sure." Brand gave her one of his charming smiles and told Raven to turn around. He scrawled quickly, using her back for support.

"And you, too, Raven," Debbie asked when he'd finished. "On the other side."

It was typical of her fans to treat her informally. They thought of her as Raven. Her spontaneous warmth made it difficult for anyone to approach her with the awe normally reserved for superstars. Raven wrote on her side of the napkin when Brand offered his back. When she had finished, she noted that Debbie's eyes were wide and fixed on Brand. The pulse in her throat was jumping like a jackhammer. Raven knew what fantasies were dancing in the girl's mind.

"Here you are, Debbie." She touched her hand to bring the girl back to reality.

"Oh." Debbie took the napkin, looked at it blankly a moment, then smiled up at Brand. "Thanks." She looked at Raven, then ran a hand through her hair as if she had just realized what she had done. "Thanks a lot."

"You're welcome." Brand smiled but began to edge Raven toward the door.

It was too much to expect that the incident had gone unnoticed or that no one else would recognize them. For the next fifteen minutes they were wedged between the crowd and the door, signing autographs and dealing with a barrage of questions. Brand made certain they weren't separated from each other as he slowly maneuvered a path through the crowd.

They were jostled and shoved a bit, but he judged the crowd to be fairly civilized. It was still early by L.A. standards, and there hadn't been too much drinking yet. Still he wanted her out. This type of situation was notoriously explosive; the mood could change abruptly. One overenthusiastic fan and it could all be different. And ugly. Raven signed and signed some more while an occasional hand reached out to touch her hair. Brand felt a small wave of relief as he finally drew her out into the fresh air. Only a few followed them out of the club, and they were able to make their way to Brand's car with just a smattering of extra autographs.

"Damn it. I'm sorry." He leaned across her to lock her door. "I should have known better than to have taken you there."

Raven took a long breath, combing her hair back from her face with her fingers as she turned to him. "Don't be silly; I wanted to go. Besides, the people were nice."

"They aren't always," he muttered as the car merged with Los Angeles traffic.

"No." She leaned back, letting her body relax. "But I've been pretty lucky. Things have only gotten out of hand once or twice. It's the hype, I suppose, and it's to be expected that fans sometimes forget we're flesh and blood."

"So they try to take little chunks of us home with them."

"That," Raven said dryly, "can be a problem. I remember seeing a film clip of a concert you gave, oh, seven or eight years ago." She leaned her elbow on the back of the seat now and cupped her cheek in her palm. "A London concert where the fans broke through the security. They seemed to swallow you whole. It must have been dreadful."

"They loved me enough to give me a couple of broken ribs."

"Oh, Brandon." She sat up straight now, shocked. "That's terrible. I never knew that."

He smiled and moved his shoulders. "We played it down. It did rather spoil my taste for live concerts for a while. I got over it." He turned, heading toward the hills. "Security's tighter these days."

"I don't know if I'd be able to face an audience after something like that."

"Where else would you get the adrenaline?" he countered. "We need it, don't we? That instant gratification of applause." He laughed and pulled her over beside him. "Why else do we do it, Raven? Why else are there countless others out there scrambling to make it? Why did you start up the road, Raven?"

"To escape," she answered before she had time to think. She sighed and relaxed against his shoulder when he didn't demand an explanation. "Music was always something I could hold on to. It was constant, dependable. I needed something that was wholly mine." She turned her head a bit to study his profile. "Why did you?"

"For most of the same reasons, I suppose. I had something to say, and I wanted people to remember I said it."

She laughed. "And you were so radical at the start of your career. Such pounding, demanding songs. You were music's bad boy for some time."

"I've mellowed," he told her.

"'Fire Hot' didn't sound mellow to me," she commented. "Wasn't that the lead cut on your last album?"

He grinned, glancing down at her briefly. "I have to keep my hand in."

"It was number one on the charts for ten consecutive weeks," she pointed out. "That isn't bad for mellow."

"That's right," he agreed as if he'd just remembered. "It knocked off a little number of yours, didn't it? It was kind of a sweet little arrangement, as I recall. Maybe a bit heavy on the strings, but..."

She gave him an enthusiastic punch on the arm.

"Raven," Brand complained mildly. "You shouldn't distract me when I'm driving."

"That sweet little arrangement went platinum."

"I said it was sweet," he reminded her. "And the lyrics weren't bad. A bit sentimental, maybe, but..."

"I like sentimental lyrics," she told him, giving him another jab on the arm. "Not every song has to be a blistering social commentary."

"Of course not," he agreed reasonably. "There's always room for cute little ditties."

"Cute little ditties," Raven repeated, hardly aware that they had fallen back into one of their oldest habits by debating each other's work. "Just because I don't go in for showboating or lyrical trickery," she began. But when he swung off to the side of the road, she narrowed her eyes at him. "What are you doing?"

"Pulling over before you punch me again." He grinned and flicked a finger down her nose. "Showboating?"

"Showboating," she repeated. "What else do you call that guitar and piano duel at the end of 'Fire Hot'?"

"A classy way to fade out a song," he returned, and though she agreed with him, Raven made a sound of derision.

"I don't need the gadgetry. My songs are..."

"Overly sentimental."

She lifted a haughty brow. "If you feel my music is overly sentimental and cute, how do you imagine we'll work together?"

"Perfectly," he told her. "We'll balance each other, Raven, just as we always did."

"We're going to have terrible fights," she predicted.

"Yes, I imagine we will."

"And," she added, failing to suppress a smile, "you won't always win."

"Good. Then the fights won't be boring." He pulled her to him, and when she resisted, he cradled her head on his shoulder again. "Look," he ordered, pointing out the window, "why is it cities always look better at night from above?"

Raven looked down on the glittering Los Angeles skyline. "I suppose it's the mystique. It makes you wonder what's going on and you can't see how fast it's moving. Up here it's quiet." She felt his lips brush her temple. "Brandon." She drew away, but he stopped her.

"Don't pull away from me, Raven." It was a low, murmured request that shot heat up her spine. "Don't pull away from me."

His head lowered slowly, and his lips nibbled at hers, hardly touching, but the hand at the back of her neck was firm. He kept her facing him while he changed the angle of the kiss. His lips were persuasive, seductive. He kissed the soft, dewy skin of her cheeks, the fragile, closed eyelids, the scented hair at her temple. She could feel herself floating toward him as she always had, losing herself to him.

Her lips parted so that when his returned, he found them inviting him to explore. The kiss deepened, but slowly, as if he savored the taste of her on his tongue. Her hand slid up his chest until she held him and their bodies touched. He murmured something, then pressed his mouth against the curve of her neck. Her scent rose and enveloped him.

She moaned when he took her breast, a sound of both hunger and protest. His mouth came back to hers, plundering now as he responded to the need he felt flowing from her. She was unresisting, as open and warm as a shaft of sunlight. Her body was yearning toward him, melting irresistibly. She thought his hand burned through the thin fabric of her dress and set fire to her naked skin. It had been so long, she thought dizzily, so long since she had felt anything this intensely, needed anything this desperately. Her whole being tuned itself to him.

"Raven." His mouth was against her ear, her throat, the hollow of her cheek. "Oh, God, I want you." The kiss was urgent now, his hands no longer gentle. "So long," he said, echoing her earlier thought. "It's been so long. Come back with me. Let me take you back with me to the hotel. Stay with me tonight."

Passion flooded her senses. His tongue trailed over her warmed skin until he came again to her mouth. Then he took possession. The heat was building, strangling the breath in her throat, suffocating her. There was a fierce tug of war between fear and desire. She began to struggle.

"No." She took deep gulps of air. "Don't."

Brand took her by the shoulders and with one quick jerk had her face turned back up to his. "Why?" he demanded roughly. "You want me, I can feel it."

"No." She shook her head, and her hands trembled as she pushed at his chest. "I don't. I can't." Raven tried to deepen her breathing to steady it. "You're hurting me, Brandon. Please let me go."

Slowly he relaxed his fingers, then released her. "The same old story," he murmured. Turning away from her, he carefully drew out a cigarette and lit it. "You still give until I'm halfway mad, then pull away from me." He took a long, deep drag. "I should have been better prepared for it."

"You're not fair. I didn't start this; I never wanted..."

"You wanted," he tossed back furiously. "Damn it, Raven, you wanted. I've had enough women to know when I'm holding one who wants me."

She stiffened against the ache that was speeding through her. "You're better off with one of your many women, Brandon. I told you I wouldn't fall at your feet this time, and I meant it. If we can have a professional relationship, fine." She swallowed and straightened the hair his fingers had so recently caressed. "If you can't work with things on that level, then you'd best find another partner."

"I have the one I want." He tossed his cigarette through the open window. "We'll play it your way for a while, Raven. We're both professionals, and we both know what this musical's going to do for our careers." He started the engine. "I'll take you home."

Chapter 5

Raven hated to be late for a party, but there was no help for it. Her schedule was drum tight. If it hadn't been important that she be there, to rub elbows with Lauren Chase and a few other principals from the cast and crew of *Fantasy*, she'd have bowed out. There were only two days left before the start of her tour.

The truth was, Raven had forgotten about the party. Rehearsals had run over, then she had found herself driving into Beverly Hills to window shop. She hadn't wanted to buy anything but had simply wanted to do something mindless. For weeks there had been nothing but demand after demand, and she could look forward only to more of the same in the weeks to come. She would steal a few hours. She didn't want to think about her mother and the clean white sanitarium or song lists and cues or her confusion over Brand as she browsed through the treasures at Neiman-Marcus and Gucci. She looked at everything and bought nothing.

Arriving home, she was met by a huge handwritten note from Julie tacked on her bedroom door.

Party at Steve Jarett's. I know—you forgot. IMPORTANT! Get your glad rags together, babe, and go. Out with Lorenzo for dinner, we'll see you there.

J.

Raven swore briefly, rebelled, then capitulated before she stalked to the closet to choose an outfit. An hour later she was cruising fast through the Hollywood hills. It was important that she be there.

Steve Jarett was directing *Fantasy*. He was, at the moment, the silver screen's boy wonder, having just directed three major successes in a row. Raven wanted *Fantasy* to be his fourth as much as he did.

The party would be crowded, she mused, and looked wistfully at the open, star-studded sky. And noisy. Abruptly she laughed at herself. Since when did a noisy, crowded party become a trial by fire? There had been a time when she had enjoyed them. And there was no denying that the people who haunted these parties were fascinating and full of incredible stories. Raven could still be intrigued. It was just that... She sighed, allowing herself to admit the real reason she had dragged her feet. Brandon would be there. He was bound to be.

Would he bring a date? she wondered. Why wouldn't he? She answered herself shortly, downshifting as she took a curve. Unless he decided to wait and take his pick from the women there. Raven sighed again, seeing the blaze of lights that told her she was approaching Jarett's house. It was ridiculous to allow herself to get tied up in knots over something that had ended years before.

Her headlights caught the dull gleam of sturdy iron gates, and she slowed. The guard took her name, checked his list, then admitted her. She could hear the music before she was halfway up the curving, palm-lined drive.

There was a white-jacketed teenager waiting to hand her out of the Lamborghini. He was probably a struggling actor or an aspiring screenwriter or cinematographer, Raven thought as she smiled at him.

"Hi, I'm late. Do you think I can slip in without anybody noticing?"

"I don't think so, Ms. Williams, not looking like that."

Raven lifted her brows, surprised that he had recognized her so quickly in the dim light. But even if he had missed the face and hair, she realized, he would never have mistaken the voice.

"That's a compliment, isn't it?" she asked.

"Yes, ma'am," he said so warmly that she laughed.

"Well, I'm going to do my best, anyway. I don't like entrances unless they're on stage." She studied the sprawling, white brick mansion. "There must be a side door."

"Around to the left." He pointed. "There's a set of glass doors that lead into the library. Go through there and turn left. You should be able to slip in without being noticed."

"Thanks." She went to take a bill out of her purse, discovered she had left it in the car and leaned in the window to retrieve it. After a moment's search, she found a twenty and handed it to him.

"Thank *you*, Raven!," he enthused as she turned away. Then he called to her, "Ms. Williams?" Raven turned back with a half-smile. "Would you sign it for me?"

She tossed back her hair. "The bill?"

"Yeah."

She laughed and shook her head. "A fat lot of good it would do you then. Here." She dug into her bag again and came up with a slip of paper. One side was scrawled on, a list of groceries Julie had given her a few weeks before, but the other side was blank. "What's your name?" she demanded.

"Sam, Sam Rheinhart."

"Here, Sam Rheinhart," she said. Dashing off a quick line on the paper, she gave him the autograph. He stared after her, the twenty in one hand and the grocery list in the other, as she rushed off.

Raven found the glass doors without trouble. Though they were closed, the sounds of the party came clearly through. There were groups of people out back listening to a very loud rock band and drifting around by the pool. She stayed in the shadows. She wore an ankle-length skirt and a dolman-sleeve pullover in a dark plum color with silver metallic threads running through which captured the moonlight. Entering through the library, she gave herself a moment to adjust to the darkness before groping her way to the door.

There was no one in the hall immediately outside. Pleased with herself, Raven stepped out and gravitated slowly toward the focus of noise.

"Why, Raven!" It was Carly Devers, a tiny blond fluff of an actress with a little-girl voice and a rapier sharp talent. Though they generally moved in different circles, Raven liked her. "I didn't know you were here."

"Hi, Carly." They exchanged obligatory brushes of the cheek. "Congratulations are in order, aren't they? I heard you were being signed as the second lead in *Fantasy*."

"It's still in the working stage, but it looks like it. It's a gem of a part, and of course, working with Steve is *the* thing to do these days." As she spoke, she gave Raven a piercing look with her baby blue eyes. "You look fabulous," she said. Raven knew she meant it. "And of course, congratulations are in order for you as well, aren't they?"

"Yes, I'm excited about doing the score."

Carly tilted her head, and a smile spread over her face. "I was thinking more about Brand Carstairs than the score, darling." Raven's smile faded instantly. "Oops." Carly's smile only widened. "Still tender." There was no malice in her amusement. She linked her arm with Raven's. "I'd keep your little collaboration very tight this time around, Raven. I'm tempted to make a play for him myself, and I guarantee I'm not alone."

"What happened to Dirk Wagner?" Raven reminded herself to play it light as they drew closer to the laughter and murmurs of the party.

"Old news, darling, do try to keep up." Carly laughed, a tinkling bell of a sound that Raven could not help but respond to. "Still, I don't make it a habit to tread on someone else's territory."

"No signs posted, Carly," Raven said carelessly.

"*Hmm.*" Carly tossed back a lock of silver-blond hair. A waiter passed by with a tray of glasses, and she neatly plucked off two. "I've heard he's a marvelous lover,'' she commented, her eyes bright and direct on Raven's.

Raven returned the look equably and accepted the offered champagne. ''Have you? But then, I imagine that's old news, too.''

''Touché,'' Carly murmured into her glass.

''Is Brandon here?'' she asked, trying to prove to herself and her companion that the conversation meant nothing.

''Here and there,'' Carly said ambiguously. ''I haven't decided whether he's been trying to avoid the flocks of females that crawl around him or if he's seeking them out. He doesn't give away much, does he?''

Raven uttered a noncommittal sound and shrugged. It was time, she decided, to change the subject. ''Have you seen Steve? I suppose I should fight my way through and say hello.''

It was a typical enough party, Raven decided. Clothes ranged from Rive Gauche to Salvation Army. There was a steady drum beat from the band by the pool underlying the talk and laughter. The doors to the terrace were open wide, letting out the clouds of smoke and allowing the warm night air to circulate freely. The expansive lawns were ablaze with colored lights. Raven was more interested in the people but gave the room itself a quick survey.

It was decorated stunningly in white—walls, furniture, rugs—with a few vivid green accents slashed here and there. Raven decided it was gorgeous and that she couldn't have lived in it in a million years. She'd never be able to put her feet up on the elegant, free-form glass coffee table. She went back to the people.

Her eyes sought out Julie with her handsome Italian millionaire. She spotted Wayne with one of his bone-thin models hanging on his arm. Raven decided that the rumors that he would design the costumes for *Fantasy* must be true. There were others Raven recognized: producers, two major stars whom she had watched countless times in darkened theaters, a choreographer she knew only by face and reputation, a screenwriter she had met before socially and several others whom she knew casually or not at all. She and Carly were both drawn into the vortex of the party.

There were dozens of greetings to exchange, along with hand-kissing and cheek-brushing, before Raven could begin to inch her way back toward the edges. She was always more comfortable with one or two people at a time than with a crowd, unless she was onstage. At a touch on her arm, she turned and found herself facing her host.

"Well, hello." Raven smiled, appreciating the chance for a tête-à-tête.

"Hi. I was afraid you weren't going to make it."

Raven realized she shouldn't have been surprised that he had noticed her absence in the crowds of people. Steve Jarett noticed everything. He was a small, slight man with a pale, intense face and dark beard who looked ten years younger than his thirty-seven years. He was considered a perfectionist, often a pain when shooting, but the maker of beautiful films. He had a reputation for patience—enough to cause him to shoot a scene over and over and over again until he got precisely what he wanted. Five years before, he had stunned the industry with a low-budget sleeper that had become the unchallenged hit of the year. His first film had received an Oscar and had opened all the doors that had previously been firmly shut in his face. Steve Jarett held the keys now and knew exactly which ones to use.

He held both of her hands and studied her face. It was he who had insisted on Brand Carstairs as the writer of the original score for *Fantasy* and he who had approved the choice of Raven Williams as collaborator. *Fantasy* was his first musical, and he wasn't going to make any mistakes.

"Lauren's here," he said at length. "Have you met her?"

"No, I'd like to."

"I'd like you to get a real feel for her. I've copies of all her films and records. You might study them before you begin work on the score."

Raven's brow rose. "I don't think I've missed any of her movies, but I'll watch them again. She is the core of the story."

He beamed suddenly, unexpectedly. "Exactly. And you know Jack Ladd."

"Yes, we've worked together before. You couldn't have picked a better Joe."

"I'm making him work off ten pounds," Jarett said, plucking a canape from a tray. "He has some very unflattering things to say about me at the moment."

"But he's taking off the ten pounds," Raven observed.

Jarett grinned. "Ounce by ounce. We go to the same gym. I keep reminding him Joe's a struggling writer, not a fulfilled hedonist."

Raven gave a low, gurgling laugh and popped a bite of cheese into her mouth. "Overweight or not, you're assembling a remarkable team. I don't know how you managed to wrangle Larry Keaston into choreographing. He's been retired for five years."

"Bribes and perseverance," Jarett said easily, glancing over to where the trim, white-haired former dancer lounged in a pearl-colored armchair. "I'm talking him into doing a cameo." He grinned at Raven again. "He's pretending dignified reluctance, but he's dying to get in front of the cameras again."

"If you can even get him to do a time step on film, you'll have the biggest coup of the decade," Raven observed and shook her head. And he'd do it, she thought. He has the touch.

"He's a big fan of yours," Jarett remarked and watched Raven's eyes widen.

"Of mine? You're joking."

"I am not." He gave Raven a curious look. "He wants to meet you."

Raven stared at Jarett, then again at Larry Keaston. Such things never ceased to amaze her. How many times, as a child, had she watched his movies on fuzzy black and white TV sets in cramped rooms while she had waited for her mother to come home? "You don't have to ask me twice," she told Jarett. She linked her arm in his.

Time passed quickly as Raven began enjoying herself. She talked at length with Larry Keaston and discovered her girlhood idol to be personable and witty. He spoke in a string of expletives delivered in his posh Boston accent. Though she spoke briefly with Jack Ladd, she had yet to meet Lauren Chase when she spotted Wayne drinking quietly in a corner.

"All alone?" she asked as she joined him.

"Observing the masses, my dear," he told her, sipping lightly from his whiskey and soda. "It's amazing how intelligent people will insist on clothing themselves in inappropriate costumes. Observe Lela Marring," he suggested, tilting his head toward a towering brunette in a narrow, pink minidress. "I have no idea why a woman would care to wear a placemat in public."

Raven suppressed a giggle. "She has very nice legs."

"Yes, all five feet of them." He swerved his line of vision. "Then, of course, there's Marshall Peters, who's trying to start a new trend. Chest hair and red satin."

Raven followed the direction of his gaze and this time did not giggle. "Not everyone has your savoir-faire, Wayne."

"Of course not," he agreed readily and took out one of his imported cigarettes. "But surely, taste."

"I like the way you've dressed your latest proté-gée," Raven commented, nodding toward the thin model speaking to a current hot property in the television series game. The model was draped in cobwebby black and gold filigree lace. "I swear, Wayne, she can't be more than eighteen. What do you find to talk about?"

He gave Raven one of his long, sarcastic looks. "Are you being droll, darling?"

She laughed in spite of herself. "Not intentionally."

He gave her a pat on the cheek and lifted his glass again. "I notice Julie has her latest conquest with her, a Latin type with cheekbones."

"Shoes," Raven said vaguely, letting her eyes drift around the room. They rested in disbelief on a girl dressed in skin-tight leather pants and a spangled sweat shirt who wore heart-shaped glasses over

heavily kohl-darkened eyes. Knowing Wayne would
be horrified, she started to call his attention to her
when she spotted Brand across the room.

His eyes were already on hers. Raven realized with
a jolt that he had been watching her for some time.
It had been at just such a party that they had first
met, with noise and laughter and music all around
them. Their eyes had found each other's then also.

It had been Raven's first Hollywood party, and she
had been unashamedly overwhelmed. There had
been people there whom she had known only as
voices over the radio or faces on the screen. She had
come alone then, too, but in that case it had been a
mistake. She hadn't yet learned how to dodge and
twist.

She remembered she had been cornered by an actor, though oddly she couldn't recall his name or his
face. She hadn't had the experience to deal with him
and was slowly being backed against the wall when
her eyes had met Brand's. Raven remembered how
he had been watching her then, too, rather lazily, a
half-smile on his mouth. He must have seen the desperation in her eyes, because his smile had widened
before he had started to weave his way through the
crowd toward her. With perfect aplomb, Brand had
slid between Raven and the actor, then had draped
his arm over her shoulders.

"Miss me?" he asked, and he had kissed her
lightly before she could respond. "There're some

people outside who want to meet you." He had shot the actor an apologetic glance. "Excuse us."

Before another word could be exchanged, he had propelled Raven through the groups of people and out to a terrace. She could still remember the scent of orange blossoms that had drifted from an orchard nearby and the silver sprinkle of moonlight on the flagstone.

Of course Raven had recognized him and had been flustered. She had managed to regain her poise by the time they were alone in the shadows on the terrace. She had brushed a hand through her hair and smiled at him. "Thanks."

"You're welcome." It had been the first time he had studied her in his direct, quiet fashion. She could still remember the sensation of gentle intrusion. "You're not quite what I expected."

"No?" Raven hadn't known exactly how to take that.

"No." He'd smiled at her. "Would you like to go get some coffee?"

"Yes." The agreement had sprung from her lips before she had given it a moment's thought.

"Good. Let's go." Brand had held out his hand. After a brief hesitation, Raven had put hers into it. It had been as simple as that.

"Raven . . . Raven."

She was tossed back into the present by the sound of Wayne's voice and his hand on her arm. "Yes . . . what?" Blandly Raven looked up at him.

"Your thoughts are written all over your face," he murmured. "Not a wise move in a room full of curious people." Taking a fresh glass of champagne from a tray, he handed it to her. "Drink up."

She was grateful for something to do with her hands and took the glass. "I was just thinking," she said inadequately, then made a sound of frustration at Wayne's dry look. "So," she tried another tactic, "it seems we'll be working on the same project."

"Old home week?" he said with a crooked grin.

She shot him a direct look. "We're professionals," she stated, aware that they both knew whom she was speaking of.

"And friends?" he asked, touching a finger to her cheek.

Raven inclined her head. "We might be; I'm a friendly sort of person."

"*Hmm.*" Wayne glanced over her shoulder and watched Brand approach. "At least he knows how to dress," he murmured, approving of Brand's casual but perfectly cut slate-colored slacks and jacket. "But are you sure Cornwall's necessary? Couldn't you try Sausalito?"

Raven laughed. "Is there anything you don't know?"

"I certainly hope not. Hello, Brand, nice to see you again."

Raven turned, smiling easily. The jolt of the memory had passed. "Hello, Brandon."

"Raven." His eyes stayed on her face. "You haven't met Lauren Chase."

With an effort Raven shifted her eyes from his. "No." She smiled and looked at the woman at his side.

Lauren Chase was a slender wisp of a woman with a thick mane of dark, chestnut hair and sea-green eyes. There was something ethereal about her. Perhaps, Raven thought, it was that pale, almost translucent skin or the way she had of walking as though her feet barely touched the ground. She had a strong mouth that folded itself in at the corners and a long, slender neck that she adorned with gold chains. Raven knew she was well into her thirties and decided she looked it. This was a woman who needn't rely on dewy youth for her beauty.

She had been married twice. The first divorce had become an explosive affair that had received a great deal of ugly press. Her second marriage was now seven years old and had produced two children. Raven recalled there was little written about Lauren Chase's current personal life. Obviously, she had learned to guard her privacy.

"Brand tells me you're going to put the heart in the music." Lauren's voice was full and rich.

"That's quite a responsibility." Raven shot Brand a glance. "Generally Brand considers my lyrics on the sentimental side; often I consider him a cynic."

"Good." Lauren smiled. "Then we should have a score with some meat in it. Steve's given me final word on my own numbers."

Raven lifted a brow. She wasn't altogether certain if this had been a warning or a passing remark. "Then I suppose we should keep you up to date on our progress," she said agreeably.

"By mail and phone," Lauren said, slanting a glance at Brand, "since you're traipsing off halfway around the world to write."

"Artistic temperament," Brand said easily.

"No question, he has it," Raven assured her.

"You should know, I suppose." Lauren lifted a shoulder. Abruptly she fixed Raven with a sharp, straight look. "I want a lot out of this score. This is the one I've been waiting for." It was both a challenge and a demand.

Raven met the look with a slow nod. Lauren Chase was, she decided, the perfect Tessa. "You'll get it."

Lauren touched her upper lip with the tip of her tongue and smiled again. "Yes, I do believe I will at that. Well," she said, turning to Wayne and linking her arm through his, "why don't you buy me a drink and tell me about the fabulous costumes you're going to design for me?"

Raven watched them move away. "That," she murmured, toying with the stem of her glass, "is a woman who knows what she wants."

"And she wants an Oscar," Brand remarked. Raven's eyes came back to his. "You'll remember she's been nominated three times and edged out three times. She's determined it isn't going to happen again." He smiled then, fingering the dangling amethyst Raven wore at her ear. "Wouldn't you like to bag one yourself?"

"That's funny, I'd forgotten we could." She let the thought play in her mind. "It sounds good, but we'd better get the thing written before we dream up an acceptance speech."

"How're rehearsals going?"

"Good. Very good." She sipped absently at her champagne. "The band's tight. You leave for Vegas soon, don't you?"

"Yes. Did you come alone?"

She glanced back at him, confused for a moment. "Here? Why, yes. I was late because I'd forgotten about it altogether, but Julie left me a note. Did she introduce you to Lorenzo?"

"No, we haven't crossed paths tonight." As she began to search the crowd for Julie, Brand took her chin to bring her eyes back to his. "Will you let me take you home?"

Her expression shifted from startled to wary. "I have my car, Brandon."

"That isn't an answer."

Raven felt herself being drawn in and struggled. "It wouldn't be a good idea."

"Wouldn't it?" She sensed the sarcasm before he smiled, bent down and kissed her. It was a light touch—a tease, a promise or a challenge? "You could be right." He touched her earring again and set it swinging. "I'll see you in a few weeks," he said with a friendly grin, then turned and merged back into the crowd.

Raven stared after him, hardly realizing she had touched her lips with her tongue to seek his taste.

Chapter 6

The theater was dark and quiet. The sound of Raven's footsteps echoed, amplified by the excellent acoustics. Very soon the quiet would be shattered by stagehands, grips, electricians, all the many backstage people who would put together the essential and hardly noticed details of the show. Voices would bounce, mingling with hammering and other sounds of wood and metal. The noise would have a hollow, empty tone, almost like her footsteps. But it was an important sound, an appealing sound, which Raven had always enjoyed.

But she enjoyed the quiet, too and often found herself roaming an empty theater long before she was needed for rehearsals, hours before the fans started to line up outside the main doors. The press would be there then, with their everlasting, eternal questions. And Raven wasn't feeling too chummy with the press at the moment. Already she'd seen a half dozen different stories about herself and Brandon— speculation about their pending collaboration on *Fantasy* and rehashes of their former relationship. Old pictures had been dredged up and reprinted. Old questions were being asked again. Each time it was like bumping the same bruise.

Twice a week she put through a call to the Fieldmore Clinic and held almost identical conversations with Karter. Twice a week he transferred her to her mother's room. Though she knew it was foolish, Raven began to believe all the promises again, all the tearful vows. She began to hope. Without the demands of the tour to keep her occupied and exhausted, she knew she would have been an emotional wreck. Not for the first time in her life, she blessed her luck and her voice.

Mounting the stage, Raven turned to face an imaginary audience. The rows of seats seemed to roll back like a sea. But she knew how to navigate it, had known from the first moment of her first concert. She was an innate performer, just as her voice was natural and untrained. The hesitation, the uncertainty she felt now, had to do with the woman, not the singer. The song had hovered in her mind, but she still paused and considered before bringing it into play. Memories, she felt, could be dangerous things. But she needed to prove something to herself, so she sang. Her voice lifted, drifting to the far corners of the theater; her only accompaniment was her imagination.

Through the clouds and the rain
You were there,
And the sun came through to find us.

Overly sentimental? She hadn't thought so when the words had been written. Now Raven sang what she hadn't sung in years. Two minutes and forty-three seconds that bound her and Brand together. Whenever it had played on the radio, she had switched it off, and never, though the requests had been many, had she ever incorporated it in an album or in a concert. She sang it now as a kind of test, remembering the drifting, almost aching harmony of her own low tones combined with Brand's clean, cool voice. She needed to be able to face the memory of working with him if she was to face the reality of doing so. The tour had reached its halfway point. There were only two weeks remaining.

It didn't hurt the way she had been afraid it would; there was no sharp slap across the face. There was more of a warm ache, almost pleasant, somehow sexual. She remembered the last time she had been in Brand's arms in the quiet car in the hills above L.A.

"I've never heard you sing that."

Caught off-guard, Raven swung around to stage
right, her hand flying in quick panic to her throat.
"Oh, Marc!" On a laugh, she let out a long breath.
"You scared the wits out of me. I didn't know anyone was here."

"I didn't want you to stop. I've only heard the cut
you and Carstairs made of that." He came forward
now out of the shadows, and she saw he had an
acoustic guitar slung over his shoulder. It was typical; she rarely saw him without an instrument in his
hands or close by. "I've always thought it was too
bad you never used it again; it's one of your best. But
I guess you didn't want to sing it with anyone else."

Raven looked at him with genuine surprise. Of
course, that had been the essential reason, but she
hadn't realized it herself until that moment. "No, I
guess I didn't." She smiled at him. "I guess I still
don't. Did you come here to practice?"

"I called your room. Julie said you'd probably be
here." He walked to her, and since there were no
chairs, he sat on the floor. Raven sat with him. She
crossed her legs in the dun-colored trousers and let
her hair fall over the soft shoulders of her topaz an-
gora sweater. She was relaxed with him, ready to talk
or jam like any musician.

Raven smiled at Marc as he went through a quick,
complicated lick. "I'm glad you came by. Sometimes I have to get the feel of the theater before a

performance. They all begin to run together at this part of a tour." Raven closed her eyes and tilted her head, shaking her hair back. "Where are we, Kansas City? God, I hate the thought of getting back on that airplane. Shuttle here, shuttle there. It always hits me like this at the halfway point. In a couple of days I'll have my second wind."

Marc let her ramble while he played quick, quiet runs on the guitar. He watched her hands as they lay still on her knees. They were very narrow, and although they were tanned golden brown, they remained fragile. There was a light tracing of blue vein just under the skin. The nails were not long but well-shaped and painted in some clear, hardening polish with a blush of pink. There were no rings. Because they were motionless, he knew she was relaxed. Whatever nerves he had sensed when he had first spoken to her were stilled now.

"It's been going well, I think," she continued. "The Glass House is a terrific warm-up act, and the band's tight, even though we lost Kelly. The new bass is good, don't you think?"

"Knows his stuff," Marc said briefly. Raven grinned and reached over to tug his beard.

"So do you," she said. "Let me try."

Agreeably Marc slipped the strap over his head, then handed Raven his guitar. She was a better-than-average player, although she took a great deal of ribbing from the musicians in her troupe whenever she attempted the guitar. Periodically she threatened them with a bogus plan to incorporate her semiskillful playing into the act.

Still she liked to make music with the six strings. It soothed her. There was something intimate about holding an instrument close, feeling its vibrations against her own body. After hitting the same wrong note twice, Raven sighed, then wrinkled her nose at Marc's grin.

"I'm out of practice," she claimed, handing him back his Gibson.

"Good excuse."

"It's probably out of tune."

He ran quickly up and down the scales. "Nope."

"You might be kind and lie." She changed position, putting her feet flat on the floor and lacing her hands over her knees. "It's a good thing you're a musician. You'd have made a lousy politician."

"Too much traveling," he said as his fingers began to move again. He liked the sound of her laughter as it echoed around the empty theater.

"Oh, you're right! How can anyone remain sane going from city to city day after day? And music's such a stable business, too."

"Sturdy as a crap table."

"You've a gift for analogy," she told him, watching the skill of his fingers on the strings. "I love to watch you play," she continued. "It's so effortless. When Brandon was first teaching me, I..." but the words trailed off. Marc glanced up at her face, but his fingers never faltered. "I—it was difficult," she went on, wondering what had made her bring up the matter, "because he was left-handed, and naturally his guitar was, too. He bought me one of my own, but watching him, I had to learn backwards." She laughed, pleased with memory. Absently she lifted a hand to toy with the thick, dangling staff of her earring. "Maybe that's why I play the way I do. I'm always having to twist it around in my head before it can get to my fingers."

She lapsed into silence while Marc continued to play. It was soothing and somehow intimate with the two of them alone in the huge, empty theater. But his music didn't sound lonely as it echoed. She began to sing with it quietly, as though they were at home, seated on a rug with the walls close and comforting around them.

It was true that the tour had tired her and that the midway point had her feeling drained. But the interlude here was lifting her, though in a different way than the audience would lift her that night. This wasn't the quick, dizzying high that shot endurance back into her for the time she was on stage and in the lights. This was a steadying hand, like a good night's sleep or a home-cooked meal. She smiled at Marc when the song was over and said again, "I'm glad you came."

He looked at her, and for once his hands were silent on the strings. "How long have I been with you, Raven?"

She thought back to when Marc had first become a semi-regular part of her troupe. "Four—four and a half—years."

"Five this summer," he corrected. "It was in August, and you were rehearsing for your second tour. You had on baggy white pants and a T-shirt with a rainbow on it. You wore barefoot. You had a lost look in your eyes. Carstairs had gone back to England about a month before."

Raven stared at him. She had never heard him make such a long speech. "Isn't it strange that you would remember what I was wearing? It doesn't sound very impressive."

"I remember because I fell in love with you on the spot."

"Oh, Marc." She searched for something to say and found nothing. Instead, she reached up and took his hand. She knew he meant exactly what he said.

"Once or twice I've come close to asking you to live with me."

Raven let out a quick breath. "Why didn't you?"

"Because it would have hurt you to have said no and it would have hurt me to hear it." He laid the guitar across his lap and leaning over it, kissed her.

"I didn't know," she murmured, pressing both of his hands to her cheeks. "I should have. I'm sorry."

"You've never gotten him out of your head, Raven. It's damn frustrating competing with a memory." Marc squeezed her hands a moment, then released them. "It's also safe. I knew you'd never make a commitment to me, so I could avoid making one to you." He shrugged his well-muscled shoulders. "I think it always scared me that you were the kind of woman who would make a man give everything because you asked for nothing."

Her brows drew together. "Am I?"

"You need someone who can stand up to you. I'd never have been able to. I'd never have been able to say no or shout at you or make crazy love. Life's nothing without things like that, and we'd have ended up hurting each other."

She tilted her head and studied him. "Why are you telling me all this now?"

"Because I realized when I watched you singing that I'll always love you but I'll never have you. And if I did, I'd lose something very special." He reached across to touch her hair. "A fantasy that warms you on cold nights and makes you feel young again when you're old. Sometimes might-have-beens can be very precious."

Raven didn't know whether to smile or to cry. "I haven't hurt you?"

"No," he said so simply she knew he spoke the truth. "You've made me feel good. Have I made you uncomfortable?"

"No." She smiled at him. "You've made me feel good."

He grinned, then rose and held out a hand to her. "Let's go get some coffee."

Brand changed into jeans in his dressing room. It was after two in the morning, but he was wide awake, still riding on energy left over from his last show. He'd go out, he decided, and put some of it to use at the blackjack table. He could grab Eddie or one of the other guys from the band and cruise the casinos.

There'd be women. Brand knew there'd be a throng of them waiting for him when he left the privacy of his dressing room. He could take his pick. But he didn't want a woman. He wanted a drink and some cards and some action; anything to use up the adrenaline speeding through his system.

He reached for his shirt, and the mirror reflected his naked torso. It was tight and lean, teetering on being thin, but there were surprising cords of muscles in the arms and shoulders. He'd had to use them often when he'd been a boy on the London streets. He always wondered if it had been the piano lessons his mother had insisted on that had saved him from being another victim of the streets. Music had opened up something for him. He hadn't been able to get enough, learn enough. It had been like food, and he had been starving.

At fifteen Brand had started his own band. He was tough and cocky and talked his way into cheap little dives. There had been women even then; not just girls, but women attracted by his youthful sexuality and arrogant confidence. But they'd only been part of the adventure. He had never given up, though the living had been lean in the beer-soaked taverns. He had pulled his way up and made a local reputation for himself; both his music and his personality were strong.

It had taken time. He had been twenty when he had cut his first record, and it had gone nowhere. Brand had recognized that its failure had been due to a combination of poor quality recording, misman-agement and his own see-if-I-care attitude. He had taken a few steps back, found a savvy manager, worked hard on arrangements and talked himself into another recording session.

Two years later he had bought his family a house in the London suburbs, pushed his younger brother into a university and set off on his first American tour.

Now, at thirty, there were times he felt he'd never been off the merry-go-round. Half his life had been given over to his career and its demands. He was tired of wandering. Brand wanted something to focus his life, something to center it. He knew he couldn't give up music, but it wasn't enough by itself anymore. His family wasn't enough, and neither was the money or the applause.

He knew what he wanted. He had known five years before, but there were times he didn't feel as sure of himself as he had when he had been a fifteen-year-old punk talking his way past the back door of a third-rate nightclub. A capacity crowd had just paid thirty dollars a head to hear him, and he knew he could afford to take every cent he made on that two-week gig and throw it away on one roll of the dice. He had an urge to do it. He was restless, reckless, running on the same nerves he had felt the night he'd taken Raven home from their dinner date. He'd only seen her once after that—at Steve Jarett's house. Almost immediately afterward he had flown to Las Vegas to begin polishing his act.

It was catching up with him now—the tension, the anger, the needs. Not for the first time, Brand wondered whether his unreasonable need for her would end if he could have her once, just once. With quick, impatient movements, he thrust the tail of his shirt into the waist of his jeans. He knew better, but there were times he wished it could be. He left the dressing room looking for company.

For an hour Brand sat at the blackjack table. He lost a little, won a little, then lost it again. His mind wasn't on the cards. He had thought the noise, the bright lights, the rich smell of gambling was what he had wanted. There was a thin, intense woman beside him with a huge chunk of diamond on her finger and sapphires around her neck. She drank and lost at the same steady rhythm. Across the table was a young couple he pegged as honeymooners. The gold band on the girl's finger looked brilliantly new and untested. They were giddy with winning what Brand figured was about thirty dollars. There was something touching in their pleasure and in the soft, exchanged looks. All around them came the endless chinkity-chink of the slots.

Brand found himself as restless as he had been an hour before in his dressing room. A half-empty glass of bourbon sat on his elbow, but he left it as he rose. He didn't want the casino, and he felt an enormous surge of envy for the man who had his woman and thirty dollars worth of chips.

When he entered his suite, it was dark and silent, a sharp contrast to the world he had just left. Brand didn't bother hitting the switches as he made his way into the bedroom. Taking out a cigarette, he sat on the bed before lighting it. The flame made a sharp hiss and a brief flare. He sat with the silence, but the adrenaline still pumped. Finally he switched on the small bedside lamp and picked up the phone.

Raven was deep in sleep, but the ringing of the phone shot panic through her before she was fully awake. Her heart pounded in her throat before the mists could clear. She'd grown up with calls coming in the middle of the night. She forgot where she was and fumbled for the phone with a sense of dread and anticipation.

"Yes . . . hello."

"Raven, I know I woke you. I'm sorry."

She tried to shake away the fog. "Brandon? Is something wrong? Are you all right?"

"Yes, I'm fine. Just unbelievably inconsiderate."

Relaxing, Raven sank back on the pillows and tried to orient herself. "You're in Vegas, aren't you?" The dim light told her it was nearing dawn. He was two hours behind her. Or was it three? She couldn't for the life of her remember what time zone she was in.

"Yes, I'm in Vegas through next week."

"How's the show going?"

It was typical of her, he mused, not to demand to know why the hell he had called her in the middle of the night. She would simply accept that he needed to talk. He drew on the cigarette and wished he could touch her. "Better than my luck at the tables."

She laughed, comfortably sleepy. The connection was clean and sharp; he didn't sound hundreds of miles away. "Is it still blackjack?"

"I'm consistent," he murmured. "How's Kansas?"

"Where?" He laughed, pleasing her. "The audience was fantastic," she continued, letting her mind wander back to the show. "Has been straight along.

That's the only thing that keeps you going on a tour like this. Will you be there in time for the show in New York? I'd love you to hear the warm-up act."

"I'll be there." He laid back on the bed as some of the superfluous energy started to drain. "Cornwall is sounding more and more appealing."

"You sound tired."

"I wasn't; I am now. Raven . . ."

She waited, but he didn't speak. "Yes?"

"I missed you. I needed to hear your voice. Tell me what you're looking at," he demanded, "what you see right now."

"It's dawn," she told him. "Or nearly. I can't see any buildings, just the sky. It's more mauve than gray and the light's very soft and thin." She smiled; it had been a long time since she had seen a day begin. "It's really lovely, Brandon. I'd forgotten."

"Will you be able to sleep again?" He had closed his eyes; the fatigue was taking over.

"Yes, but I'd rather go for a walk, though I don't think Julie would appreciate it if I asked her to come along."

Brand pried off his shoes, using the toe of one foot, then the other. "Go back to sleep, and we'll walk on the cliffs one morning in Cornwall. I shouldn't have woken you."

"No, I'm glad you did." She could hear the change; the voice that had been sharp and alert was now heavy. "Get some rest, Brandon. I'll look for you in New York."

"All right. Good night, Raven."

He was asleep almost before he hung up. Fifteen hundred miles away, Raven laid her cheek on the pillow and watched the morning come.

Chapter 7

Raven tried to be still while her hair was being twisted and knotted and groomed. Her dressing room was banked with flowers; they had been arriving steadily for more than two hours. And it was crowded with people. A tiny little man with sharp, black eyes touched up her blusher. Behind her, occasionally muttering in French, was the nimble-fingered woman who did her hair. Wayne was there, having business of his own here in New York. He'd told Raven that he'd come to see his designs in action and was even now in deep discussion with her dresser. Julie opened the door to another flower delivery.

"Have I packed everything? You know, I should have told Brandon to give me an extra day in town for shopping. There're probably a dozen things I need." Raven turned in her seat and heard the swift French oath as her partially knotted hair flew from the woman's fingers. "Sorry, Marie. Julie, did I pack a coat? I might need one." Slipping the card from the latest arrangement of flowers, she found it was from a successful television producer with whom she'd worked on her last TV special. "They're from Max.... There's a party tonight. Why don't you go?" She handed the card to Julie and allowed her lip liner to be straightened by the finicky makeup artist.

"Yes, you packed a coat, your suede, which you could need this early in the spring. And several sweaters," Julie added distractedly, checking her list. "And maybe I will."

"I can't believe this is it, the last show. It's been a good tour, hasn't it, Julie?" Raven turned her head and winced at the sharp tug on her hair.

"I can't remember you ever getting a better response or deserving one more...."

"And we're all glad it's over," Raven finished for her.

"I'm going to sleep for a week." Julie found space for the flowers, then continued to check off things in her notebook. "Not everyone has your constant flow of energy."

"I love playing New York," she said, tucking up her legs to the despair of her hairdresser.

"You must hold still!"

"Marie, if I hold still much longer, I'm going to explode." Raven smiled at the makeup artist as he fussed around her face. "You always know just what to do. It looks perfect; I feel beautiful."

Recognizing the signal, Julie began nudging people from the room. Eventually they went, and soon only Julie and Wayne were left. The room quieted considerably; now the walls hummed gently with the vibrations of the warm-up act. Raven let out a deep sigh.

"I'll be so glad to have my face and body and hair back," she said and sprawled in the chair. "You should have seen what he made me put all over my face this morning."

"What was it?" Wayne asked absently as he smoothed the hem of one of her costumes.

"Green," she told him and shuddered.

He laughed and turned to Julie. "What are you going to do when this one takes off to the moors?"

"Cruise the Greek Islands and recuperate." She pushed absently at the small of her back. "I've already booked passage on the ninth. These tours are brutal."

"Listen to her." Raven sniffed and peered at herself critically in the glass. "She's the one who's held the whip and chair for four weeks. He certainly makes me look exotic, doesn't he?'' She wrinkled her nose and spoiled the effect.

"Into costume," Julie commanded.

"See? Orders, orders." Obediently Raven rose.

"Here." Wayne lifted the red and silver dress from the hanger. "Since I nudged your dresser along, I'll be your minion."

"Oh, good, thanks." She stepped out of her robe and into the dress. "You know, Wayne," she continued as he zipped her up, "you were right about the black number. It gets a tremendous response. I never know if they're applauding me or the costume after that set."

"Have I ever let you down?" he demanded as he tucked a pleat.

"No." She turned her head to smile at him over her shoulder. "Never. Will you miss me?"

"Tragically." He kissed her ear.

There was a brief, brisk knock at the door. "Ten minutes, Ms. Williams."

She took a long breath. "Are you going to go out front?"

"I'll stay back with Julie." He glanced over at her, lifting a brow in question.

"Yes, thanks. Here, Raven, don't forget these wonderfully gaudy earrings." She watched Raven fasten one. "Really, Wayne, they're enough to make me shudder, but they're fabulous with that dress."

"Naturally."

She laughed, shaking her head. "The man's ego," she said to Raven, "never ceases to amaze me."

"As long as it doesn't outdistance the talent," he put in suavely.

"New York audiences are tough." Raven spoke quickly, her voice jumping suddenly with nerves and excitement. "They scare me to death."

"I thought you said you loved playing New York." Wayne took out a cigarette and offered one to Julie.

"I do, especially at the end of a tour. It keeps you sharp. They're really going to know if I'm not giving them everything. How do I look?"

"The dress is sensational," Wayne decided. "You'll do."

"Some help you are."

"Let's go," Julie urged. "You'll miss your cue."

"I never miss my cue." Raven fussed with the second earring, stalling. He'd said he'd be here, she told herself. *Why isn't he?* He could have gotten the time mixed up, or he could be caught in traffic. Or he could simply have forgotten that he'd promised to be here for the show.

The quick knock came again. "Five minutes, Ms. Williams."

"Raven." Julie's voice was a warning.

"Yes, yes, all right." She turned and gave them both a flippant smile. "Tell me I'm wonderful when it's over, even if I wasn't. I want to end the tour feeling marvelous."

Then she was dashing for the door and hurrying down the hall where the sounds of the warm-up band were no longer gentle; now they shook the walls.

"Ms. Williams, Ms. Williams! Raven!"

She turned, breaking the concentration she'd been building and looked at the harried stage manager. He thrust a white rose into her hand.

"Just came back for you."

Raven took the bud and lifted it, wanting to fill herself with the scent. She needed no note or message to tell her it was from Brand. For a moment she simply dreamed over it.

"Raven." The warm-up act had finished; the transition to her own band would take place on the darkened stage quickly. "You're going to miss your cue."

"No, I'm not." She gave the worried stage manager a kiss, forgetful of her carefully applied lipstick. Twirling the rose between her fingers, she took it with her. They were introducing her as she reached the wings.

Big build-up; don't let the audience cool down. They were already cheering for her. *Thirty seconds; take a breath.* Her band hit her introduction. Music crashed through the cheers. *One, two, three!*

She ran out, diving into a wave of applause.

The first set was hot and fast, staged to keep the audience up and wanting more. She seemed to be a ball of flame with hundreds of colored lights flashing around her. Raven knew how to play to them, play with them, and she pumped all her energy into a routine she had done virtually every night for four weeks. Enthusiasm and verve kept it fresh. It was hot under the lights, but she didn't notice. She was wrapping herself in the audience, in the music. The costume sizzled and sparked. Her voice smoked.

It was a demanding forty minutes, and when she rushed offstage during an instrumental break, she had less than three minutes in which to change costumes. Now she was in white, a brief, shimmering top covered with bugle beads matched with thin harem pants. The pace would slow a bit, giving the audience time to catch their breath. The balance was in ballads, the slow trembling ones she did best. The lighting was muted, soft and moody.

It was during a break between songs, when she traditionally talked to the audience, that someone in the audience spotted Brand in their midst. Soon more people knew, and while Raven went on unaware of the disturbance, the crowd soon became vocal. Shielding her eyes, she could just make out the center of the commotion. Then she saw him. It seemed they wanted him up on stage.

Raven was a good judge of moods and knew the value of showmanship. If she didn't invite Brand on stage, she'd lose the crowd. They had already taken the choice out of her hands.

"Brandon." Raven spoke softly into the mike, but her voice carried. Though she couldn't see his eyes with the spotlight in her own, she knew he was looking at her. "If you come up and sing," she told him lightly, "we might get you a refund on your ticket." She knew he'd grin at that. There was an excited rush of applause and cheers as he rose and came to the stage.

He was all in black: trim, well-cut slacks and a casual polo sweater. The contrast was striking as he stood beside her. It might have been planned. Smiling at her, he spoke softly, out of the range of the microphone. "I'm sorry, Raven, I should have gone backstage. I wanted to watch you from out front."

She tilted her head. It was, she discovered, more wonderful to see him than she had imagined. "You're the one being put to work. What would you like to do?"

Before he could answer, the demand sprang from the crowd. Once the idea formed, it was shouted over and over with growing enthusiasm. Raven's smile faded. "Clouds and Rain."

Brand took her wrist and lifted the rose she held. "You remember the words, don't you?"

It was a challenge. A stagehand rushed out with a hand mike for Brand.

"My band doesn't know it," she began.

"I know it." Marc shifted his guitar and watched them. The crowd was still shouting when he gave the opening chords. "We'll follow you."

Brand kept his hand on Raven's wrist and lifted his own mike.

Raven knew how it needed to be sung: face to face, eye to eye. It was a caress of a song, meant for lovers. The audience was silent now. Their harmony was close, intricate. Raven had once thought it must be like making love. Their voices flowed into each other. And she forgot the audience, forgot the stage and for a moment forgot the five years.

There was more intimacy in singing with him than she had ever allowed in any other aspect of their relationship. Here she could not resist him. When he sang to her, it was as if he told her there wasn't anyone else, had never been anyone else. It was more moving than a kiss, more sexual than a touch.

When they finished, their voices hung a moment, locked together. Brand saw her lips tremble before he brought her close and took them.

They might have been on an island rather than on stage, spotlighted for thousands. She didn't hear the tumultuous applause, the cheers, the shouting of their names. Her arms went around him, one hand holding the mike, the other the rose. Cameras flashed like fireworks, but she was trapped in a velvet darkness. She lost all sense of time; her lips might have moved on his for hours or days or only seconds. But when he drew her away, she felt a keener sense of loss than any she had ever known before. Brand saw the confusion in her eyes, the dazed desire, and smiled.

"You're better than you ever were, Raven." He kissed her hand. "Too bad about those sentimental numbers you keep sticking into the act."

Her brows rose. "Try to boost your flagging career by letting you sing with me, and you insult me." Her balance was returning as they took a couple of elaborate bows, hands linked.

"Let's see if you can carry the rest on your own, love. I've warmed them back up for you." He kissed her again, but lightly now, on the cheek, before he waved to the audience and strolled offstage left.

Raven grinned at his back, then turned to her audience. "Too bad he never made it, isn't it?"

Raven should have been wrung dry after the two hours were over. But she wasn't. She'd given them three encores, and though they clamored for more, Brand caught her hand as she hesitated in the wings.

"They'll keep you out there all night, Raven." He could feel the speed of her pulse under his fingers. Because he knew how draining two hours onstage could be, he urged her back down the hall toward her dressing room.

There were crowds of people jammed in together in the hallway, congratulating her, touching her. Now and then a reporter managed to elbow through to shoot out a question. She answered, and Brandon tossed off remarks with quick charm while steering her determinedly toward her dressing room. Once inside, he locked the door.

"I think they liked me," she said gravely, then laughed and spun away from him. "I feel so good!" Her eyes lit on the bucket of ice that cradled a bottle. "Champagne?"

"I thought you'd need to console yourself after a flop like that." Brand moved over and drew out the bottle. "You'll have to open the door soon and see people. Do try to put on a cheerful front, love."

"I'll do my best." The cork popped, and the white froth fizzed a bit over the mouth of the bottle.

Brand poured two glasses to the rim and handed her one. "I meant it, Raven." He touched his glass to hers. "You were never better."

Raven smiled, bringing the glass to her lips. Again, he felt the painful thrust of desire. Carefully Brand took the glass from her, then set both it and his own down again. "There's something I didn't finish out there tonight."

She was unprepared. Even though he drew her close slowly and took his time bringing his mouth to hers, Raven wasn't ready. It was a long, deep kiss that mingled with the champagne. His mouth was warm on hers, seeking. His hands ran over her hips, snugly encased in the thin black jumpsuit, but she could sense he was under very tight control.

His tongue made a thorough, lengthy journey through the moist recesses of her mouth, and she responded in kind. But he wanted her to do more than give; he wanted her to want more. And she did, feeling the pull of need, the flash of passion. She could feel the texture of his long, clever fingers through the sheer material of her costume, then flesh to flesh as he brought them up to caress the back of her neck.

Her head was swimming with a myriad of sensations: excitement and power still clinging from her performance; the heady, heavy scent of mixed flowers which crowded the air; the firm press of his body against her; and desire, more complex, more insistent than she had been prepared for.

"Brandon," she murmured against his lips. She wanted him more, wanted him desperately, and was afraid.

Brand drew her away, then carefully studied her face. Her eyes were like thin glass over her emotions. "You're beautiful, Raven, one of the most beautiful women I know."

She was unsteady and tried to find her balance without clinging to him. She stepped back, resting her hand on the table that held their glasses. "One of the most?" she challenged, lifting her champagne.

"I know a lot of women." He grinned as he lifted his own glass. "Why don't you take that stuff off your face so I can see you?"

"Do you know how long I had to sit still while he troweled this stuff on?" Moving to the dressing table, she scooped up a generous glob of cold cream. Her blood was beginning to settle. "It's supposed to make me glamorous and alluring." She slathered it on.

"You make me nervous when you're glamorous, and you'd be alluring in a paper sack."

She lifted her eyes to his in the mirror. His expression was surprisingly serious. "I think that was a compliment." She smeared the white cream generously over her face and grinned. "Am I alluring now?"

Brand grinned back, then slowly let his eyes roam down her back to focus on her snugly clad bottom. "Raven, don't fish. The answer is obvious."

She began to tissue off the cream and with it the stage makeup. "Brandon. It was good to sing with you again." After removing the last of the cream from her face, Raven toyed with the stem of her champagne glass. "I always felt very special when I sang with you. I still do." He watched her chew for a moment on her bottom lip as if she was unsure about what she should say. "I imagine they'll play up that duet in the papers. They'll probably make

something else out of it, especially—especially with
the way we ended it."

"I like the way we ended it." Brand came over and
laid his hands on her shoulders. "It should always be
ended that way." He kissed the back of her neck
while his eyes smiled into hers in the glass. "Are you
worried about the press, Raven?"

"No, of course not. But, Brandon..."

"Do you know," he interrupted, brushing the hair
away from her neck with the back of his hand, "no
one else calls me that but my mother. Strange." He
bent, nuzzling his lips into the sensitive curve of her
neck. "You affect me in an entirely different way."

"Brandon..."

"When I was a boy," he continued, moving his
lips up to her ear, "and she called me Brandon, I
knew that was it. Whatever crime I'd committed had
been found out. Justice was about to strike."

"I imagine you committed quite a few crimes."
She forced herself to speak lightly. When she would
have moved away, he turned her around to face him.

"Too many to count." He leaned to her, but instead of the kiss she expected and prepared for, he
caught her bottom lip between his teeth. She clutched
at his shirt as she struggled for breath and balance.
Their eyes were open and on each other's, but his
face dimmed, then faded, as passion clouded her vision.

Brand released her, then gave her a quick kiss on the nose. Raven ran a hand through her hair, trying to steady herself. He was tossing her back and forth too swiftly, too easily.

"Do you want to change before we let anyone in?" he asked. When she could focus again, Raven saw he was drinking champagne and watching her. There was an odd look on his face, as if, she thought, he were a boxer checking for weaknesses, looking for openings.

"I—yes." Raven brought herself back. "Yes, I think I would, but..." She glanced around the dressing room. "I don't know what I did with my clothes."

He laughed, and the look was gone from his face. Relieved, Raven laughed with him. They began to search through the flowers and sparkling costumes for her jeans and tennis shoes.

Chapter 8

It was late when they arrived at the airport. Raven was still riding on post-performance energy and chattered about everything that came into her head. She looked up at a half-moon as she and Brand transferred from limo to plane. The private jet wasn't what she had been expecting, and studying the comfortably lush interior of the main cabin helped to allay the fatigue of yet one more flight.

It was carpeted with a thick, pewter-colored shag and contained deep, leather chairs and a wide, plush sofa. There was a padded bar at one end and a doorway at the other which she discovered led into a tidy galley. "You didn't have this before," she com-

mented as she poked her head into another room and
found the bath, complete with tub.

"I bought it about three years ago." Brand
sprawled on the sofa and watched her as she explored. She looked different than she had a short
time before. Her face was naked now, and he found
he preferred it that way. Makeup seemed to need-
lessly gloss over her natural beauty. She wore faded
jeans and sneakers, which she immediately pried off
her feet. An oversized yellow sweater left her shape-
less. It made him want to run his hands under it and
find her. "Do you still hate to fly?"

Raven gave him a rueful grin. "Yes. You'd think
after all this time I'd have gotten over it, but..." She
continued to roam the cabin, not yet able to settle. If
she had to, Raven felt she could give the entire performance again. She had enough energy.

"Strap in," Brand suggested, smiling at the quick,
nervous gestures. "We'll get started, then you won't
even know you're in the air."

"You don't know how many times I've heard that
one." Still she did as he said and waited calmly
enough while he told the pilot they were ready. In a
few minutes they were airborne, and she was able to
unstrap and roam again.

"I know the feeling," Brand commented, watching her. She turned in silent question. "It's as though
you still have one last burst of energy to get rid of.

It's the way I felt that night in Vegas when I called and woke you up."

She caught back her hair with both hands. "I feel I should jog for a few miles. It might settle me down."

"How about some coffee?"

"Yes." She wandered over to a porthole and pressed her nose against it. It was black as pitch outside the glass. "Yes, coffee would be nice, then you can tell me what marvelous ideas you have forming for the score. You've probably got dozens of them."

"A few." She heard the clatter of cups. "I imagine you've some of your own."

"A few," she said, and he chuckled. Turning away from the dark window, she saw him leaning against the opening between the galley and the main cabin. "How soon do you think we'll start to fight?"

"Soon enough. Let's wait at least until we're settled into the house. Is Julie going back to L.A., or have you tied up all your loose ends there?"

A shadow crossed her face. Raven thought of the one brief visit she had paid to her mother since the start of the tour. They had had a day's layover in Chicago, and she had used the spare time to make the impossible flight to the coast and back. There had been the inevitable interview with Karter and a brief, emotional visit with her mother. Raven had been relieved to see that the cast had gone from her mother's skin and that there was more flesh to her face.

There had been apologies and promises and tears, just as there always were, Raven thought wearily. And as she always did, she had begun to believe them again.

"I never seem to completely tie up the loose ends," she murmured.

"Will you tell me what's wrong?"

She shook her head. She couldn't bear to dwell on unhappiness now. "No, nothing, nothing really." The kettle sang out, and she smiled. "Your cue," she told him.

He studied her for a moment while the kettle spit peevishly behind him. Then, turning, he went back into the galley to fix the coffee. "Black?" he asked, and she gave an absent assent.

Sitting on the sofa, Raven let her head fall back while the energy began to subside. It was almost as if she could feel it draining. Brand recognized the signs as soon as he came back into the room. He set down her mug of coffee, then sipped thoughtfully from his own as he watched her. Sensing him, Raven slowly opened her eyes. There was silence for a moment; her body and her mind were growing lethargic.

"What are you doing?" she murmured.

"Remembering."

Her lids shuttered down, concealing her eyes and their expression. "Don't."

He drank again, letting his eyes continue their slow, measured journey over her. "It's a bit much to ask me not to remember, Raven, isn't it?" It was a question that expected no answer, and she gave it none. But her lids fluttered up again.

He didn't have her full trust, nor did he believe he had ever had it. That was the root of their problems. He studied her while he stood and drank his coffee. There was high, natural color in her cheeks, and her eyes were dark and sleepy. She sat, as was her habit, with her legs crossed under her and her hands on her knees. In contrast to the relaxed position, her fingers moved restlessly.

"I still want you. You know that, don't you?"

Again Raven left his question unanswered but he saw the pulse in her throat begin to thump. When she spoke, her voice was calm. "We're going to work together, Brandon. It's best not to complicate things."

He laughed, not in mockery but in genuine amusement. She watched his eyes lose their brooding intensity and light. "By all means, let's keep things simple." After draining his coffee, he walked over and sat beside her. In a smooth, practiced move he drew her against his side. "Relax," he told her, annoyed when she resisted. "Give me some credit. I know how tired you are. When are you going to trust me, Raven?"

She tilted her head until she could see him. Her look was long and eloquent before she settled into the crook of his shoulder and let out a long sigh. Like a child, she fell asleep quickly, and like that of a child, the sleep was deep. For a long moment he stayed as he was, Raven curled against his side. Then he laid her down on the sofa, watching as her hair drifted about her.

Rising, Brand switched off the lights. In the dark he settled into one of the deep cabin chairs and lit a cigarette. Time passed as he sat gazing out at a sprinkle of stars and listening to Raven's soft, steady breathing. Unable to resist, he rose, and moving to her, laid down beside her. She stirred when he brushed the hair from her cheek, but only to snuggle closer to him. Over the raw yearning came a curiously sweet satisfaction. He wrapped his arm around her, felt her sigh, then slept.

It was Brand who awoke first. As was his habit, his mind and body came together quickly. He laid still and allowed his eyes to grow accustomed to the darkness. Beside him, curled against his chest, Raven slept on.

He could make out the curve of her face, the pixie sharp features, the rain straight fall of hair. Her leg was bent at the knee and had slipped between his. She was soft and warm and tempting. Brand knew he had experience enough to arouse her into submission before she was fully awake. She would be drowsy and disoriented.

The hazy gray of early dawn came upon them as he watched her. He could make out her lashes now, a long sweep of black that seemed to weigh her lids down. He wanted her, but not that way. Not the first time. Asleep, she sighed and moved against him. Desire rippled along his skin. Carefully Brand shifted away from her and rose.

In the kitchen he began to make coffee. A glance at his watch and a little arithmetic told him they'd be landing soon. He thought rather enthusiastically about breakfast. The drive from the airport to his house would take some time. He remembered an inn along the way where they could get a good meal and coffee better than the instant he was making.

Hearing Raven stir, he came to the doorway and watched her wake up. She moaned, rolled over and unsuccessfully tried to bury her face. Her hand reached out for a pillow that wasn't there, then slowly, on a disgusted sigh, she opened her eyes. Brand watched the stages as her eyes roamed the room. First came disinterest, then confusion, then sleepy understanding.

"Good morning," he ventured, and she shifted her eyes to him without moving her head. He was grinning at her, and his greeting was undeniably cheerful. She had a wary respect for cheerful risers.

"Coffee," she managed and shut her eyes again.

"In a minute." The kettle was beginning to hiss behind him. "How'd you sleep?"

Dragging her hands through her hair, she made a courageous attempt to sit up. The light was still gray now but brighter, and she pressed her fingers against her eyes for a moment. "I don't know yet," she mumbled from behind her hands. "Ask me later."

The whistle blew, and as Brand disappeared back into the galley, Raven brought her knees up to her chest and buried her face against them. She could hear him talking to her, making bright, meaningless conversation, but her mind wasn't yet receptive. She made no attempt to listen or to answer.

"Here, love." As Raven cautiously raised her head, Brand held out a steaming mug. "Have a bit, then you'll feel better." She accepted with murmured thanks. He sat down beside her. "I've a brother who wakes up ready to bite someone's— anyone's—head off. It's metabolism, I suppose."

Raven made a noncommittal sound and began to take tentative sips. It was hot and strong. For some moments there was silence as he drank his own cream-cooled coffee and watched her. When her cup was half empty, she looked over and managed a rueful smile.

"I'm sorry, Brandon. I'm simply not at my best in the morning. Especially early in the morning." She tilted her head so that she could see his watch, made a brave stab at mathematics, then gave up. "I don't suppose it matters what time it actually is," she decided, going back to the coffee. "It'll take me a few days to adjust to the change, anyway."

"A good meal will set you up," he told her, lazily sipping at his own coffee. "I read somewhere where drinking yeast and jogging cures jet lag, but I'll take my chances with breakfast."

"Yeast?" Raven grimaced into her mug, then drained it. "I think sleep's a better cure, piles of it." The mists were clearing, and she shook back her hair. "I guess we'll be landing soon, won't we?"

"Less than an hour, I'd say."

"Good. The less time I spend awake on a plane, the less time I have to think about being on one. I slept like a rock." With another sigh, Raven stretched her back, letting her shoulders lift and fall with the movement. "I made poor company." Her system was starting to hum again, though on slow speed.

"You were tired." Over the rim of his cup he watched the subtle movements of her body beneath the oversized sweater.

"I turned off like a tap," she admitted. "It happens that way sometimes after a concert." She lifted one shoulder in a quick shrug. "But I suppose we'll both be better today for the rest. Where did you sleep?"

"With you."

Raven closed her mouth on a yawn, swallowed and stared at him. "What?"

"I said I slept with you, here on the couch." Brand made a general gesture with his hand. "You like to snuggle."

She could see he was enjoying her dismayed shock. His eyes were deep blue with amusement as he lifted his cup again. "You had no right..." Raven began.

"I always fancied being the first man you slept with," he told her before draining his cup. "Want some more coffee?"

Raven's face flooded with color; her eyes turned dark and opaque. She sprang up, but Brand managed to pluck the cup from her hand before she could hurl it across the room. For a moment she stood, breathing hard, watching him while he gave her his calm, measuring stare.

"Don't flatter yourself," she tossed out. "You don't know how many men I've slept with."

Very precisely, he set down both coffee cups, then looked back up at her. "You're as innocent as the day you were born, Raven. You've barely been touched by a man, much less made love to."

Her temper flared like a rocket. "You don't know anything about who I've been with in the last five years, Brandon." She struggled to keep from shouting, to keep her voice as calm and controlled as his. "It's none of your business how many men I've slept with."

He lifted a brow, watching her thoughtfully. "Innocence isn't something to be ashamed of, Raven."

"I'm not..." She stopped, balling her fists. "You had no right to—" She swallowed and shook her head as fury and embarrassment raced through her. "—While I was asleep," she finished.

"Do what while you were asleep?" Brandon demanded, lazing back on the sofa. "Ravish you?" His humor shimmered over the old-fashioned word and made her feel ridiculous. "I don't think you'd have slept through it, Raven."

Her voice shook with emotion. "Don't laugh at me, Brandon."

"Then don't be such a fool." He reached over to the table beside him for a cigarette, then tapped the end of it against the surface without lighting it. His eyes were fixed on hers and no longer amused. "I could have had you if I'd wanted to, make no mistake about it."

"You have colossal nerve, Brandon. Please remember that you're not privy to my sex life and that you wouldn't have had me because I don't want you. I choose my own lovers."

She hadn't realized he could move so fast. The indolent slouch on the sofa was gone in a flash. He reached up, seizing her wrist, and in one swift move had yanked her down on her back, trapping her body with his. Her gasp of surprise was swallowed as his weight pressed down on her.

Never, in all the time they had spent together past and present, had Raven seen him so angry. An iron taste of fear rose in her throat. She could only shake her head, too terrified to struggle, too stunned to move. She had never suspected he possessed the capacity for violence she now read clearly on his face. This was far different from the cold rage she had seen before and which she knew how to deal with. His fingers bit into her wrist while his other hand came to circle her throat.

"How far do you think I'll push?" he demanded. His voice was harsh and deep with the hint of Ireland more pronounced. Her breathing was short and shallow with fear. Laying completely still, she made no answer. "Don't throw your imaginary string of lovers in my face, or, by God, you'll have a real one quickly enough whether you want me or not." His fingers tightened slightly around her throat. "When the time comes, I won't need to get you drunk on champagne or on exhaustion to have you lie with me. I could have you now, this minute, and after five minutes of struggle you'd be more than willing." His voice lowered, trembling along her skin. "I know how to play you, Raven, and don't you forget it."

His face was very close to hers. Their breathing mixed, both swift and strained, the only sound coming from the hum of the plane's engines. The fear in her eyes leaped out, finally penetrating his fury. Swearing, Brand pushed himself from her and rose. Her eyes stayed on his as she waited for what he would do next. He stared at her, then turned sharply away, moving over to a porthole.

Raven lay where she was, not realizing she was massaging the wrist that throbbed from his fingers. She watched him drag a hand through his hair.

"I slept with you last night because I wanted to be close to you." He took another long, cleansing breath. "It was nothing more than that. I never touched you. It was an innocent and rather sweet way to spend the night." He curled his fingers into a fist, remembering the frantic flutter of her pulse under his hand when he had circled it around her throat. It gave him no pleasure to know he had frightened her. "It never occurred to me that it would offend you like this. I apologize."

Raven covered her eyes with her hand as the tears began. She swallowed sobs, not wanting to give way to them. Guilt and shame washed over her as fear drained. Her reaction to Brand's simple, affectionate gesture had been to slap his face. It had been embarrassment, she knew, but more her own suppressed longing for him that had pushed her to react with anger and spiteful words. She'd tried to provoke him and had succeeded. But more, she knew now she had hurt him. Rising from the sofa, she attempted to make amends.

Though she walked over to stand behind him, Raven didn't touch him. She couldn't bear the thought that he might stiffen away from her.

"Brandon, I'm so sorry." She dug her teeth into her bottom lip to keep her voice steady. "That was stupid of me, and worse, unkind. I'm terribly ashamed of the way I acted. I wanted to make you angry; I was embarrassed, I suppose, and . . . ." The words trailed off as she searched for some way to describe the way she had felt. Even now something inside her warmed and stirred at the knowledge that she had lain beside him, sharing the intimacy of sleep.

Raven heard him swear softly, then he rubbed a hand over the back of his neck. "I baited you."

"You're awfully good at it," she said, trying to make light of what had passed between them. "Much better than I am. I can't think about what I'm saying when I'm angry."

"Obviously, neither can I. Look, Raven," Brand began and turned. Her eyes were huge, swimming with restrained tears. He broke off what he had been about to say and moved to the table for his cigarettes. After lighting one, he turned back to her. "I'm sorry I lost my temper. It's something I don't do often because it's a nasty one. And you've got a good aim with a punch, Raven, and it reminded me of the last time we were together five years ago."

She felt her stomach tighten in defense. "I don't think either of us should dwell on that."

"No." He nodded slowly. His eyes were calm again and considering. Raven knew he was poking into her brain. "Not at the moment, in any case. We should get on with today." He smiled, and she felt each individual muscle in her body relax. "It seems we couldn't wait until we settled in before having a fight."

"No." She answered his smile. "But then I've always been impatient." Moving to him, Raven rose on her toes and pressed her lips lightly to his. "I'm really sorry, Brandon."

"You've already apologized."

"Yes, well just remember the next time, it'll be your turn to grovel."

Brand tugged on her hair. "I'll make some more coffee. We should have time for one more cup before we have to strap in."

When he had gone into the galley, Raven stood where she was a moment. The last time, she thought, five years ago.

She remembered it perfectly: each word, each hurt. And she remembered that the balance of the fault then had also been hers. They'd been alone; he'd wanted her. She had wanted him. Then everything had gone wrong. Raven remembered how she had shouted at him, near hysteria. He'd been patient, then his patience had snapped, though not in the way it had today. Then, she remembered, he'd been cold, horribly, horribly cold. Comparing the two reactions, Raven realized she preferred the heat and violence to the icy disdain.

Raven could bring the scene back with ease. They'd been close, and the desire had risen to warm her. Then it was furnace hot and she was smothering, then shouting at him not to touch her. She'd told him she couldn't bear for him to touch her. Brand had taken her at her word and left her. Raven could easily remember the despair, the regret and confusion—and the love for him outweighing all else.

But when she had gone to find him the next morning, he had already checked out of his hotel. He had left California, left her, without a word. And there'd been no word from him in five years. No word, she mused, but for the stories in every magazine, in every newspaper. No word but for the whispered comments at parties and in restaurants whenever she would walk in. No word but for the constant questions, the endless speculation in print as to why they were no longer an item—why Brand Carstairs had begun to collect women like trophies.

So she had forced him out of her mind. Her work, her talent and her music had been used to fill the holes he had left in her life. She'd steadied herself and built a life with herself in control again. That was for the best, she had decided. Sharing the reins was dangerous. And, she mused, glancing toward the galley, it would still be dangerous. *He* would still be dangerous.

Quickly Raven shook her head. Brandon was right, she told herself. It was time to concentrate on today. They had work to do, a score to write. Taking a deep breath, she walked to the galley to help him with the coffee.

Chapter 9

Raven fell instantly in love with the primitive countryside of Cornwall. She could accept this as the setting for Arthur's Camelot. It was easy to imagine the clash of swords and the glint of armor, the thundering gallop of swift horses.

Spring was beginning to touch the moors, the green blooms now just emerging. Here and there was the faintest touch of pink from wild blossoms. A fine, constant drizzling mist added to the romance. There were houses, cottages really, with gardens beginning to thrive. Lawns were a tender, thin green, and she spotted the sassy yellow of daffodils and the sleepy blue of wood hyacinths. Brand drove south toward the coast and cliffs and Land's End.

They had eaten a country breakfast of brown eggs, thick bacon and oat cakes and had set off again in the little car Brand had arranged to have waiting for them at the airport.

"What's your house like, Brandon?" Raven asked as she rummaged through her purse in search of something to use to secure her hair. "You've never told me anything about it."

He glanced at her bent head. "I'll let you decide for yourself when you see it. It won't be long now."

Raven found two rubber bands of differing sizes and colors. "Are you being mysterious, or is this your way of avoiding telling me the roof leaks?"

"It might," Brand considered. "Though I don't recall being dripped on. The Pengalleys would see to it; they're quite efficient about that sort of thing."

"Pengalleys?" Raven began to braid her hair.

"Caretakers," he told her. "They've a cottage a mile or so off from the house. They keep an eye on the place, and she does a bit of housekeeping when I'm in residence. He does the repairs."

"Pengalley," she murmured, rolling the name over on her tongue.

"Cornishmen, tried and true," Brand remarked absently.

"I know!" Raven turned to him with a sudden smile. "She's short and a bit stout, not fat, just solidly built, with dark hair pulled back and a staunch, rather disapproving face. He's thinner and going gray, and he tipples a bit from a flask when he thinks she's not looking."

Brand quirked a brow and shot her another brief glance. "Very clever. Just how did you manage it?"

"It had to be," Raven shrugged as she secured one braid and started on the next, "if any gothic novel I've ever read had a dab of truth in it. Are there any neighbors?"

"No one close by. That's one of the reasons I bought it."

"Antisocial?" she asked, smiling at him.

"Survival instinct," Brand corrected. "Sometimes I have to get away from it or go mad. Then I can go back and slip into harness again and enjoy it. It's like recharging." He felt her considering look and grinned. "I told you I'd mellowed."

"Yes," she said slowly, "you did." Still watching him, Raven twisted the rubber band around the tip of the second braid. "Yet you've still managed to put out quite a bit. All the albums, the double one last year; all but five of the songs were yours exclusively. And the songs you wrote for Cal Ripley—they were the best cuts on his album."

"Did you think so?" he asked.

"You know they were," she said, letting the rubber band snap into place.

"Praise is good for the ego, love."

"You've had your share now." She tossed both braids behind her back. "What I was getting at was that for someone who's so mellow, you're astonishingly productive."

"I do a lot of my writing here," Brand explained. "Or at my place in Ireland. More here, actually, because I've family across the channel, so there's visiting to be done if I'm there."

Raven gave him a curious look. "I thought you still lived in London."

"Primarily, but if I've serious work or simply need to be alone, I come here. I've family in London as well."

"Yes." Raven looked away again out into the misty landscape. "I suppose large families have disadvantages."

Something in her tone made him glance over again, but her face was averted. He said nothing, knowing from experience that any discussion of Raven's family was taboo. Occasionally in the past, he had probed, but she had always evaded him. He knew that she had been an only child and had left home at seventeen. Out of curiosity, Brand had questioned Julie. Julie knew all there was to know about Raven, he was certain, but she had told him nothing. It was yet another mystery about Raven which alternately frustrated and attracted Brand. Now he put the questions in the back of his mind and continued smoothly.

"Well, we won't be troubled by family or neighbors. Mrs. Pengalley righteously disapproves of show people, and will keep a healthy distance."

"Show people?" Raven repeated and turning back to him, grinned. "Have you been having orgies again, Brandon?"

"Not for at least three months," he assured her and swung onto a back road. "I told you I'd mellowed. But she knows about actors and actresses, you see, because as Mr. Pengalley tells me, she makes it her business to read everything she can get her hands on about them. And as for musicians, *rock* musicians, well..." He let the sentence trail off meaningfully, and Raven giggled.

"She'll think the worst, I imagine," she said cheerfully.

"The worst?" Brand cocked a brow at her.

"That you and I are carrying on a hot, illicit love affair."

"Is that the worst? It sounds rather appealing to me."

Raven colored and looked down at her hands. "You know what I meant."

Brand took her hand, kissing it lightly. "I know what you meant." The laugh in his voice eased her embarrassment. "Will it trouble you to be labeled a fallen woman?"

"I've been labeled a fallen woman for years," she returned with a smile, "every time I pick up a mag-

azine. Do you know how many affairs I've had with
people I've never even spoken to?''

"Celebrities are required to have overactive libi-
dos,'' he murmured. ''It's part of the job.''

"Your press does yours credit,'' she observed
dryly.

Brand nodded gravely. ''I've always thought so. I
heard about a pool going around London last year.
They were betting on how many women I'd have in
a three-month period. The British,'' he explained,
"will bet on anything.''

Raven allowed the silence to hang for a moment.
"What number did you take?''

"Twenty-seven,'' he told her, then grinned. ''I
thought it best to be conservative.''

She laughed, enjoying him. He would have done
it, too, she reflected. There was enough of the cocky
street kid left in him. ''I don't think I'd better ask
you if you won.''

"I wish you wouldn't,'' he said as the car began to
climb up a macadam drive.

Raven saw the house. It was three stories high,
formed of sober, Cornish stone with shutters of deep,
weathered green and a series of stout chimneys on the
roof. She could just make out thin puffs of smoke
before they merged with the lead-colored sky.

"Oh, Brandon, how like you,'' she cried, enchanted. ''How like you to find something like this.''

She was out of the car before he could answer. It was then that she discovered the house had its back to the sea. There were no rear doors, she learned as she dashed quickly to the retaining wall on the left side. The cliff sheared off too close to the back of the house to make one practical. Instead, there were doors on the sides, set deep in Cornish stone.

Raven could look down from the safety of a waist-high wall and watch the water foam and lash out at jagged clumps of rock far below. The view sent a thrill of terror and delight through her. The sea roared below, a smashing fury of sound. Raven stood, heedless of the chill drizzle, and tried to take it all in.

"It's fabulous. Fabulous!" Turning, she lifted her face, studying the house again. Against the stone, in a great tangle of vines, grew wild roses and honey-suckle. They were greening, not yet ready to bloom, but she could already imagine their fragrance. A rock garden had been added, and among the tender green shoots was an occasional flash of color.

"You might find the inside fabulous too," Brand ventured, laughing when she turned her wet face to him. "And dry."

"Oh, Brandon, don't be so unromantic." She turned a slow circle until she faced the house again. "It's like something out of *Wuthering Heights*."

He took her hand. "Unromantic or not, mate, I want a bath, a hot one, and my tea."

"That does have a nice sound to it," she admitted but hung back as he pulled her to the door. She thought the cliffs wonderfully jagged and fierce. "Will we have scones? I developed a taste for them when I toured England a couple years ago. Scones and clotted cream—why does that have to sound so dreadful?"

"You'll have to take that up with Mrs. Pengalley," Brand began as he placed his hand on the knob. It opened before he could apply any pressure.

Mrs. Pengalley looked much as Raven had jokingly described her. She was indeed a sturdily built woman with dark hair sternly disciplined into a sensible bun. She had dark, sober eyes that passed briefly over Raven, took in the braids and damp clothing, then rested on Brandon without a flicker of expression.

"Good morning, Mr. Carstairs, you made good time," she said in a soft, Cornish burr.

"Hullo, Mrs. Pengalley, it's good to see you again. This is Ms. Williams, who'll be staying with me."

"Her room's ready, sir. Good morning, Miss Williams."

"Good morning, Mrs. Pengalley," said Raven, a trifle daunted. This, she was sure, was what was meant by "a formidable woman." "I hope I haven't put you to too much trouble."

"There's been little to do." Mrs. Pengalley's dark eyes shifted to Brand again. "There be fires laid, and the pantry's stocked, as you instructed. I've done you a casserole for tonight. You've only to heat it when you've a mind to eat. Mr. Pengalley laid in a good supply of wood; the nights're cool, and it's been damp. He'll be bringing your bags in now. We heard you drive up.''

''Thanks.'' Brand glanced over, seeing that Raven was already wandering around the room. ''We're both in need of a hot bath and some tea, then we should do well enough. Is there anything you want in particular, Raven?''

She glanced back over at the sound of her name but hadn't been attentive to the conversation. ''I'm sorry. What?''

He smiled at her. ''Is there anything you'd like before Mrs. Pengalley sees to tea?''

''No.'' Raven smiled at the housekeeper. ''I'm sure everything's lovely.''

Mrs. Pengalley inclined her head, her body bending not an inch. ''I'll make your tea, then.'' As she swept from the room, Raven shot Brand a telling glance. He grinned and stretched his back.

''You continually amaze me, Brandon,'' she murmured, then went back to her study of the room.

It was, Raven knew, the room in which they would be doing most of their work over the next weeks. A grand piano, an old one which, she discovered on a quick testing run, had magnificent tone, was set near a pair of narrow windows. Occasional rag rugs dotted the oak-planked floor. The drapes were cream-colored lace and obviously handworked. Two comfortable sofas, both biscuit-colored, and a few Chippendale tables completed the furniture.

A fire crackled in the large stone fireplace. Raven moved closer to examine the pictures on the mantel.

At a glance, she could tell she was looking at Brand's family. There was a teenage boy in a black leather jacket whose features were the same as Brand's though his dark hair was a bit longer and was as straight as Raven's. He wore the same cocky grin as his brother. A woman was next; Raven thought her about twenty-five and astonishingly pretty with fair hair and slanted green eyes and a true English rose complexion. For all the difference in coloring, however, the resemblance to Brand was strong enough for Raven to recognize his sister. She was in another picture along with a blond man and two boys. Both boys had dark hair and the Carstairs mischief gleaming in their eyes. Raven decided Brand's sister had her hands full.

Raven studied the picture of Brand's parents for some time. The tall, thin frame had been passed down from his father, but it seemed only one of the children had inherited his fair, English looks. Raven judged it to be an old snapshot—twenty, perhaps twenty-five, years old. It had been painstakingly staged, with the man and woman dead center, standing straight in their Sunday best. The woman was dark and lovely. The man looked a bit self-conscious and ill at ease having to pose, but the woman beamed into the camera. Her eyes bespoke mischief and her mouth a hint of the cockiness so easily recognized in her children.

There were more pictures: family groups and candid shots, with Brand in several of them. The Carstairses were very much a family. Raven felt a small stir of envy. Shaking it off, she turned back to Brand and smiled.

"This is quite a group.". She flicked her fingers behind her toward the mantel. "You're the oldest, aren't you? I think I read that somewhere. The resemblance is remarkable."

"Sweeney genes from my mother's side," Brand told her, looking beyond her shoulder at the crowded grouping of frames. "The only one they slipped up on a bit was Alison." He ran a hand through his damp hair and came to stand beside her. "Let me take you upstairs, love, and get you settled in. The grand tour can wait until we're dry." He slipped an arm around her. "I'm glad you're here, Raven. I've never seen you with things that are mine before. And hotel rooms, no matter how luxurious, are never home."

Later, lounging in a steaming tub, Raven thought over Brand's statement. It was part of the business of being an entertainer to spend a great many nights in hotel rooms, albeit luxury suites, in their positions, but they were hotel rooms nonetheless. Home was a place for between concerts and guest appearances, and to her, it had become increasingly important over the years. It seemed the higher she rose, the more she needed a solid base. She realized it was the same with Brand.

They'd both been on the road for several weeks. He was home now, and somehow Raven knew already that she, too, would be at home there. For all its age and size, there was something comforting in the house. Perhaps, Raven mused as she lazily soaped a leg, it's the age and size. Continuity was important to her, as she felt she'd had little of it in her life, and space was important for the same reason.

Raven had felt an instant affinity for the house. She liked the muffled roar of the sea outside her window and the breathtaking view. She liked the old-fashioned porcelain tub with the curved legs and the oval mahogany-framed mirror over the tiny pedestal sink.

Rising from the tub, she lifted a towel from the heated bar. When she had dried herself, she wrapped a thick, buff-colored towel around her before letting down her hair. The two braids fell from where she had pinned them atop of her head. Absently, as she wandered back into the bedroom, she began to undo them.

Her luggage still sat beside an old brass chest, but she didn't give much thought to unpacking. Instead she walked to the window seat set in the south wall and knelt on the padded cushion.

Below her the sea hurled itself onto the rocks, tossed up by the wind. There was a sucking, drawing sound before it crashed back onto the shingles and cliffs. Like the sky, they were gray, except for where the waves crested in stiff, white caps. The rain drizzled still, with small drops hitting her window to trail lazily downward. Placing her arms on the wide sill, Raven rested her chin on them and lost herself in dreamy contemplation of the scene below.

"Raven."

She heard Brand's call and the knock and answered both absently. "Yes, come in."

"I thought you might be ready to go downstairs," he said.

"In a minute. What a spectacular view this is! Come look. Does your room face the sea like this? I think I could sit here watching it forever."

"It has its points," he agreed and came over to stand behind her. He tucked his hands into his pockets. "I didn't know you had such a fondness for the sea."

"Yes, always, but I've never had a room where I felt right on top of it before. I'm going to like hearing it at night." She smiled over her shoulder at him. "Is your house in Ireland on the coast, too?"

"No, it's more of a farm, actually. I'd like to take you there." He ran his fingers through her hair, finding it thick and soft and still faintly damp. "It's a green, weepy country, and as appealing as this one, in a different way."

"That's your favorite, isn't it?" Raven smiled up at him. "Even though you live in London and come here to do work, it's the place in Ireland that's special."

He returned the smile. "If it wasn't that there'd have been Sweeneys and Hardestys everywhere we looked, I'd have taken you there. My mother's family," he explained, "are very friendly people. If the score goes well, perhaps we can take a bit of a vacation there when we're done."

Raven hesitated. "Yes . . . I'd like that."

"Good." The smile turned into a grin. "And I like your dress."

Puzzled, Raven followed his lowered glance. Stunned, she gripped the towel at her breasts and scrambled to her feet. "I didn't realize . . . I'd forgotten." She could feel the color heating her cheeks. "Brandon, you might have said something."

"I just did," he pointed out. His eyes skimmed down to her thighs.

"Very funny," Raven retorted and found herself smiling. "Now, why don't you clear out and let me change?"

"Must you? Pity." He hooked his hand over the towel where it met between her breasts. The back of his fingers brushed the swell of her bosom. "I was just thinking I liked your outfit." Without touching her in any other way, he brought his mouth down to hers.

"You smell good," he murmured, then traced just the inside of her mouth with his tongue. "Rain's still in your hair."

A roaring louder than the sea began in her brain. Instinctually she was kissing him back, meeting his tongue with hers, stepping closer and rising on her toes. Though her response was quick and giving, he kept the kiss light. She sensed the hunger and the strength under tight control.

Under the towel, his finger swept over her nipple, finding it taut with desire. Raven felt a strong, unfamiliar ache between her thighs. She moaned with it as each muscle in her body went lax. He lifted his face and waited until her eyes opened.

"Shall I make love to you, Raven?"

She stared at him, aching with the churn of rising needs. He was putting the decision in her hands. She should have been grateful, relieved, yet at that moment she found she would have preferred it if he had simply swept her away. For an instant she wanted no choice, no voice, but only to be taken.

"You'll have to be sure," he told her quietly. Lifting her chin with his finger, he smiled. His eyes were a calm blue-green. "I've no intention of making it easy for you."

He dropped his hand. "I'll wait for you downstairs, though I still think it's a pity you have to change. You're very attractive in a towel."

"Brandon," she said when he was at the door. He turned, lifting a brow in acknowledgement. "What if I'd said yes?" Raven grinned, feeling a bit more steady with the distance between them. "Wouldn't that have been a bit awkward with Mrs. Pengalley still downstairs?"

Leaning against the door, he said lazily, "Raven, if you'd said yes, I wouldn't give a damn if Mrs. Pengalley and half the country were downstairs." He shut the door carefully behind him.

Chapter 10

Both Raven and Brand were anxious to begin. They started the day after their arrival and soon fell into an easy, workable routine. Brand rose early and was usually finishing up a good-sized breakfast by the time Raven dragged herself downstairs. When she was fortified with coffee, they started their morning stretch, working until noon and Mrs. Pengalley's arrival. While the housekeeper brought in the day's marketing and saw to whatever domestic chores needed to be seen to, Brand and Raven would take long walks.

The days were balmy, scented with sea spray and spring. The land was rugged, even harsh, with patches of poor ground covered with heather not yet in bloom. The pounding surf beat against towering granite cliffs. Hardy birds built their nests in the crags. Their cries could be heard over the crash of the waves. Standing high, Raven could see down to the village with its neat rows of cottages and white church spire.

They'd work again in the afternoon with the fire sizzling in the grate at their backs. After dinner they went over the day's work. By the end of the week they had a loosely based outline for the score and the completed title song.

They didn't work without snags. Both Raven and Brand felt too strongly about music for any collaboration to run smoothly. But the arguments seemed to stimulate both of them; and the final product was the better for them. They were a good team.

They remained friends. Brand made no further attempt to become Raven's lover. From time to time Raven would catch him staring intently at her. Then she would feel the pull, as sensual as a touch, as tempting as a kiss. The lack of pressure confused her and drew her more effectively than his advances would have. Advances could be refused, avoided. She knew he was waiting for her decision. Underneath the casualness, the jokes and professional disagreements, the air throbbed with tension.

The afternoon was long and a bit dreary. A steady downpour of rain kept Raven and Brand from walking the cliffs. Their music floated through the house, echoing in corners here and there and drifting to forgotten attics. They'd built the fire high with Mr. Pengalley's store of wood to chase away the dampness that seemed to seep through the windows. A tray of tea and biscuits that they had both forgotten rested on one of the Chippendale tables. Their argument was reaching its second stage.

"We've got to bring up the tempo," Raven insisted. "It just doesn't work this way."

"It's a mood piece, Raven."

"Not a funeral dirge. It drags this way, Brandon. People are going to be nodding off before she finishes singing it."

"Nobody falls asleep while Lauren Chase is singing," Brand countered. "This number is pure sex, Raven, and she'll sell it."

"Yes, she will," Raven agreed, "but not at this tempo." She shifted on the piano bench so that she faced him more directly. "All right, Joe's fallen asleep at the typewriter in the middle of the chapter he's writing. He's already believing himself a little mad because of the vivid dreams he's having about his character, Tessa. She seems too real, and he's fallen in love with her even though he knows she's a product of his own imagination, a character in a novel he's writing, a fantasy. And now, in the middle of the day, he's dreaming about her again, and this time she promises to come to him that night."

"I know the plot, Raven," Brand said dryly.

Though she narrowed her eyes, Raven checked her temper. She thought she detected some fatigue in his voice. Once or twice she'd been awakened in the middle of the night by his playing. "'Nightfall' is hot, Brandon. You're right about it being pure sex, and your lyrics are fabulous. But it still needs to move."

"It moves." He took a last drag on his cigarette before crushing it out. "Chase knows how to hang on to a note."

Raven made a quick sound of frustration. Unfortunately he was usually right about such things. His instincts were phenomenal. This time, however, she was certain that her own instincts—as a songwriter and as a woman—were keener. She knew the way the song had to be sung to reap the full effect. The moment she had read Brand's lyrics, she had known what was needed. The song had flowed, completed, through her head.

"I know she can hang on to a note, and she can handle choreography. She'll be able to do both and still do the song at the right tempo. Let me show you." She began to play the opening bars. Brand shrugged and rose from the bench.

Raven moved the tempo to *andante* and sang to her own accompaniment. Her voice wrapped itself around the music. Brand moved to the window to watch the rain. It was the song of a temptress, full of implicit, wild promises.

Raven's voice flowed over the range of notes, then heated when it was least expected until Brand felt a tight knot of desire in the pit of his stomach. There was something not quite earthly in the melody she had created. The quicker tempo made a sharp contrast, much more effective than the pace Brand had wanted. She ended abruptly in a raspy whisper without any fade-out. She tossed her hair, then shot him a look over her shoulder.

"Well?" There was a half-smile on her face.

He had his back to her and kept his hands tucked into his pockets. "You have to be right now and again, I suppose."

Raven laughed, spinning around on the bench until she faced the room. "You've a way with compliments, Brandon. It sets my heart fluttering."

"She doesn't have your range," he murmured. Then, making an impatient movement, he wandered over to the teapot. "I don't think she'll get as much out of the low scale as you do."

"*Mmm.*" Raven shrugged as she watched him pour out a cup of tea. "She's got tremendous style, though; she'll milk every ounce out of it." He set the tea down again without touching it and roamed to the fire. As she watched him, a worried frown creased Raven's brow. "Brandon, what's wrong?"

He threw another log on the already roaring fire. "Nothing, just restless."

"This rain's depressing." She rose to go to the window. "I've never minded it. Sometimes I like a dreary, sleepy day. I can be lazy without feeling guilty. Maybe that's what you should do, Brandon, be lazy today. You've got that marvelous chessboard in the library. Why don't you teach me to play?" She lifted her hands to his shoulders and feeling the tension, began to knead absently. "Of course, that might be hard work. Julie gave up playing backgammon with me. She says I haven't any knack for strategy."

Raven broke off when Brand turned abruptly around and removed her hands from his shoulders. Without speaking, he walked away from her. He went to the liquor cabinet and drew out a bottle of bourbon. Raven watched as he poured three fingers into a glass and drank it down.

"I don't think I've the patience for games this afternoon," he told her as he poured a second drink.

"All right, Brandon," she said. "No games." She walked over to stand in front of him, keeping her eyes direct. "Why are you angry with me? Certainly not because of the song."

The look held for several long moments while the fire popped and sizzled in the grate. Raven heard a log fall as the one beneath it gave way.

"Perhaps it's time you and I talked," Brandon said as he idly swirled the remaining liquor in the glass. "It's dangerous to leave things hanging for five years; you never know when they're going to fall."

Raven felt a ripple of disquiet but nodded. "You may be right."

Brand gave her a quick smile. "Should we be civilized and sit down or take a few free swings standing up?"

She shrugged. "I don't think there's any need to be civilized. Civilized fighting never clears the air."

"All right," he began but was interrupted by the peal of the bell. Setting down his glass, Brand shot her a last look, then went to answer.

Alone, Raven tried to control her jitters. There was a storm brewing, she knew, and it wasn't outside the windows. Brand was itching for a fight, and though the reason was unclear to her, Raven found herself very willing to oblige him. The tension between them had been glossed over in the name of music and peace. Now, despite her nerves, she was looking forward to shattering the calm. Hearing his returning footsteps, she walked back to the tea tray and picked up her cup.

"Package for you." Brand gestured with it as he came through the doorway. "From Henderson."

"I wonder what he could be sending me," she murmured, already ripping off the heavy packing tape. "Oh, of course." She tossed the wrappings carelessly aside and studied the album jacket. "They're sample jackets for the album I'm releasing this summer." Without glancing at him, Raven handed Brand one of the covers, then turned to another to read the liner notes.

For the next few minutes Brand studied the cover picture without speaking. Again, a background of white, Raven sitting in her habitual cross-legged fashion. She was looking full into the camera with only a tease of a smile on her lips. Her eyes were very gray and very direct. Over her shoulders and down to her knees, her hair spilled—a sharp contrast against the soft-focused white of the background. The arrangement appeared to be haphazard but had been cleverly posed nonetheless. She appeared to be nude, and the effect was fairly erotic.

"Did you approve this picture?"

"Hmm?" Raven pushed back her hair as she continued to read. "Oh, yes, I looked over the proofs before I left on tour. I'm still not completely sure about this song order, but I suppose it's a bit late to change it now."

"I always felt Henderson was above packaging you this way."

"Packaging me what way?" she asked absently.

"As a virgin offering to the masses." He handed her the cover.

"Brandon, really . . . how ridiculous."

"I don't think so," he said. "I think it's an uncannily apt description: virgin white, soft focus, and you sitting naked in the middle of it all."

"I'm not naked," she retorted indignantly. "I don't do nudes."

"The potential buyer isn't supposed to know that, though, is he?" Brand leaned against the piano and watched her through narrowed eyes.

"It's provocative, certainly. It's meant to be." Raven frowned down at the cover again. "There's nothing wrong with that. I'm not a child to be dressed up in Mary Janes and a pink pinafore, Brandon. This is business. There's nothing extreme about this cover. And I'm more modestly covered than I would be on a public beach."

"But not more decently," he said coldly. "There's a difference."

Color flooded her face, now a mixture of annoyance and embarrassment. "It's not indecent. I've never posed for an indecent picture. Karl Straighter is one of the finest photographers in the business. He doesn't shoot indecent pictures."

"One man's art is another's porn, I suppose."

Her eyes widened as she lowered the jackets to the piano bench. "That's a disgusting thing to say," she whispered. "You're being deliberately horrible."

"I'm simply giving you my opinion," he corrected, lifting a brow. "You don't have to like it."

"I don't need your opinion. I don't need your approval."

"No," he said and crushed out his cigarette. "You bloody well don't, do you? But you're going to have it in any case." He caught her by the arm when she would have turned away. The power of the grip contrasted the cool tone and frosty eyes.

"Let go of me," Raven demanded, putting her hand on top of his and trying unsuccessfully to pry it from her arm.

"When I'm finished."

"You have finished." Her voice was abruptly calm, and she stopped her frantic attempts to free herself. Instead she faced him squarely, emotion burning in her eyes. "I don't have to listen to you when you go out of your way to insult me, Brandon. I won't listen to you. You can prevent me from leaving because you're stronger than I am, but you can't make me listen." She swallowed but managed to keep her voice steady. "I run my own life. You're entitled to your opinion, certainly, but you're not entitled to hurt me with it. I don't want to talk to you now; I just want you to let me go."

He was silent for so long, Raven thought he would refuse. Then, slowly, he loosened his grip until she could slip her arm from his fingers. Without a word she turned and left the room.

* * *

Perhaps it was the strain of her argument with Brand or the lash of rain against the windows or the sudden fury of thunder and lightning. The dream formed out of a vague montage of childhood re-membrances that left her with impressions rather than vivid pictures. Thoughts and images floated and receded against the darkness of sleep. There were rolling sensations of fear, guilt, despair, one lapping over the other while she moaned and twisted be-neath the sheets, trying to force herself awake. But she was trapped, caught fast in the world just below consciousness. Then the thunder seemed to explode inside her head, and the flash of lightning split the room with a swift, white flash. Screaming, Raven sat up in bed.

The room was pitch dark again when Brand rushed in; he found his way to the bed by following the sounds of Raven's wild weeping. "Raven. Here, love." Even as he reached her, she threw herself into his arms and clung. She was trembling hard, and her skin was icy. Brand pulled the quilt up over her back and cuddled her. "Don't cry, love, you're safe here." He patted and stroked as he would for a child frightened of a storm. "It'll soon be over."

"Hold me." She pressed her face into his bare shoulder. "Please, just hold me." Her breathing was quick, burning her throat as she struggled for air. "Oh, Brandon, such an awful dream."

He rocked her and laid a light kiss on her temple. "What was it about?" The telling, he recalled from childhood, usually banished the fear.

"She'd left me alone again," Raven murmured, shuddering so that he drew her closer in response. The words came out as jumbled as her thoughts, as tumbled as the dream. "How I hated being alone in that room. The only light was from the building next door—one of those red neon lights that blinks, on and off, so that the dark was never still. And so much noise out on the street, even with the windows closed. Too hot . . . too hot to sleep," she murmured into his shoulder. "I watched the light and waited for her to come back. She was drunk again." She whimpered, her fingers opening and closing against his chest. "And she'd brought a man with her. I put the pillow over my head so I wouldn't hear."

Raven paused to steady her breath. It was dark and quiet in Brand's arms. Outside, the storm rose in high fury.

"She fell down the steps and broke her arm, so we moved, but it was always the same. Dingy little rooms, airless rooms that smelled always of gin no matter how you scrubbed. Thin walls, walls that might as well not have existed for the privacy they gave you. But she always promised that this time, this time it'd be different. She'd get a job, and I'd go to school . . . but always one day I'd come home and there'd be a man and a bottle."

She wasn't clinging any longer but simply leaning against him as if all passion were spent. Lightning flared again, but she remained still.

"Raven." Brand eased her gently away and tilted her face to his. Tears were still streaming from her eyes, but her breathing was steadier. He could barely make out the shape of her face in the dark. "Where was your father?"

He could see the shine of her eyes as she stared at him. She made a soft, quiet sound as one waking. He knew the words had slipped from her while she had been vulnerable and unaware. Now she was aware, but it was too late for defenses. The sigh she made was an empty, weary sound.

"I don't know who he was." Slowly she drew out of Brand's arms and rose from the bed. "She didn't, either. You see, there were so many."

Brand said nothing but reached into the pocket of the jeans he had hastily dragged on and found a pack of matches. Striking one, he lit the bedside candle. The light wavered and flickered, hardly more than a pulse beat in the dark. "How long," he asked and shook out the match, "did you live like that?"

Raven dragged both hands through her hair, then hugged herself. She knew she'd already said too much for evasions. "I don't remember a time she didn't drink, but when I was very young, five or six, she still had some control over it. She used to sing in clubs. She had big dreams and an average voice, but she was very lovely...once.''

Pausing, Raven pressed her fingers against her eyes and wiped away tears. ''By the time I was eight, she was...her problem was unmanageable. And there were always men. She needed men as much as she needed to drink. Some of them were better than others. One of them took me to the zoo a couple of times....''

She trailed off and turned away. Brand watched the candlelight flicker over the thin material of her nightgown.

''She got steadily worse. I think part of it was from the frustration of having her voice go. Of course, she abused it dreadfully with smoking and drinking, but the more it deteriorated, the more she smoked and drank. She ruined her voice and ruined her health and ruined any chance she had of making something of herself. Sometimes I hated her. Sometimes I know she hated herself.''

A sob escaped, but Raven pushed it back and began to wander the room. The movement seemed to make it easier, and the words tumbled out quicker, pressing for release. ''She'd cry and cling to me and beg me not to hate her. She'd promise the moon, and more often than not, I'd believe her. 'This time'— that was one of her favorite beginnings. It still is.'' Raven let out a shaky sigh. ''She loved me when she wasn't drinking and forgot me completely when she was. It was like living with two different women, and neither one of them was easy. When she was sober, she expected an average mother-and-daughter relationship. Had I done my homework? Why was I five minutes late getting home from school? When she was drunk, I was supposed to keep the hell out of her way. I remember once, when I was twelve, she went three months and sixteen days without a drink. Then I came home from school and found her passed out on the bed. She'd had an audition that afternoon for a gig at this two-bit club. Later she told me she'd just wanted one drink to calm her nerves. Just one…'' Raven shivered and hugged herself tighter. ''It's cold,'' she murmured.

Brand rose and stooped in front of the fire. He added kindling and logs to the bed of coals in the grate. Raven walked to the window to watch the fury of the storm over the sea. Lightning still flashed sporadically, but the violence of the thunder and the rain were dying.

''There were so many other times. She was working as a cocktail waitress in this little piano bar in Houston. I was sixteen then. I always came by on payday so I could make certain she didn't spend the money before I bought food. She'd been pretty good then. She'd been working about six weeks straight and had an affair going with the manager. He was one of the better ones. I used to play around at the piano if the place was empty. One of my mother's lovers had been a musician; he'd taught me the basics and said I had a good ear. Mama liked hearing me play.'' Her voice had quieted. Brand watched her trail a finger down the dark pane of window glass.

"Ben, the manager, asked me if I wanted to play during the lunch hour. He said I could sing, too, as long as I kept it soft and didn't talk to the customers. So I started." Raven sighed and ran a hand over her brow. Behind her came the pop and crackle of flame. "We left Houston for Oklahoma City. I lied about my age and got a job singing in a club. It was one of Mama's worst periods. There were times I was afraid to leave her alone, but she wasn't working then, and..." She broke off with a sound of frustration and rubbed at an ache in her temple. She wanted to stop, wanted to block it all out, but she knew she had come too far. Pressing her brow against the glass, she waited until her thoughts came back into order.

"We needed the money, so I had to risk leaving her at night. I suppose we exchanged roles for a time," she murmured. "The thing I learned young, but consistently forgot, was that an alcoholic finds money for a bottle. Always, no matter what. One night during my second set she wove her way into the club. Wayne was working there and caught on to the situation quickly. He managed to quiet her down before it got too ugly. Later he helped me get her home and into bed. He was wonderful: no lecture, no pity, no advice. Just support."

Raven turned away from the window again and wandered to the fire. "But she came back again, twice more, and they let me go. There were other towns, other clubs, but it was the same then and hardly matters now. Just before I turned eighteen I left her." Her voice trembled a bit, and she took a moment to steady it. "I came home from work one night, and she was passed out at the kitchen table with one of those half-gallon jugs of wine. I knew if I didn't get away from her I'd go crazy. So I put her to bed, packed a bag, left her all the money I could spare and walked out. Just like that." She covered her face with her hands a moment, pressing her fingers into her eyes. "It was like being able to breathe for the first time in my life."

Raven roamed back to the window. She could see the vague ghost of her own reflection. Studying it, listening to the steady but more peaceful drum of rain, she continued. "I worked my way to L.A., and Henderson saw me. He pushed me. I'm not certain what my ambition was before I signed with him. Just to survive, I think. One day and then the next. Then there were contracts and recording sessions and the whole crazy circus. Doors started opening. Some of them were trap doors, I've always thought." She gave a quick, wondering laugh. "God, it was marvelous and scary and I don't believe I could ever go through those first few months again. Anyway, Henderson got me publicity, and the first hit single got me more. And then I got a call from a hospital in Memphis.''

Raven turned and began to pace. The light silk of her nightgown clung, then swirled, with her movements. "I had to go, of course. She was in pretty bad shape. Her latest lover had beaten her and stolen what little money she had. She cried. Oh, God, all the same promises. She was sorry; she loved me. Never again, never again. I was the only decent thing she'd ever done in her life." The tears were beginning to flow again, but this time Raven made no attempt to stop them. "As soon as she could travel, I brought her back with me. Julie had found a sanitarium in Ojai and a very earnest young doctor. Justin Randolf Karter. Isn't that a marvelous name, Brandon?" Bitterness spilled out with the tears. "A marvelous name, a remarkable man. He took me into his tasteful, leather-bound office and explained the treatment my mother would receive."

Whirling, Raven faced Brand, her shoulders heaving with sobs. "I didn't want to know! I just wanted him to do it. He told me not to set my hopes too high, and I told him I hadn't any hopes at all. He must have found me cynical, because he suggested several good organizations I could speak to. He reminded me that alcoholism is a disease and that my mother was a victim. I said the hell she was; *I* was the victim!'' Raven forced the words out as she hugged herself tightly. ''*I* was the victim; *I* had had to live with her and deal with her lies and her sickness and her men. It was so safe, so easy, for him to be sanctimonious and understanding behind that tidy white coat. And I *hated* her.'' The sobs came in short, quick jerks as she balled her hands and pressed them against her eyes. ''And I loved her.'' Her breath trembled in and out as everything she had pent up over the weeks of her mother's latest treatment poured through her. ''I still love her,'' she whispered.

Weary, nearly spent, she turned to the fire, resting her palms on the mantel. ''Dr. Karter let me shout at him, then he sat with me when I broke down. I went home, and they started her treatment. Two days later I met you.''

Raven didn't hear him move, didn't know he stood behind her, until she felt his hands on her shoulders. Without speaking she turned and went into his arms. Brand held her, feeling the light tremors while he stared down at the licking, greedy flames. Outside, the storm had become only a patter of rain against the windows.

''Raven, if you had told me, I might have been able to make things easier for you.''

She shook her head, then buried her face against his chest. ''No, I didn't want it to touch that part of my life. I just wasn't strong enough.'' Taking a deep

breath, she pulled back far enough to look in his
eyes. "I was afraid that if you knew you wouldn't
want anything to do with me."

"Raven." There was hurt as well as censure in his
voice.

"I know it was wrong, Brandon, even stupid, but
you have to understand: everything seemed to be
happening to me at once. I needed time. I needed to
sort out how I was going to live my life, how I was
going to deal with my career, my mother, everything." Her hands gripped his arms as she willed him
to see through her eyes. "I was nobody one day and
being mobbed by fans the next. My picture was
everywhere. I heard myself every time I turned on the
radio. You know what that's like."

Brand brushed her hair from her cheek. "Yes, I
know what that's like." As he spoke, he could feel
her relax with a little shudder.

"Before I could take a breath, Mama walked back
into my life. Part of me hated her, but instead of realizing that it was a normal reaction and dealing with
it, I felt an unreasonable guilt. And I was ashamed.
No," she shook her head, anticipating him, "there's
no use telling me I had no need to be. That's an in-
tellectual statement, a practical statement; it has
nothing to do with emotion. I don't expect you to
understand that part of it. You've never had to deal
with it. She's my mother. It isn't possible to completely separate myself from that, even knowing that

the responsibility for her problem isn't mine." Raven gave him one last, long look before turning away. "And on top of everything that was happening to me, I fell in love with you." The flames danced and snapped as she watched. "I loved you," she murmured so quietly he strained to hear, "but I couldn't be your lover."

Brand stared at her back, started to reach for her, then dropped his hands to his sides. "Why?"

Only her head turned as she looked over her shoulder at him. Her face was in shadows. "Because then I would be like her," she whispered, then turned away again.

"You don't really believe that, Raven." Brand took her shoulders, but she shook her head, not answering. Firmly he turned her to face him, making a slow, thorough study of her. "Do you make a habit of condemning children for their parents' mistakes?"

"No, but I . . ."

"You don't have the right to do it to yourself."

She shut her eyes on a sigh. "I know, I know that, but . . ."

"There're no buts on this one, Raven." His fingers tightened until she opened her eyes again. "You know who you are."

There was only the sound of the sea and the rain and fire. "I wanted you," she managed in a trembling voice, "when you held me, touched me. You were the first man I'd ever wanted." She swallowed, and again he felt the shudder course through her. "Then I'd remember all those cramped little rooms, all those men with my mother...." She broke off and would have turned away again if his hands hadn't held her still.

Brand removed his hands from her arms, then slowly, his eyes still on hers, he used them to frame her face. "Sleeping with a stranger is different from making love with someone you care for."

Raven moistened her lips. "Yes, I know that, but..."

"Do you?" The question stopped her. She could do no more than let out a shaky breath. "Let me show you, Raven."

Her eyes were trapped by his. She knew he would release her if she so much as shook her head. Fear was tiny pinpoints along her skin. Need was a growing warmth in her blood. She lifted her hands to his wrists. "Yes."

Again Brand gently brushed the hair away from her cheeks. When her face was framed by his hands alone, he lowered his head and kissed her eyes closed. He could feel her trembling in his arms. Her hands still held his wrists, and her fingers tightened when he brought his mouth to hers. His was patient, waiting until her lips softened and parted.

The kisses grew deeper, but slowly, now moister until she swayed against him. His fingers caressed, his mouth roamed. Firelight flickered over them in reds and golds, casting its own shadows. Raven could feel the heat from it through the silk she wore, but it was the glow inside of her which built and flamed hot.

Brand lowered his hands to her shoulders, gently massaging as he teased her lower lip with his teeth. Raven felt the gown slip down over her breasts, then cling briefly to her hips before it drifted to the floor. She started to protest, but he deepened the kiss. The thought spiraled away. Down the curve of her back, over the slight flare of her hips, he ran his hands. Then he picked her up in his arms. With her mind spinning, she sank into the mattress. When Brand joined her, the touch of his naked body against hers jolted her, bringing on a fresh surge of doubts and fears.

"Brandon, please, I..." The words were muffled, then died inside his mouth.

Easily, his hands caressed her, stroking without hurry. Somewhere in the back of her mind she knew he held himself under tight control. But her mind had relaxed, and her limbs were heavy. His mouth wandered to her throat, tasting, giving pleasure, arousing by slow, irresistible degrees. He worked her nipple with his thumb, and she moaned and moved against him. Brand allowed his mouth to journey downward, laying light, feathering kisses over the curve of her breast. Lightly, very lightly, he ran his tongue over the tip. Raven felt the heat between her thighs, and tangling her fingers in his hair, pressed him closer. She arched and shuddered not from fear but from passion.

Heat unlike anything she had ever known or imagined was building inside her. She was still aware of the flicker of the fire and candlelight on her closed lids, of the soft brush of linen sheets against her back, of the faint, pleasant smell of wood smoke. But these sensations were dim, while her being seemed focused on the liquefying touch of his tongue over her skin, the feathery brush of his fingers on her thighs. Over the hiss of rain and fire, she heard him murmur her name, heard her own soft, mindless response.

Her breath quickened, and her mouth grew hungry. Suddenly desperate, she drew his face back to hers. She wrapped her arms around him tightly as the pressure of the kiss pushed her head deep into the pillow. Brand lay across her, flesh to flesh, so that her breasts yielded to his chest. Raven could feel the light mat of his hair against her skin.

His hand lay on her stomach and drifted down as she moved under him. There was a flash of panic as he slid between her thighs, then her breath caught in a heady rush of pleasure. He was still patient, his fingers gentle and unhurried as they gradually increased her rhythm.

For Raven, there was no world beyond the firelit room, beyond the four-poster bed. His mouth took hers, his tongue probing deeply, then moving to her ear, her throat, her neck and back to her lips. All the while, his hands and fingers were taking her past all thought, past all reason.

Then he was on top of her, and she opened for him, ready to give, to receive. She was too steeped in wonder to comprehend his strict, unwavering control. She knew only that she wanted him and urged him to take her. There was a swift flash of pain, dulled by a pleasure too acute to be measured. She cried out, but the sound was muffled against his mouth, then all was lost on wave after wave of delight.

Chapter 11

With her head in the curve of Brand's shoulder, Raven watched the fire. Her hand lay over his heart. She could feel its quick, steady rhythm under her palm.

The room was quiet, and outside, the rain had slackened to a murmur. Raven knew she would remember this moment every time she lay listening to rain against windows. Brand's arm was under her, curled over her back with his hand loosely holding her arm. Since he had rolled from her and drawn her against his side, he had been silent. Raven thought he slept and was content to lay with him, watching the fire and listening to the rain. She shifted her head, wanting to look at him and found he wasn't asleep.

She could see the sheen of his eyes as he stared at the ceiling. Raven lifted a hand to his cheek.

"I thought you were asleep."

Brand caught her hand and pressed it to his lips. "No, I . . ." Looking down at her, he broke off, then slowly brushed a tear from her lash with his thumb. "I hurt you."

"No." Raven shook her head. For a moment she buried her face in the curve of his neck, where she could feel his warmth, smell his scent. "Oh, no, you didn't hurt me. You made me feel wonderful. I feel...free." She looked up at him again and smiled. "Does that sound foolish?"

"No." Brand ran his fingers through the length of her hair, pushing it back when it would have hidden her face from him. Her skin was flushed. In her eyes he could see the reflected flames from the fire. "You're so beautiful."

She smiled again and kissed him. "I've always thought the same about you."

He laughed, drawing her closer. "Have you?"

She lay half across him, heated flesh to heated flesh. "Yes, I always thought you'd make a remarkably lovely girl, and I see by your sister's picture that I was right."

He lifted a brow. "Strange, I never realized the direction of your thoughts. Perhaps it's best I didn't."

Raven gave one of her low, rich chuckles and pressed her lips against the column of his throat. She loved the way his tones could become suddenly suavely British. "I'm sure you make a much better man."

"That's comforting," he said dryly as he began to stroke her back, "under the circumstances." His fingers lingered at her hip to caress.

"I'm sure I like you much better this way." Raven kissed the side of his throat again, working her way up to his ear. Under her breast she felt the sudden jump and scramble of his heartbeat. "Brandon . . ." She sighed, nuzzling his ear. "You're so good to me, so kind, so gentle."

She heard him groan before he rolled over, reversing their positions. His eyes were heated and intense and very green, reminding her of the moment he had held her like this on the plane. Now again her pulse began to hammer, but not with fear.

"Love isn't always kind, Raven," he said roughly. "It isn't always gentle."

His mouth came down on hers crushingly, urgently, as all the restraints he had put on himself snapped. There was no patience in him now, only passion. Where before he had taken her up calmly, easily, now he took her plummeting at a desperate velocity. Her mouth felt bruised and tender from his, yet she learned hunger incited hunger. Raven wanted more, and still more, so she caught him closer.

Demanding, possessing, he took his hands over her. "So long," she heard him mutter. "I've wanted you for so long." Then his teeth found the sensitive area of her neck, and she heard nothing. She plunged toward the heat and the dark.

Brand felt her give and respond and demand. He was nearly wild with need. He wanted to touch all of her, taste all of her. He was as desperate as a starving man and as ruthless. Where before, responding to her innocence, he had been cautious, now he took what he had wanted for too many years. She was his as he had dreamed she would be: soft and yielding, then soft and hungry beneath him.

He could hear her moan, feel the bite of her fingernails in his shoulders as he took his mouth down the curve of her breast. The skin of her stomach was smooth and quivered under his tongue. He slipped a hand between her thighs, and she strained against him so that he knew she was as desperate as he. Yet he wouldn't take her, not yet. He felt an impossible greed. His tongue moved to follow the path of his hands. All the years he'd wanted her, all the frustrated passion, burst out, catching them both in the explosion. Not knowing the paths, Raven went where he led her and learned that desire was deeper, stronger, than anything she had known possible.

He was pulling her down—down until the heat was too intense to bear. But she wanted more. His hands were rough, bruising her skin. But she craved no gentleness. She was steeped in passion too deep for escape. She called out for him, desperately, mindlessly, for him to take her. She knew there couldn't be more; they'd gone past all the rules. Pleasure could not be sharper; passion could not be darker than it was at that moment.

Then he was inside her, and everything that had gone before paled against the color and the heat.

His mouth was buried at her neck. From far off he heard her gasps for breath merge with his own. They moved together like lightning, so that he could no longer think. There was only Raven. All passion intensified, concentrated, until he thought he would go mad from it. The pain of it shot through him, then flowed from him, leaving him weak.

They lay still, with Brand over her, his face buried in her hair. His breathing was ragged, and he gave no thought to his weight as he relaxed completely. Beneath him Raven shuddered again and again with the release of passion. She gripped his shoulders tightly, not wanting him to move, not wanting to relinquish the unity. If he had shown her the tenderness and compassion of loving the first time, now he had shown her darker secrets.

A log fell in the grate, scattering sparks against the screen. Brand lifted his head and looked down at her. His eyes were heavy, still smoldering, as they lowered to her swollen mouth. He placed a soft kiss on them, then, shifting his weight, prepared to rise.

"No, don't go." Raven took his arm, sitting up as he did.

"Only to bank the fire."

Bringing her knees to her chest, Raven watched as Brand stacked the fire for the night. The light danced over his skin as she stared, entranced. The ripple of muscles was surprising in one so lean. She saw them in his shoulders, his back, his thighs. The passion in the cool, easygoing man was just as surprising, but she knew the feel of it now, just as she knew the feel of the muscles. He turned and looked at her with the fire leaping at his back. They studied each other, both dazed by what had passed between them. Then he shook his head.

"My God, Raven, I want you again."

She held her arms out to him.

There was a brilliant ribbon of sunlight across Raven's eyes. It was a warm, red haze. She allowed her lids to open slowly before turning to Brand. ·

He slept still, his breathing deep and even. She had to suppress the urge to brush his hair away from his face because she didn't want to wake him. Not yet. For the first time in her life she woke to look at her lover's face. She felt a warm, settled satisfaction.

He *is* beautiful, she thought, remembering how he had been faintly distressed to hear her say so the night before. *And I love him*. Raven almost said the words aloud as she let herself think them. I've al-

ways loved him, right from the beginning, all
through the years in between—and even more now
that we're together. But no mistakes this time. She
closed her eyes tight on the sudden fear that he could
walk out of her life again. *No demands, no pres-
sures.* We'll just be together; that's all I need.

She dropped her eyes to his mouth. It had been
tender in the night, she remembered, then hungry,
almost brutal. She hadn't realized how badly he had
wanted her, or she him, until the barriers had shattered. *Five years, five empty years.* Raven pushed the
thought away. There was no yesterday, no tomorrow; only the present.

Suddenly she smiled, thinking of the enormous
breakfasts he habitually ate. She would usually
stumble into the kitchen for coffee as he was cleaning off a plate. Cooking wasn't her best thing, she
mused, but it would be fun to surprise him. His arm
was tossed around her waist, holding her against him
so that their bodies had warmed each other even in
sleep. Carefully Raven slipped out from under it.
Padding to the closet, she found a robe, then left
Brand sleeping to go downstairs.

The kitchen was washed in sunlight. Raven went
straight to the percolator. First things first, she decided. Strangely, she was wide awake, there was none
of the drowsy fogginess she habitually used coffee to
chase away. She felt vital, full of energy, very much
the way she felt when finishing a live concert, she re-

alized as she scooped out coffee. Perhaps there was
a parallel. Raven fit the lid on the pot, then plugged
it in. She had always felt that performing for an audience was a bit like making love: sharing yourself,
opening your emotions, pulling down the barriers.
That's what she had done with Brand. The thought
made her smile, and she was singing as she rummaged about for a frying pan.

Upstairs, Brand stirred, reached for her and found
her gone. He opened his eyes to see that the bed beside him was empty. Quickly he pushed himself up
and scanned the room. The fire was still burning. It
had been late when he had added the last logs. The
drapes were open to the full strength of the sun. It
spilled across the bed and onto the floor. Raven's
nightgown lay where it had fallen the night before.

Not a dream, he told himself, tugging a hand
through his hair. They'd been together last night,
again and again until every ounce of energy had been
drained. Then they had slept, still holding each other,
still clinging. His eyes drifted to the empty pillow
beside him again. *But where—where the devil is she
now?* Feeling a quick flutter of panic, he rose, tugged
on his jeans and went to find her.

Before Brand reached the bottom of the stairs, her
voice drifted to him.

Every morning when I wake,
I'll see your eyes.

And there'll only be the love we make,
No more good-byes.

He recognized the song as the one he had teased
her about weeks before when they had sat in his car
in the hills above Los Angeles. The knot in his stomach untied itself. He walked down the hall, listening
to the husky, morning quality of her voice, then
paused in the doorway to watch her.

Her movements suited the song she sang: cheerful, happy. The kitchen was filled with morning
noises and scents. There was the popping rhythm of
the percolator as the coffee bubbled on the burner,
the hiss and sizzle of the fat sausage she had frying
in a cast-iron skillet, the clatter of crockery as she
searched for a platter. Her hair was streaming down
her back, still tumbled from the night, while the
short terry robe she wore rode high up on her thighs
as she stretched to reach the top shelf of a cupboard.

Raven stopped singing for a moment to swear
good-naturedly about her lack of height. After
managing to get a grip on the platter, she lowered her
heels back to the floor and turned. She gave a gasp
when she spotted Brand, dropped the fork she held
and just managed to save the platter from following
it.

"Brandon!" Raven circled her throat with her hand a moment and took a deep breath. "You scared me! I didn't hear you come down."

Brand didn't answer her smile. He didn't move but only looked at her. "I love you, Raven."

Her eyes widened, and her lips trembled open, then shut again. The words, she reminded herself, mean so many different things. It was important not to take a simple statement and deepen its meaning. Raven kept her voice calm as she stooped to pick up the fork. "I love you, too, Brandon."

He frowned at the top of her head, then at her back as she turned away to the sink. She turned on the tap to rinse off the fork. "You sound like my sister. I've already two of those; I don't need another."

Raven took her time. She turned off the tap, composed her face into a smile, then turned. "I don't think of you as a brother, Brandon." The tension at the back of her neck made it difficult to move calmly back to the cupboard for cups and saucers. "It isn't easy for me to tell you how I feel. I needed your support, your compassion. You helped me last night more than I can say."

"Now you make me sound like a bloody doctor. I said I love you, Raven." There was a snap of anger in the words this time. When Raven turned back to him, her eyes were eloquent.

"Brandon, you don't have to feel obligated..."
She broke off as his eyes flared. Storming into the
room, he flicked off the gas under the smoking sausage, then yanked the percolator cord from the wall.
Coffee continued to pop for a few moments, then
subsided weakly.

"Don't tell me what I have to do!" he shouted. "I
know what I have to do." He grabbed her by the
shoulders and shook her. "I *have* to love you. It's not
an obligation, it's a fact, it's a demand, it's a terror."

"Brandon..."

"Shut up," he commanded. He pulled her close,
trapping the dishes she held between them before he
kissed her. She tasted the desperation, the temper.
"Don't tell me you love me in that calm, steady
voice." Brand lifted his head only to change the angle of the kiss. His mouth was hard and insistent before it parted from hers. "I need more than that from
you, Raven, much more than that." His eyes blazed
green into hers. "I'll have more, damn it!"

"Brandon." She was breathless, dizzy, then
laughing. This was no dream. "The cup's digging a
permanent hole in my chest. Please, let me put the
dishes down." He said something fierce about the
dishes, but she managed to pull away from him
enough to put them on the counter. "Oh, Brandon!" Immediately Raven threw her arms around his
neck. "You have more; you have everything. I was

afraid—and a fool to be afraid—to tell you how much I love you." She placed her hands on his cheeks, holding his face away from hers so that he could read what was in her eyes. "I love you, Brandon."

Quick and urgent, their lips came together. They clung still when he swept her up in his arms. "You'll have to do without your coffee for a while," he told her as she pressed a kiss to the curve of his neck. She only murmured an assent as he began to carry her down the hall.

"Too far," she whispered.

"Mmm?"

"The bedroom's much too far away."

Brand turned his head to grin at her. "Too far," he agreed, taking a sharp right into the music room. "Entirely too far." They sank together on a sofa. "How's this?" He slipped his hands beneath the robe to feel her skin.

"We've always worked well together here." Raven laughed into his eyes, running her fingers along the muscles of his shoulders. It was real, she thought triumphantly, kissing him again.

"The secret," Brand decided, then dug his teeth playfully into her neck, "is a strong melody."

"It's nothing without the proper lyric."

"Music doesn't always need words." He switched to the other side of her neck as his hand roamed her breast.

"No," she agreed, finding that her own hands refused to be still. They journeyed down his back and up again. "But harmony—two strong notes coming together and giving a bit to each other."

"Melding," he murmured. "I'm big on melding." He loosened the belt of her robe.

"Oh, Brandon!" she exclaimed suddenly, remembering. "Mrs. Pengalley...she'll be here soon."

"This should certainly clinch her opinion of show people," he decided as his mouth found her breast.

"Oh, no, Brandon, stop!" She laughed and moaned and struggled.

"Can't," he said reasonably, trailing his lips back up to her throat. "Savage lust," he explained and bit her ear. "Uncontrollable. Besides," he said as he kissed her, then moved to her other ear, "it's Sunday, her day off."

"It is?" Raven's mind was too clouded to recall trivial things like days of the week. "Savage lust?" she repeated as he pushed the robe from her shoulders. "Really?"

"Absolutely. Shall I show you?"

"Oh, yes," she whispered and brought his mouth back to hers. "Please do."

A long time later Raven sat on the hearth rug and watched Brand stir up the fire. She had reheated the coffee and brought it in along with the sausages. Brand had pulled a sweater on with his jeans, but she still wore the short, terry robe. Holding a coffee cup in both hands, she relaxed. She felt like a cat sitting in her square of sunlight, watching Brand fix a log onto snapping flames. He turned to find her smiling at him.

"What are you thinking?" He stretched out on the floor beside her.

"How happy I am." She handed him his coffee, leaning over to kiss him as he took it. It all seemed so simple, so right.

"How happy?" he demanded. He smiled at her over the rim of the cup.

"Oh, somewhere between ecstatic and delirious, I think." She sought his hand with hers. Their fingers linked. "Bordering on rapturous."

"Just bordering on?" Brand asked with a sigh. "Well, we'll work on it." He shook his head, then kissed her hand. "Do you know you nearly drove me mad in this room yesterday?"

"Yesterday?" Raven tossed her hair back over her shoulder with a jerk of her head. "What are you talking about?"

"I don't suppose you'll ever realize just how arousing your voice is," he mused as he sipped his coffee and studied her face. "That might be part of the reason—that touch of innocence with a hell-smoked voice."

"I like that." Raven reached behind her to set down her empty cup. The movement loosened the tie of her robe, leaving it open to brush the curve of her breasts. "Do you want one of these sausages? They're probably awful."

Brand lifted his eyes from the smooth expanse of flesh that the shift of material had revealed. He shook his head again and laughed. "You make them sound irresistible."

"A starving man can't be picky," she pointed out. Raven plucked one with her fingers and handed it over. "They're probably greasy."

He lifted a brow at this but took a bite. "Aren't you going to have one?"

"No. I know better than to eat my own cooking." She handed him a napkin.

"We could go out to eat."

"Use your imagination," she suggested, resting her hands on her knees. "Pretend you've already eaten. It always works for me."

"My imagination isn't as good as yours." Brand finished off the sausage. "Maybe if you tell me what I've had."

"An enormous heap of scrambled eggs," she decided, narrowing her eyes. "Five or six, at least. You really should watch your cholesterol. And three pieces of toast with that dreadful marmalade you pile on."

"You haven't tried it," he reminded her.

"I imagined I did," she explained patiently. "You also had five slices of bacon." She put a bit of censure in her voice, and he grinned.

"I've a healthy morning appetite."

"I don't see how you could eat another bite after all that. Coffee?" Raven reached for the pot.

"No, I imagine I've had enough."

She laughed and leaning over, linked her arms around his neck. "Did I really drive you mad, Brandon?" She found the taste of her own power delicious and sweet.

"Yes." He rubbed her nose with his. "First it was all but impossible to simply be in the same room with you, wanting you as I did. Then that song." He gave a quiet laugh, then drew back to look at her. "Music doesn't always soothe the savage beast. And then that damn album jacket. I had to be furious, or I'd have thrown you down on the rug then and there."

He saw puzzlement, then comprehension, dawn in her eyes. "Is that why you..." She stopped, and the smile grew slowly. Raven tilted her head and ran the tip of her tongue over her teeth. "I suppose that now that you've had your way with me, I won't drive you mad any more."

"That's right." He kissed her lightly. "I can take you or leave you." Brand set down his empty cup, then ruffled her hair, amused by her wry expression. "It's noon," he said with a glance at the clock. "We'd best get to it if we're going to get any work done today. That novelty number we were toying with, the one for the second female lead—I'd an idea for that."

"Really?" Raven unhooked her hands from behind his neck. "What sort of idea?"

"We might bounce up the beat, a bit of early forties jive tempo, you know. It'd be a good contrast to the rest of the score."

"*Hmmm,* could be a good dance number." Raven slipped her hands under his sweater and ran them up his naked chest. She smiled gently at the look of surprise that flickered in his eyes. "We need a good dance number there."

"That's what I was thinking," Brand murmured. The move had surprised him, and the light touch of her fingers sent a dull thud of desire hammering in his stomach. He reached for her, but she rose and moved to the piano.

"Like this, then?" Raven played a few bars of the melody they had worked with, using the tempo he had suggested. "A little boogie-woogie?"

"Yes." He forced his attention to the bouncing, repetitive beat but found his blood beating with it. "That's the idea."

She looked back over her shoulder and smiled at him. "Then all we need are the lyrics." She experimented a moment longer, then went to the coffeepot. "Cute and catchy." Raven drank, smiling down at Brand. "With a chorus."

"Any ideas?"

"Yes." She set down the cup. "I have some ideas." Raven sat down beside him, facing him, and thoughtfully brushed the hair back from his forehead. "If they're going to cast Carly, as it appears they're going to do, we need something to suit that baby-doll voice of hers. Her songs should be a direct foil for Lauren's." She pressed her lips lightly to his ear. "Of course, the chorus could carry the meat of it." Again she slipped a hand under his sweater, letting her fingertips toy with the soft mat of hair on his chest. She slid her eyes up to his. "What do you think?"

Brand took her arm and pulled her against him, but she turned her head so that the kiss only brushed her cheek. "Raven," he said after a laughing moan. But when she trailed her fingers down to his stomach, she felt him suck in air. Again he moaned her name and crushed her against him.

Raven tilted her head back for the kiss. It was deep and desperate, but when he would have urged her down, she shifted so that her body covered his. She buried her mouth at his neck and felt the pulse hammering against her lips. Her hands were still under his sweater so that she was aware of the heating of his skin. He tugged at her robe, but she only pressed harder against him, lodging the fabric between them. She nipped at the cord of his neck.

"Raven." His voice was low and husky. "For God's sake, let me touch you."

"Am I driving you mad, Brandon?" she murmured, nearly delirious with her own power. Before he could answer, she brought her lips to his and took her tongue deep into his mouth. Slowly she hiked up his sweater, feeling the shudders of his skin as she worked it over his chest and shoulders. Even as she tossed it aside, Raven began journeying down his chest, using her lips and tongue to taste him.

It was a new sensation for her; the knowledge that he was as vulnerable to her as she was to him. There was harmony between them and the mutual need to make the music real and full. Before, he had guided her, but now she was ready to experiment with her own skill. She wanted to toy with tempos, to take the lead. She wanted to flow *pianissimo,* savoring each touch, each taste. Now it was her turn to teach him as he had taught her.

His skin was hot under her tongue. He was moving beneath her, but the first wave of desperation had passed into a drugged pleasure. Her fingers weren't shy but rather sought curiously, stroking over him to find what excited, what pleased. His taste was something she knew now she would starve without. She could feel his fingers in her hair tightening as his passion built. As she had the night before, she sensed his control, but now the challenge of breaking it excited her.

His stomach was taut and tightened further when she glided over it. She heard his breathing catch. Finding the snap to his jeans, she undid it, then began to tug them down over his hips. The rhythm was gathering speed.

Then her mouth was on his, ripping them both far beyond the gentle pace she had initiated. She was suddenly starving, trembling with the need. Pushing herself up, Raven let the robe fall from her shoulders. Her hair tumbled forward to drape her breasts.

"Touch me." Her eyes were heavy but locked on his. "Touch me now."

Brand's fingers tangled in her hair as they sought her flesh. When she would have swayed back down to him, he held her upright, wanting to watch the pleasure and passion on her face. Her eyes were blurred with it. The need built fast and was soon too great.

"Raven." There was desperate demand in his voice as he took her hips.

She let him guide her, then gave a sharp gasp of pleasure. Their bodies fused in a soaring rhythm, completely tuned to each other. Raven shuddered from the impact. Then, drained, she lowered herself until she lay prone on him. He brought his arms around her to hold her close as the two of them flowed from passion to contentment.

Tangled with him, fresh from loving in a room quiet and warm, Raven gave a long, contented sigh. "Brandon," she murmured, just wanting to hear the sound of his name.

"Hmm?" He stroked her hair, seemingly lost somewhere in a world between sleep and wakefulness.

"I never knew it could be like this."

"Neither did I."

Raven shifted until she could look at his face. "But you've been with so many women." She curled up at his side, preparing to rest her head in the curve of his shoulder.

Brand rose on his elbow, then tilted her face up to his. He studied her softly flushed cheeks, the swollen mouth and drowsy eyes. "I've never been in love with my lover before," he told her quietly.

For a moment there was silence. Then she smiled. "I'm glad. I suppose I've never been sure of that until now."

"Be sure of it." He kissed her, hard and quick and possessively.

She settled against him again but shivered, then laughed. "A few moments ago I'd have sworn I'd never be cold again."

Grinning, Brand reached for her robe. "I seriously doubt we'll get any work done unless you get dressed. In fact, I'd suggest unattractive clothes."

After tugging her arms through the sleeves, Raven put her hands on his shoulders. Her eyes were light and full of mischief. "Do I distract you, Brandon?"

"You might put it that way."

"I'll probably be tempted to try all the time, now that I know I can." Raven kissed him, then gave a quick shrug. "I won't be able to help myself."

"I'll hold you to that." Brand lifted a brow. "Would you like to start now?"

She gave his hair a sharp tug. "I don't think that's very flattering. I'm going to go see about those unattractive clothes."

"Later," he said, pulling her back when she started to rise.

Raven laughed again, amazed with what she saw in his eyes. "Brandon, really!"

"Later," he said again and pressed her back gently to the floor.

Chapter 12

Summer came to Cornwall in stages. Cool mornings turned to warm afternoons that had bees humming outside the front windows. The stinging chill of the nights mellowed. The first scent of honeysuckle teased the air. Then the roses, lush wild roses, began to bloom. And all through the weeks the countryside blossomed, Raven felt that she, too, was blooming. She was loved.

Throughout her life, if anyone had asked her what one thing she wanted most, Raven would have answered, "To be loved." She had starved for it as a child, had hungered as an adolescent when she had been shuffled from town to town, never given the opportunity to form lasting friendships and affections. It was this need, in part, that had made her so successful as a performer. Raven was willing to let the audience love her. She never felt herself beyond their reach when she stood in the spotlight. And they knew it. The love she had gained from her audiences had filled an enormous need. It had filled her but had not satisfied her as much, she discovered, as Brand's love.

As the weeks passed, she forgot the demands and responsibilities of the performer and became more and more in tune with the woman. She had always known herself; it had been important early that she grasp an identity. But for the first time in her life Raven focused on her womanhood. She explored it, discovered it, enjoyed it.

Brand was demanding as a lover, not only in the physical sense but in an emotional one as well. He wanted her body, her heart, her thoughts, with no reservations. His need for an absolute commitment was the only shadow in the summery passing of days. Raven found it impossible not to hold parts of herself in reserve. She'd been hurt and knew how devastating pain could be when you loved without guard. Her mother had broken her heart too many times to count, with always a promise of happiness after the severest blow. Raven had learned to cope with that, to guard against it to some extent.

She had loved Brand before, naïvely perhaps, but totally. When he had walked out of her life, Raven had thought she would never be whole again. For five years she had insulated herself against the men who had touched her life. They could be friends— loving friends—but never lovers. The wounds had healed, but the scar had been a constant reminder to be careful. She had promised herself that no man would ever hurt her as Brand Carstairs had. And Raven discovered the vow she had made still held true. He was the only man who would ever have the power to hurt her. That realization was enough to both exhilarate and frighten.

There was no doubt that he had awakened her physically. Her fears had been swept away by the tides of love. Raven found that in this aspect of their relationship she could indeed give herself to Brand unreservedly. Knowing she could arouse him strengthened her growing confidence as a woman. She learned her passions were as strong and sensitive as his. She had kept them restricted far too long. If Brand could heat her blood with a look, Raven was aware he was just as susceptible to her. There was nothing of the cool, British reserve in his lovemaking; she thought of him as all Irish then, stormy and passionate.

One morning he woke her at dawn by strewing the bed with wild rosebuds. The following evening he surprised her with iced champagne while she bathed in the ancient footed tub. At night he could be brutally passionate, waking and taking her with a desperate urgency that allowed no time for surprise, protest or response. At times he appeared deliriously happy; at others she would catch him studying her with an odd, searching expression.

Raven loved him, but she could not yet bring herself to trust him completely. They both knew it, and they both avoided speaking of it.

Seated next to Brand at the piano, Raven experimented with chords for the opening bars of a duet. "I really think a minor mode with a raised seventh." She frowned thoughtfully. "I imagine a lot of strings here, a big orchestration of violins and cellos." She played more, hearing the imagined arrangement rather than the solitary piano. "What do you think?" Raven turned her head to find Brand looking down at her.

"Go ahead," he suggested, drawing on a cigarette. "Play the lot."

She began, only to have him interrupt during a bridge. "No." He shook his head. "That part doesn't fit."

"That was your part," she reminded him with a grin.

"Genius is obliged to correct itself," he returned, and Raven gave an unladylike snort. He looked down his very straight British nose. "Had you a comment, then?"

"Who, me? I never interrupt genius."

"Wise," he said and turned back to spread his own fingers over the keys. "Like this." Brand played the same melody from the beginning, only altering a few notes on the bridge section.

"Did you change something?"

"I realize your inferior ear might not detect the subtlety," he began. She jammed her elbow into his ribs. "Well said," he murmured, rubbing the spot. "Shall we try again?"

"I love it when you're dignified, Brandon."

"Really?" He lifted an inquiring brow. "Now, where was I?"

"You were about to demonstrate the first movement from Tchaikovsky's Second Symphony."

"Ah." Nodding, Brand turned back to the keys. He ran through the difficult movement with a fluid skill that had Raven shaking her head.

"Show-off," she accused when he finished with a flourish.

"You're just jealous."

With a sigh she lifted her shoulders. "Unfortunately, you're right."

Brand laughed and put his hand palm to palm with hers. "I have the advantage in spread."

Raven studied her small, narrow-boned hand. "It's a good thing I didn't want to be a concert pianist."

"Beautiful hands," Brand told her, making one of his sudden and completely natural romantic gestures by lifting her fingers to his lips. "I'm quite helplessly in love with them."

"Brandon." Disarmed, Raven could only look at him. A tremble of warmth shot up her spine.

"They always smell of that lotion you have in that little white pot on the dresser."

"I didn't think you'd notice something like that." She shivered in response when his lips brushed the inside of her wrist.

"There's nothing about you I don't notice." He kissed her other wrist. "You like your bath too hot, and you leave your shoes in the most unexpected places. And you always keep time with your left foot." Brand looked back up at her, keeping one hand entwined with hers while he reached up with the other to brush the hair from her shoulder. "And when I touch you like this, your eyes go to smoke." He ran a fingertip gently over the point of her breast and watched her irises darken and cloud. Very slowly he leaned over and touched his lips to hers. Lazily he ran his finger back and forth until her nipple was taut and straining against the fabric of her blouse.

Her mouth was soft and opened willingly. Raven tilted her head back, inviting him to take more. Currents of pleasure were already racing along her skin. Brand drew her closer, one hand lingering at her breast.

"I can feel your bones melt," he murmured. His mouth grew hungrier, his hand more insistent. "It drives me crazy." His fingers drifted from her breast to the top button of her blouse. Even as he loosened it, the phone shrilled from the table across the room. He swore, and Raven gave a laugh and hugged him.

"Never mind, love," she said on a deep breath. "I'll remind you where you left off this time, too." Slipping out of his arms, she crossed the room to answer. "Hello."

"Hello, I'd like to speak with Brandon Carstairs, please," a voice said.

Raven smiled at the musical lilt in the voice and wondered vaguely how one of Brand's fans had gotten access to his number. "Mr. Carstairs is quite busy at the moment." She grinned over at him and got both a grin and a nod of approval before he crossed to her. He began to distract her by kissing her neck.

"Would you ask him to call his mother when he's free?"

"I beg your pardon?" Raven stifled a giggle and tried to struggle out of Brand's arms.

"His mother, dear," the voice repeated. "Ask him to call his mother when he has a minute, won't you? He has the number."

"Oh, please, Mrs. Carstairs, wait! I'm sorry." Wide-eyed, she looked up at Brand. "Brandon's right here. Your mother," Raven said in a horrified whisper that had him grinning again. Still holding her firmly to his side, he accepted the receiver.

"Hullo, Mum." Brand kissed the top of Raven's head, then chuckled. "Yes, I was busy. I was kissing a beautiful woman I'm madly in love with." The color rising in Raven's cheeks had him laughing. "No, no, it's all right, love, I intend to get back to it. How are you? And the rest?"

Raven nudged herself free of Brand's arm. "I'll make some tea," she said quietly, then slipped from the room.

Mrs. Pengalley had left the kitchen spotlessly clean, and Raven spent some time puttering around it aimlessly while the kettle heated on the stove. She found herself suddenly hungry, then remembered that she and Brand had worked straight through lunch. She got out the bread, deciding to make buttered toast fingers to serve with the tea.

Afternoon tea was one of Brand's rituals, and Raven had grown fond of it. She enjoyed the late afternoon breaks in front of the fireplace with tea and biscuits or scones or buttered toast. They could be any two people then, Raven mused, two people sitting in front of a fireplace having unimportant conversations. The kettle sang out, and she moved to switch off the flame.

Raven went about the mechanical domestic tasks of brewing tea and buttering toast, but her thoughts kept drifting back to Brand. There had been such effortless affection in his voice when he had spoken to his mother, such relaxed love. And Raven had felt a swift flash of envy. It was something she had experienced throughout childhood and adolescence, but she hadn't expected to feel it again. Raven reminded herself she was twenty-five and no longer a child.

The chores soothed her. She loaded the tray and started back down the hall with her feelings more settled. When she heard Brand's voice, she hesitated, not wanting to interrupt his conversation. But the weight of the tray outbalanced her sense of propriety.

He was sunk into one of the chairs by the fire when Raven entered. With a smile he gestured her over so that she crossed the room and set the tray on the table beside him. "I will, Mum, perhaps next month. Give everyone my love." He paused and smiled again, taking Raven's hand. "She's got big gray eyes, the same color as the dove Shawn kept in the coop on the roof. Yes, I'll tell her. Bye, Mum. I love you."

Hanging up, Brand glanced at the ladened tea tray, then up at Raven. "You've been busy."

She crouched down and began pouring. "I discovered I was starving." She watched with the usual shake of her head as he added milk to his tea. That was one English habit Raven knew she would never comprehend. She took her own plain.

"My mother says to tell you you've a lovely voice over the phone." Brand picked up a toast finger and bit into it.

"You didn't have to tell her you'd been kissing me," Raven mumbled, faintly embarrassed. Brand laughed, and she glared at him.

"Mum knows I have a habit of kissing women," he explained gravely. "She probably knows I've occasionally done a bit more than that, but we haven't discussed that particular aspect of my life for some time." He took another bite of toast, studying Raven's face. "She wants to meet you. If the score keeps going along at this pace, I thought we might drive up to London next month."

"I'm not used to families, Brandon," she said. Raven reached for her cup, but he placed his hand over hers, waiting until she looked back up at him.

"They're easy people, Raven. They're important to me. You're important to me. I want them to know you."

She felt her stomach tighten, and lowered her eyes.

"Raven." Brand gave a short, exasperated sigh. "When are you going to talk to me?"

She couldn't pretend not to understand him. She could only shake her head and avoid the subject a little while longer. The time when they would have to return to California and face reality would come soon enough. "Please, tell me about your family. It might help me get used to being confronted with all of them if I know a bit more than I've read in the gossip columns." Raven smiled. Her eyes asked him to smile back and not to probe. Not yet.

Brand struggled with a sense of frustration but gave in. He could give her a little more time. "I'm the oldest of five." He gestured toward the mantel. "Michael's the distinguished-looking one with the pretty blond wife. He's a solicitor." Brand smiled, remembering the pleasure it had given him to send his brother to a good university. He'd been the first Carstairs to receive that sort of education. "There was nothing distinguished about him at all as a boy," Brand remarked. "He liked to give anyone within reach a bloody nose."

"Sounds like a good lawyer," Raven observed dryly. "Please go on."

"Alison's next. She graduated from Oxford at the top of her class." He watched Raven glance up at the photo of the fragile, lovely blond. "An amazing brain," Brand continued, smiling. "She does something incomprehensible with computers and has a particular fondness for rowdy rugby matches. That's where she met her husband."

Raven shook her head, trying to imagine the delicate-looking woman shouting at rugby games or programming sophisticated computers. "I suppose your other brother's a physicist."

"No, Shawn's a veterinarian." Affection slipped into Brand's voice.

"Your favorite?"

He tilted his head as he reached for more tea. "If one has a favorite among brothers and sisters, I suppose so. He's simply one of the nicest people I know. He's incapable of hurting anyone. As a boy he was the one who always found the bird with the broken wing or the dog with a sore paw. You know the type.''

Raven didn't, but she murmured something and continued to sip at her tea. Brand's family was beginning to fascinate her. Somehow, she had thought that people raised in the same house under the same circumstances would be more the same. These people seemed remarkably diverse. ''And your other sister?''

''Moria.'' He grinned. ''She's in school yet, claims she's going into finance or drama. Or perhaps,'' he added, ''anthropology. She's undecided.''

''How old is she?''

''Eighteen. She thinks your records are smashing, by the way, and had them all the last time I was home.''

''I believe I'll like her,'' Raven decided. She let her gaze sweep the mantel again. ''Your parents must be very proud of all of you. What does your father do?''

''He's a carpenter.'' Brand wondered if she was aware of the wistful look in her eyes. ''He still works six days a week, even though he knows money isn't a problem anymore. He has a great deal of pride.'' He paused a moment, stirring his tea, his eyes on Raven. ''Mum still hangs sheets out on a line, even though I bought her a perfectly good dryer ten years ago. That's the sort of people they are."

"You're very lucky," Raven told him and rose to wander about the room.

"Yes, I know that." Brand watched her move around the room with her quick, nervous stride. "Though I doubt I thought a great deal about it while I was growing up. It's very easy to take it all for granted. It must have been very difficult for you."

Raven lifted her shoulders, then let them fall. "I survived." Walking to the window, she looked out on the cliffs and the sea. "Let's go for a walk, Brandon. It's so lovely out."

He rose and walked to her. Taking her by the shoulders, Brand turned her around to face him. "There's more to life than surviving, Raven."

"I survived intact," she told him. "Not everyone does."

"Raven, I know you call home twice a week, but you never tell me anything about it." He gave her a quick, caring shake. "Talk to me."

"Not about that, not now, not here." She slipped her arms around him and pressed her cheek to his chest. "I don't want anything to touch us here—nothing from the past, nothing from tomorrow. Oh, there's so much ugliness, Brandon, so many responsibilities. I want time. Is that so wrong?" She held him tighter, suddenly possessive. "Can't this be our fantasy, Brandon? That there isn't anybody but us? Just for a little while.''

She heard him sigh as his lips brushed the crown of her head. "For a little while, Raven. But fantasies have to end, and I want the reality, too.''

Raven lifted her face, then framed his with her hands. "Like Joe in the script,'' she reflected and smiled. "He finds his reality in the end, doesn't he?''

"Yes.'' Brand bent to kiss her and found himself lingering over it longer than he had intended. "Proving dreams come true,'' he murmured.

"But I'm not a dream, Brandon.'' She took both of his hands in hers while her eyes smiled at him. "And you've already brought me to life.''

"And without magic.''

Raven lifted a brow. "That depends on your point of view,'' she countered. "I still feel the magic.'' Slowly she lifted his hand to the neckline of her blouse. "I think you were here when we left off.''

"So I was.'' He loosened the next button, watching her face. "What about that walk?''

"Walk? In all that rain?'' Raven glanced over to the sun-filled window. "No.'' Shaking her head, she looked back at Brand. "I think we'd better stay inside until it blows over.''

He ran his finger down to the next button, smiling at her while he toyed with it. "You're probably right.''

Chapter 13

Mrs. Pengalley made it a point to clean the music room first whenever Raven and Brand left her alone in the house. It was here they spent all their time working—if what show people did could be considered work. She had her own opinion on that. She gathered up the cups, as she always did, and sniffed them. Tea. Now and again she had sniffed wine and occasionally some bourbon, but she was forced to admit that Mr. Carstairs didn't seem to live up to the reputation of heavy drinking that show people had. Mrs. Pengalley was the smallest bit disappointed.

They lived quietly, too. She had been sure when Brand had notified her to expect him to be in residence for three months that he would have plans to entertain. Mrs. Pengalley knew what sort of entertainment show business people went in for. She had waited for the fancy cars to start arriving, the fancy people in their outrageous clothes. She had told Mr. Pengalley it was just a matter of time.

But no one had come, no one at all. There had been no disgraceful parties to clean up after. There had only been Mr. Carstairs and the young girl with the big gray eyes who sang as pretty as you please. But of course, Mrs. Pengalley reminded herself, she was in *that* business, too.

Mrs. Pengalley walked over to shake the wrinkles from the drapes at the side window. From there she could see Raven and Brand walking along the cliffs. Always in each other's pockets, she mused and sniffed to prevent herself from smiling at them. She snapped the drape back into place and began dusting off the furniture.

And how was a body supposed to give anything a proper dusting, she wanted to know, when they were always leaving their papers with the chicken scratchings on them all over everywhere? Picking up a piece of staff paper, Mrs. Pengalley scowled down at the lines and notes. She couldn't make head nor tail out of the notations; she scanned the words instead.

Loving you is no dream / I need you here to hold on to / Wanting you is everything / Come back to me.

She clucked her tongue and set the paper back down. Fine song, that one, she thought, resuming her dusting. Doesn't even rhyme.

Outside, the wind from the sea was strong, and Brand slipped his arm over Raven's shoulders. Turning her swiftly to face him, he bent her backward and gave her a long, lingering kiss. She gripped his shoulders for balance, then stared at him when his mouth lifted.

"What," she began and let out a shaky breath, "was that for?"

"For Mrs. Pengalley," he answered easily. "She's peeking out the music room window."

"Brandon, you're terrible." His mouth came down to hers again. Her halfhearted protest turned into total response. With a quiet sound of pleasure, Brand deepened the kiss and dragged her closer to him. Raven could feel the heat of the sun on her skin even as the sea breeze cooled it. The wind brought them the scent of honeysuckle and roses.

"That," he murmured as his mouth brushed over her cheeks, "was for me."

"Have you any other friends?" Raven asked.

Laughing, Brand gave her a quick hug and released her. "I suppose we've given her enough to cluck her tongue over today."

"So that's what you want me for." Raven tossed her head. "Shock value."

"Among other things."

They wandered to the sea wall, for some moments looking out in comfortable silence. Raven liked the cliffs with their harsh faces and sheer, dizzying drop. She liked the constant, broiling noise of the sea, the screaming of the gulls.

The score was all but completed, with only a few minor loose ends and a bit of polishing to be done. Copies of completed numbers had been sent back to California. Raven knew they were drawing out a job that could be finished quickly. She had her own reasons for procrastinating, though she wasn't wholly certain of Brand's. She didn't want to break the spell.

Raven wasn't sure precisely what Brand wanted from her because she hadn't permitted him to tell her yet. There were things, she knew, that had to be settled between them—things that could be avoided for the time being while they both simply let themselves be consumed by love. But the time would come when they would have to deal with the everyday business of living.

Would their work be a problem? That was one of the questions Raven refused to ask herself. Or if she asked it, she refused to answer. Commitments went with their profession, time-consuming commitments that made it difficult to establish any sort of a normal life. And there was so little privacy. Every detail of their relationship would be explored in the press. There would be pictures and stories, true and fabricated. The worst kind, Raven mused, were those with a bit of both. All of this, she realized, could be handled with hard work and determination if the love was strong enough. She had no doubts theirs was, but she had other doubts.

Would she ever be able to rid herself of the nagging fear that he might leave her again? The memory of the hurt kept her from giving herself to Brand completely. And her feelings of responsibility to her mother created yet another barrier. This was something she had always refused to share with anyone. She couldn't even bring herself to share it with the person she cared for most in the world. Years before, she had made a decision to control her own life, promising herself she would never depend too heavily on anything or anyone. Too often she had watched her mother relinquish control and lose.

If she could have found a way, Raven would have prolonged the summer. But more and more, the knowledge that the idyll was nearly at an end intruded into her thoughts. The prelude to fantasy was over. She hoped the fantasy would become a reality.

Brand watched Raven's face as she leaned her elbows on the rough stone wall and looked out to sea. There was a faraway look in her eyes that bothered him. He wanted to reach her, but their time alone together was slipping by rapidly. A cloud slid across the sun for a moment, and the light shifted and dimmed. He heard Raven sigh.

"What are you thinking?" he demanded, catching her flying hair in his hand.

"That of all the places I've ever been, this is the best." Raven tilted her head to smile up at him but didn't alter her position against the wall. "Julie and I took a break in Monaco once, and I was sure it was the most beautiful spot on earth. Now I know it's the second."

"I knew you'd love it if I could ever get you here," Brand mused, still toying with the ends of her hair. "I had some bad moments thinking you'd refuse. I'm not at all sure I could have come up with an alternate plan."

"Plan?" Raven's forehead puckered over the word. "I don't know what you mean. What plan?"

"To get you here, where we could be alone."

Raven straightened away from the wall but continued looking out to sea. "I thought we came here to write a score."

"Yes." Brand watched the flight of a bird as it swooped down over the waves. "The timing of that was rather handy."

"Handy?" Raven felt the knot start in her stomach. The cloud shifted over the sun again.

"I doubt you'd have agreed to work with me again if the project hadn't been so tempting," he said. Brand frowned up at a passing cloud. "You certainly wouldn't have agreed to live with me."

"So you dangled the score in front of my nose like a meaty bone?"

"Of course not. I wanted to work with you on the project the moment it was offered to me. It was all just a matter of timing, really."

"Timing and planning," she said softly. "Like a chess game. Julie's right; I've never been any good at strategy." Raven turned away, but Brand caught her arm before she could retreat.

"Raven?"

"How could you?" She whirled back to face him. Her eyes were dark and hot, her cheeks flushed with fury. Brand narrowed his eyes and studied her.

"How could I what?" he asked coolly, releasing her arm.

"How could you use the score to trick me into coming here?" She dragged at her hair as the wind blew it into her face.

"I'd have used anything to get you back," Brand said. "And I didn't trick you, Raven. I told you nothing but the truth."

"Part of the truth," she countered.

"Perhaps," he agreed. "We're both rather good at that, aren't we?" He didn't touch her, but the look he gave her became more direct. "Why are you angry? Because I love you or because I made you realize you love me?"

"Nobody *makes* me do anything!" She balled her hands into fists as she whirled away. "Oh, I detest being maneuvered. I run my own life, make my own decisions.''

''I don't believe I've made any for you.''

''No, you just led me gently along by the nose until I *chose* what was best for myself.'' Raven turned back again, and now her voice was low and vibrant with anger. ''Why couldn't you have been honest with me?''

''You wouldn't have let me anywhere near you if I'd been completely honest. I had experience with you before, remember?''

Raven's eyes blazed. ''Don't you tell me what I would've done, Brandon. You're not inside my head.''

''No, you've never let me in there.'' He pulled out a cigarette, cupped his hands around a match and lit it. Before speaking, he took a long, contemplative drag. ''We'll say I wasn't in the mood to be taking chances, then. Will that suit you?''

His cool, careless tone fanned her fury. ''You had no right!'' she tossed at him. ''You had no right to arrange my life this way. Who said I had to play by your rules, Brandon? When did you decide I was incapable of planning for myself?''

''If you'd like to be treated as a rational adult, perhaps you should behave as one,'' he suggested in a deceptively mild tone. ''At the moment I'd say you're being remarkably childish. I didn't bring you here under false pretenses, Raven. There was a score to be written, and this was a quiet place to do it. It was also a place I felt you'd have the chance to get used to being with me again. I wanted you back."

"*You* felt. *You* wanted!" Raven tossed back her hair. "How incredibly selfish! What about *my* feelings? Do you think you can just pop in and out of my life at your convenience?"

"As I remember, I was pushed out."

"You left me!" The tears came from nowhere and blinded her. "Nothing's ever hurt me like that before. Nothing!" Tears of hurt sprang to her eyes. "I'll be damned if you'll do it to me again. You went away without a word!"

"You mightn't have liked the words I wanted to say." Brand tossed the stub of his cigarette over the wall. "You weren't the only one who was hurt that night. How the hell else could I be rational unless I put some distance between us? I couldn't have given you the time you seemed to need if I'd stayed anywhere near you."

"Time?" Raven repeated as thoughts trembled and raced through her mind. "You gave me time?"

"You were a child when I left," he said shortly. "I'd hoped you'd be a woman when I came back."

"You had hoped . . ." Her voice trailed off into an astonished whisper. "Are you telling me you stayed away, giving me a chance to—to grow up?"

"I didn't see I had any choice." Brand dug his hands into his pockets as his brows came together.

"Didn't you?" She remembered her despair at his going, the emptiness of the years. "And of course, why should you have given me one? You simply took it upon yourself to decide for me."

"It wasn't a matter of deciding." He turned away from her, knowing he was losing his grip on his temper. "It was a matter of keeping sane. I simply couldn't stay near you and not have you."

"So you stayed away for five years, then suddenly reappeared, using my music as an excuse to lure me into bed. You didn't give a damn about the quality of *Fantasy*. You just used it—and the talent and sweat of the performers—for your own selfish ends."

"That," he said in a deadly calm voice, "is beyond contempt." Turning, he walked away. Within moments Raven heard the roar of an engine over the sound of the sea.

She stood, watching the car speed down the lane. If she had meant to deal a savage blow, she had succeeded. The shock of her own words burned in her throat. She shut her eyes tightly.

Even with her eyes closed, she could see clearly the look of fury on Brand's face before he had walked away. Raven ran a shaking hand through her hair. Her head was throbbing with the aftereffects of temper. Slowly she opened her eyes and stared out at the choppy green sea.

Everything we've had these past weeks was all part of some master plan, she thought. Even as she stood, the anger drained out of her, leaving only the weight of unhappiness.

She resented the fact that Brand had secretly placed a hand on the reins of her life, resented that he had offered her the biggest opportunity in her career as a step in drawing her to him. And yet . . . Raven shook her head in frustration. Confused and miserable, she turned to walk back to the house.

Mrs. Pengalley met her at the music room door. "There's a call for you, miss, from California." She had watched the argument from the window with a healthy curiosity. Now, however, the look in the gray eyes set her maternal instincts quivering. She repressed an urge to smooth down Raven's hair. "I'll make you some tea," she said.

Raven walked to the phone and lifted the receiver. "Yes, hello."

"Raven, it's Julie."

"Julie." Raven sank down in a chair. She blinked back fresh tears at the sound of the familiar voice. "Back from the isles of Greece?"

"I've been back for a couple weeks, Raven."

Of course. She should have known that. "Yes, all right. What's happened?"

"Karter contacted me because he wasn't able to reach you this morning. Some trouble on the line or something."

"Has she left again?" Raven's voice was dull.

"Apparently she left last night. She didn't go very far." Hearing the hesitation in Julie's voice, Raven felt the usual tired acceptance sharpen into apprehension.

"Julie?" Words dried up, and she waited.

"There was an accident, Raven. You'd better come home."

Raven closed her eyes. "Is she dead?"

"No, but it's not good, Raven. I hate having to tell you over the phone this way. The housekeeper said Brand wasn't there."

"No." Raven opened her eyes and looked vaguely around the room. "No, Brandon isn't here." She managed to snap herself back. "How bad, Julie? Is she in the hospital?"

Julie hesitated again, then spoke quietly. "She's not going to make it, Raven. I'm sorry. Karter says hours at best."

"Oh, God." Raven had lived with the fear all her life, yet it still came as a shock. She looked around the room again a little desperately, trying to orient herself.

"I know there's no good way to tell you this, Raven, but I wish I could find a better one."

"What?" She brought herself back again with an enormous effort. "No, I'm all right. I'll leave right away."

"Shall I meet you and Brand at the airport?"

The question drifted through Raven's mind. "No. No, I'll go straight to the hospital. Where is she?"

"St. Catherine's, intensive care."

"Tell Dr. Karter I'll be there as soon as I can. Julie . . ."

"Yes?"

"Stay with her."

"Of course I will. I'll be here."

Raven hung up and sat staring at the silent phone.

Mrs. Pengalley came back into the room carrying a cup of tea. She took one look at Raven's white face and set it aside. Without speaking, she went to the liquor cabinet and took out the brandy. After pouring out two fingers, she pressed the snifter on Raven.

"Here now, miss, you drink this." The Cornish burr was brisk.

Raven's eyes shifted to her. "What?"

"Drink up, there's a girl."

She obeyed as Mrs. Pengalley lifted the glass to her lips. Instantly Raven sucked in her breath at the unexpected strength of the liquor. She took another sip, then let out a shaky sigh.

"Thank you." She lifted her eyes to Mrs. Pengalley again. "That's better."

"Brandy has its uses," the housekeeper said righteously.

Raven rose, trying to put her thoughts in order. There were things to be done and no time to do them.

"Mrs. Pengalley, I have to go back to America right away. Could you pack some things for me while I call the airport?"

"Aye." She studied Raven shrewdly. "He's gone off to cool his heels, you know. They all do that. But he'll be back soon enough."

Realizing Mrs. Pengalley spoke of Brand, Raven dragged a hand through her hair. "I'm not altogether certain of that. If Brandon's not back by the time I have to go to the airport, would you ask Mr. Pengalley to drive me? I know it's an inconvenience, but it's terribly important."

"If that's what you want." Mrs. Pengalley sniffed. Young people, she thought, always flying off the handle. "I'll pack your things, then."

"Thank you." Raven glanced around the music room, then picked up the phone.

An hour later she hesitated at the foot of the stairs. Everything seemed to have happened at once. She willed Brand to return, but there was no sign of his car in the driveway. Raven struggled over writing a note but could think of nothing to say on paper that could make up for the words she had thrown at him. And how could she say in a few brief lines that her mother was dying and she had to go to her?

Yet there wasn't time to wait until he returned. She knew she couldn't risk it. Frantically she pulled a note pad from her purse. "Brandon," she wrote quickly, "I had to go. I'm needed at home. Please forgive me. I love you, Raven."

Dashing back into the music room, she propped the note against the sheet of staff paper on top of the pile on the piano. Then, hurrying from the room, she grabbed her suitcases and ran outside. Mr. Pengalley was waiting in his serviceable sedan to drive her to the airport.

Chapter 14

Five days passed before Raven began thinking clearly again. Karter had been right about there only being a matter of hours. Raven had had to deal not only with grief but also an unreasonable guilt that she hadn't been in time. The demand of details saved her from giving in to the urge to sink into self-pity and self-rebuke. She wondered once, during those first crushing hours, if that was why people tied so many traditions and complications to death: to keep from falling into despair.

She was grateful that Karter handled the police himself in a way that ensured the details would be kept out of the papers.

After the first busy days there was nothing left but to accept that the woman she had loved and despised was gone. There was no more she could do. The disease had beaten them, just as surely as if it had been a cancer. Gradually she began to accept her mother's death as the result of a long, debilitating illness. She didn't cry, knowing she had already mourned, knowing it was time to put away the unhappiness. She had never had control of her mother's life; she needed the strength to maintain control of her own.

A dozen times during those days Raven phoned the house in Cornwall. There was never an answer. She could almost hear the hollow, echoing sound of the ring through the empty rooms. More than once she considered simply getting on a plane and going back, but she always pushed the thought aside. He wouldn't be there waiting for her.

Where could he be? she wondered again and again. *Where would he have gone? He hasn't forgiven me.* And worse, she thought again and again, *he'll never forgive me.*

After hanging up the phone a last time, Raven looked at herself in her bedroom mirror. She was pale. The color that had drained from her face five days before in Cornwall had never completely returned. There was too much of a helpless look about her. Raven shook her head and grabbed her blusher.

Borrowed color, she decided, was better than none at all. She had to start somewhere.

Yes, she thought again, still holding the sable brush against her cheek. I've got to start somewhere. Turning from the mirror, Raven again picked up the phone.

Thirty minutes later she came downstairs wearing a black silk dress. She had twisted her hair up and was setting a plain, stiff-brimmed black hat over it as she stepped into the hall.

"Raven?" Julie came out of the office. "Are you going out?"

"Yes, if I can find that little envelope bag and my car keys. I think they're inside it." She was already poking into the hall closet.

"Are you all right?"

Raven drew her head from the closet and met Julie's look. "I'm better," she answered, knowing Julie wouldn't be satisfied with a clichéd reply. "The lecture you gave me after the funeral, about not blaming myself? I'm trying to put it into practice."

"It wasn't a lecture," Julie countered. "It was simply a statement of facts. You did everything you could do to help your mother; you couldn't have done any more."

Raven sighed before she could stop herself. "I did everything I knew how to do, and I suppose that's the same thing." She shook off the mood as she shut the closet door. "I *am* better, Julie, and I'm going to be fine." She smiled, then, glimpsing a movement, looked beyond Julie's shoulder. Wayne stepped out of the office. "Hello, Wayne, I didn't know you were here."

He moved past Julie. "Well, I can definitely approve of that dress," he greeted her.

"And so you should," Raven returned dryly. "You charged me enough for it."

"Don't be a philistine, darling. Art has no price." He flicked a finger over the shoulder of the dress. "Where are you off to?"

"Alphonso's. I'm meeting Henderson for lunch."

Wayne touched Raven's cheek with a fingertip. "A bit heavy on the blush," he commented.

"I'm tired of looking pale. Don't fuss." She placed a hand on each of his cheeks, urging him to bend so that she could kiss him. "You've been a rock, Wayne. I haven't told you how much I appreciate your being here these last few days."

"I needed to escape from the office."

"I adore you." She lowered her hands to meet his arms and squeezed briefly. "Now, stop worrying about me." Raven shot a look past his shoulder to Julie. "You, too. I'm meeting Henderson to talk over plans for a new tour."

"New tour?" Julie frowned. "Raven, you've been working nonstop for over six months. The album, the tour, the score." She paused. "After all of this you need a break."

"After all this the thing I need least is a break," Raven corrected. "I want to work."

"Then take a sabbatical," Julie insisted. "A few months back you were talking about finding a mountain cabin in Colorado, remember?"

"Yes." Raven smiled and shook her head. "I was going to write and be rustic, wasn't I? Get away from the glitter-glamour and into the woods." Raven grinned, recalling the conversation. "You said something about not being interested in anything more rustic than a margarita at poolside."

Julie lifted a thin, arched brow. "I've changed my mind. I'm going shopping for hiking boots."

Wayne's comment was a dubious *"hmmm."*

Raven smiled. "You're sweet," she said to Julie as she kissed her cheek. "But it isn't necessary. I need to do something that takes energy, physical energy. I'm going to talk to Henderson about a tour of Australia. My records do very well there."

"If you'd just talk to Brand..." Julie began, but Raven cut her off.

"I've tried to reach him; I can't." There was something final and flat in that statement. "Obviously he doesn't want to talk to me. I'm not at all sure I blame him."

"He's in love with you," Wayne said from behind her. Raven turned and met the look. "A few thousand people saw the sparks flying the night of your concert in New York."

"Yes, he loves me, and I love him. It doesn't seem to be enough, and I can't quite figure out why. No, please." She took his hand, pressing it between both of hers. "I have to get my mind off it all for a while. I feel as if I had been having a lovely picnic and got caught in a landslide. The bruises are still a bit sore. I could use some good news," she added, glancing from one of them to the other, "if the two of you are ever going to decide to tell me."

Raven watched as Wayne and Julie exchanged glances. She grinned, enjoying what she saw. "I've been noticing a few sparks myself. Isn't this a rather sudden situation?"

"Very," Wayne agreed, smiling at Julie over Raven's head. "It's only been going on for about six years."

"Six years!" Raven's brows shot up in amazement.

"I didn't choose to be one of a horde," Wayne said mildly, lighting one of his elegant cigarettes.

"And I always thought he was in love with you," Julie stated, letting her gaze drift from Raven to Wayne.

"With *me?*" Raven laughed spontaneously for the first time in days.

"I fail to see the humor in that," Wayne remarked from behind a nimbus of smoke. "I'm considered by many to be rather attractive."

"Oh, you are," she agreed, then giggled and kissed his cheek. "Madly so. But I can't believe anyone could think you were in love with me. You've always dated those rather alarmingly beautiful models with their sculptured faces and long legs."

"I don't think we need to bring all that up at the moment," Wayne retorted.

"It's all right." Julie smiled sweetly and tucked her hair behind her ear. "I haven't any problem with Wayne's checkered past."

"When did all this happen, please?" Amused, Raven cut into their exchange. "I turn my back for a few weeks, and I find my two best friends making calf's eyes at each other."

"I've never made calf's eyes at anyone," Wayne remonstrated, horrified. "Smoldering glances, perhaps." He lifted his rakishly scarred brow.

"When?" Raven repeated.

"I looked up from my deck chair the first morning out on the cruise," Julie began, "and who do you suppose is sauntering toward me in a perfectly cut Mediterranean white suit?"

"Really?" Raven eyed Wayne dubiously. "I'm not certain whether I'm surprised or impressed."

"It seemed like a good opportunity," he explained, tapping his expensive ashes into a nearby dish, "if I could corner her before she charmed some shipping tycoon or handy sailor."

"I believe I charmed a shipping tycoon a few years ago," Julie remarked lazily. "And as to the sailor..."

"Nevertheless," Wayne went on, shooting her a glance. "I decided a cruise was a very good place to begin winning her over. It was," he remarked, "remarkably simple."

"Oh?" Julie's left brow arched. "Really?"

Wayne tapped out his cigarette, then moved over to gather her in his arms. "A piece of cake," he added carelessly. "Of course, women habitually find me irresistible."

"It would be safer if they stopped doing so. I might be tempted to wring their necks," Julie cooed, winding her arms around his neck.

"The woman's going to be a trial to live with." Wayne kissed her as though he'd decided to make the best of it.

"I can see you two are going to be perfectly miserable together. I'm so sorry." Walking over, Raven slipped an arm around each of them. "You will let me give you the wedding?" she began, then stopped. "That is, are you having a wedding?"

"Absolutely," Wayne told her. "We don't trust each other enough for anything less encumbering." He gave Julie a flashing grin that inexplicably made Raven want to weep.

Raven hugged them both again fiercely. "I needed to hear something like this right now. I'm going to leave you alone. I imagine you can entertain yourselves while I'm gone. Can I tell Henderson?" she asked. "Or is it a secret?"

"You can tell him," Julie said, watching as Raven adjusted her hat in the hall mirror. "We're planning on taking the plunge next week."

Raven's eyes darted up to Julie's in the mirror. "My, you two move fast, don't you?"

"When it's right, it's right."

Raven smiled in quick agreement. "Yes, I suppose it is. There's probably champagne in the refrigerator, isn't there, Julie?" She turned away from the mirror. "We can have a celebration drink when I get back. I'll just be a couple of hours."

"Raven." Julie stopped her as she headed for the door. Raven looked curiously over her shoulder. "Your purse." Smiling, Julie retrieved it from a nearby table. "You won't forget to eat, will you?" she demanded as she placed it in Raven's hand.

"I won't forget to eat," Raven assured her, then dashed through the door.

Within the hour Raven was seated in the glassed-in terrace room of Alphonso's toying with a plate of scampi. There were at least a dozen people patronizing the restaurant whom she knew personally. A series of greetings had been exchanged before she had been able to tuck herself into a corner table.

The room was an elaborate jungle, with exotic plants and flowers growing everywhere. The sun shining through the glass and greenery gave the terrace a warmth and glow. The floor was a cool ceramic tile, and there was a constant trickle of water from a fountain at the far end of the room. Raven enjoyed the casual elegance, the wicker accessories and the pungent aromas of food and flowers that filled the place. Now, however, she gave little attention to the terrace room as she spoke with her agent.

Henderson was a big, burly man whom Raven had always thought resembled a logjammer rather than the smooth, savvy agent he was. He had a light red thatch of hair that curled thinly on top of his head and bright, merry blue eyes that she knew could sharpen to a sword's point. There was a friendly smattering of freckles over his broad, flat-featured face.

He could smile and look genial and none too bright. It was one of his best weapons. Raven knew Henderson was as sharp as they came, and when necessary, he could be hard as nails. He was fond of her, not only because she made him so rich, but because she never resented having done so. He couldn't say the same about all of his clients.

Now Henderson allowed Raven to ramble on about ideas for a new tour, Australia, New Zealand, promotion for the new album that was already shooting up the charts a week after its release. He ate his veal steadily, washing it down with heavy red wine while Raven talked and sipped occasionally from her glass of white wine.

He noticed she made no mention of the *Fantasy* score or of her time in Cornwall. The last progress report he had received from her had indicated the project was all but completed. The conversations he had had with Jarett had been enthusiastic. Lauren Chase had approved each one of her numbers, and the choreography had begun. The score seemed to be falling into place without a hitch.

So Henderson had been surprised when Raven had returned alone so abruptly from Cornwall. He had expected her to phone him when the score was completed, then to take the week or two she had indicated she and Brand wanted to relax and do nothing. But here she was, back early and without Brand.

She chattered nervously, darting from one topic to another. Henderson didn't interrupt, only now and again making some noncommittal sounds as he attended to his meal. Raven talked nonstop for fifteen minutes, then began to wind down. Henderson waited, then took a long swallow of wine.

"Well, now," he said, patting his lips with a white linen napkin. "I don't imagine there should be any problem setting up an Australian tour." His voice suited his looks.

"Good." Raven pushed the scampi around on her plate. She realized she had talked herself out. Spearing a bit of shrimp, she ate absently.

"While it's being set up, you could take yourself a nice little vacation somewhere."

Raven's brows rose. "No, I thought you could book me on the talk-show circuit, dig up some guest shots here and there."

"Could do that, too," he said genially. "After you take a few weeks off."

"I want gigs, not a few weeks off." Her brows lowered suspiciously. "Have you been talking to Julie?"

He looked surprised. "No, about what?"

"Nothing." Raven shook her head, then smiled. "Gigs, Henderson."

"You've lost weight, you know," he pointed out and shoveled in some more veal. "It shows in your face. Eat."

Raven gave an exasperated sigh and applied herself to her lunch. "Why does everyone treat me like a dimwitted child?" she mumbled, swallowing shrimp. "I'm going to start being temperamental and hard to get along with until I get some star treatment." Henderson said something quick and rude between mouthfuls which she ignored. "What about Jerry Michaels? Didn't I hear he was lining up a variety special for the fall? You could get me on that."

"Simplest thing in the world," Henderson agreed. "He'd be thrilled to have you."

"Well?"

"Well, what?"

"Henderson." Resolutely, Raven pushed her plate aside. "Are you going to book me on the Jerry Michaels show?"

"No." He poured more wine into his glass. The sun shot through it, casting a red shadow on the tablecloth.

"Why?" Annoyance crept into Raven's tone.

"It's not for you." Henderson lifted a hand, palm up, as she began to argue. "I know who's producing the show, Raven. It's not for you."

She subsided a bit huffily, but she subsided. His instincts were the best in the field. "All right, forget the Michaels gig. What, then?"

"Want some dessert?"

"No, just coffee."

He signaled the waiter, then, after ordering blueberry cheesecake for himself and coffee for both of them, he settled back in his chair. "What about *Fantasy?*"

Raven twirled her wineglass between her fingers. "It's finished," she said flatly.

"And?"

"And?" she repeated, looking up. His merry blue eyes were narrowed. "It's finished," she said again. "Or essentially finished. I can't foresee any problem with the final details. Brandon or his agent will get in touch with you if there are, I'm sure."

"Jarett will probably need the two of you off and on during the filming," Henderson said mildly. "I wouldn't consider myself finished with it for a while yet.''

Raven frowned into the pale golden liquid in her glass. "Yes, you're right, of course. I hadn't thought about it. Well . . ." She shook her head and pushed the wine away. "I'll deal with that when the time comes."

"How'd it go?"

She looked at Henderson levelly, but her thoughts drifted. "We wrote some of the best music either one of us has ever done. That I'm sure of. We work remarkably well together. I was surprised."

"You didn't think you would?" Henderson eyed the blueberry cheesecake the waiter set in front of him.

"No, I didn't think we would. Thank you," this to the waiter before she looked at Henderson again. "But everything else apart, we did work well together."

"You'd worked well together before," he pointed out. " 'Clouds and Rain.' " He saw her frown but continued smoothly. "Did you know sales on that have picked up again after your New York concert? You got yourself a lot of free press, too."

"Yes," Raven mumbled into her coffee. "I'm sure we did."

"I've had a lot of questions thrown at me during the last weeks," he continued blandly, even when her eyes lifted and narrowed. "From the inside," he said with a smile, "as well as the press. I was at a nice little soirée just last week. You and Brand were the main topic of conversation."

"As I said, we work well together." Raven set down her cup. "Brandon was right; we are good for each other artistically."

"And personally?" Henderson took a generous bite of cheesecake.

"Well." Raven lifted a brow. "You certainly get to the point."

"That's all right, you don't have to answer me." He swallowed the cake, then broke off another piece. "You can tell *him*."

"Who?"

"Brand," Henderson answered easily and added cream to his coffee. "He just walked in."

Raven whirled around in her chair. Instantly her eyes locked on Brand's. With the contact came a wild, swift surge of joy. Her first instinct was to spring from the table and run to him. Indeed, she had pushed her chair back, preparing to do so, when the expression on his face cut through her initial spring of delight. It was ice cold fury. Raven sat where she was, watching as he weaved his way through the crowded restaurant toward her. There were casual greetings along the way which he ignored. Raven heard the room fall silent.

He reached her without speaking once or taking his eyes from her. Raven's desire to hold out a hand to him was also overcome. She thought he might strike it away. The look in his eyes had her blood beating uneasily. Henderson might not have been sitting two feet away.

"Let's go."

"Go?" Raven repeated dumbly.

"Now." Brand took her hand and yanked her to feet. She might have winced at the unexpected pressure if she hadn't been so shocked by it.

"Brandon..."

"Now," he repeated. He began to walk away, dragging her behind him. Raven could feel the eyes following them. Shock, delight, anxiety all faded into temper.

"Let go of me!" she demanded in a harsh undertone. "What's the matter with you? You can't drag me around like this." She bumped into a lunching comedian, then skirted around him with a mumbled apology as Brand continued to stalk away with her hand in his. "Brandon, stop this! I will not be dragged out of a public restaurant."

He halted then and turned so that their faces were very close. "Would you prefer that I say what I have to say to you here and now?" His voice was clear and cool in the dead silence of the room. It was very easy to see the violence of temper just beneath the surface. Raven could feel it in the grip of his hand on hers. They were spotlighted again, she thought fleetingly, but hardly in the manner in which they had been in New York. She took a deep breath.

"No." Raven struggled for dignity and kept her voice lowered. "But there isn't any need to make a scene, Brandon."

"Oh, I'm in the mood for a scene, Raven," he tossed back in fluid British tones that carried well. "I'm in the mood for a bloody beaut of a scene."

Before she could comment, Brand turned away again and propelled her out of the restaurant. There was a Mercedes at the curb directly outside. He shoved her inside it, slamming the door behind her.

Raven straightened in the seat, whipping her head around as he opened the other door. "Oh, you're going to get one," she promised and ripped off her hat to throw it furiously into the back seat. "How *dare* you..."

"Shut up. I mean it." Brand turned to her as she started to speak again. "Just shut up until we get where we're going, otherwise I might be tempted to strangle you here and be done with it."

He shot away from the curb, and Raven flopped back against her seat. I'll shut up, all right, she thought on wave after wave of anger. I'll shut up. It'll give me time to think through exactly what I have to say.

Chapter 15

By the time Brand stopped the car in front of the Bel-Air, Raven felt she had her speech well in order. As he climbed out of his side, she climbed out of hers, then turned to face him on the sidewalk. But before she could speak, he had her arm in a tight grip and was pulling her toward the entrance.

"I told you not to drag me."

"And I told you to shut up." He brushed past the doorman and into the lobby. Raven was forced into an undignified half-trot in order to keep up with his long-legged stride.

"I will *not* be spoken to like that," she fumed and gave her arm an unsuccessful jerk. "I will *not* be carted through a hotel lobby like a piece of baggage."

"I'm tired of playing it your way." Brand turned, grabbing both of her shoulders and dragging her against him. His fingers bit into her skin and shocked her into silence. "My game now, my rules."

His mouth came down hard on hers. It was a kiss of rage. His teeth scraped across her lips, forcing them open so that he could plunder and seek. He held her bruisingly close, as if daring her to struggle.

When Brand pulled away, he stared at her for a long, silent moment, then swore quickly, fiercely. Turning, he pulled her to the elevators.

Though she was no longer certain if it was fear or anger, Raven was trembling with emotion as they took the silent ride up. Brand could feel the throbbing pulse as he held her arm. He swore again, pungently, but she didn't glance at him. As the doors slid open, he pulled her into the hall and toward the penthouse.

There were no words exchanged between them as he slid the key into the lock. He released her arm as he pushed the door open. Without protest, Raven walked inside. She moved to the center of the room.

The suite was elegant, even lush, in a dignified, old-fashioned style with a small bricked fireplace and a good, thick carpet. Behind her the door slammed— a final sound—and she heard Brand toss the key with a faint metallic jingle onto a table. Raven drew a breath and turned around.

"Brandon..."

"No, I'll do the talking first." He crossed to her, his eyes locked on hers. "My rules, remember?"

"Yes." She lifted her chin. Her arm throbbed faintly where his fingers had dug into it. "I remember."

"First rule, no more bits and pieces. I won't have you closing parts of yourself off from me any more." They were standing close. Now that the first dazed shock and surprise were passing, Raven noticed signs of strain and fatigue on his face. His words were spilling out so quickly, she couldn't interrupt. "You did the same thing to me five years ago, but then we weren't lovers. You were always holding out, never willing to trust."

"No." She shook her head, scrambling for some defense. "No, that's not true."

"Yes, it's true," he countered and took her by the shoulders again. "Did you tell me about your mother all those years ago? Or how you felt, what you were going through? Did you bring me into your life enough to let me help you, or at least comfort you?"

This was not what she had expected from him. Raven could only press her hand to her temple and shake her head again. "No, it wasn't something..."

"Wasn't something you wanted to share with me." He dropped her arms and stepped away from her.

"Yes, I know." His voice was low and furious again as he pulled out a cigarette. He knew he had to do something with his hands or he'd hurt her again. He watched as she unconsciously nursed her arm where he had gripped her. "And this time, Raven, would you have told me anything about it if it hadn't been for the nightmare? If you hadn't been half asleep and frightened, would you have told me, trusted me?"

"I don't know." She made a small sound of confusion. "My mother had nothing to do with you."

Brand hurled the cigarette away before he lit it. "How can you say that to me? How can you stand there and say that to me?" He took a step toward her, then checked himself and stalked to the bar. "Damn you, Raven," he said under his breath. He poured bourbon and drank. "Maybe I should have stayed away," he managed in a calmer tone. "You'd already tossed me out of your life five years ago."

"*I* tossed *you* out?" This time her voice rose. "You walked out on me. You left me flat because I wouldn't be your lover." Raven walked over to the bar and leaned her palms on it. "You walked out of my house and out of my life, and the only word I had from you was what I read in the paper. It didn't take you long to find other women—several other women."

"I found as many as I could," Brand agreed and drank again. "As quickly as I could. I used women, booze, gambling—anything—to try to get you out of my system." He studied the dregs of liquor in his glass and added thoughtfully, "It didn't work." He set the glass down and looked at her again. "Which is why I knew I had to be patient with you."

Raven's eyes were still dark with hurt. "Don't talk to me about tossing you out."

"That's exactly what you did." Brand grabbed her wrist as she turned to swirl away from him. He held her still, the narrow, mahogany bar between them. "We were alone, remember? Julie was away for a few days."

Raven kept her eyes level. "I remember perfectly."

"Do you?" He arched a brow. Both his eyes and his voice were cool again. "There might be a few things you don't remember. When I came to the house that night I was going to ask you to marry me."

Raven could feel every thought, every emotion, pour out of her body. She could only stare at him.

"Surprised?" Brand released her wrist and again reached in his pocket for a cigarette. "Apparently we have two different perspectives on that night. I *loved* you." The words were an accusation that kept her speechless. "And God help me, all those weeks we were together I was faithful to you. I never touched another woman." He lit the cigarette, and as the end flared, Raven heard him say softly, "I nearly went mad."

"You never told me." Her voice was weak and shaken. Her eyes were huge gray orbs. "You never once said you loved me."

"You kept backing off," he retorted. "And I knew you were innocent and afraid, though I didn't know why." He gave her a long, steady look. "It would have made quite a lot of difference if I had, but you didn't trust me."

"Oh, Brandon."

"That night," he went on, "you were so warm, and the house was so quiet. I could feel how much you wanted me. It drove me crazy. Good God, I was trying to be gentle, patient, when the need for you was all but destroying me." He ran a tense hand through his hair. "And you were giving, melting, everywhere I touched you. And then—then you were struggling like some terrified child, pushing at me as if I'd tried to kill you, telling me not to touch you. You said you couldn't bear to have me touch you."

He looked back at her, but his eyes were no longer cool. "You're the only woman who's ever been able to hurt me like that."

"Brandon." Raven shut her eyes. "I was only twenty, and there were so many things . . ."

"Yes, I know now; I didn't know then." His tone was flat. "Though there really weren't so many changes this time around." Raven opened her eyes and started to speak, but he shook his head. "No, not yet. I've not finished. I stayed away to give you

time, as I told you before. I didn't see any other way.
I could hardly stay, kicking my heels in L.A., waiting for you to make up your mind. I didn't know
how long I'd stay away, but during those five years I
concentrated on my career. So did you."

Brand paused, spreading his long, elegant hands
on the surface of the bar. "Looking back, I suppose
that's all for the best. You needed to establish yourself, and I had a surge of productivity. When I
started reading about you regularly in the gossip
columns I knew it was time to come back." He
watched her mouth fall open at that, and her eyes
heat. "Get as mad as you damn well like when I've
finished," he said shortly. "But don't interrupt."

Raven turned away to search for control. "All
right, go on," she managed and faced him again.

"I came to the States without any real plan, except to see you. The solid idea fell into my lap by way
of *Fantasy* when I was in New York. I used the score
to get you back," he said simply and without apology. "When I stood up in that recording booth
watching you again, I knew I'd have used anything,
but the score did nicely." He pushed his empty glass
aside with his fingertip. "I wasn't lying about wanting to work with you again for professional reasons
or about feeling you were particularly right for *Fantasy*. But I would have if it had been necessary. So
perhaps you weren't so far wrong about what you
said on the cliffs that day." He moved from the bar

to the window. "Of course, there was a bit more to it in my mind than merely getting you to bed."

Raven felt her throat burn. "Brandon." She swallowed and shut her eyes. "I've never been more ashamed of anything in my life than what I said to you. Anger is hardly an excuse, but I'd hoped—I'd hoped you'd forgiven me."

Brand turned his head and studied her a moment. "Perhaps if you hadn't left, it would have been easier."

"I had to. I told you in the note..."

"What note?" His voice sharpened as he turned to face her.

"The note." Raven was uncertain whether to step forward or back. "I left it on the piano with the music."

"I didn't see any note. I didn't see anything but that you were gone." He let out a long breath. "I dumped all the music into a briefcase. I didn't notice a note."

"Julie called only a little while after you'd left to tell me about the accident."

His eyes shot back to hers again. "What accident?"

Raven stared at him.

"Your mother?" he said, reading it in her eyes.

"Yes. She'd had an accident. I had to get back right away."

He jammed his hands into his pockets. "Why didn't you wait for me?"

"I wanted to; I couldn't." Raven laced her fingers together to prevent her hands from fluttering. "Dr. Karter said it would only be a matter of hours. As it was..." She paused and turned away. "I was too late, anyway."

Brand felt the anger drain from him. "I'm sorry. I didn't know."

Raven didn't know why the simple, quiet statement should bring on the tears she hadn't shed before. They blinded her eyes and clogged her throat so that speech was impossible.

"I went a bit crazy when I got back to the house and found you'd packed and gone." Brand spoke wearily now. "I don't know exactly what I did at first; afterwards I got roaring drunk. The next morning I dumped all the music together, packed some things and took off for the States.

"I stopped off for a couple of days in New York, trying to sort things out. It seems I spend a great deal of time running after you. It's difficult on the pride. In New York I came up with a dozen very logical, very valid reasons why I should go back to England and forget you. But there was one very small, very basic point I couldn't argue aside." He looked at her again. Her back was to him, her head bent so that with her hair pulled up he could see the slender length of her neck. "I love you, Raven."

"Brandon." Raven turned her tear-drenched face toward him. She blinked at the prisms of light that blinded her, then shook her head quickly when she saw him make a move to come to her. "No, please don't. I won't be able to talk if you touch me." She drew in a deep breath, brushing the tears away with her fingertips. "I've been very wrong; I have to tell you."

He stood away from her, though impatience was beginning to simmer through him again. "I had my say," he agreed. "I suppose you should have yours."

"All those years ago," she began. "All those years ago there were things I couldn't say, things I couldn't even understand because I was so—dazzled by everything. My career, the fame, the money, the perpetual spotlight." The words came quickly, and her voice grew stronger with them. "Everything happened at once; there didn't seem to be any time to get used to it all. Suddenly I was in love with Brandon Carstairs." She laughed and brushed at fresh tears. "*The* Brandon Carstairs. You have to understand, one minute you were an image, a name on a record, and the next you were a man, and I loved you."

Raven moistened her lips, moving to stare from the window as Brand had. "And my mother—my mother was my responsibility, Brandon. I've felt that always, and it isn't something that can be changed overnight. You were the genuine knight on a charger.

I couldn't—wouldn't talk to you about that part of my life. I was afraid, and I was never sure of you. You never told me you loved me, Brandon.''

''I was terrified of you,'' he murmured, ''of what I was feeling for you. You were the first.'' He shrugged. ''But you were always pulling back from me. Always putting up No Trespassing signs whenever I started to get close.''

''You always seemed to want so much.'' She hugged her arms. ''Even this time, in Cornwall, when we were so close. It didn't seem to be enough. I always felt you were waiting for more.''

''You still put up the signs, Raven.'' She turned, and his eyes locked on hers. ''Your body isn't enough. That isn't what I waited five years for.''

''Love should be enough,'' she tossed back, suddenly angry and confused.

''No.'' Brand shook his head, cutting her off. ''It isn't enough. I want a great deal more than that.'' He waited a moment, watching the range of expressions on her face. ''I want your trust, without conditions, without exceptions. I want a commitment, a total one. It's all or nothing this time, Raven.''

She backed away. ''You can't own me, Brandon.''

A quick flash of fury shot into his eyes. ''Damn it, I don't want to own you, but I want you to belong to me. Don't you know there's a difference?''

Raven stared at him for a full minute. She dropped her arms, no longer cold. The tension that had begun to creep up the back of her neck vanished. "I didn't," she said softly. "I should have."

Slowly she crossed to him. She was vividly aware of every detail of his face: the dark, expressive brows drawn together now with thought, the blue-green eyes steady but with the spark of temper, the faint touch of mauve beneath them that told her he'd lost sleep. It came to her then that she loved him more as a woman than she had as a girl. A woman could love without fear, without restrictions. Raven lifted her fingertip to his cheek as if to smooth away the tension.

Then they were locked in each other's arms, mouth to mouth. His hands went to her hair, scattering pins until it tumbled free around them. He murmured something she had no need to understand, then plunged deep again into her mouth. Hurriedly, impatiently, they began to undress each other. No words were needed. They sought only to touch, to give, to fulfill.

His fingers fumbled with the zipper of her dress, making him swear and her laugh breathlessly until he pulled her with him to the rug. Then, somehow, they were flesh to flesh. Raven could feel the shudders racing through him to match her own as they touched. His mouth was no more greedy than hers, his hands no less demanding. Their fire blazed clean and bright. Need erupted in them both so that she pulled him to her, desperate to have him, frantic to give.

Raw pleasure shot through her, rocking her again and again as she moved with him. His face was buried in her hair, his body damp to her touch. Air was forcing its way from her lungs in moans and gasps as they took each other higher and faster. Then the urgency passed, and a sweetness took its place.

Time lost all meaning as they lay together. Neither moved nor spoke. Tensions and angers, ecstasies and desperations, had all passed. All that was left was a soft contentment. She could feel his breath move lightly against her neck.

"Brandon," Raven murmured, letting her lips brush his skin.

"Hmm?"

"I think I still had something to say, but it's slipped my mind." She gave a low laugh.

Brand lifted his head and grinned. "Maybe it'll come back to you. Probably wasn't important."

"You're right, I'm sure." She smiled, touching his cheek. "It had something to do with loving you beyond sanity or some such thing and wanting more than anything in the world to belong to you. Nothing important."

Brand lowered his mouth to hers and nipped at her still tender lip. "You were distracted," he mused, seeking her breast with his fingertip.

Raven ran her hands down his back. "I was in a bit of a hurry."

"This time..." He began to taste her neck and shoulder. "This time we'll slow down the tempo. A bit more orchestration, don't you think?" His fingers slid gently and teasingly over the point of her breast.

"Yes, quite a bit more orchestration. Brandon..." Her words were lost on a sound of pleasure as his tongue found her ear. "Once more, with feeling," she whispered.

SONG OF
THE WEST

NORA ROBERTS

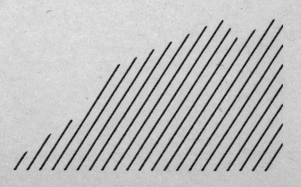

Chapter 1

The land in southeast Wyoming is a magnificent paradox. Spreading plains and rolling hills coexist with rocky mountains and thick velvet pines. From the kitchen window, the view was astounding, and Samantha Evans halted in her duties for a moment to drink it in.

The Rockies dominated the vast curtain of sky, their peaks laced with snow, though it was late March.

Samantha wondered if she would still be in Wyoming the following winter. She dreamed of long walks with the air biting and sharp on her cheeks, or wild rides on a spirited mount with hooves kicking up a flurry of white. But none of that could happen until her sister was well enough to be left alone.

A frown creased her smooth brow. Sabrina was her reason for being in Wyoming, with its majestic mountains and quiet plains, rather than in the more familiar surroundings of Philadelphia's tall buildings and traffic-choked streets.

The two sisters had always been close, that special, magical intimacy which twins share. They were not identical. Though they were the same in height and build, Samantha's eyes were a dark, cornflower blue widely set with thick, spikey lashes, while Sabrina's eyes were a light gray. Both faces were oval, set with small, straight noses and well-shaped mouths, but while Samantha's rich brown hair, with its highlights of gold, was shoulder length with a fringe of bangs, Sabrina's ash blonde was short, framing her face with delicate curls. The bond between them was strong and enduring. Even when Sabrina had married Dan Lomax and moved so many miles away to settle on his ranch in the Laramie Basin, their devotion had remained constant and unwavering.

They kept in touch by phone and letter which helped to mitigate Samantha's aching loneliness. And she was happy in her sister's delight in the coming baby. The two women had laughed and planned together over the phone. But that was before Dan's call. Samantha had been aroused from a deep predawn sleep by the shrill ringing of the phone. She reached groggily for it, but was instantly alerted by the anxious tone of her brother-in-law's voice. "Sam," he said without any preamble. "Bree's been very ill. We did manage to save the baby, but she has to be very careful for a while now. She will have to stay in bed and have constant round-the-clock care. We are trying to find someone to—"

Samantha had only one thought—her sister, the person she loved best in the world. "Don't worry, Dan, I will come immediately."

She was on the plane to Wyoming less than twenty-four hours later....

The whistle of the kettle brought Samantha back to the present. She began to brew the herbal tea, placing delicate floral cups on a silver tray.

"Tea time," she called as she entered the living room. Sabrina was propped up with pillows and comforters on the long wood-edged sofa. Though her smile was warm, her cheeks still retained a delicate pallor.

"Just like the movies," Sabrina commented as her sister set the tray on the pine table. "But the role of Camille is getting to be a bore."

"I imagine so." Samantha poured the fragrant tea into the cups. "But you may as well get used to it, Bree, you've got the part for a month's run." She transferred a large gray striped cat from Sabrina's lap to her own, offered Sabrina a steaming cup and sat on the rug. "Has Shylock been keeping you company?"

"He's a terrible snob." With a wry smile, Sabrina sipped at her tea. "He did graciously allow me to scratch his ears. I have to admit, I'm glad you brought him with you, he's my biggest entertainment." She sighed and lay back against the pillows, regarding her sister seriously. "I'm ashamed to be lying here feeling sorry for myself. I'm lucky." She rested her hand on her stomach in a protective gesture. "I shall have my baby, and I sit here moaning about your waiting on me."

"You're entitled to moan a bit, Bree," said Samantha, immediately sympathetic. "You're used to being active and busy."

"I've no right to complain. You gave up your job and left home to come out here and take care of me." Another deep sigh escaped, and her gray eyes were dangerously moist. "If Dan had told me what you were planning to do, I would never have allowed it."

"You couldn't have stopped me." Samantha attempted to lighten the mood. "That's what older sisters are for."

"You never forget those seven minutes, do you?" Sabrina's eyes cleared and a reluctant smile curved her generous mouth.

"Nope, it gives me seniority."

"But your job, Sam."

"Don't worry." Samantha made another dismissive gesture. "I'll get another job in the fall. There's more than one high school in the country and they all have gym teachers. Besides, I needed a vacation."

"Vacation!" Sabrina exclaimed. "Cleaning, cooking, caring for an invalid. You call that a vacation?"

"My dear Sabrina, have you ever tried to teach an overweight, totally uncoordinated teenager the intricacies of the parallel bars? Well, the stories I could tell you would curl your hair, so don't tell me about vacations."

"Sam, what a pair we are. You with your teenagers and me with my pre-adolescent Mozarts. Lord knows how many times I cleaned peanut butter off the keys of that old Wurlitzer before Dan came along and took me away from scales and infant prodigies. Do you think Mom expected us to come to this when she dragged us to all those lessons?"

"Ah, but we're well-rounded." Samantha's grin was faintly wicked. "Aren't you grateful? She always told us we'd be grateful one day for the ballet and the piano lessons."

"The voice lessons and the riding lessons," Sabrina continued, ticking them off on her fingers.

"Gymnastics and swimming lessons," Samantha added.

"Cooking and sewing lessons," Sabrina concluded with a giggle.

"Poor Mom." Samantha shifted Shylock to a more comfortable position. "I think she expected one of us to marry the president, and she wanted us to be prepared."

"We shouldn't make fun." Samantha wiped her eyes with a tissue. "The lessons did give us our living."

"True. And I can still whip up a mean spinach soufflé."

"Ugh." Sabrina grimaced, and Samantha lifted her brows.

"Exactly."

"You have your medals," Sabrina reminded her. Her smile warmed with pride and a trace of awe.

"Yes, I have the medals and the memories. Sometimes, it feels like yesterday instead of nearly ten years ago."

Sabrina smiled. "I can still remember my terrified excitement when you first swung onto the uneven bars. Even though I'd watched the routine countless times, I couldn't quite believe it was you. When they put that first Olympic medal around your neck, it was one of the happiest moments of my life."

"I remember thinking just before that competition, after I'd botched the balance beam so badly, that I couldn't do it. My legs felt like petroleum jelly, and I was mortally afraid I was going to be sick and disgrace myself. Then I saw Mom in the stands, and it ran through my mind how much she'd sacrificed.

Not the money. The bending of those rather strange values of hers to allow me those years of training and those few heady moments of competition. I had to prove it was justified, I had to pay her back with something, even though I knew she'd never be able to say she was proud of me."

"You proved it was justified." Sabrina gave her twin a soft smile. "Even if you hadn't won on the bars and the floor exercises, you'd proved it by just being there. And she was proud of you, even if she didn't say it."

"You've always understood. So get over the idea I'm doing you a favor coming here. I want to be here. I *belong* here."

"Sam." Sabrina held out a hand. "I don't know what I'd do without you. I don't know what I *ever* would have done without you."

"You'd manage," Samantha returned, giving the frail hand a squeeze. "You have Dan."

"Yeah, I do." The smile became soft. "This is the time of day that I miss him most. He should be home soon." Her gaze wandered to the glass-domed anniversary clock on the mantel above the fire.

"He said something about checking fences today. I can't quite get away from the image of him chasing rustlers or fighting off renegade Indians."

With a light laugh, Sabrina settled back among the cushions. "City slicker. You know, Sam, sometimes I can't even remember what Philadelphia looks like.

Jake Tanner was riding along with Dan today to make sure the boundary fences were in good repair.''

"Jake Tanner?" Samantha's question was idle.

"Oh, that's right, you haven't met him yet. The northwest corner of the ranch borders his. Of course, the Lazy L would fit into one corner of his ranch. He owns half the county."

"Ah, a land baron," Samantha concluded.

"A very apt description," Sabrina agreed. "The Double T, his ranch, is the most impressive I've seen. He runs it like clockwork, super efficient. Dan says he's not only an incredible rancher, but a very crafty businessman."

"Sounds like a bore," Samantha commented, wrinkling her nose. "Steel gray hair around a leathered face, a handlebar moustache drooping over his mouth and a generous belly hanging over his belt..."

Sabrina's laughter rang out, high and sweet. "You're about as far off the mark as you can get. Jake Tanner is anything but a bore, and speaking from the safety of marital bliss, he's a fascinating man to look at. And, being rich, successful and unattached, all the females under forty buzz around him like bees around honey."

"Sounds like a good catch," Samantha said dryly. "Mom would love him."

"Absolutely," Sabrina agreed. "But Jake has eluded capture so far. Though from what Dan says, he does enjoy the chase."

"Now he sounds like a conceited bore." Samantha tickled Shylock's smooth belly.

"You can hardly blame him for taking what's offered." Sabrina defended the absent Jake Tanner with a vague movement of her shoulders. "I imagine he'll settle down soon. Lesley Marshall—her father's ranch borders the other side of the Double T—has her sights set on him. She's a very determined woman as well as being more than a little spoiled, and dreadfully rich."

"Sounds like a perfect match."

"Mmm, maybe," Sabrina murmured. Her face creased in a small frown. "Lesley's nice enough when it suits her, and it's about time Jake had a wife and family. I'm fond of Jake. I'd like to see him set up with someone with more warmth."

"Listen to the old married woman." Samantha addressed a dozing and unconcerned Shylock. "A year of nuptial bliss, and she can't stand to see anyone unattached."

"True. I'm going to start on you next."

"Thanks for the warning."

"Wyoming's full of good-looking cowboys and handsome ranchers." Sabrina continued to smile as her sister grimaced. "You could find a worse place to settle down."

"I have no objection to settling here, Bree. I've become quite attached to the wide open spaces. But," she paused significantly, "cowboys and ranchers are not among my immediate plans for the future." She rose from the floor in a fluid motion. "I've got to check on that roast. Here." She handed her sister the novel which rested on the table. "Read your love stories, you incurable romantic."

"You won't be so cynical when you fall in love," Sabrina predicted with the wisdom of experience.

"Sure." Samantha's grin was indulgent.

"There'll be bells ringing and fireworks shooting and trumpets blaring." She patted her sister's hand and strolled from the room, calling over her shoulder. "Angels singing, flames leaping . . ."

"Just you wait," Sabrina shouted after her.

Samantha busied herself preparing vegetables for the evening meal, clucking her tongue at her sister's nonsense. *Love,* she sniffed derisively. Her only experience with that complex emotion had been fending off unwanted attentions from eager males. Not once had any man lit an answering spark in her. But whatever this love was, it worked for Bree. The younger twin had always been more delicate, softer and more dependent. And though Sabrina was trying to be brave and strong, her sister knew the fear of miscarriage still lurked in the back of her mind. She needed Dan's support and love, and right now, she needed to feel his arms around her.

Like the answer to a prayer, Samantha spotted two figures on horseback approaching from the lower pasture. Grabbing her heavy jacket from the hook by the back door, she scurried out of the kitchen and into the cold March air.

As Dan and his companion drew closer, Samantha greeted him with a smile and a wave. She had noticed, even at a distance, Dan's expression of concern. But a smile relaxed his features when he spotted Samantha.

"Sabrina's all right?" he asked as he reined in next to her.

"She's fine," Samantha assured him. "Just a trifle restless and tremendously lonely for her husband."

"Did she eat better today?"

Samantha's smile warmed, lighting her face with a quick flash of astonishing beauty.

"Her appetite was much better. She's trying very hard." Samantha lifted a hand to stroke the smooth flank of the gelding he rode. "What she needs now is you."

"I'll be in in as soon as I stable my horse."

"Oh, Dan, for heaven's sake. Let your hand do it, or I'll do it myself. Bree needs you."

"But..."

"'S all right, boss," the other horseman interrupted, and Samantha spared him a brief glance.
"I'll tend to your horse; you go on and see the mis-
sus."

Dan flashed his companion a wide grin and dismounted. "Thanks," he said simply as he handed
over the reins and turned to Samantha. "Coming
in?"

"No." She shook her head and hunched her
shoulders in the confines of her jacket. "You two
could use some time alone, and I'd like some air."

"Thanks, Sam." He pinched her cheek with
brotherly affection and moved off toward the house.

Waiting until the door closed behind him,
Samantha walked over and dropped wearily onto the
stump used for splitting wood. Resting her back
against the fence, she breathed deeply, devouring the
brisk, cold air. The strain of caring for her sister in
addition to running the house and cooking the meals,
including, over his objection, Dan's pre-dawn
breakfast, had taken its toll.

"A few more days," she whispered as she closed
her eyes. "A few more days and I'll have adjusted to
the routine and feel more like myself." The heavy
corded jacket insulated her from the bite of the cold,
and she tilted back her head, allowing the air to play
on her cheeks as her mind drifted on the edge of exhaustion.

* * *

"Funny place to take a nap."

Samantha sat up with a jerk, confused and disoriented by sleep. Her eyes traveled up to the speaker's face. It was a lean face, skin bronzed by the sun and stretched tightly over cheekbones, all lines and shadows, hollows and angles. The eyes were arresting, deep-set and heavily lashed. But it was their color, a deep pure jade, which caught and held her attention. His dusky gold hair curled from under a well-battered Stetson.

"Evening, ma'am." Though he touched the brim of his hat with due respect, his extraordinary eyes were faintly mocking.

"Good evening," she returned, struggling for dignity.

"Person could catch a bad chill sitting out too long after the sun's low. Wind's picking up too." His speech was slow and thickly drawled. His weight was distributed evenly on both legs, hands deep in pockets. "Oughtn't to be out without a hat." His comment was accompanied by a fractional movement of his head toward her unadorned one. "Hat helps keep the heat in."

"I'm not cold." She feared for a moment her teeth would chatter and betray her. "I was... I was just getting some air."

"Yes, ma'am." He nodded in agreement, glancing behind her at the last, dying brilliance of the sun as it slipped behind circling peaks. "Fine evening for setting out and watching the sunset."

Her eyes flashed at the teasing. She was embarrassed to have been caught sleeping. He smiled a slow, careless smile which crept unhurried across his face. The movement of his lips caused the hollows to deepen, the shadows to shift. Unable to resist, Samantha's lips curved in response.

"All right, I confess. You caught me napping. I don't suppose you'd believe I was just resting my eyes."

"No, ma'am." His answer was grave with just a hint of apology.

"Well." She rose from her seat and was dismayed at how far she still had to look up to meet his eyes. "If you keep quiet about it, I'll see to it that you get a piece of the apple pie I baked for dinner."

"That's a mighty tempting offer." He considered it with a long-fingered hand reaching up to stroke his chin. "I'm partial to apple pie. Only one or two things I'm more partial to." His eyes roamed over her in a thorough and intense study which caused her heart to pound with unaccustomed speed.

There was something different about this man, she thought swiftly, something unique, a vitality at odds with lazy words and careless smiles. He pushed his hat back further on his head, revealing more disorderly curls. "You've got yourself a deal." He held out his hand to confirm the agreement, and she placed her small hand in his.

"Thanks." The single word was breathless, as she found her speech hampered by the currents running up her arm. Abruptly, she pulled her hand away, wondering what it was about him which disturbed her equilibrium. "I'm sorry if I was short before about Dan's horse." She spoke now in a rush to conceal a reaction she could not understand.

"No need to apologize," he assured her, and the new soft texture in his tone both warmed and unnerved her. "We're all fond of Mrs. Lomax."

"Yes, well I..." she stammered, suddenly needing to put a safe distance between herself and this slow talking man. "I'd better go inside. Dan must be hungry." She looked past him and spotted his horse, still saddled, waiting patiently. "You didn't stable your horse. Aren't you finished for the day?" Hearing the concern in her own voice, she marveled at it. Really, she thought, annoyed, why should I care?

"Oh, yes, ma'am, I'm finished." There was laughter in his voice now, but Samantha failed to notice. She began to study the mount with care.

It was a magnificent animal, dark, gleaming chestnut, at least sixteen hands, she estimated, classic lines, fully flowing mane and proud, dished face. Arabian. Samantha knew horses and she recognized a full-blooded Arabian stallion when she saw one.

What in the world...? "That's an Arabian." Her words interrupted her thoughts.

"Yes, ma'am," he agreed easily, entirely too easily. Her eyes narrowed with suspicion as she turned to him.

"No ranch hand is going to be riding around on a horse that's worth six months' pay." She stared at him and he returned the steady survey with a bland, poker face. "Who are you?"

"Jake Tanner, ma'am." The slow grin appeared again, widening, deepening, then settling as he lifted the brim of his hat at the introduction. "Pleased to meet you."

The land baron with the women at his feet, Samantha's brain flashed. Anger darkened her eyes.

"Why didn't you say so?"

"Just did," he pointed out.

"Oh." She tossed back her thick fall of hair. "You know very well what I meant. I thought you were one of Dan's men."

"Yes, ma'am." He nodded.

"Stop ma'aming me," she commanded. "What a mean trick! All you had to do was open your mouth and say who you were. I would have stabled Dan's horse myself."

"I didn't mind." His expression became annoyingly agreeable. "It wasn't any trouble, and you had a nice rest."

"Well, Mr. Tanner, you had a fine laugh at my expense. I hope you enjoyed it," she said coldly.

"Yes, ma'am." The grin widened without seeming to move at all. "I did."

"I told you to stop..." She halted, biting her lip with frustration. "Oh, forget it." Tossing her head she took a few steps toward the house, then turned back crossly. "I notice your accent has modified quite a bit, Mr. Tanner."

He did not reply, but continued to stand negligently, his hands in his pockets, his face darkened by the late afternoon shadows. Samantha spun back around and stomped toward the house.

"Hey," he called out, and she turned toward him before she could halt the reflex. "Do I still get that pie?"

She answered his question with a glare. His laughter, deep and rich, followed her into the house.

Chapter 2

The sound of the slamming door reverberated through the ranch house as Samantha struggled out of her jacket and marched into the living room. At the sight of her sister's face Sabrina slipped down into the pillows, picked up the novel lying on her lap and buried her nose in its pages. Dan, however, did not recognize the storm warning in his sister-in-law's blue eyes and flushed cheeks. He greeted her with a friendly ingenuous smile.

"Where's Jake?" His gaze slid past her. "Don't tell me he went home without a cup of coffee?"

"He can go straight to the devil without his coffee."

"I expect he wanted to get home before dark," Dan concluded. His nod was sober, his eyes brilliant with merriment.

"Don't play innocent with me, Dan Lomax." Samantha advanced on him. "That was a rotten trick, letting me think he was one of your hands, and..." A giggle escaped from behind the paperback. "I'm glad you think it's amusing that your sister's been made a fool of."

"Oh, Sam, I'm sorry." Warily, Sabrina lowered the book. "It's just hard to believe anyone could mistake Jake Tanner for a ranch hand." She burst out laughing and Samantha was torn between the pleasure of seeing her sister laugh and irritation at being the brunt of the joke.

"Well, really, what makes him so special?" she demanded. "He dresses like every other cowboy I've seen around here, and that hat of his has certainly seen better days." But, she remembered, there *had* been something special about him which she had not quite been able to define. She firmly dismissed this disquieting thought. "The nerve of him." She rounded on Dan again. "Calling you boss and ma'aming me in that exaggerated drawl."

"Reckon he was just being polite," Dan suggested. His smile was amiable and pure. Samantha sent him the look which terrified her students.

"Men." Raising her eyes, she searched the ceiling in hopes of finding the answer there. "You're all

alike, and you all stick together.'' She bent and
scooped up the sleeping Shylock and marched into
the kitchen.

Time at the ranch passed quickly. Though her days
were full and busy, Samantha fretted for some of the
physical outlet which had so long been part of her
life. At times, the confinement of the house was suffocating. Years of training and discipline had left her
with an inherent need for activity.

Unconsciously, she separated her life into three
categories: the pre-Olympic years, the Olympic
years, and the post-Olympic years.

The pre-Olympic years were a blur of lessons,
piano teachers, dance instructors, her mother's
gentle but inescapable admonishments to ''Be a
Lady.'' Then, the first time she had gripped the lower
bar of the unevens, the new chapter had begun.

By the time she was twelve years old she had remarkable promise. The gymnastics instructor had
informed her mother, who was more distressed than
pleased at the praise. Though her mother had ob-
jected to more intense training, Samantha had ulti-
mately prevailed.

The hours of training became months, county
meets became state meets, and national competitions became international competitions. When
Samantha was picked for the Olympic team it was
just another step down a road she was determined to

follow. Weariness and aching muscles were accepted without hesitation.

Then it was over, and at fifteen, she had found it necessary to alter what had become a way of life. College had to be considered, and earning a living. The years passed into the post-Olympic period, and she remembered her days of athletic competitions as a dream. Now her life was shifting again, though she was unsure as to the direction. The mountains and plains were calling to her, inviting her to explore, but she buried her desires, remaining indoors to see to her sister's needs. Dan is a busy man, she thought as she prepared lunch, and Bree needs someone within calling distance during this critical period. When she's better there will be plenty of time to see the country.

She arched her back and rubbed a small spot of tension at the base of her neck. The kitchen door opened and Dan burst in accompanied by Jake Tanner. Samantha met the amused green eyes levelly, though once more she felt treacherously at a disadvantage.

Her hair had been carelessly scooped on the top of her head that morning, and now, with their usual abandonment, stray locks were beginning to escape confinement. She was dressed in a black ribbed sweater, which had seen too many washings, and ancient jeans, splattered, faded, patched and too tight. She resisted the urge to raise her hand to her tumbling hair, forced a smile and turned to her brother-in-law.

"Hello, Dan. What are you doing home this time of day?" Purposefully, she ignored the tall figure beside him.

"Wasn't too far out," Dan explained. Slipping off his jacket and hat, he tossed both over the hooks provided. "Jake was giving me a hand, so I figured it was only neighborly to bring him back for lunch."

"Hope I'm not imposing, ma'am." The slow smile spread, once more rearranging the angles of his face.

"No imposition, Mr. Tanner. But you'll have to settle for pot luck."

"My favorite dish—" he paused, giving her a cheeky wink, "—next to apple pie."

Samantha sent him a withering glance and turned away to warm the previous evening's stew.

"I'll just go tell Sabrina I'm home," Dan announced to the room in general and strode away. Samantha did her best to ignore Jake's disturbing presence. She stirred the stew busily.

"Smells good." Jake moved over to the stove and lounged against it. Samantha went to the cupboard to get the bowls.

When she turned back to place them on the round kitchen table, she noticed that he had shed his outdoor clothing. The slim fitting jeans, snug and low on narrow hips, accentuated his leanness. His flannel shirt fitted over his broad shoulders and hard chest before tapering down to a narrow waist. The athlete in her immediately responded to the firm, well-proportioned body; there was not an ounce of spare flesh on him.

"Don't talk much, do you?" The drawl was there again, the exaggerated twang of the previous evening. Samantha turned her head, preparing to freeze him with her eyes.

His face was barely inches from hers as he slouched by the stove. For a moment, her mind ceased to function.

"I really have nothing to say to you, Mr. Tanner." She struggled to keep her voice cold and detached, but she could feel the blood rush to her face.

"Well now, we'll have to see if we can change that." He spoke with easy confidence as he straightened to his full height. "We're not much on formalities around here. Just make it Jake." Though his words were spoken with his usual lazy delivery, there was an undertone of command. Samantha's chin rose in defense.

"Maybe I prefer to keep things formal between us, Mr. Tanner."

His lips were curved in his careless smile, but in his eyes she now recognized that special something that separated him from an ordinary ranch hand. *Power.* She wondered how she had missed it at their first meeting.

"I don't think there's much chance of that," he paused, and tugged at a loose lock of his hair, before adding with irritating emphasis, "ma'am. Nope, I don't think there's much chance of that at all."

Samantha was saved from coming up with a suitable rebuttal by Dan's reappearance. She began to spoon the stew into ceramic bowls, noting to her dismay that her hands were not altogether steady. This man was infuriating her with his arrogantly lazy confidence. I have never met a more irritating male, she thought. He thinks he can switch on that rugged cowboy charm and women will drop in droves at his feet. Well, maybe some do, but not this one.

"O.K., Sam?" Dan's voice shattered the electric silence.

"What? I'm sorry, I wasn't listening."

"You'll keep Jake company over lunch, won't you? I'll have mine in the living room with Sabrina."

She swore silently. "Of course," she answered with an impersonal smile.

Within a short time, Samantha found herself sitting across from the man she wanted most to avoid.

"You've a fine hand with dumplings, Sam." Her brows rose involuntarily at his easy use of her nickname, but she kept her voice even.

"Thank you, Mr. Tanner. It's just one of my many talents."

"I'm sure it is," he agreed with an inclination of his head.

"You haven't changed much from the girl in the picture in Sabrina's parlor." Samantha was astonished.

"You'd have been about fifteen," he continued. "A bit skinnier than you are now, but your hair was the same, not quite willing to stay bundled on top of your head." Samantha's blank expression had turned to a frown at the word skinnier. She remembered the photo clearly.

"You'd just finished winning your second medal." She had indeed been fifteen. The picture had been snapped at the moment she had completed her floor routine. It had captured the look of stunned triumph, for she had known in that instant a medal was hers.

"Sabrina's just about as proud of you as you are worried about her." Samantha said nothing, only staring into the lean, handsome features. His brows rose ever so slightly, a movement which would have gone unnoticed had she not been so intent on his face. For a moment, she forgot the thread of the conversation, caught up suddenly in a series of small, irrelevant details; the curling gold which spilled over his brow, the tiny white scar on his jawline, the thickness of his long lashes. Confused, she dropped her eyes to her bowl and struggled to bring her thoughts to order.

"I'd forgotten Bree had that picture," she said. "It was a long time ago."

"So now you teach. You don't look like any gym teacher I ever knew."

"Oh really?"

"No, ma'am." He shook his head slowly and considered her through another mouthful of stew. "Don't look strong enough or old enough."

"I assure you, Jake, I'm both strong enough and old enough for my profession."

"What made you become a gym teacher?" His sudden question caught her off balance, and she stared at him.

"Well, I..." Her shoulders moved restlessly. "Our mother was a fanatic on lessons when Bree and I were growing up." She smiled in spite of herself. "We took lessons in everything, Mom's theory on being well-rounded. Anyway, Bree found her talent in music and I developed a knack for the physical. For awhile I focused on gymnastics, then when the time came to work it seemed natural. Bree taught little people to play the classics, and I teach bigger people to tumble."

"Do you like your work? Are you happy with it?"

"As a matter of fact, I do," she retorted. "I like the activity, I like being involved in a physical type of work. It can be frustrating at times, of course. Some of the girls I teach would rather be flirting with their boyfriends than learning gymnastics, I suspect."

"And you yourself are more interested in calisthenics than men?" The question was delivered with a broad masculine smile.

"That's hardly relevant," she snapped, annoyed that she had lowered her guard.

"You don't think so?"

Samantha scraped back her chair and moved to the stove. "Coffee?"

"Yes, ma'am, black." It was unnecessary to turn around; she felt the slow grin crease his face as clearly as if she had witnessed it with her eyes. She set the cup down on the table with a bang. Before she could spin back to pour her own, her hand was captured in a firm grip. There was nothing soft about the hand. It was hard and masculine.

Completely outmatched in the short battle which ensued, Samantha discovered that under the lean, lanky exterior lay an amazing strength. Deciding that it was undignified to grapple in her sister's kitchen, she allowed her hand to rest quietly in his, meeting his laughing eyes with a resentful glare. Her heart began to pound uncomfortably against her ribs.

"What do you want?" Her voice came out in a husky whisper. His eyes left hers to travel slowly down to the generous curve of her mouth, lingering until she could taste the heat on her lips, as real as a kiss. Taking his time, he moved his gaze back to her eyes.

"You're jumpy." His observation was laconic, as if none of the heat had touched him though she herself was beginning to suffocate. "Powerful strong for such a little bit of a thing."

"I'm not little," she retorted. "You're just so big." She began to tug at her hand again, feeling a near desperate urgency to shake off the contact which was infusing her with an unexplained weakness around the knees.

"Your eyes are fabulous when you're angry, Sam." His tone was conversational. "Temper agrees with you. You grow beautiful with it." He laughed and pulled her closer.

"You're insufferable," she said, still struggling to escape his grasp.

"For telling you you're beautiful? I was just stating the obvious. I'm sure it's been mentioned to you once or twice before."

"You men are all the same." She ceased her struggles long enough to aim a lethal glare. "Always grabbing and groping."

"I don't grope, Samantha." His drawl was feather soft. For an instant, the cocky cowboy vanished, and she glimpsed the man, shrewd and ruthless, beneath. Here was a man who not only expected to have his own way, but would. "And the next time I grab you, it won't only be to hold your hand." Releasing her, he leaned back in his chair. "You have been warned."

Later, as Sabrina napped and the house grew still around her, Samantha found herself staring blankly at the pages of a novel. Scowling, she tossed it aside and rose from the sofa to pace to the window. What an infuriating man. Obviously, he considers himself irresistible. She began to wander the room, attempting to block out the effect his blatant virility had had on her.

It was too bad, she decided on her fourth circle, that all those good looks, strength and appeal had to belong to such a rude, arrogant man.

Deciding that a brisk walk was just what she needed to get Jake Tanner out of her mind, she stopped her pacing and grabbed a warm jacket. Moments later she was out the door, gazing around her in delight at the beauty of the starlit Wyoming night. Her breath puffed out in thin white mists as she moved. The air, tinged with frost, carried the aroma of pine, and she drank it in greedily, enjoying the mixed scent of hay and horses and aged wood. She could hear the lonely sound of a coyote calling to the full silver moon. And suddenly she realized that she had fallen in love with Wyoming. The spell of the mountains and plains was on her, and she was inexplicably glad she had come.

"Goodness, you were out a long time," her sister commented as Samantha plopped down in a wing-backed chair in front of the fire a few minutes later. "You must be frozen."

"No." Samantha stretched out her legs and sighed. "I love it out there. It's fantastic! I never realized how big the sky was before, and I don't think I'll ever get used to the space, the openness."

She turned her attention to the powerfully built man sitting next to her sister on the sofa. "I wonder if you appreciate it, Dan, living here all of your life? Even your letters, Bree, didn't do justice to that world out there." Running her fingers through her hair, she made a small sound of pleasure. "To someone used to traffic-choked streets and huge buildings, all this . . ." Her hands moved in an inadequate gesture.

"You haven't had much of a chance to see anything since you've been here," Dan observed. "You've been with us a month and you haven't gone a quarter mile away from the house. And that's been mostly to fetch the mail in the mornings."

"I'll have plenty of time to explore later. I'll be around through the summer."

"Just the same, we're not having you tied to the house while you're here, Sam," Dan announced, and sat back against the cushions. "Even the most devoted sister is entitled to a day off."

"Don't be silly. You make it sound as though I were slaving from dawn to dusk. Half the time I'm not doing anything."

"We know how hard you're working, Sam," Sabrina said quietly, glancing up at Dan before returning her gaze to her twin. "And I know the lack of activity is harder on you than the work. I also know how you disrupted your life to come out here and take care of me."

"Oh, Bree, for heaven's sake," Samantha began, shifting uncomfortably. "I never would have found out how much I love Wyoming if I hadn't come."

"Don't try to shrug it off, Sam." Dan grinned at the embarrassed motion of her shoulders. "We're grateful, and you'll just have to get used to us telling you so. But tomorrow, we're going to show we're grateful instead of just talking about it. We're kicking you out for the day."

"Huh?" Blankly, Sam blinked at the bland smile before shifting her gaze to Sabrina's serene one.

"That's right." His grin widened as she drew her brows together. "Tomorrow's Sunday, and I'm staying home with my wife. And you…." He pointed a warning finger at his sister-in-law. "You're going to have your pick of the horses and take off."

Samantha sprung up from her slouched position. "Do you mean it?" Her face was glowing with pleasure, and Dan's smile warmed with affection.

"Yes, little sister, I mean it. It should be more."

"The dapple gray gelding," she began in a rush, ignoring the last part of his comment. "Can I take him?"

"Already inspected the stock, and it appears you know your horses." Dan chuckled and shook his head. "Spook's a good mount. A little frisky, but from what Sabrina's told me, you can handle him."

"Oh, I can and I promise I'll be careful with him." She sprang from her chair and crossed the room, flinging her arms around his neck. "Thanks, Dan. You are absolutely my favorite brother-in-law, bar none."

"I think she likes the idea, Sabrina," Dan commented as he met his wife's eyes over Samantha's head. "In fact, I'd say she's downright pleased about it."

"And I thought I hid my emotions so effectively." She gave his cheek a loud, smacking kiss.

"You be ready to start out about nine." He patted Samantha's slim shoulder. "Jake'll be around then."

"Jake?" Samantha repeated. Her smile froze.

"Yeah, he'll be riding out with you. Actually," Dan continued, "he suggested the idea this afternoon. He thought it would do you good to get out of the house for awhile." He sighed and scratched his dark head, managing to appear sheepish for all his size. "I'm ashamed I didn't think of it first. I guess I've been a bit preoccupied and didn't notice you were looking a little tired and hemmed in."

"I'm not tired," she denied automatically.

"Hemmed in?" Sabrina offered with a knowing smile.

"A little maybe, but I'm hardly in the last stages of cabin fever. I'm sure it's very kind of Mr. Tanner to be so concerned about my welfare." She managed to say his name in a normal voice. "But there's certainly no need for him to go with me. I know he has hundreds of more important things to do with his Sunday."

"Well now, he didn't seem to think so," Dan said. "It was his suggestion, and he seemed keen on the idea, too."

"I don't know why he would be," she muttered. "Besides, I don't want to impose on him. We're practically strangers. I can just go by myself."

"Nonsense." Dan's refusal was good-natured but firm. "I couldn't possibly let you ride out by yourself just yet, no matter how good you are on a horse. You don't know the country, and it's easy to get lost. There's always the possibility of an accident. Besides," he added, and his grin was expansive, "you're part of the family, and I grew up with Jake, so you're not strangers. If anyone knows his way around this part of Wyoming, he does." He shrugged and rested his back against the cushions. "He owns half of it, anyway." Samantha glanced at her sister for help. Sabrina, however, appeared to be engrossed in her needlepoint.

Frowning at the lack of support, Samantha stewed over her predicament. If she refused Jake's company, she would not only forfeit the opportunity to ride the Wyoming countryside, but she would spoil Sabrina's and Dan's plans for a day alone together. She shrugged in resignation and offered a smile.

"I'll be ready at nine." She added to herself: If Jake Tanner can stand a day in my company, I guess I can stand a day in his.

Chapter 3

Sunday dawned with a sky as cold and clear as sapphire. The sun offered thin light and little warmth. To her annoyance, she had overslept. Hurriedly, she showered and dressed in forest green cords and a chunky beige pullover.

Her riding boots clattered on the parquet floor as she hurried from her room and down the hall to the kitchen. She frowned as she reached the doorway. Jake was sitting at the table, enjoying a cup of coffee with the air of one very much at home.

He was, she noted with illogical irritation, every bit as attractive as she remembered.

"Oh, you're here." Her greeting was hardly welcoming, but he returned it with his slow smile.

"Morning, ma'am."

"Don't start ma'aming me again," she said.

He remained silent as she clattered the cups in the cupboard and filled one with the steaming liquid from the pot on the stove.

"Sorry." She popped a piece of bread in the toaster and turned to offer a peace-time smile. "My! I overslept. I hope you haven't been waiting long."

"I've got all day," he answered, leaning back in his chair as if to emphasize his words.

She drew a slab of bacon and a carton of eggs from the refrigerator. "Have you eaten?" she asked in invitation.

"Yeah, thanks." He rose, poured himself another cup of coffee and resumed his position at the table. "Dan's already seen to breakfast for himself and Sabrina. They're having it in their room."

"Oh." She replaced the items and pulled out the butter.

"Aren't you going to eat?"

"Toast and coffee. I'm not much on breakfast."

"If you always eat like that," he observed over the rim of his cup, "it's no wonder you never grew any bigger."

"For goodness sake." She whirled around, brandishing the butter knife. "I'm hardly a midget. I'm five-four, that's tall enough for anybody."

He held up his hands in mock surrender. "I never argue with an armed woman."

"Ready?" He rose when she had finished both the toast and another cup of coffee.

When she mumbled her assent, he plucked her jacket from its hook, holding it out so that she had no choice but to allow him to help her into it. She stiffened as his hands touched her shoulders and turned her to face him. Her pulses responded immediately. As if he were aware of her reaction, he began to do up her leather buttons with slow care. She jerked back, but his hold on the front of her coat prevented her from a clean escape.

"You're a pretty little thing," he drawled, completing his task with his eyes directly on hers. "Can't have you catching cold." He reached out and plucked Sabrina's dark, wide-brimmed hat from a peg and placed it neatly on her head. "This'll keep your head warm."

"Thanks." She pushed the hat firmly in place.

"Anytime, Sam." His face was unperturbed as he pulled his own sheepskin jacket over his flannel shirt and jeans.

On the way to the stables, Samantha increased her pace to a trot to keep up with Jake's long, careless stride. Despite herself, she admired the confident, loose-limbed grace of his movement. He took his time, she noted, and decided he probably did nothing quickly, and more than likely, still finished ahead of everyone else.

The dapple gray had been saddled and led outside by a smiling ranch hand.

"Howdy, ma'am. Dan said to have Spook ready for you."

"Thanks." She returned his friendly smile and patted the gelding's neck. "But I could have done it. I don't like to give you extra work."

"No trouble, ma'am. Dan said you weren't to do a lick of work today. You just go and have yourself a good time, and I'll rub old Spook down when you get back."

Samantha vaulted easily onto the horse's back, happy to feel a mount beneath her again. Riding was an old pleasure, to be enjoyed only when finances allowed.

"Now, you take good care of Miss Evans, Jake," the cowboy admonished with a conspirator's wink Samantha failed to catch. "Dan sets great store by this little lady."

Little again, Samantha thought.

"Don't you worry about Miss Evans, Lon." Jake mounted his stallion with a fluid motion. Again Samantha noticed he wasted no time on superfluous movement. "I intend to keep a close eye on her."

Samantha acknowledged Jake's statement with a wrinkled nose, then following the direction his hand indicated, set off in a brisk canter.

As the neat cluster of ranch buildings was left behind, her irritation vanished. The rushing air was exciting, filling her lungs and whipping roses into her cheeks. She had almost forgotten the sense of liberation riding gave her. It was the same sensation that she had experienced many times when flying from top to bottom or springing high in a double twist.

They rode in silence for a quarter of an hour. Jake allowed her to fill her being with the thrill of movement and the beauty of the countryside. Wild peaks jutted arrogantly into the sky. The rolling plains below were yellow-green with winter. They rode by Herefords, white-faced and sleek, who noted their passage with a lazy turn of the head before resuming their grazing.

A shape darted across an open field, and Samantha slowed her horse to a walk and pointed. "What's that?"

"Antelope," Jake answered, narrowing his eyes against the sun.

"Oh!" She halted her mount and watched the animal's graceful, bounding progress until it streaked over a hill and out of her view. "It must be marvelous to run like that, graceful and free." She turned her unguarded face to the man beside her and found him regarding her intently. His eyes held an expression she did not understand. A strange tingling raced along her spine, like warm fingers on cold skin. The tingling increased, the sensation spreading to settle somewhere in her stomach. Suddenly, his expression changed. The shadows of his face shifted as his lips moved into a smile.

"Someday you will be caught, little antelope."

She blinked at him, totally disoriented, trying to remember what they had been talking about. His grin increased. He pointed to a large, bare-limbed tree a quarter of a mile away.

"Race you." There was challenge under the lazy dare.

Her eyes brightened with excitement. "Fine chance I'd have against a horse like that. What handicap do I get?"

Jake pushed his hand back as if to view her more completely. "From the look of you, I'd say you've got a good fifty-pound advantage. That should balance the odds some."

"No head start?"

"No, ma'am."

She pouted for a moment, then grinned. "All right, Jake Tanner, I'll give you a run for your money."

"Whenever you say, Sam." He pulled the brim of his hat low over his forehead.

"Now!"

She met the gelding's sides with her heels and spurted forward in a gallop. The quiet morning air vibrated with the thunder of hooves. Samantha, her hair flowing behind her, gave herself over to the thrill of the race. She reached the finish just ahead of her competitor and reined in, filling the morning with dusty, breathless laughter.

"Oh, that was wonderful, absolutely wonderful."

"Anytime you want to give up teaching, Sam, you can work for me. I can use a hand who rides like you."

"I'll keep that in mind, even though I know you let me beat you."

"Now what makes you think that." He leaned his arm on the horn of his saddle and watched her thoughtfully.

"I'm not stupid." Her grin was good-natured and friendly. "I couldn't beat that Arabian in a million years. You, maybe," she added with a touch of arrogance, "but not that horse."

"Pretty sharp, aren't you?" he returned, answering her grin.

"As a tack," she agreed. "And," she continued, brushing her hair from her shoulders, "I am not a weak female who needs to be placated. With my background, I know how to compete, I know how to lose, and," she grinned and lifted her brows, "I know how to win."

"Point taken." He tilted his head as if to view her from a different angle. "From now on, Sam, we play head-to-head." He smiled, and she was no longer sure they were talking about the same thing. "I know how to win, too," he added slowly. They continued at a leisurely pace for a time, crossing a narrow branch of the Medicine Bow River. They paused there for the horses to quench their thirst in the icy water which forced its way over shining rocks with hisses and whispers. At Samantha's request, Jake began to identify the surrounding mountains.

Pointing to the long fingers of peaks at the south, he told her they extended from eastern Colorado, the Laramie Range. The middle section was the Medicine Bow Range, and the Sierra Madre loomed westward. The vast ranges were separated by broad tongues of the Wyoming Basin. Silver-blue, they gleamed in the sunlight, lacings of snow trembling from their summits.

She had reined in without being aware of her action. "I can never look at them long enough. I suppose you're used to them."

"No." There was no laughter or mockery in his tone. "You never get used to them."

She smiled a bit uncertainly, not at all sure she could deal with this side of him.

"Are there bears up there?" she asked.

He glanced up at the mountains, smiled, then looked back at her. "Black bear and grizzly," he informed her. "Elk, coyotes, mountain lions..."

"Mountain lions?" she repeated a little nervously.

"You're not likely to run into one down here," he returned with an indulgent smile.

She ignored the mockery in his voice and looked around her, again awed by the miles of open space. "I wonder if this looked the same a century ago."

"Some of it. Those don't change much." He indicated the Rockies with an inclination of his head. "The Indians are gone," he continued, as if thinking aloud. "There were Arapaho, Sioux, Cheyenne, Crow, Shoshone, all roaming free over the state before the first white man set foot here. Then trappers came, trading with Indians, dressing like them, living like them, and the beaver was nearly driven into extinction." He turned back to her, as if suddenly remembering she was there. "You're the teacher." His smile appeared. "You should be telling me."

Samantha shook her head in mock despair. "My knowledge of Wyoming's history is limited to late-night westerns." They were walking their horses slowly, side by side. She had completely forgotten her aversion to the man beside her. "It's impossible to believe the killing and cruelty that must have gone on here. It's so serene, and so vast. It seems there would have been room enough for everyone."

This time it was Jake who shook his head. "In 1841 more than a hundred and fifty thousand people crossed the South Pass going west, and a few years later, fifty thousand more came through on their way to California looking for gold. This was Indian land, had been Indian land for generations. Game disappeared, and when people get hungry, they fight. Treaties were signed, promises made by both sides, broken by both sides." He shrugged.

"In the 1860s, they tried to open the Bozeman Pass from Fort Laramie to Montana, and open war broke out. The trail ran through the Sioux hunting ground. The fighting was of the worst kind, massacres, indiscriminate killing of women and children, butcheries by both white and Indian. More treaties were signed, more misunderstandings, more killing, until the whites outnumbered the Indians, drove them away or put them on reservations."

"It doesn't seem fair," Samantha whispered, feeling a wave of sadness wash over her.

"No, it doesn't." He heard the wistful note in her voice and turned to regard her. "Life isn't always fair though, is it, Samantha?"

"I suppose not." She sighed. "You seem to know quite a bit about what happened here. You must have had a good history teacher."

"I did." He held her curious look with a teasing half-smile on his lips. "My great-grandmother lived to be ninety-eight. She was Sioux."

Samantha lifted her brows in surprised interest. "Oh, I'd love to have met her. The things she must have seen, the changes in nearly a century of living."

"She was quite a woman." His smile faded a moment. "She taught me a lot. Among other things she told me that the land goes on no matter who walks on it, that life moves on whether you fight against it or flow with it, that when you want something, you go after it until it's yours.''

Suddenly, she felt he was leading her out of her depth, reaching for something she was not sure she possessed. She turned from the directness of his eyes to search the land.

"I'd like to have seen all this before there were any fences, before there was any fighting.''

Jake pointed skyward. Glancing up, Samantha watched the graceful flight of an eagle. For a timeless moment, he soared overhead, the undisputed sovereign of the skies. They moved off in companionable silence. "I hope you're getting some fun out of this trip, some compensation for taking care of your sister," Jake said at last.

"I don't need any compensation for taking care of Bree, she's my sister, my..."

"Responsibility?"

"Well...yes. I've always looked out for Bree, she's more delicate, more...dependent than I am." She shrugged and felt uncomfortable without knowing why. "Dad always joked that I took my share of strength and half of Bree's while we were still in the womb. She needs me," she added, feeling compelled to defend what she had always taken for granted.

"She has Dan," Jake reminded her. "And she's a grown woman now—just as you are. Did it ever occur to you that you have your own life to lead now that Sabrina has a husband to care for her?''

''I'm not trying to take over for Dan,'' she said quickly. ''Perhaps you can figure out how he could see to her needs and tend to the house and the ranch all at the same time, but I can't.'' She glared at him, half in anger, half in exasperation. ''What do you expect me to do? Sit up in Philadelphia teaching kids to jump on a tramp while my sister needs my help?''

''No, Samantha.'' He met her eyes with a quiet patience which was more disturbing than angry words and shouts. ''What you're doing is very kind and unselfish.''

''There's nothing kind or unselfish about it,'' she interrupted, shrugging the words away. ''We're sisters. More than that, we're twins. We shared life from its beginning. You can't understand the kind of bond that creates. I'd give up a hundred jobs to help Bree if she needed me.''

''No one's condemning your loyalty, Samantha; it's an admirable trait.'' He gave her a long, level look. ''Just a word of advice. Don't become so involved that you forget who Samantha Evans is, and that she just might have the right to her own woman's life.''

Samantha drew herself up to her full height in the saddle. "I hardly need your advice on how to run my life. I've been managing nicely for some time now."

His face creased in a lazy smile. "Yes, ma'am, I'm sure you have."

Chapter 4

Samantha had been riding the dapple gray in stubborn silence for nearly thirty minutes when she noticed more cattle. Her guide seemed unperturbed by her silence and slowed his Arabian's gait to the gelding's meandering walk. She would never have admitted to the man at her side that his words had disturbed her peace of mind.

What business is it of his how she chose to run her life? What gave Jake Tanner the right to question her relationship with Sabrina? No one asked him for his advice. And why in heaven's name should anything he said matter in the first place?

They were approaching a large ranch house. A redwood porch skirted the building's front, graced by evergreen shrubs. A gray wisp of smoke rose in a welcoming spire from the chimney. Ranch buildings sat neat and unobtrusive in the background.

"Welcome to the Double T, ma'am."

Jake drew her eyes with the uncharacteristic formality in his tone. She turned to see him smile and touch the brim of his well-worn Stetson.

"Thank you, Mr. Tanner. I can honestly say your ranch is spectacular. But what, may I ask, are we doing here?"

"Well now." Jake shifted in the saddle to face her directly. "I don't know about you, but nearly three hours in the saddle gives me a powerful appetite. I figured here we might do a bit better than beef jerky."

"Three hours?" Samantha repeated, and pushed Sabrina's hat from her head so it lay against her back. "Has it really been that long?"

The angles of his face moved slowly with his grin, and she found herself once more intrigued by the process. "I'll take that to mean you were so delighted with my company, time stood still."

She answered with a toss of her head. "I hate to tread on your ego, Jake, but the credit goes to Wyoming."

"Close enough for now." Reaching over, he plopped the brimmed hat back in place on Samantha's head and urged his mount into a canter.

Samantha stared after him in exasperation, watching the confidence with which he rode the Arabian. They moved like one form rather than horse and man. Scowling, she pressed her heels to the gelding's side and raced forward to join him.

As she reached his side, he skirted the ranch house and rode toward the buildings in the rear, following the left fork on a long hard-packed road. A large, sleepy-eyed St. Bernard rose from his siesta and romped forward to greet them. A deep, hoarse bark emitted from his throat. Jake halted in front of the stables. He slid off the Arabian's back, running his hand through the dog's thick fur as he hit the ground.

"Wolfgang's harmless." He acknowledged the loving, wet kisses with another brief caress and moved to the gelding's side. "He's just a puppy."

"A puppy," Samantha repeated. "You don't see many hundred-and-fifty-pound puppies." Tilting her head, she gave the overgrown baby a thorough examination before she brought her leg over the saddle to dismount.

Jake gripped her waist as she made her descent, holding her off the ground a moment as if she were weightless. As her boots touched earth, she was turned around and drawn against a hard chest. She tilted her head to inform him that his assistance was unnecessary, but saw only a brief blur of his face before his lips captured hers.

Her mind whirled with the touch and scent of him. She felt as though she were falling into a deep well and her heart began to beat a mad tempo against her ribs. She clutched at his jacket in defense. Perhaps the kiss was brief. It could have lasted no more than a portion of a minute, but it felt like forever. She knew his mouth was warm and sure on hers while decades flew into centuries.

The strange sensations of timelessness and loss of control frightened her. She stiffened and began to struggle against his grasp. He released her immediately, staring down at her clouded blue eyes with a satisfied smile. The smile transformed terror into fury.

"How dare you?"

"Just testing, ma'am." His answer was complacent, as though the kiss had been no more than that, a traditional touching of lips.

"Testing?" she repeated, running an agitated hand through her hair. "Testing what?"

"I've always wanted to kiss a teacher." Grinning, he gave her a friendly pat on the cheek. "I think there're some holes in your education."

"I'll show you holes, you conceited, high-handed—" her mind searched for something appropriately derogatory and settled on a generality, "—*man*. If I didn't consider that kiss so insignificant, you'd be lying on your back checking out the sky."

He surveyed her as she trembled with a mixture of fury and wounded pride. He rubbed his chin thoughtfully. "You know, Sam, I almost believe you could do it."

"You can bank on it," she confirmed with an arrogant toss of her head. "And the next time you..." Feeling her arm sharply pulled she glanced down to see the sleeve of her jacket captured in the awesome jaws of the St. Bernard. "What'd you do, teach him to eat unwilling females?"

"He just wants to make your acquaintance," Jake laughed, as he led the horses to the stable to turn them over to one of his men.

Samantha was not normally timid, and her pride refused to allow her to call Jake to untangle her from the teeth of his puppy. She swallowed and spoke to her canine captor.

"Hello... Wolfgang, wasn't it?" she muttered. "I'm Sam. You, ah, wouldn't consider letting go of my jacket, would you?" The dog continued to stare with droopy, innocent eyes. "Well, that's all right," she said, trying out magnanimity. "It's just an old one anyway. I'm very fond of dogs, you know." Tentatively, she brought her free hand up to touch the fur on his huge head. "Well, actually, I have a cat," she admitted in apology, "but I have absolutely no prejudices."

Though his expression did not alter, she decided it was prudent to give him time for consideration. Her patience was rewarded when he released her sleeve and bathed her hand with his enormous tongue.

"Well, I see you two have made friends," Jake drawled, coming up behind her.

"No thanks to you," she said. "He might have eaten me alive."

"Not you, Sam," Jake disagreed, taking her hand and striding toward the house. "Too tough for Wolfgang's taste."

Jake led her to the back entrance through a paneled, tiled-floor mud room and into the kitchen. A large square room, it was bright and cheery with tangerine curtains framing the wide windows. The pleasant looking woman who stood by the sink smiled at Samantha. "Jake, you scoundrel, have you had this poor little lady out in the cold all this time?" Samantha met the warm brown eyes with a returning smile.

Jake grinned, unabashed. "Samantha Evans, meet Annie Holloway, my cook, housekeeper and best girl."

"Don't you try soft soaping me, you young devil." She brushed off his words with indulgent affection, but pleased color rose to her pudgy cheeks. "Thinks he can get around me with sweet talk. Pleased to meet you, Miss Evans." Samantha found her hand enclosed in a firm grip.

"Hello, Miss Holloway, I hope I'm not putting you out."

"Putting me out?" Annie let out a rich, full laugh, her ample bust heaving with the sound. "Isn't she the sweet one? Don't you be silly, now, and you just call me Annie like everyone else."

"Thank you, Annie." Samantha's smile warmed. "Everyone calls me Sam."

"Now that's a pretty thing," Annie commented, peering candidly into Samantha's face. "Yes sir, a right pretty thing. You two run along," she commanded with an attempt at sternness. "Out of my kitchen. Lunch will be along, and I'll bring you in some tea to warm you up. Not you," she said with a scowl as Jake grimaced. "For the little lady. You don't need any warming up."

"Annie runs things," Jake explained as he led Samantha down a wide hall into the living room.

"I can see she does, even when she's securely wrapped around your little finger."

For a moment, his smile was so boyish and full of mischief, she nearly gave into the urge to brush the curls from his forehead.

The paneling in the living room was light. The expanse of wood was broken by a large stone fireplace and wide windows framed with cinnamon-colored sheers. The dark gleaming furniture had been upholstered in gold, burnt sienna and rich browns. There was a comfortable hodgepodge of Hepplewhites and Chippendales with pie-crust tilt-top tables and pembrokes, ladderback chairs and candlestands. In the center of the hardwood floor lay a wide rug of Indian design, so obviously old and handworked, that Samantha wondered if it had been his great grandmother's fingers that had hooked it perhaps nearly a century ago. The room reflected a quiet, understated wealth, a wealth she somehow did not associate with the rangy, brash cowboy side of Jake.

A Charles Russell painting caught her eye. She turned to study it, attempting to sort out her new impressions of this complex man. Turning back, she found him watching her reaction with unconcealed amusement.

"I have a feeling you were expecting bear skins and oil cloth."

Samantha focused her attention on the inviting fire. "I never know what to expect from you," she muttered.

"No?" He dropped his lanky form into a wingedback chair and pulled out a long, thin cigar. "I thought you were pretty bright."

Samantha seated herself in the chair across from him, keeping the warmth and hiss of the fire between them. "This is a lovely room, very appealing and very warm."

"I'm glad you like it." If he noticed her blatant change of subject, he gave no sign. Lighting his cigar, he stretched out his legs and looked totally relaxed and content.

"I have a weakness for antiques," she continued, deciding the topic was safe and impersonal.

He smiled, the smoke curling lazily above his head. "There's a piece in one of the bedrooms you might like to see. A blanket chest in walnut that was brought over from the East in the 1860s."

"I'd like that very much." She returned his smile and settled back as Annie wheeled a small tea cart into the room.

"I brought you coffee," she said to Jake and passed him a cup. "I know you won't take tea unless you douse it with bourbon. Something not quite decent about doing that to a good cup of tea."

"Tea is an old ladies' drink," he stated, ignoring her rapidly clucking tongue.

"How do you think Sabrina looks?" Samantha asked him when Annie had bustled back to the kitchen.

"I think you worry too much about her."

She bristled instinctively before replying. "Perhaps you're right," she surprised herself by admitting. "Our mother always said Bree and I were mirror images, meaning, I discovered after a while, opposites."

"Right down to Sabrina being right-handed, and you being left."

"Why, yes." She looked at him in faint surprise. "You don't miss much, do you?" He merely shook his head and gave her an enigmatic smile. "Well," she plunged on, not sure she liked his expression, a bit like a cat who already had the mouse between his paws. "I suppose the summary of my discrepancies was that I could never keep the hem in my white organdy party dress. You'd have to know my mother to understand that. She would have Bree and me all decked out in these frilly white organdy dresses and send us off to a party. Bree would come back, spotless, pure and angelic. I'd come back with dirt on my frills, bloody knees and trailing a hem."

During her story, Jake's smile had widened. The coffee in his cup cooled, unattended as he watched her. "There're doers and there're watchers, Samantha. I imagine you had fun scraping up your knees."

As ridiculous as it seemed, she felt she'd just been complimented, and was both pleased and faintly embarrassed.

"I suppose you're a doer, too." She dropped her eyes. "You couldn't run a ranch like this and not be. Cattle ranching sounds romantic, but I imagine it's long hours, hot summers and cold winters. I don't suppose it's really all that different from the way it used to be a hundred years ago."

"The range isn't open anymore," he corrected. "You don't find cowboys going off to Texas to punch cattle with a ten-dollar horse and a forty-dollar saddle." He shrugged and set his empty cup on the table beside him. "But some change slow, and I'm one who likes to take my time."

She was frowning into his smile when Annie announced lunch. It was not until they were settled in the dining room that she spoke directly to him again, pressing him for more details on how the ranch was run.

He explained how roundups, which had once been accomplished on the vast open range with only men and horses, were now aided by fences and technology. But it was still men and ponies who moved the cattle into corrals. Over a few states there were still strongholds of riders and ropers, men who cultivated the old technique and blended it with the new. On the Double T, Jake employed the best of both.

"If roundups aren't what they once were, they still accomplish the same end. Getting the cattle together and branding them."

"Branding?" Samantha interrupted and shuddered.

"Your Philadelphia's showing, Sam." He grinned. "Take my word for it, branding is a good deal more unpleasant for the branders than the brandees."

She decided to ignore his comments and changed the subject abruptly. "Bree told me your ranch borders Dan's. This place must be huge for it to have taken us three hours to get here."

Jake's deep, rich laughter filled the room, and she decided unwillingly that she liked the sound very much. "It's a pretty big spread, Sam, but if you take the straight road north from the Lazy L, you can be here in twenty minutes on horseback. I took you on a big circle today," he explained. "Just a small taste of our part of the Laramie Basin."

They lingered over coffee, relaxed in each other's company.

"We'd better get started back," Jake said after awhile. He rose and extended his hand. Her own slipped without hesitation into it as he pulled her to her feet. When she looked up at him her smile was warm and spontaneous.

"Annie was right, that's a pretty thing." He lifted his hand and traced his fingers over the curve of her mouth. She started. "Now don't go skittish on me, Sam, I'm not going to use spurs and a whip."

His mouth lowered, gentle and persuasive. One hand held hers while the other circled the back of her neck to soothe with coaxing fingers. She had only to sway forward to feel his body against hers, had only to lift her hand to bring his mouth firmer and warmer on hers. Before the choice could be made, he drew her away and the decision was taken out of her hands.

"Sam." He shook his head as if exasperated and lightly amused. "You're enough to try a man's patience."

With this, he pulled her through to the kitchen.

"Well, so you're off again." Annie wiped one hand on her apron and wagged the other at Jake. "And don't be keeping her out in that cold too long."

"No, ma'am," Jake returned with suspicious respect.

"Thank you, Annie," Samantha broke in. "Lunch was wonderful."

"Well now, that's fine then." She gave Samantha a friendly pat on the cheek. "You just come back real soon, and you say hi to Sabrina for me, and that young rascal Dan, too. As soon as she's fit again, I'll be coming by to see her. Oh, Jake, I clean forgot." Annie turned to him and sighed at her absentmindedness. "Lesley Marshall called earlier, something about dinner tonight. I told her you'd give her a call, then it went straight out of my mind."

"No problem," Jake said easily. "I'll get back to her later. Ready, Sam?"

"Yes, I'm ready." She kept her smile in place, though a large black cloud seemed to have suddenly smothered the sunshine.

Lesley Marshall, she mused, automatically going through the motions of securing her hat and coat. That was the woman Bree had predicted would marry Jake when he decided to settle down. Why should it matter to me? She straightened her spine and accompanied Jake to the waiting horses. I have absolutely no interest in Jake Tanner's affairs.

He's probably had dozens of girlfriends. Well it's no concern of mine. Vaulting into the saddle, she followed as he set off down the hard-packed road.

They spoke little on the return journey. Samantha pretended an engrossment with the scenery she was far from feeling. Unhappily, she realized Wyoming's magic was not quite enough to lift her flagging spirits. Snow-capped peaks glistened just as brightly in the late afternoon sun, and the land still spread and beckoned, but as she surveyed them now she felt strangely depressed.

It had been an unusual day, she concluded. Jake had annoyed her, charmed her, angered her and delighted her, all in a handful of hours. His kiss had aroused excitement and a deeper feeling she could not explain.

The knowledge that he was dining with another woman that evening depressed her beyond belief. She stole a sidelong look at his lean, tanned features.

He was undeniably attractive, she admitted, pulling her eyes away from him before he could sense her study. There was a powerful aura of virility about him, which alternately intrigued her and made her wary. Perhaps it would be wise to avoid his company. He confused her, and Samantha liked to know precisely where she stood with a man. She wanted to call the shots, and she realized that this man would never allow anyone to call the shots but himself.

She would keep her distance from now on. Let him spread his charm over this Lesley Marshall, or any of the other women who were undoubtedly thirsting for his attention. Samantha Evans could get along very easily without him. As the Lazy L grew closer, she resolved to be polite and casually friendly to her escort. After all, she reflected, there was no reason to be rude. He was perfectly free to dine with whomever he chose; his life was most assuredly his own. Besides, she added to herself, if she had anything to say about it, they would be seeing very little of each other in the future.

When they reached the ranch she dismounted, handing Spook's reins to a waiting cowboy. "I had a wonderful time, Jake." Samantha's smile was faultless in its social politeness as he walked her toward the ranch house, leading his stallion behind him. "I appreciate your time and hospitality."

Jake's mouth lifted at one corner. "It was my pleasure, ma'am."

If there was mockery in his tone, Samantha chose to ignore it. Reaching the back door, she turned to smile at him again as he stood, tall and lean, beside the gleaming chestnut.

"Would you like some coffee before you go?" she invited, determined to be polite.

"No, thanks, Sam." He continued to watch her, his eyes shaded by the brim of his hat. "I'd best be getting along."

"Well." She breathed a small sigh of relief as her hand touched the doorknob and safety was in easy reach. "Thanks again."

"Sure." He nodded briefly and turned to his horse, paused and turned back to look at her with a penetrating intensity which turned her legs to water. When he spoke, it was soft and final. "I mean to have you, you know."

Several moments of silence passed before she could summon up an answer.

"D-do you?" Her voice was a shaky whisper, unlike the coolly flippant tone she would have wished for.

"Yes, ma'am." He vaulted onto the chestnut's back and pushed the Stetson back on his head so that she had a disturbingly clear view of his eyes. "I do," he confirmed, turning his mount and galloping away.

Chapter 5

Often over the next few days, Samantha told herself that her reaction to Jake's kiss had been merely a passing physical attraction. She was a normal woman, wasn't she? So why feel guilty about it?

Jake Tanner *was* a very attractive man. *Too attractive,* she added to herself. And he knew too much about charming women. The fact that Jake was abrasive, smug and irritating had nothing to do with the way she had acted. It had just been a passing fancy. *And would certainly not occur again.*

Finally Sabrina was allowed up from the confinement of her bed. Samantha decided it was safe to leave her sister for a few hours. With a light heart, she saddled Spook and set off from the ranch at a brisk canter. For a while she enjoyed the feeling of Spook's hooves pounding the hard road. The sky hung low above her and heavy, leaden gray clouds draped the distant mountains in mysterious gloom. There was a stillness, a waiting in the air unnoticed by Samantha in her eagerness to escape the close confines of the house.

She rode swiftly past the bored, white-faced cattle and the stretches of barbed wire, eager to explore new territory, tasting the joy of motion and freedom. The mountains, grim sentinels above her, stood stone-gray under the unbroken sky. Remembering Dan's instructions, Samantha took care to mark her route, choosing a clump of rocks, a cottonwood tree with a broken limb, and a gnarled stump as landmarks for her return trip.

She led her mount to a crest of a hill, watching as a jackrabbit, startled by her intrusion, darted across the road and out of sight.

Nearly an hour passed before the first flakes began to drift lazily from sky to earth. She stopped and watched their progress in fascination. The snow fell slowly. Lifting her face, she let it caress her cheeks and closed her lids. The air was moist, coming to life around her, and she stirred herself out of her dream.

"Well, Spook, this is my first Wyoming snow. I'd like to stay here all day and watch it fall, but duty calls. We'd better head back.'' Patting the horse's neck, she turned back toward the ranch.

They rode slowly. Samantha was enchanted with the fairyland which was forming around her. Cottonwoods and aspens were draped in white, their branches a stark contrast to the brilliant etchings of snow. The ground was cloaked quickly. Though the beauty was breathtaking, Samantha began to feel uncomfortably alone.

She took Spook into a canter. The sound of his hooves was soft and muffled. The quiet surrounding her was unearthly, almost as though the world had ceased to breathe. She shivered, suddenly cold in the warm confines of her jacket. To her annoyance, she saw that in her preoccupation with the landscape she had taken a wrong turn, and she began to backtrack, berating herself for carelessness.

The snow increased, plunging down from a sky she could no longer see. She cursed herself for having come so far, fighting down a sudden surge of panic. ''Don't be silly, Sam,'' she spoke aloud, wanting the reassurance of her own voice. ''A little snow won't hurt you.''

The cold became more intense, piercing the layers of her skin. Samantha tried to concentrate on steaming coffee and a blazing fire as she looked around for a familiar landmark. Nothing was the same as it had been. She clamped her lips tight to still the chattering of her teeth, telling herself that it was impossible that she could be lost. But it was a lie. The trees and hills around her were strangers blanketed in white.

The snow fell thickly, a blinding white wall blocking her vision. A wind had sprung up, breaking the silence with its moans and tossing snow hard and bitter into her face. She was forced to slow the gelding to a walk, afraid of tangling with the sharp teeth of barbed wire she was unable to see. Her teeth savaged her lips in an effort to control a growing terror.

It's so cold, she thought as she began to shiver convulsively, so unbelievably cold.

The snow had soaked through the wool of her slacks and slipped mercilessly down the neck of her coat. She hunched her shoulders against the driving wind. Snow was everywhere, blocking her in and seeping into her clothing.

She let the reins hang limp, praying that the horse's instinct would guide him back to the warm shelter of his stables. They trudged on, the vortex of white begun so innocently now whirling around her. Time and direction had lost all meaning, and though she tried calling out, her voice was soundless against the fierce breath of the wind.

Now she felt the cold. Her body was numbed into submission. Her mind was following suit. The swirling snow was hypnotic, and a growing lethargy was creeping over her. In a small part of her mind, she knew her survival depended on remaining alert.

Horse and rider plodded on. There was no time, no world beyond the unbroken curtain of white. Samantha felt her eyelids heavy, but she willed them open with all her strength. The snow piled onto her back, weighing her down until she slumped onto the gelding's mane and clung to him. Staring down at the gelding's front hoof, she began to count each drudging step that Spook took as he continued his slow progress through the blinding storm.

Samantha's concentration on the horse's halting steps began to fade.

If I close my eyes, she thought dimly, I won't see all that white and I can sleep. Oh, how I want to sleep....

The snow was talking, she mused deliriously. Well, why not? It's alive. Why should it sound like Jake? Helplessly, she began to giggle. Well, why shouldn't it? *They both play to win.*

"Samantha!" The snow was shouting at her. "Open your eyes. Stop that insane laughing and open your eyes!"

Wearily, she forced herself to obey the command. Dimly she saw the blur of Jake's features through the flurries of snow. "You would be the last thing I see before I die." With a moan, she closed her eyes again and sought the silence.

"Tell Dan we've found her," Jake shouted against the howl of the wind. "I'm taking her back to the Double T."

The darkness was comforting. Samantha gave over to it, feeling herself falling slowly into a hole with no bottom. She burrowed deeper into it. Her consciousness swam to the surface.

Bemused, she looked around a dimly lit room. The snow which pooled around her was not snow at all, but a bed with a thick warm quilt. She allowed her heavy lids to close again.

"Oh no you don't." The lids opened fractionally, and Samantha saw Jake standing in the open doorway.

"Hello."

His mouth thinned as he advanced to the bed to tower over her. It seeped through the misty reaches of her brain that he was angry. She stared at him with lazy fascination.

"What in heaven's name were you doing out in such a storm? I've seen some dumb stunts, but taking a joy ride in the middle of a blizzard tops them all."

She wanted to ask him to stop shouting at her, but lacked the energy. "Where am I?" was all she could find to say.

Sitting on the edge of the bed, he drew her head from the pillow, then held a cup to her lips. "Here, drink this first, then we'll talk."

The brandy was warm and strong, and she sputtered and gasped as he poured it down her throat. Its power spread through her, pushing back the mists of unconsciousness.

"Now, to answer your question, you're at the Double T." Jake set the empty cup aside, and lay her head back on the mound of pillows.

"Oh."

"Is that all you can say?" He was shouting again. He took her shoulders as if to shake her. "Just 'oh'? What in heaven's name were you doing out there?"

"It seems so long ago." She frowned in concentration, closing her eyes with the effort. "It wasn't snowing when I left," she said in weak defense.

"Wasn't snowing?" Jake repeated, incredulous. "Samantha, didn't you see the sky? Where are your brains?"

"There's no excuse for insults," she retorted with a small flash of spirits.

"No excuse for insults? Are you stark raving mad? Do you realize what nearly happened to you?" His hands retreated to his pockets as though he could barely prevent them from throttling her. "Out here in the middle of a blizzard, half-frozen and helplessly lost! It was a miracle we found you. A little longer, and you'd be lying somewhere buried in it, and no one would have found what was left until spring. Dan was half out of his mind when he got through to me and told me you'd gone out in this."

"Bree?"

"Knew nothing." He whirled to face her again. "She was taking a nap. It never occurred to her that you had gone out with a storm brewing." He laughed harshly.

The memory of the snow and the terror washed over her, and she began to shake. "I'm sorry," she managed through the tears which threatened to flow. With a brief oath, Jake ran a hand through his hair. He closed the distance between them and gathered her in his arms. "Samantha," he murmured against her hair. "What hell you put us all through."

"I'm sorry," she repeated, and she began to sob in earnest. "I was so scared, so cold."

He rocked and murmured words she could not understand, his lips brushing through her hair and over her damp cheeks until they met hers. The kiss mingled with the salt of her tears. "I've gotten your shirt all wet," she murmured after a while.

He let out a deep breath. She saw his smile begin to spread before he rested his brow against hers. "That is without doubt the worst calamity of the day."

"It's dark," she said with sudden realization. "How long...?"

"Too long. What you need now is rest."

"Spook?" she began as he lay her down on the pillows.

"Is sleeping off his adventure in the stables. He looks a lot better than you, I might add."

"I want to thank you for everything." Samantha reached for his hand. In that instant she discovered there was nothing covering her save sheets and blankets. "M-my clothes," she stammered, drawing the quilt higher in a purely feminine gesture which caused Jake's mouth to twitch.

"Soaked through, Sam." Rising, he stood, rocking gently on his heels. "It was necessary to get you warm and dry."

"Did Annie?" she managed a smile at the thought of the matronly presence of Jake's housekeeper. "I seem to have put everyone to a lot of trouble. Will you thank her for me?"

"Well, Sam, I'd like to oblige you, but Annie left yesterday for Colorado to spend a week with her nephew." Jake's grin broadened.

"Then who...?" The question caught in her throat, and her eyes became round and impossibly dark. "Oh, no," she whispered, closing her eyes in humiliation.

"No need to be embarrassed, Sam, you have a beautiful body."

"Oh, no." With a moan, she squeezed her eyes tighter.

"Now, don't you fret." His tone took on the light insolence of the cowboy she met a month before in the cold March sunset. "When I took off your clothes and rubbed you down, it was strictly medical. I'd do as much for any stray." He patted her hand, and her eyes opened warily at his touch.

"Yes, of course." Moistening her lips, she attempted to see the practical side. "I, well...thank you."

"'S all right, don't give it another thought." He moved toward the door, then paused and turned back. "Now, the next time I get your clothes off, my purposes'll be completely different."

He strolled casually from the room leaving a speechless Samantha.

Chapter 6

Samantha looked around her. She remembered with a shock that she was in Jake's house—and worse yet, *naked* in bed. She was debating the wisdom of wrapping the quilt around her and searching for a more appropriate attire when footsteps sounded down the hall outside her room. She pulled the covers to her chin as Jake strode through the open door.

"So, you're awake. How do you feel?"

"Fine." Her respiratory system behaved erratically as he continued toward her and dropped onto the bed. "I'm just fine," she repeated, then added unnecessarily, "It's still snowing."

"So it is," he agreed without taking his eyes from her face. "Slowing down though."

"Is it?" She forced herself to look out the window.

"The worst'll be over by midday." He reached up and pried one of her hands loose from the death grip on the blanket. "Calm down, Sam, I'm not going to ravish you, I'm going to check your pulse."

"I'm fine," she repeated again.

"Far from fine, Samantha," he corrected. His fingers brushed against her cheek as if to test its substance. "The first thing is to get some food into you." Rising, he held out a large flannel robe which he had dropped at the foot of the bed. "You'd probably feel better if you had something on." His smile was gently mocking. "Can you manage to get into this by yourself?"

"Of course." Plucking it from him, she kept a cautious grip on the blankets. "I'm not an invalid."

"You best think like one. Put that on, then get back in bed. I'll bring you some breakfast."

"I don't . . ."

"Don't argue." The two words were swift and final. He was gone before she could say another word.

He had shut the door, however, and grateful for the concession, Samantha tossed back the covers and slipped her arm into the robe. When she stood, the room swayed and spun around her. She sank back onto the bed and slipped her other arm into its sleeve, pulling the robe about her before attempting to stand again. Her limbs felt heavy and weak, and she noted with puzzlement that her ankle was throbbing lightly. Gripping one poster of the bed until the room steadied, she rolled up the sleeves of the robe several times until her hands became visible, then moved to the bathroom to study herself in the mirror.

The sight of her own face caught at her breath. Her skin seemed nearly transparent, her eyes darker and larger in contrast. The breath of color which resulted as she pinched her cheeks faded instantly. She ran a hand through her hair falling on the shoulders of the dark green robe.

It must be this, she realized, looking down at the sleeves which swallowed her arms, and the hem which fell nearly to her ankles. A strange sensation flowed over her as she felt the material on her skin. Turning away from the mirror she studied the bed.

"I'm not getting in there again," she muttered, and with a small gesture of defiance, belted the robe more securely. "I can eat at the table like a normal person."

After a moment, her progress down the hall seemed more of a crawl than a walk. Her legs were heavy with a weakness which infuriated her. The stillness of the house vibrated around her, playing havoc with her nerves, and the need to hear the natural, everyday movements of another human being became increasingly important. She cursed the waves of giddiness which swam around in her head, forcing her to stop time after time to rest her hand against the wall.

"This is ridiculous."

"You're right."

The harsh agreement came from behind as Jake's hands gripped her shoulders.

"What are you doing out of bed?"

"I'm all right." She swayed against his chest. He gripped her waist to support her, and she rested her hands on his arms.

"I'm just a bit wobbly, and I'm having some trouble with my ankle."

He let his gaze travel down to rest on her bare feet. "Probably turned it when you fell off the horse."

"I fell off Spook?" Her expression was incredulous.

"You were unconscious at the time. Now, get back into bed and stay there." Effortlessly, he swept her into his arms, and she laid her head against his shoulder.

"Jake, don't make me go back to bed. It's so quiet in there, and I don't feel like being alone now."

He bent and brushed the lips which parted in confusion. "If you think you can sit in a chair without sliding on your face, you can come in the kitchen."

She nodded, sighed and closed her eyes. "I hate being so much trouble."

She felt him shift her in his arms before he began the journey down the hall. "I knew you were trouble the minute I set eyes on you."

"Don't tease, Jake, I'm trying to thank you."

"What for?"

She lifted a hand to his cheek, turning his face so that he would look at her. "For my life."

"Then take better care of it in the future," he suggested.

"Jake, please, I'm serious. I owe you..."

"Nothing, you owe me nothing." His voice had hardened with annoyance. "I don't want your gratitude." They had reached the kitchen, and he placed her in a chair at the table. "Which ankle did you hurt?" He crouched down by her feet.

"The left one. Jake, I, ouch!"

"Sorry." He grinned up at her, then rested his hand with friendly ease on her knee. "It's not swollen."

"It still hurts," she said stubbornly.

"Keep off it then," he advised with simple logic, and turned away to finish breakfast.

"You've got some bedside manners, Dr. Tanner," she observed sharply.

"Yes, ma'am, so I've been told." When he turned to face her, his smile was bland. "Tell me, Sam, does Sabrina have a mole on her left hip too?"

Color flooded her face. "You...you," she faltered, and clutched the robe tight at her throat.

"Around here, we call that locking the barn door after the cow's got loose. Have some coffee," he invited with sudden graciousness, pouring a cup and setting it on the table. "Start on this bacon," he ordered, sliding a plate in front of her. "That color didn't last long, you're pale as a ghost again. When did you eat last?"

"I . . . at breakfast yesterday, I guess."

"Toast and coffee, I imagine," he said disgustedly. "It's a wonder you can manage to sit up at all. Eat." He plucked a piece of bacon from the plate and held it out to her. "I'll have some eggs ready in a minute."

Obediently, she accepted the bacon and took a bite. "Are you going to have something?"

"In a minute," he answered absently, involved with breaking and beating eggs in a bowl.

With the first bite of bacon Samantha realized she was ravenous. Through her preoccupation with food, she watched Jake cook with a deftness which amused and surprised her.

In a moment, he sat across from her, his plate piled high. She wondered how he could eat with such abandon and remain hard and lean.

She watched him under the cover of her lashes, and the thought came unbidden to her mind that never before had she shared the breakfast table with a man. The intimacy of their situation washed over her; the scent of bacon and coffee drifting through the air, the house quiet and empty around them, the soft flannel of his robe against her skin, the faint masculine scent of him clinging to it. It was as if they were lovers, she thought suddenly, as if they had shared the night, and now they were sharing the morning. Her face grew warm.

"I don't know what thought put roses back in those cheeks, Sam, but keep it up."

Her eyes lifted to his, and she had the uncomfortable feeling he knew very well what road her thoughts had taken. She dropped her eyes to her plate. "I should call Bree and let her know I'm all right."

"Phones are out," he said simply, and her eyes flew back to his.

"The phones are out?" she repeated.

No telephone, her mind said again. Without a telephone they might as well be on an island a thousand miles from anyone. Their isolation was complete, and the snow was still falling as though it would never stop.

"With a storm like this, it's not surprising to lose the phones. Power's out, too. We're on generator. Don't worry about Sabrina, she knows you're with me." His words did nothing to erase her tension.

"When... when do you think I'll be able to get back?"

"Couple of days," he returned with an easy shrug and sipped his coffee. "The roads'll have to be cleared after the storm lets up, and you're not in any shape to travel through a mess like that yet. In a day or two, you'll be more up to it."

"A couple of days?"

He leaned back comfortably in his chair, his voice smooth as a quiet river. "Of course, by then you'll be hopelessly compromised, not a scrap of your sterling reputation left. Alone with me for two or three days, without Annie to add a thread of decency to the situation." His eyes traveled down her slim figure. "Wearing my bathrobe, too." He shook his head. "Not too many years back, I'd have had to marry you."

"Thank goodness for progress," she retorted smartly.

"Oh, I don't know, Sam." His sigh was convincing. "I'm an old-fashioned sort of man."

"It's only a matter of circumstance that we're alone here in the first place." With great dignity, she folded her arms. "And I've hardly been compromised, as you so quaintly put it."

"No?" He watched her through lazily narrowed eyes. "So far, I've undressed you, tucked you in and fixed your breakfast. Who knows what that might lead to?"

His smile may have been lazy, but it was full of meaning. Suddenly Samantha found it difficult to swallow.

"Relax, Sam." His laugh was full of arrogant enjoyment. "I told you I mean to have you, but it's not in my plans to take on a pale child who barely has the strength to stand." He paused, lit one of his long, thin cigars and blew smoke at the ceiling. "When I make love to you, I want you to have your wits about you. I don't want you passing out in my arms."

The man's arrogance was amazing! "You conceited mule," she began. "How dare you sit there and tell me you're going to make love to me? You seem to think you're irresistible! Well, you have another think coming—"

"I'm going to remind you of that one day, Sam," Jake said mildly as he crushed out his cigar. "Now, I think you better lie down again. You're not quite up to sparring with me yet."

"I do not have to lie down. And I certainly don't need you carting me around. I can manage." She stood up, then was forced to grasp the table as the room revolved around her.

"You don't look ready to turn cartwheels, teacher," Jake observed as he took her arm.

"I'm all right." Her hand which she had lifted to push him away lay weakly on his chest for support. He tilted her chin, and he was no longer smiling. "Samantha, sometimes you have to be strong enough to let someone else take care of things. You've going to have to hand over the reins to me for a couple of days. If you fight it, you're only going to make it harder on yourself."

With a sigh, she allowed her head to fall against his chest, not protesting as his arms encircled her. "Do I have to like it?"

"Not necessarily." He gave a short laugh and lifted her easily and carried her back to bed.

Her small spurt of energy deserted her. With an odd feeling of contentment, she settled down under the covers. She was asleep even before his lips had lightly touched her forehead in a farewell kiss....

"I was beginning to think you'd sleep through the night."

She turned her head quickly. Jake was sitting across the room, the smoke of his cigar spiraling upward, the flickering lights from the fire shooting specks of gold into his eyes. Samantha brushed the tousled hair from her face and struggled into a sitting position.

"It's dark," she said. "What time is it?"

He glanced at the gold watch on his wrist and took a slow drag from his cigar. "It's a bit past six."

"Six? I've slept for hours. I feel as if I've slept for weeks."

"You needed it." Tossing the stub of his cigar into the mouth of the fire, Jake rose and moved toward her. His concerned eyes roamed over her sleep-flushed cheeks and heavy eyes. Gradually, his expression lightened, the angles of his face moving into a satisfied smile. "Your color's coming back." He took her wrist, and her eyes dropped from his to study the dancing flames of the fire. "Pulse's a bit jumpy." The smile reflected in his voice. "Strong though. Hungry?"

"I shouldn't be." She forced her eyes to meet his. "I've done nothing but lie around all day, but I'm starved."

He smiled again, lifting her without comment. She felt small and vulnerable in his arms, a sensation which was both pleasant and disturbing. She found it difficult to resist the impulse to rest her head against the strong curve of his shoulder. Instead, she concentrated on the sharp, clean lines of his profile.

"I'm sure I can walk. I really feel fine."

"I doubt it." She could feel his warm breath on her face. "Besides, you seem to fit in my arms pretty well."

Finding no quick comeback to this comment, she took the journey to the kitchen in silence.

Leaning back in her chair, replete and content, Samantha sipped the cool white wine in her glass and gave Jake a nod of approval.

"You're going to make some woman a terrific husband. You're an outstanding cook."

"I think so." He nodded smugly. "My wife wouldn't have to be a gourmet cook," he added with casual consideration. "I'd demand other qualities."

"Adoration," Samantha suggested. "Obedience, unswerving loyalty, solicitude."

"That's all right for a start."

"Poor woman."

"Of course, I don't want her to be a doormat. Let's say I like a woman who knows how to think, one who doesn't pretend to be anything but who she is. Of course," he added, finishing off his wine, "I'm also partial to good looks."

"Well, so far it doesn't sound as though you're asking for much," Samantha giggled. "Just perfection."

"The woman I have in mind can handle it," he smiled broadly as he rose to pour coffee. Samantha stared at his back, feeling as though her heart had been dropped into a deep hole. *Lesley Marshall.* Her mind flashed the name like a neon sign in bright red letters.

Jake squelched her offer to do the dishes and swooped her from her chair and deposited her on the living room sofa.

"I feel useless," she muttered, helplessly cocooned by blankets and pillows. "I'm not mad for lying around. I'm never sick." She gave Jake a sulky glare as if the entire matter was his fault. "I don't

know how Bree coped with this sort of thing for a
month.''

"Could be you got her share of strength, and she
got your share of patience," he considered, then
shrugged. "Of course, I could be wrong." She heard
his chuckle and the quiet click of his lighter as he lit
a cigar.

Well, Samantha, she chided herself, you've really
done it this time. Not only are you isolated with a
man who constantly confuses you, but you can't
even stand on your own feet. They say people learn
about each other quickly when they live together, but
I think it's going to take much more than one day to
learn what this man is all about. *Living together,* she
repeated, finding herself more amused than embarrassed. If Momma could see me now, we'd need a
gallon of smelling salts.

Chapter 7

Dawn was breaking. Pink and gold streaks split the hazy blue of the sky, and light tumbled through to rest on Samantha's closed lids.

Morning? Sitting up with a start, she shook her head vigorously to dispel the last remnants of sleep. Pulling on the borrowed robe, she set her feet on the floor, took three deep breaths and stood. When both the room and her head remained stable, she let out a long sigh of relief. Her legs were weak, but they no longer felt as if they would melt from under her, and the stiffness in her ankle had disappeared.

Mobility, she thought with arrogant glee. I've never truly appreciated it until now. Coffee. One thought followed swiftly on the trail of the other, and she deserted the room with the intention of making fantasy fact. A door opened as she passed it, and with a cry of surprise, she fell against the opposite wall.

Jake stood in the doorway, rubbing a towel briskly through his damp hair, a terry cloth robe tied loosely around his waist. "Morning, ma'am."

"You startled me." She swallowed, overpowered by the lean, bronzed maleness which the terry cloth did little to hide. He took a step toward her, and her breath caught instinctively. "I—I'm much better." She began to babble, unconsciously cowering against the smooth paneling. "I can actually walk a straight line."

Her voice died to a whisper as he stood directly in front of her. Her eyes were on a line with the tanned column of throat revealed by the open neck of the robe. His hand lifted her chin, and she trembled.

"Relax, Sam." His laughter sounded deep in his throat. "I just want to look you over. You must have the constitution of an elephant," he concluded with unflattering candor. "You look as though you've been on vacation instead of battling blizzards. One day's rest after nearly freezing to death; most women would have been stretched out for a week."

"I'm not most women." She pushed his hand away from her face. "I'm not fragile and delicate, and I'm not going back to bed. I'm going to fix breakfast.'' She nudged him out of her path and started down the hall.

"Coffee's already on," he called after her.

Samantha had breakfast under way by the time Jake joined her. Clad in the less disturbing attire of corded jeans and flannel shirt, he watched her prepare the meal as he silently sipped at the coffee at the kitchen table.

"I'm getting used to having a pretty face across from me at breakfast," he commented when she sat down to join him.

"I'm sure I'm not the first," she commented with studied indifference. Nor, she added to herself, will I be the last.

"Nope," he agreed easily, "but there's something to be said for big blue eyes first thing in the morning."

"Blue eyes are common enough," she muttered, and lowered them to the contents of her plate. "Besides, this is hardly a long-term arrangement." He did not speak for a moment, and her fork moved restlessly among her eggs.

"We should have the road clear enough sometime tomorrow."

"Tomorrow?" she repeated. A hollow feeling spread through her stomach.

"There's a lot of snow out there, some of the drifts are small mountains. It's going to take a little time to move it."

"I see."

"Do you think you could manage on your own for a while today?"

"What? Oh sure, I'll be fine."

"There's a lot I should see to. My foreman was in charge yesterday, but the men need all the help they can get." He was frowning. "Cattle need hay brought out to them. They haven't the sense to dig through to the grass; they'll just stand there and starve to death."

"I suppose the storm did a lot of damage."

"It's only minor from the reports I've gotten. We were hit worse a couple years ago."

"Reports?"

"One of my men came by yesterday afternoon to fill me in." Pouring more coffee in his cup, he reached for the cream. "You were asleep."

"Oh." Strange, she thought, there had been a ripple in their isolation and she had been totally unaware of it.

Lifting his cup, he studied her over the rim. "I don't like leaving you alone, especially with the phones out."

Her shoulders moved. "Don't worry about me, I'll be fine." Glancing up, she met his speculative gaze.

"I don't know how long I'll be gone."

"Jake, stop fussing. I feel fine."

He tilted his head to the side, his eyes still narrowed. "Stand up. I want to see how you feel for myself."

Before she realized his intent, his arms were around her, and his mouth was on hers. Her legs buckled.

His mouth was light, teasing, his teeth nibbling at the fullness of her bottom lip until she moaned from the exquisite agony. She gripped his shoulders as a dim light of control seeped into the darkness. Pulling away, she shook her head in refusal.

"Now, Sam." His voice was soft and persuasive, but the hands which descended to her hips were firm. "You wouldn't send a man out in the cold without something warm to remember, would you?"

Insistently, he brought her closer, molding her hips, exploring the soft roundness until she was pressed against him with exciting intimacy. His mouth closed over her protest, his tongue moving with slow devastation to tease hers until she felt the room spinning as wildly as it had the day before. Slowly, his hands ascended, his thumbs circling the side of her breasts while his mouth and tongue destroyed all resistance. She was straining against him, moving against him, reason forgotten. Her body heated urgently at his touch. Her sigh was a moan as his mouth descended to her throat. His lips tasted, lingered, traveled to new territories, the tip of his tongue moist and warm against her ear until her mouth was desperate for its return to hers.

Her mouth was to go unsatisfied. He pulled her away with the same arrogance as he had pulled her to him. Dazed and limp, she could do no more than stare up at him as her body throbbed with a myriad of newly discovered desires.

"You're learning fast, Sam. That was enough to keep any man moving through a six-foot snow-drift."

Furious, and humiliated by her own response, she drew back her hand.

"Now, Sam." He caught her wrist easily, holding it aloft ignoring her efforts to escape. "You're not strong enough yet for wrestling. Give yourself a couple more days." Turning her hand over, his lips brushed her palm, causing her struggles to cease abruptly. "I'm going to bring in Wolfgang to keep an eye on you. Take it easy today and try to remember, you're not as tough as you'd like to think."

Ruffling her hair as though she were a child, he disappeared into the adjoining mud room.

Later Samantha indulged in a hot, steaming shower, attempting to forget, as she soaped her skin, the feel of Jake's hands running over her. In the bedroom, she noticed her clothes piled neatly on the spoon-back chair. She slipped them on and wandered through the house in aimless exploration, the St. Bernard lumbering at her heels.

The house abounded in small, delightful treasures, an oak roll-top desk, a wall box with Friesian carving, a Windsor cradle. With a small sigh, she wondered if the latter had rocked the baby Jake. Opening yet another door, she found Jake's library.

It smelled of leather and age, and her fingers ran over volume after volume. She pulled out a small volume of love poetry and opened the cover. Light, feminine handwriting adorned the top corner, and her mouth turned down at the inscription.

Darling Jake... To remind you.
Love, Lesley.

Shutting the book with a snap, Samantha held it for one heat-blinded moment over the wastebasket, then, grinding her teeth, stuck it firmly back in place.

"It makes no difference to me," she informed Wolfgang. "She can give him a hundred books of poetry, she can give him a thousand books of poetry. It's her privilege."

She nudged the big dog with her toe. "Come on, Wolfgang, let's get moving."

She returned to the living room and built up the fire which had burned down to a hissing pile of embers. She curled up beside it.

One hour slipped into two, two slipped into three. Surely, Jake should be home by now, she told the silent clock as the hands crept past six. It was getting dark. Rising, Samantha stared out into the diminishing light.

What if something had happened to Jake? Her throat went dry, fear creeping along her skin. Nothing could happen to him, she told herself, running her hands over her arms to combat the sudden chill. He's strong and self-reliant.

But why am I so worried about him?

"Because," she said aloud, slowly, *"I love him. I've lost my mind and fallen in love with him."* Her hands lifted to cover her eyes as the weight of the knowledge crushed down on her. "Oh, how could I be so stupid? Of all the men in the world, I had to fall in love with this one."

A man, she remembered, who had chosen *Lesley Marshall to be his wife.* Is that why I've felt pulled in two? Is that why I responded to him when I've never responded to anyone else? Looking out into the darkness she shuddered. I might as well admit that I don't care about anything except his getting home....

When finally the sound of the outside door slamming reached her ears, she ran into the mud room and threw herself at an astonished, snow-covered Jake.

"Sam, what's going on?" He tried to pull her away from his cold, wet jacket.

"I was afraid something had happened to you." Her voice was muffled against his chest, her cheek oblivious to the frigid dampness.

"Nothing's happened, except I'm half-frozen and soaked to the skin." Firmly now, he took her shoulders, disentangling himself from her arms. "You're getting covered with snow." His grip was gentle. She stared up at him with huge, swimming eyes. "I'm sorry I was gone so long, but things were piled up, and it's slow working in a mess like this."

Embarrassed by her outburst, she backed away. "You must be exhausted. I'm sorry, it was stupid to go on like that. It must come from being alone in the house all day." As she babbled, she was backing purposefully toward the door. "You probably want a shower and something hot to drink. I—I've got dinner on."

"Something smells good," he commented. His eyes roamed over her flushed face, and a smile spread over his features.

"S—spaghetti," she stammered and despised herself. "I'll go finish it up."

Retreating into the kitchen, Samantha kept her back toward him when he emerged and announced casually that he would have a hot shower before dinner. She mumbled a vague reply, pretending a complete involvement with her dinner preparation. Listening to his receding footsteps she let out a long, pent-up breath.

"Oh, idiot that I am," she sighed, and pushed her hair from her face in an angry gesture. The type of behavior she had displayed in the mud room would only lead to trouble. She took a solemn oath to keep her emotions on a tight leash as long as Jake Tanner was around.

Tomorrow, she remembered, with a mixture of relief and disappointment, she would be back with her sister, and avoiding Jake would be a great deal easier. She had only to get through one more evening without making a fool of herself, and then she would sort out her thinking.

She was setting the table when Jake returned.

"If that tastes as good as it smells, I'll die a happy man." He lifted the lid on the pot and gave a sigh of approval. Grinning he disappeared for a moment, then returned with a bottle of wine just as she was placing the pot on the table.

"A nice burgundy," he said, opening the bottle and setting out two glasses.

"Samantha, this is fantastic." He broke off eating long enough to give her a smile. "Where'd you learn to cook like this?"

"More of my mother's famous lessons."

"What else can you do?"

"Well, let's see. I do a rather superb swan dive, a very graceful arabesque, I can walk on my hands as easily as some walk on their feet, whip up an incredible quiche, and waltz without counting the time."

"I am suitably impressed. How did a woman of your talents spend the day?"

She sighed and grimaced and began to toy with her spaghetti. "Sleeping mostly."

"Hmm." His cough did not quite cover his laugh.

After dinner, Samantha insisted on seeing to the washing up herself. She wanted to avoid the intimacy of working side by side with him in the confines of the kitchen.

When the last signs of the meal had vanished, she walked down the hall to the living room. Jake was adding another log to the low, shifting blaze. As she entered, he turned to smile at her. "Want some brandy?"

"No, no, thank you." She took a deep breath and willed her legs to carry her to the sofa.

"Not in training are you?" He moved from the hearth to join her on the sofa.

Smiling, she shook her head. "The fire's wonderful." Grasping the first topic which came to mind, she riveted her eyes on the flames. "I always wanted one in my apartment. We had one at home, and Bree and I used to pop corn over it. We'd always burn it, and..."

The rest of her rush of words was lost as Jake placed his finger under her chin and turned her face to his. His face moved closer, and when she jerked back in defense, his brow lifted in amusement. He bent toward her again, and again she started.

"I'm only going to kiss you, Samantha." His grip tightened on her chin. Sliding from her chin his hand framed her face as his lips moved over hers, soft as a whisper. In spite of herself, she relaxed against him. Her lips parted, inviting him to explore, begging him to take.

"Samantha." Her name was a sigh.

"Kiss me again," she whispered slowly as she lifted her mouth to his.

With a low groan, he brought his lips down on hers. She clung to him, her body throbbing with heat, her heart desperate against his while a part of her looked on, aghast, as she answered his kiss.

Her mouth clung, avid and sweet to his. Dormant passion exploded into life until there remained only man and woman and the need, older than time, to love and be loved, to possess and be possessed.

He opened her shirt and claimed her breast. The first desperation mellowed into slow exploration as his fingers trailed lightly, drugging her with a new delirious languor. His mouth moved to sample the taste of her neck, his face buried in the spreading lushness of her hair. She pressed against the rippling muscles of his back as his mouth and tongue and hands raged fire over her.

She felt rather than heard him say her name against her mouth, sensed rather than felt the tension enter his body before her lips were set free.

Dimly, she heard the strident insistence of bells ringing as she groped to bring heaven back within reach.

"Hell of a time for them to fix the phones." She opened her eyes, dark as sapphires, and stared without comprehension. "There's nothing I'd like more than to ignore it, Samantha, but it might be important." Her lids fluttered in confusion. She could feel the warm raggedness of his breath against her cheek. "The phones have been out for two days, and there's a lot of damage out there."

His body left hers and took the warmth with it. She struggled to sit up, pulling her shirt closed. The hands which worked at the buttons were unsteady, and rising on weak legs, she sought the warmth of the fire. Pushing at tumbled hair, she wrapped her arms around her body and closed her eyes.

What had she done, losing herself that way? Tossing away pride like damaged goods! What if the phone hadn't rung? Her arms closed tighter. Does love always hurt? Does it always make a fool of you?

"Samantha." She whirled at the sound of her name, her arms still tight in protection. "It's Sabrina." Dropping her eyes from his, she moved into the hall.

Samantha picked up the phone and swallowed. "Hi, Bree." Her voice sounded strangely high-pitched to her ears, and her fingers gripped hard on the receiver.

"Sam, how are you?"

Taking a deep breath, she answered. "Fine. How *you* are is more important."

"Stronger every minute. I'm so glad you had the sense to head for the Double T when the snow started. The thought of you getting caught in that blizzard makes my blood turn cold."

"That's me, a steady head in a crisis." Samantha nearly choked on a gurgle of hysterical laughter.

"Are you sure you're all right? You sound strange. You aren't coming down with a cold, are you?"

"It's probably the connection."

"I thought they'd never get the phones fixed! I guess I just couldn't really relax until I'd talked to you and made sure you were safe! Of course, I know Jake would take care of you, but it's not the same as hearing your voice. I won't keep you, Sam, we'll see you tomorrow. By the way, I think Shylock misses you."

"Probably indigestion. Tell him I'll see him tomorrow." After replacing the receiver, she stared at it for a full minute.

"Samantha." She whirled again at Jake's voice, finding him watching her from the living room archway.

"I—ah—Bree seems fine." She avoided his eyes and toyed with the ink pot by the phone. She took a step backward as Jake advanced. "She said she thought Shylock misses me. That's quite an accomplishment, he's so self-sufficient and aloof."

"Samantha. Come, sit down." He held out his hand for hers. She knew if he touched her, she would be lost.

"No, no, I think I'll go to bed, I'm still not quite myself." Her color had ebbed again, leaving pale cheeks and darkened eyes.

"Still running, Sam?" The anger in his tone was well controlled.

"No, no, I . . ."

"All right then, for the moment we seem to be at a stalemate." He captured her chin before she could avoid the gesture. "But we haven't finished by a long shot. Do you understand?"

She nodded, then broke away to flee to the sanctuary of her room.

Chapter 8

As each day passed, Sabrina became more cheerful. Her features took on a roundness giving her a contented appearance. And as Samantha watched her, she wondered if Sabrina possessed more strength than she had ever given her credit for. It was a sobering experience to see her usually dreamy sister grabbing life with determination and purpose while she herself couldn't seem to stop daydreaming. Jake Tanner, she had to admit, was disturbing her days and sneaking into her dreams.

Stuffing her hands in her pockets, she scowled and continued her morning trudge to the mailbox. He meant to have her, did he? Well, Samantha Evans had no intention of being had by anyone, especially some annoying cowboy with too much charm for his own good . . . and fascinating green eyes, and that beautiful mouth. . . .

Now the days began to lengthen. The sun grew in strength. Spring began to drift over the basin greening the grass and teasing the crocuses to push their heads from the earth.

Scurrying down the hall as the doorbell interrupted her latest project—painting the nursery—Samantha wiped a few streaks of canary yellow on her jeans, and opened the door.

The woman in the doorway smiled, her almond-shaped dark eyes making a thorough survey. "Hello, you must be Samantha. I'm Lesley Marshall."

The introduction was unnecessary, for with an instinct she had been unaware of possessing, Samantha had recognized the woman instantly. "Please, come in. It's still rather cold, isn't it?" She smiled, refusing to acknowledge the effort it cost her, and shut the nippy May air outside.

"I'm so glad to meet you at last." The dark eyes swept down, then up Samantha briefly. "I've heard so much about you." There was light amusement in her voice.

"Oh really? I'm afraid I can't say the same." Her smile was faintly apologetic. "But, of course, I've been rather busy."

"I would have been by sooner, but I wanted to wait until Sabrina was more up to company."

"Bree's feeling much better these days. I'm sure she'll be glad to see you. Let me take your coat." Samantha hung the soft fur in the hall closet. Turning back to her visitor, she needed all her willpower to keep the social smile in place. The oatmeal slacks accentuated Lesley's sleekness; the trim cerise blouse set off her delicately feathered ebony hair and the perfect ivory of her skin. Desperately, Samantha wished a miracle would transform her navy sweat-shirt with its Wilson High School banner and paint-streaked jeans into something smart and sophisti-cated. As usual, her hair was escaping from its pins. She resisted the urge to bring her hand up to it and jam them in tightly.

"Bree's in the living room," she announced, knowing the pale gray eyes had studied her and found her wanting. "I was just about to make some tea."

Sabrina appeared at that moment, and Samantha gladly relinquished the role of hostess and escaped to the kitchen.

"So, she's beautiful," she grumbled to an uncon-cerned Shylock as she set the kettle on to boil. "So, she's smooth and sophisticated and makes me feel like a pile of dirty laundry." Turning, she lowered her face to his and scowled. "Who cares?" Shylock scowled back and went to sleep. Her thoughts wandered on. "I don't imagine he's ever laughed at her and patted her head as though she were a slow-witted child," she muttered as she gathered up the tea tray.

"Sabrina, you look wonderful," Lesley commented sometime later, sipping from a dainty china cup. "I'm sure having your sister with you must be very good for you. I don't have to tell you how concerned everyone has been."

"No, and I appreciate it. Sam's made everything so easy. I didn't have anything to do but sit and heal." She shot her sister an affectionate glance. "I don't know what we would have done without her these past two months."

Lesley followed her gaze. "Jake was telling me that you're a gym teacher, Samantha," she purred, managing to make this sound faintly disgusting.

"Physical Education instructor," Samantha corrected, slipping into a vague southern drawl.

"And you were in the Olympics as well. I'm sure it must have been fascinating. You don't look the sturdy, athletic type." The shrug of her shoulders was elegant, as was the small gesture of her hand. "I suppose one can never tell." Samantha gritted her teeth against a biting retort and was vastly relieved when, glancing at a slender gold watch, Lesley suddenly rose from her chair. "I must run now, Sabrina, I have a dinner engagement." Turning to Samantha, she offered a small smile. "So happy to have met you. I'm sure we'll be seeing each other again soon."

She left amidst a swirl of fur and the drifting scent of roses. Samantha sat back in the cushioned chair, relaxing for the first time in more than an hour.

"Well, what did you think of Lesley?" Sabrina questioned, shifting into a more comfortable position on the sofa.

"Very sophisticated."

"Come on, Sam." Sabrina grinned, her hands folding across the mound of her belly. "This is Bree."

"I don't know why I should have to comment, since you seem to be reading me so well. But," her mouth curved into a rueful smile, "I suppose she's a bit smooth for my taste, and I didn't much care for the way she looked down that aristocratic nose at me."

"Actually, you really don't appear very sturdy." The observation was made with wide-eyed innocence. Samantha grimaced, pulling pins from her hair with a sharp tug until a cascade of golden brown tumbled in confusion about her shoulders.

"She'd have gotten her own back on that one if you hadn't sent me that 'Don't make a scene' look."

"Oh well, Lesley can be nice enough when it suits her. Her father spoils her dreadfully. Her mother died when she was barely into her teens, and he transferred all his attention to Lesley. An overabundance of clothes, the best horses, and as she grew older, cars and European tours and so on. Whatever Lesley wants, Lesley gets.''

"Poor thing." The sarcasm caused her to feel spiteful and unjust. She sighed. "I suppose too much is as bad as too little. It was nice of her to come and see how you were getting along."

Sabrina's laughter floated through the room. "Sam, darling, I've never known you to be so slow." At her sister's puzzled expression, she continued. "Lesley didn't come to see me, she came to get a look at you."

"At me?" Finely etched brows disappeared under a fringe of bangs. "What for? I wouldn't think a lowly gym teacher from Philadelphia would interest Lesley Marshall."

"Any teacher who caught Jake Tanner's attention the way you have would interest Lesley. He wouldn't have gone out of his way to show just anyone around the ranch, you know."

A light color rose in Samantha's cheeks. "I think Miss Marshall's mind was put to rest after she got a good look." Her hand moved expressively down her sweatshirt and jeans. "She'd hardly see any danger here."

"Don't underestimate yourself, Sam."

"No false modesty." Samantha's sigh came from nowhere. "If a man's attracted to silk and champagne, cotton and beer are no competition. I'm cotton and beer, Bree," she murmured. Her voice trailed away with her thoughts. "I couldn't be anything else if I wanted to."

The following day, Samantha's continuing battle with her paints and brushes was interrupted by a more welcome visitor. Annie Holloway arrived at the ranch's kitchen door with a beaming smile and a chocolate cake.

"Hi." Samantha opened the door wide in welcome. "It's nice to see you again, and bearing gifts too."

"Never like to come empty handed," Annie announced, handing the thickly frosted cake to Samantha. "Dan always had a partiality for chocolate cake."

"Me too." She eyed the cake hungrily. "He's not here right now, and I was just going to make some coffee. Do you suppose we could start without him?"

"Good idea." Setting herself comfortably in a chair, Annie waved a wide-palmed hand. "I reckon it wouldn't hurt for us to have a slice or two."

"Bree's taking a nap," Samantha explained as she put down the mugs of steaming coffee. "The doctor says she still has to lie down every day, but she's beginning to grumble about it a bit. Very quietly, of course."

"You're keeping an eye on her." Annie nodded and added two generous spoons of sugar to her coffee. "Dan says she's up to company now."

"Oh, yes, people have been dropping by now and again. Ah..." Samantha added cream to her own cup. "Lesley Marshall was by yesterday."

"I wondered how long it would be before Lesley hauled herself over to get a look at you."

"You sound like Bree." Sipping her coffee, Samantha shook her head. "I don't know why Lesley Marshall would want to meet me."

"Easy. Lesley's a mite stingy with her possessions, and she'd like to group Jake among them. She hasn't figured out yet that Jake is his own man, and all her daddy's money can't buy him for her. When my Jake picks his woman, he'll decide the time and place. He's always been an independent rascal. He was barely twenty when he lost his folks, you know." Samantha lifted her eyes to the warm brown ones. "It wasn't an easy time for him, they'd been close. They were a pair, Jake's folks, always squabbling and loving. You're a bit like her when she was a young thing." Annie smiled, her head tilting with it as Samantha remained silent. "Nobody's going to ride roughshod over you, at least not for long. I saw that straight off. She was stubborn as a mule with two heads, and there's times, though it's been better than ten years, I still miss her."

"It must have been hard on Jake, losing his parents and having all the responsibility of the ranch when he was still so young," Samantha murmured.

"Seemed to change from boy to man overnight, just out of college and still green. 'Course," she continued, "he'd been in the saddle since childhood and what he hadn't learned about ranching from his father and that fancy college, he learned from doing. He picked up the reins of that ranch with both hands. There's not a man who works for him wouldn't wrestle a long-horned bull if he asked them to. He can fool you with that easy-going way of his, but nobody gets the better of Jake Tanner. He runs the ranch like his life, and Lesley's going to find him a hard steer to rope and brand."

"Maybe it's more the other way around," Samantha suggested. Annie's response was prevented by the appearance at the kitchen door of the man in question.

He entered with the easy familiarity of an old friend.

"Howdy, ma'am." He broke the silence with a cocky smile, removed his battered Stetson and glanced at her attire. "Been painting?"

"Obvious, isn't it?" Samantha said sharply.

"Nice colors." He helped himself to a cup of coffee. "Are you going to part with another piece of that cake?"

"Jake Tanner!" Annie exclaimed in disgust. "You should be ashamed of gobbling Dan's cake when you've got a perfectly good one of your own at home."

"Somebody else's always tastes better, Annie." He slipped off his jacket, tossing it over a hook, and grinned boyishly. "He won't miss it anyway. I brought you and the cake over, didn't I? You're not going to begrudge me one little piece?"

"Don't waste those eyes on me, you young devil." Annie attempted to sniff and look indignant. "I'm not one of your fillies."

Jake's appearance had successfully shattered Samantha's peace of mind. After a reasonable period of politeness, she excused herself to Annie and Jake and went back to her job in the nursery.

Samantha's artistic talent was decidedly impressionistic. The floor, protected by plastic, was splotched and splattered, but the walls were coming to life with a joy of brilliant colors. Of the four walls, two were yellow and two were white, each trimmed with its opposite's color. On the one wall which was unbroken by door or windows, she had begun the construction of a wide, arching rainbow, carefully merging blues into pinks into greens.

Time passed, and in the quiet concentration of her work she forgot her preoccupation with Jake. Sitting on the ladder's top step, she paused, brushing the back of her hand across her cheek absently as she viewed the results.

"That's a mighty pretty sight."

She jolted, dropping the brush with a clatter, and would have fallen from the ladder had Jake's arms not gripped her waist and prevented the tumble.

"Sure spook easy," Jake commented, removing the dangerously sloshing paint bucket from her hand.

"You shouldn't come up behind a person like that," she complained. "I might have broken my neck." She wiped her hands on the legs of her jeans. "Where's Annie?"

"With your sister. She wanted to show Annie some things she's made for the baby." He set the bucket on the floor and straightened. "I didn't think they needed me."

"No, I'm sure they didn't. I need that paint though, and the brush you made me drop." She glanced down, but his eyes remained on hers.

"I like the blue, especially that spot on your cheek," Jake said.

She rubbed at the offending area in annoyance. "If you'd just hand those things back to me, I could finish up."

"Green's nice too," he said conversationally, and ran a finger over a long streak on her thigh. "Wilson High." His eyes lowered to the letters on her shirt. "Is that where you taught back East?"

"Yes." She shifted, uncomfortable that the name was prominent over her breasts. "Are you going to hand me my things?"

"What are your plans for tonight?" he countered easily, ignoring her request. She stared, completely thrown off balance by his unexpected question.

"I, ah, I have a lot of things to do." She searched her mind for something vital in her schedule.

"Things?" he prompted. His smile grew as his finger began to twist through a stray curl which had escaped its confines.

"Yes, things," she retorted, abandoning the attempt to elaborate. "I'm going to be very busy, and I really want to finish this room."

"I suppose I could let you get by with that, even though we both know better. Well." He smiled and shrugged. "Come down and kiss me goodbye then. I've got to get back to work."

"I will not kiss you goodbye . . ." she began, the words trailing off as he gripped her waist. Her hands automatically went to his arms, and he plucked her from her perch.

He lowered her slowly, his eyes never leaving hers, and her mouth was roughly claimed before her feet could reach the floor. His hands slipped under her shirt to roam the smooth skin of her back, pressing her closer as her body betrayed her and dissolved against his. Slowly he explored her soft, firm breasts, subtly rounded hips, lean thighs.

Every time, every time, her mind murmured. Every time he kisses me I go under deeper, and one day I'll never find my way back. His teeth moved to nip at her ear and neck, searching and finding new vulnerabilities before returning to ravage her mouth again. Without will, without choice, she rested in his arms, surrendering to forces she could never defeat.

He drew her away, breaking the intimacy, but his mouth returned to hers to linger briefly before he spoke. "About tonight, Samantha."

"What?" she murmured as his tongue traced the softness of her lips.

"I want to see you tonight."

Jerking herself back into reality, she pressed her hands against his chest, but did not manage to break away. "No, no, I'm busy. I told you."

"So you did," he acknowledged, and his eyes narrowed in speculation.

His words were cut off by the sound of Sabrina's laughter drifting down the hall. Samantha wiggled against Jake's hold. "Let me go, will you?"

"Why?" He was grinning now, enjoying the flood of color in her cheeks.

"Because..."

"Don't ever play poker, Sam." The warning was curt. "You'd lose your shirt."

"I...I..."

"Sabrina's due in September, right?"

The sudden question caused her to blink in confusion. "Well, yes, she..."

"That gives you a little breathing space, Samantha." He leaned down, and his kiss was hard and brief and to the point. "After that, don't expect to get away so lightly."

"I don't know what..."

"You know exactly what I mean," he interrupted. "I told you I meant to have you, and I always get what I want."

Her eyes flashed. "If you think I'm going to let you make love to me just because you say so, then you..."

The suggestion she would have made died as his mouth took hers again. She went rigid, telling herself she would not amuse him with a response this time. As she told herself she would not, her arms circled his neck. Her body became pliant, her lips parted with the hunger she had lived with all through the past month. As he took, she offered more, as he demanded, she gave. Her own mouth was mobile, her own hands seeking, until it seemed the month of fasting had never been.

"I want you, I don't have to tell you that, do I?"

She shook her head, trying to steady her breathing as his eyes alone caused her pulse to triple its rate.

"We'll settle this in September, unless you decide to come to me sooner." She began to shake her head again, but the fingers on the back of her neck halted the movement. "If you don't come to me, I'll wait until after the baby's born and you've got that much off your mind. I'm a patient man, Sam, but . . ." He stopped talking as Annie and Sabrina stepped into the room.

"Well." Annie shook her head at the two of them. "I can see he's been giving you a hard time." She turned to Sabrina with a half-exasperated shrug. "He's always been fresh as a new-laid egg. This is going to be a beautiful room, Sam." She glanced around at Samantha's handiwork, nodding in approval. "Let go of the little lady now, Jake, and take me back home, I've got dinner to fix."

"Sure. I've already said what I came to say." He released Samantha with a last, penetrating look and strode from the room, calling a goodbye over his shoulder.

"Fresh as a new-laid egg," Annie reiterated, and echoing his goodbye, followed him.

When the guests had departed, Samantha began to gather up paint buckets and brushes.

"Sam." Walking over, Sabrina placed a hand on her sister's arm. "I had no idea."

"No idea about what?" Bending, she banged the lid securely on rose pink.

"That you were in love with Jake." The truth she had avoided for so long was out in the open now: She had fallen hopelessly, irrevocably in love with Jake

Tanner! Standing, Samantha searched in vain for words of denial.

"We know each other too well, Sam," Sabrina said before she could answer. "How bad is it?"

Samantha lifted her hands and let them fall to her sides. "Terminal."

"Well, what are you going to do about it?"

"Do about it?" Samantha repeated. "What can I do about it? After the baby comes, I'll go back East and try to forget about him."

"I've never known you to give up without a fight," Sabrina spoke sharply. At the unexpected tone, Samantha's brows rose.

"I'd fight for something that belonged to me, Bree, but I don't move in on someone else's territory."

"Jake's not engaged to Lesley Marshall. Nothing's official."

"I'm not interested in semantics." Samantha began to fiddle with the paint cans. "Jake wants an affair with me, but he'll marry Lesley Marshall."

"Are you afraid to compete with Lesley?" Bree asked.

Samantha whirled around, eyes flashing. "I'm not afraid of anyone," she stormed. Sabrina's lips curved in a smug smile. "Don't try your psychology on me, Sabrina! Lesley Marshall and I don't belong in the same league, but I'm not afraid of her. I *am* afraid of getting hurt though.'' Her voice wavered and Sabrina's arm slipped over her shoulder.

"All right, Sam, we won't talk about it any more right now. Leave those brushes, I'll wash them out. Go take a ride. You know the only way to clear your head is to go off by yourself.''

"I'm beginning to think you know me too well.'' With a wry smile Samantha wiped her hands on her jeans.

"I know you all right, Samantha.'' Sabrina patted her cheek and urged her from the room. "I just haven't always known what to do about you.''

Chapter 9

During the months since their first meeting, Samantha had grown to know Jake Tanner, and to realize when he wanted something, he made certain he got it. And she knew he wanted her.

If, when she rode out on horseback, she kept closer to the ranch than had been her habit, she told herself it was not fear of encountering Jake which prompted the action, but simply her desire to spend more of her free time with Sabrina. Now Sabrina was growing cumbersome in her pregnancy, there was a grain of truth to this, so Samantha found it easy to accept the half-truth.

Every day she fell more under the spell of Wyoming. Bare branches were now fully cloaked in green.

The cattle grew sleek and fat. The land was fully awakened and rich.

"I think you may just have twins in there, Bree," Samantha commented as the two sisters took advantage of golden sun and fragrant warmth. Sabrina glanced down to where Samantha sat cross-legged on the wide front porch. "Dr. Gates thinks not." She patted the mound in question. "He says there's only one, and I'm just getting fat. One of us should have twins though."

"I'm afraid that's going to be up to you, Bree. I think I'll revive the tradition of old-maid school teachers."

Sabrina was sensitive to the wistfulness in the words. "Oh no, you'll have to get married, Sam. You can't let all those lessons go to waste."

This brought the light laugh it had intended. "I'm perfectly serious. Remember what Madame Dubois always said: 'Von must reach for ze stars.'"

"Oh, yes, Madame Dubois." Samantha smiled at the memory of their former ballet teacher. "You know, of course, that accent was a phoney. She came from New Jersey."

"I'm suitably crushed. She did think she had a genuine protégé in you."

"Yes, I was magnificent." Samantha sighed with exaggerated pride.

"Let's see a few of your famous leaps now, Sam."

"Not on your life!"

"Come on, cut-offs are as good as tu-tu any day. I'd join you in a *pas de deux,* but it would actually be a *pas de trois.*"

Samantha rose reluctantly from her seat on the porch. "All right, I don't mind showing off a little."

With quiet dignity, Sabrina began to hum a movement from Swan Lake, and Samantha lowered into a purposefully dramatic body sweep before exploding with an energetic series of grand jetés, stageleaps and cabrioles. She concluded the performance with a group of pirouettes, ended by dropping in a dizzy heap on the grass.

"That's what you get," she said, closing her eyes and shaking her head at the giddyness, "when you forget to spot focus."

"Is this show open to the public?"

Samantha glanced sharply toward the sound of the all-too-familiar voice.

"Dan!" Sabrina exclaimed. "I didn't expect you back so early."

"Ran into Lesley and Jake out on the north boundary," he explained, striding over and planting a firm kiss. "I thought you and Sam might like some company."

"Hello, Lesley, Jake." Sabrina included them both in her smile. "Have a seat, I'll bring out something cool."

Samantha had been sitting, praying without result for the ground to open up and swallow her. "I'll do it, Bree." She jumped at the opportunity of escape. "Don't get up."

"I'm up," Sabrina pointed out, disappearing inside before Samantha could argue.

"Do you teach ballet as well, Samantha?" Lesley asked. She surveyed Samantha's outfit of semi-ragged cut-offs and T-shirt with dark mocking eyes.

"No, no," Samantha muttered, feeling once more desperately at a disadvantage next to the slim woman in elegantly tailored breeches and silk shirt.

"I thought it was real nice," Dan commented, innocently turning the knife.

"Samantha's just full of surprises," Jake said.

Now that he had spoken again, Samantha was forced to give Jake a portion of her attention. He looked devastatingly male, the denim shirt rolled past his elbows to expose bronzed, corded arms, the low slung belt in his jeans accentuating his leanness. She concentrated on a spot approximately six inches to the left of his face in order to avoid the smile which had already mastered his face.

"Yeah," she returned. "I'm just a bushel of surprises."

"Anything you can't do, Sam?"

"A few things." She attempted a cool sophistication.

"You're so energetic," Lesley commented, slipping her hand through Jake's arm. "You must be horribly strong and full of bulging muscles."

For one heady moment, Samantha considered flight. She was opening her mouth to make her excuses when Dan effectively cut off all hope.

"Sit down, Sam, I want to talk over a little idea with you and Sabrina." Sinking down on the porch steps, Samantha avoided any glimpse of Jake's face. "Do you think Sabrina's up to a little party?" Samantha looked up at Dan's question and attempted to marshal her thoughts.

"A party?" she repeated, drawing her brows together in concentration. "I suppose so. Dr. Gates says she's doing very well, but you could always ask to be sure. Did you want to go to a party?"

"I was thinking of having one," he corrected with a grin. "There're these twins I know who have this birthday in a couple of weeks." Bending over, he tugged at Samantha's loosened locks. "Seems like a good excuse for having a party."

"Oh, our birthday." Samantha's response was vague. The impending anniversary had slipped her mind.

"Did I hear someone say party?" Sabrina emerged through the screen door with a tray of iced tea.

Samantha sipped the cool, sweet tea her sister handed her and watched Sabrina's face light up with anticipation.

"A birthday party, Sam." She turned to her sister, eyes shining with excitement. "When's the last time we had one?"

"When we were twelve and Billy Darcy got sick all over Mom's new carpet." Leaning back against the porch rail, Samantha unwittingly lifted her face to Jake's.

"Well, then, it's high time for another," Dan said. "What do you say, Sam? I know it means extra work for you."

"Huh?" Tearing her eyes from Jake's smile, she endeavored to pick up the threads of the conversation. "What? Oh, no, it's no trouble. It'll be fun." Concentrating on Dan's face, she blocked out the sight of Lesley lounging intimately against Jake. "How many people did you have in mind?"

"Just neighbors and friends." He reached up to rub his chin. "About thirty or forty, I'd say. What do you think, Lesley?"

The full mouth pouted a moment in thought. "If you want to keep it small, Dan," she agreed after a short deliberation. Samantha's eyes grew wide. These people definitely had a different idea of small than she did.

"Oh, Lesley, come take a look at this punch bowl I've got, see if you think we should use it." Rising, Sabrina took Dan's hand. "Come, get it down for me, Dan." Throwing her sister an innocent smile,

Sabrina disappeared inside and left her alone with Jake.

"How's the painting coming?" Jake stretched both arms over the back of the swing.

"Painting? Oh, the nursery. It's finished."

That, she recalled with a frown, was just one of many times he had come upon her in a ridiculous situation. Sleeping on stumps, covered with paint, and now leaping across the lawn like some crazed ballerina. Samantha, she told herself, you have class.

"What do you want for your birthday, Sam?" He prodded her with the toe of his boot and earned a scowl.

Blowing a wisp of hair from her eyes, she moved her shoulders. "Fur, diamonds."

"No, you're not the type for furs." Taking out a cigar, he lit it and blew a lazy stream of smoke. "You'd be thinking about all the little minks that were scalped to make it. And diamonds wouldn't suit you."

"I suppose I'm more the quartz type." She rose irritated.

"No, I was thinking more of sapphires." He caught her wrist. "To go with your eyes, or maybe rubies to go with your temper."

"I'll be sure to put both on my list. Now, if you'll excuse me." She glanced at her captured hand, then back at him. "I've got to go feed my cat." She gestured to where Shylock lay on the far side of the porch.

"He doesn't look very hungry."

"He's pretending to be dead," she muttered. "Shylock, let's eat."

Amber eyes opened and blinked, then to her pleasure, Shylock rose and padded toward her. However, upon reaching his mistress, he gave her a disinterested stare, leaped into Jake's lap and began to purr with wicked enjoyment.

"No, ma'am." Jake glanced down at the contented cat. "He doesn't look hungry at all."

With a final glare, Samantha turned, stalked to the door and slammed the screen smartly behind her.

The sun shone warm and friendly on the morning of the twins' birthday. Samantha carried a large parcel into the kitchen. Dumping her burden on the table where her sister was enjoying a cup of tea, she nudged Shylock away with her foot. She had not yet decided to forgive him for his treacherous advances to Jake.

"This just came, it's from the folks."

"Open it, Sam." Sabrina poked an experimental finger at the package. "Dan refuses to give me my present yet, and I've searched everywhere I can think of."

"I bet it's six books on child rearing for you, and six on etiquette for me."

"A present's a present," Sabrina stated, and tore the mailing paper from the box.

"Here's a note." After breaking the seal, Samantha produced a sheet of paper and read aloud.

"To Samantha and Sabrina:

A very happy birthday and our love to you both. Sabrina, I do hope you are taking good care of yourself. As you know, proper diet and rest are essential. I'm sure having Samantha with you during the last weeks of your confinement is a great comfort. Samantha, do look after your sister and see that she takes the necessary precautions. However, I hope you're not overlooking your own social life. As your mother, it is my duty to remind you that you are long past the marriageable age. Your father and I are looking forward to seeing you and our first grandchild in a few weeks. We will be in Wyoming the first part of September, if Dad's schedule holds true.

With love, Mom and Dad

"There's a postscript for you, Bree.

"Sabrina, doesn't Daniel know any suitable men for your sister?"

With a sigh, Samantha folded the letter and

dropped it on the table. "She never changes." Dipping into the box, Samantha plucked out a smaller one with Sabrina's name on it and handed it to her. "Marriageable age," she muttered and shook her head.

"Did you peek in here before?" Sabrina accused, dumping out volumes of infant and child care.

"No," Samantha denied with a superior smirk. "I just know Mom." Drawing out her own package, she ripped off the concealing paper. "Good grief." She let the box drop to the table and held up a brief black lace negligée.

"I thought I knew Mom." Both sisters burst into laughter. "She must be getting desperate," Samantha concluded, holding the negligée in front of her.

"Now that's a pretty thing," Jake observed as he and Dan entered the kitchen. "But it's even prettier with something in it." Samantha bundled the garment behind her and flushed scarlet.

"Presents from Mom and Dad," Sabrina explained, indicating her stack of books.

"Very suitable." Dan grinned as he glanced through the volumes.

"Doesn't look like Sam feels the same about hers." Jake smiled. Samantha felt her already alarming color deepen. "Let's see it again."

"Don't tease, Jake." Sabrina turned to her husband. "Mom says they'll be here the first part of September."

"I'll put this stuff away." Samantha tossed the gown into the box and began to bury it under books.

"Leave that till later." Dan took her hand and pulled her away. "I need you outside for a minute."

She went willingly. Escape was escape. Imagining it had something to do with Sabrina's gift, she was surprised when Dan slowed his pace and allowed his wife to join them in their walk toward the ranch buildings. He kept her involved in a running conversation about the party until they came to a halt at the paddock fence.

"Happy birthday, Sam." Sabrina kissed her sister's cheek as Samantha's eyes focused on the golden Arabian mare.

"Oh." She could manage no more.

"She's from a good line," Dan informed her, his arm slipping around Sabrina's shoulders. "She's out of the Double T Stock, no finer in Wyoming."

"But I..." Words faltered, and she swallowed and tried to begin again.

"What do you give someone who packs their own life away for six months without hesitation, without asking for anything in return?" Dan's free arm slipped around Samantha and pulled her to his side.

"We figured if you insisted on going back East, we'd always have a hold on you. You'd have to come visit us to ride your mare."

"I don't know how to thank you."

"Then don't," Dan ordered. "Go try her out."

"Now?"

"Now's as good a time as any." Not needing a second urging, Samantha was over the fence, stroking the mare and murmuring.

"We may convince her to stay yet," Dan commented, watching as she slipped into the saddle and took the mare around the paddock. "I could have a word with Jake."

Sabrina shook her head. "No, Sam would be furious if we interfered. She'd bolt back to Philadelphia before we could take a breath. For now, we'd better keep out of it." She lowered her voice as a beaming Samantha trotted around to them and slipped off the little mare.

"She's a real beauty," she sighed. "I don't know how I can ever bear to leave her...."

Sabrina's eyes met her husband's in silent satisfaction. Perhaps it will not be necessary, their unspoken message said.

"Come, little sister," Dan said. "If you can tear yourself away from your new friend, I sure could use a cup of coffee now."

As the trio trouped back toward the house, Jake swung through the back door. "Delivery just came. It's in the living room."

"Oh," Dan murmured, looking entirely too innocent. "Come on, Sabrina, we'd best see what it is."

"Is it the piano?" Sam asked Jake, and Dan and Sabrina disappeared inside.

"Looked like one to me. I guess that's another present that'll go over big. Walk to the truck with me," Jake commanded and captured her hand before she could protest.

"Really, Jake, I have a million things to do." She trotted to keep pace with his loose, lanky stride.

"I know, you're indispensable." Stopping by his truck, he reached in the cab and produced a package. "But this seems to be the time for gift giving. I thought I'd let you have your present now."

"You didn't have to get me anything."

"Samantha." His drawl was lazy, but his eyes narrowed in annoyance. "I never do anything unless I want to." Taking her hand from behind her back, he placed the box in it. "Open it."

Lifting the statue from its tissue bedding, she examined it in silent amazement. The alabaster was smooth and cool in her hands, carved into the shape of a horse and rider in full gallop. The artist had captured the fluid grace, the freedom of motion. She ran a hesitant finger over the delicate features.

"It looks like me." She lifted her eyes to Jake's.

"And so it should," he answered easily. "It's supposed to be you."

"But how?" She shook her head, torn between pleasure and confusion.

"A man I know does this kind of thing. I described you to him."

For the second time that day, Samantha found herself at a loss for words.

"Why?" The question was out before she could swallow it. Slowly, a smile drifted across his face. He pushed back his hat. "Because it suits you better than furs and diamonds."

She braced herself to meet his eyes again.

"Thank you."

He nodded, his face solemn. He took the box from her hands and placed it on the hood of the truck. "I think a birthday kiss is traditional."

Swallowing, she took an instinctive step in retreat, but he gripped her arms and held her still. She offered her cheek, and his laughter broke out, full and rich on the summer air. "Sam," he turned her face to his, and his eyes sparkled with humor, "you're incredible."

His lips met hers. His hand moved from her arms to her hips, drawing her firmly against the hard lines of his body. She submitted to the embrace, as long as his arms held her, as long as they were mouth to mouth, as long as the heat from his body infused into hers, he owned her, and she could not run.

Finally he drew her away, bringing his hands to her shoulders while hers rested on his chest for support.

"Happy birthday, Sam."

"Thank you," she managed, still breathless from the impact of his embrace.

He lifted the box from the hood of the truck and placed it in her hands before sliding into the cab. "See you tonight." With a salute, he started the engine. The truck moved down the road, leaving her staring after it.

Chapter 10

Party sounds filled the house. Laughter and voices and music mingled and drifted through open windows to float on the night air.

On this evening, the twins were dramatically different in their appearance. Sabrina's pale blue gown floated about her, cunningly masquerading her pregnancy. Her hair was a glinting halo around rose-tinted cheeks. Samantha's black-striped satin clung to her body, her halter neckline plunging deep to a wide, gathered waist. Her hair was free and thick around her shoulders.

As she moved and mingled with the crowd, Samantha searched for a tall, lanky form, noting with increasing despair and a gnawing jealousy, that a slim, dark woman had also as yet failed to put in an appearance.

Cornered by an enthusiastic young cowboy, Samantha's attention began to wander from the detailed account of horse breeding when her eyes met dark jade across the room.

He was standing with two men she did not recognize, and Lesley Marshall stood beside him. She was elegant in an oyster white gown. Her fine-boned ivory hand was placed from time to time on Jake's arm, as if, Samantha thought grimly, flaunting her possession.

Furious with the sudden feeling of inadequacy, Samantha turned to her companion with a dazzling smile. He stammered over his lecture, his words grinding to a halt. She tucked her arm in his and used her eyes without shame.

"Howdy, Tim." Jake appeared from nowhere and placed a hand on the young man's shoulder. "I'm going to steal this little lady for a moment." He paused and smiled easily into Samantha's mutinous face. "There're a couple of people she hasn't met yet."

Without waiting for an assent, he had her unwilling hand in his, propelling her through the crowd. "Tim won't be the same for weeks," he whispered close to her ear. "A woman could get run out of town for using her eyes that way on susceptible young boys," he warned, pulling her through the sea of people.

"You don't have to drag me."

"I know a stubborn mule when I see one," he countered, without bothering to lower his voice. Her furious retort was swallowed as Jake presented her to the two men who flanked Lesley.

"Sam, I'd like you to meet George Marshall, Lesley's father." Samantha's hand was enveloped in a hearty grip. "And Jim Bailey," he continued, nodding toward the second man.

"Jim only works with cattle on paper. He's a lawyer."

"My, this is a mighty pretty girl!" George Marshall boomed. Giving Jake a sly wink, he patted his daughter's shoulder.

"You always manage to rope in the pick of the herd, don't you, Jake?"

Jake slipped his hands easily into his pockets. "I do my best. But then roping them's one thing, getting them's another."

"Well now, little lady," George's genial voice continued, "Les tells me you're a gym teacher."

"That's right, Mr. Marshall."

"Now, you just call me George," he instructed, squeezing her shoulder with genial affection. "Tell me, why isn't a pretty little thing like you married and settled down instead of running around some gymnasium?"

Jake was grinning with obvious enjoyment. Samantha tossed her hair behind her back, but before she could think of a suitable answer George's laughter boomed through the room.

"I like this girl," George announced to the group. "Looks like she has spirit. You come over to our ranch anytime, little lady, any time at all."

In spite of herself, Samantha found herself liking his expansive hospitality. "If you'll excuse me now, I've got . . . got to get a tray out of the kitchen." She gave the group an all-encompassing smile and melted into the crowd.

In the kitchen, she pulled a tray from the refrigerator to give her excuse credibility and was glad she had when Jake followed her in a moment later.

"George is a good man. He has the right ideas when it comes to women." Smiling knowingly at her, he leaned against the door watching her every move.

"That's your opinion," she returned tartly, bustling around the kitchen in an attempt to ignore him.

"Sit down a minute, Sam."

She glanced up, immediately wary, then lifted the tray as defense. "No, I've got to get back."

"Please."

Despite herself, she lowered the tray to the table and herself into a chair.

"I ran into Jack Abbot the school principal, the other day."

"Oh?"

"He told me the girls' Phys. Ed. instructor isn't coming back next term." Leaning back in his chair, Jake studied her. "He's going to offer you the job."

"Oh," she repeated before she could stop herself.

"He wants you pretty bad. He really needs someone this fall. I told him I'd be seeing you, and that I'd mention it. He's going to call you officially, of course."

How simple, Samantha thought.

How simple it would all be if I didn't love this man. I could stay where I want to stay, work where I want to work. But now, I've got to refuse, I've got to go away.

"I appreciate your telling me, and I appreciate Mr. Abbot wanting me, but . . ."

"Don't appreciate it, Samantha, think about it."

"You don't know what you're asking me to do."

He rose to pace the room, his hands seeking the depths of his pockets. "I'm just asking you to think about it. You like it here. You've made friends. You like being near your sister. You'd still have the satisfaction of doing what you feel you're suited for. Is it so much to ask that you consider it?"

"Yes, it's quite a lot. Jake, I don't want to argue with you. There are things I have to do the same way there are things you have to do."

"All right." He nodded, then repeated slowly as if coming to a decision. "All right, there *are* things I have to do." Moving over he captured her chin between his thumb and fingers.

His arms slipped around her waist to bring her close, his mouth lowering to brush her cheeks and the corners of her lips. "Come home with me now, Samantha. We can be alone there." His voice had become low and seductive, as his fingers trailed over the bare skin of her back.

"No, please don't." She turned her face away.

"I want to make love to you. I want to feel your skin under my hands, all of you. I want to hear you sigh when I touch you."

"Jake, please." She dropped her head to his chest. "It's unfair, here, like this."

"Then come home with me."

"No, I can't." She shook her head without raising it. "I won't."

"All right, Samantha." He framed her face and brought it up to his. "I said I'd give you until the baby was born. We'll stick to that. We won't argue tonight. Let's call it a truce for your birthday. Agreed?"

He kissed her once, briefly, and turned to lift the tray. "Then we'll both do what we have to do when the time comes."

Leaving her confused, Jake moved through the doorway.

Rejoining the festivities, Samantha moved from group to group, but her thoughts were only about

Jake. Why was he so interested in her career choices? Why did he want her to take the job in Wyoming? *Maybe he cared for her.* For a brief moment, she allowed hope to shimmer. Her eyes swept the room to find him. Finally she spotted him. He was dancing with Lesley. The shining cap of her raven hair brushing his cheek, the ivory of her hand entwined with the bronze of his. Samantha winced as he threw back his head and laughed at something Lesley had said for his ears alone.

Care for me? her mind repeated in a scathing whisper. Grow up, Samantha, *caring* and *wanting* don't always mean the same thing. In a few weeks, she comforted herself, she would no longer be subjected to this constant pain. When the ache had eased, she could visit Bree again. Jake would probably be too busy with his wife to spare time for visits to the Lazy L. Samantha felt her heart contract with pain.

She turned away and bumped solidly into Jim Bailey.

"Sorry." He took her shoulders to steady her. "I didn't see you."

"It's all right," she returned, offering a smile. "Besides, I think I ran into you."

"Well, no harm done either way." She watched his eyes slide past her and focus on Jake and Lesley. "They look nice together, don't they?"

Embarrassed that he must have seen her staring at them, Samantha nodded, and looked down at her empty glass. "Come on, we better get you a refill."

A few moments later, they joined the group around the piano as Sabrina played.

"So, you're a lawyer." She smiled at Jim. "I don't think I've ever met a lawyer before."

Jim returned her smile. "And you're a gymnast."

"No, actually, I'm a gym teacher now."

He lifted his glass in toast and drank. "I remember you. I've always been an avid fan of the Olympics. I thought you were fabulous."

"Well, that's nice to hear after a decade."

He tapped his glass to hers. "Well, Olympic Star, would you like to dance?"

"I'd love to."

Samantha enjoyed Jim Bailey's easy conversation. She learned during their two dances that he was interested in getting into politics. His dark good looks and ready wit would certainly be assets, she decided.

"Sam." Sabrina motioned to her as they moved back toward the piano. "It's your turn. Union rules."

"O.K.," Samantha agreed, sliding onto the bench.

She played with practiced ease, moving from one song to the next. Time slipped through her fingers. As in a dream, she was aware of the voices behind her, the faint, drifting breeze of Wyoming through the opened windows.

Someone sat beside her. Recognizing the lean fingers which lifted to turn the page of her sheet music, she faltered and missed a note.

"You and Jim seem to have hit it off." Samantha heard the click of his lighter over the sounds of the party.

"He's a very nice man. Have you known him long?"

"Oh, only since we were about eight and I gave him a black eye and he loosened a few of my teeth."

"Sounds like a loving relationship."

Jake again turned the page before she could do so herself. "Well, after that we sort of stuck together." He pushed the curtain of hair behind her shoulder, and Samantha struggled not to break the thread of the melody. "The two of you seemed to have a lot to talk about."

"He's very charming, and we have a few mutual interests."

"Hmm." Jake shifted slightly in his seat. His thigh brushed hers, and her fingers responded by hitting three wrong notes.

"You play very well."

Was he being ironic? She turned to look at him, but found no mockery in his jade eyes.

"Pleasantly," she corrected. "I get the general melody, but the details are a bit fuzzy."

"I've noticed that you have a tendency to shrug off your own capabilities. Are you aware of that?"

"That's not true. I just know what I do well and what I don't."

"You're a very tough critic, and you're inclined to underestimate."

"Honesty," she countered, finishing the song with a flourish. "I am a totally honest person."

"Are you, Samantha?" he said softly. "That's what I plan to find out."

Chapter 11

The days grew hot and sultry. The skies were improbably blue, rarely softened by clouds.

Long hours in the sun had deepened the honey of Samantha's skin, teasing out the gold in her hair. As long as she was occupied, she had no time for soul searching. She could enjoy the long summer days without thinking of the fall. As Sabrina wilted like a thirsty rose in the searing heat, Samantha confined her own activities to the early morning hours. In the long, hot haze of the afternoon, Sabrina moved slowly through the house, her body clumsy. Samantha did not dare leave her. The baby was due in two weeks and Samantha wanted to remain within calling distance of her sister as much as possible.

One particularly humid afternoon, the two women were sitting idly in the living room. Sabrina got up heavily from her chair to look out the window. "Sam," she said, "before Dan left for town, he said a storm was brewing. From the looks of the sky, I'd say he was right."

Before Samantha could answer there was a sudden flash of lightning. A blast of thunder rolled in on the wind and the rain began to fall in sheets.

"It's coming down fast," Samantha agreed. "It should cool us off a bit." She looked sympathetically at her sister's bulky form.

The storm built in power. Jagged flashes of lightning illuminated the room and an angry wind hurled the rain against the windows. The two women watched in fascination as the storm exhausted itself. Soon rain dripped tentatively from the eaves and the thunder was a mere grumble in the distance.

The sun struggled to reappear, breaking through the gloom with a hazy promise of light.

"That," Sabrina commented with an enormous sigh, "was a mean one."

Samantha turned from her place by the window and again slumped into a chair. "Remember when you used to hide in the closet whenever we had a thunder storm?"

"All too well." She gave her sister a pained smile. "And you used to stand on the porch loving every minute of it until Mom dragged you in, soaking wet. On that note from the past," Sabrina announced and struggled to her feet, "I'm going to take a nap, Sam." She turned at the doorway and studied the woman slouched in the chair, bare legs and feet stretched out in unconscious grace. "I love you."

With a rather puzzled smile, Samantha watched her walk away.

Wandering out to the porch, Samantha drank in the rain-fresh air. Everything sparkled. Raindrops clung like jewels to blossoms and leaves. Though the flowers had drooped with the weight of the storm, their colors had been washed into brilliant life. A bird, flying by on a shaft of light, trilled above her. She could hear the steady dripping of the rain off the eaves above the whisper of the dying wind. Satisfied, she curled up on a porch rocker and instantly fell asleep.

She had no idea how long she had drifted in the soft twilight world when, with reluctance, she woke at the touch of a hand on her shoulder. She looked up drowsily and yawned. "Oh, Bree, I must have fallen asleep. It's so wonderfully cool out here."

"Sam, I think the baby's decided to put in an unscheduled appearance."

"Huh? Oh!" Springing to her feet, she was instantly awake. "Right now? Dan's not here, and it's not time yet. Sit down, sit," she ordered, running agitated fingers through her hair.

"I think the first thing to do is to calm down," Sabrina suggested.

"You're right. I'm not going to fall apart, it was just a shock. I wasn't expecting this for another week or two."

"Neither was I." Sabrina's smile was half-amused, half-apologetic.

"All right, how long have you been having contractions, and how far apart are they?"

"Only for an hour or so."

"That should give us plenty of time." Samantha patted Sabrina's hand.

"But, they've been getting awfully strong, and..." Breaking off, she closed her eyes and began to breathe in a deep, methodical rhythm. "And," she continued, after a final long breath, "awfully close together."

"How close?" Samantha asked, feeling new tension at the base of her neck.

"Ten minutes."

"Ten minutes," Samantha repeated. "I'd better get you to the hospital. I'll bring the car around. Stay put," she told her sister and raced to the garage.

Upon reaching Sabrina's compact and sliding behind the wheel, Samantha was horrified to find the engine unresponsive to the turn of the key. The little car sputtered, emitted an apologetic groan and died.

"You can't," she insisted, and smacked the steering wheel. "We just had you fixed."

There was no use wasting more time trying to figure out what was wrong with the car. It was clearly not going to start, and Samantha hadn't the first idea of where to look for the problem.

Rushing back to the house, she picked up the phone in the kitchen. At least she could call Dr. Gates. A groan of despair was wrenched from her as she heard the dead silence on the line. Oh no, the storm must have knocked out the phones!

Forcing herself to appear calm, she returned to the living room where Sabrina was waiting for her.

Reaching her sister again, Samantha knelt down so their eyes were level. "Bree, the car won't start. All the trucks and jeeps are out with the men, and the storm must have knocked down the phone lines."

"Looks like we've got a few problems." Sabrina took a deep breath.

"It's going to be all right." Samantha took her hand in reassurance. "I'll help you get into bed, and then I'll take a horse and ride toward the Double T. If I don't see any of the men on the way, I'll get a truck there and bring it back. Most of them have radios, and I can call ahead to the doctor."

"Sam, it's going to take time for you to get there, and to get back. I don't think I'll make it in time to get to the hospital after that. You'll have to have the doctor come here."

"Here?" Samantha repeated. Her throat closed on the word. Sabrina nodded. "All right. Don't worry, I won't be long. I'll be back as soon as I can." Samantha raced off to the stables and without wasting time for a saddle, she leaped on her mare's back.

The familiar landscape was a blur, as she urged more speed out of the powerful horse. The sound of her own breath was masked by the sound of thudding hooves. Every minute she took was a minute longer Sabrina was alone. She crouched lower on the horse and dug in her bare heels.

When Samantha spotted the men on horseback she spurred the Arabian over the fence in a fluid leap. As her hooves touched earth, she met the horse's sides again. They streaked across the field, scattering annoyed cattle.

When she reached the group she reined in sharply. The mare reared, nearly unseating her. Her breath came in gasps as she struggled to keep her seat.

"What are you trying to do, break your neck?" Furiously, Jake snatched the reins from her hands. "If you're stupid enough not to care about yourself, think of your horse. What do you mean riding like a fool and jumping fences? Where's your saddle? Have you lost your mind?"

"Bree," she managed at last between giant gulps of air. "The baby's coming, and the phone's out. The car wouldn't start, and there's nobody around. Dan's in town. Bree says there's no time to get her into the hospital now, and I have to call the doctor." She felt tears of fear burning at her eyes and bit her lip.

"All right, take it easy." Twisting in the saddle, Jake called out to one of his men. "Get back to the ranch and get hold of Dr. Gates on the C.B. Tell him

Sabrina Lomax is in labor and to get to the Lazy L in a hurry.'' Turning back, he handed the reins to Samantha. "Let's go."

"Are you coming back with me?" Flooded with relief, she gripped tight on the leather.

"What do you think?"

Together, they sprang forward in a gallop.

Speed and thundering hooves were all Samantha ever remembered of the ride back. There was no time for conversation, no time for thought. She was sliding to the ground before coming to a full stop and Jake once more secured her reins.

"Keep your head, Samantha," he ordered, watching her bound up the steps and through the front door.

The house was silent. Her stomach tightened as she rushed to the master bedroom. Sabrina sat up in bed, propped by a mound of pillows and greeted her with a cheerful smile.

"That was quick, did you fly?"

"Just about," Samantha returned, faint with relief.

"We've sent for the doctor. Everything's under control." She sat down on the bed, taking her sister's hand. "How're you doing?"

"Not too bad." Her hand closed over Samantha's as much to reassure as seeking reassurance. "I'm glad you're back. Here comes another one."

Samantha looked on with unfamiliar helplessness. Her fingers grew tighter over her twin's as if to steal some of her pain.

"We can thank Mom for that book on natural childbirth." Sabrina gave a long, shaky sigh and relaxed against the pillows.

"Don't look so worried, I'm doing fine. Oh, hello Jake." Glancing at the doorway, Sabrina greeted him with friendly cheerfulness. "I didn't know you were here. Come in. It's not contagious."

He advanced into the room, looking tall, male and out of place. His hands retreated to his pockets. "How're you doing?"

"Oh well, you've seen a cow in labor before, I don't imagine there's much difference." The small hand tightened on Samantha's. "Here we go again."

Samantha lifted the hand to her cheek. *Where was the doctor?* Sabrina should be in the hospital surrounded by experts.

"This baby's in a big hurry," Sabrina announced with a small moan. "I'm sorry, Sam, it's not going to wait much longer."

I don't know anything about childbirth, Samantha thought in a moment of terror. *What am I going to do? What do I do first?*

Standing, she turned to Jake. "Go sterilize some towels, lots of them, and some string and scissors."

"All right." His hand rested on her shoulder a moment. "If you need me, give a call."

Nodding, she moved into the adjoining bath and scrubbed her hands and arms until they hurt.

"You're going to be fine," she stated as she reentered the bedroom.

"Yes, I am." Sabrina lay back on the pillows and closed her eyes. "I'm going to have this baby, Sam, and I'm going to do a good job of it. You can't do this for me, I have to be strong."

"You are strong." Brushing away the hair from Sabrina's cheeks, she realized with a sudden jolt that it was true. "You're stronger than I ever knew."

Her calm had returned, and she took over the duties of midwife with an instinct as old as time. She wiped moisture from her sister's face, working with her, breathing with her, uttering soothing encouragements. Sabrina had not gone through all she had to lose now, and Samantha would not allow anything to go wrong.

"All right." Wiping beads of sweat from her own brow, Samantha straightened. "I think she's going to come this time, it's almost over. You have to help."

Sabrina nodded, her face pale and composed. Her hair had darkened with dampness. She shuddered and moaned with the final pang of childbirth. A thin shrill cry pierced the stillness of the room. Samantha held new life in her hands.

"Oh, Bree." She stared down at the tiny, wriggling form.

Dan burst into the room two steps ahead of the doctor.

Suddenly, it was all so simple, Dan standing by Sabrina's side, his large hand clutching hers, the small, fresh form swaddled in the curve of her mother's arms.

"Only one." Sabrina sighed, her eyes luminous. "You'll have to handle the twins, Sam. One at a time is enough for me."

Sometime later, Samantha shut the door behind her and walked toward the kitchen. Jake looked up at her approach.

"A girl." She lowered herself into a chair. "The doctor says she's perfect, almost seven pounds. Bree's fine." She pushed at her tumbled hair and ran a hand across her brow. "I want to thank you."

"I didn't do anything."

"You were here." She lifted her eyes, and they were young and vulnerable. "I needed to know you were here."

"Samantha." He smiled and shook his head. "You sure find a man's weak points. I'll get you a drink."

He was back in a moment with a decanter of brandy and two snifters. Sitting across from her, he filled both generously. "It's not champagne, but it'll do." Lifting his glass, he touched it solemnly to hers. "To mother and child, and to Samantha Evans." He paused, his smile fading into seriousness. "She's one hell of a woman."

Samantha folded her arms on the table, lay her head on them and burst into tears.

"I was so scared." She found her voice muffled against his shoulder as he brought her against him. "I've never been so scared. I thought I would lose them both."

He tilted her chin as one hand rubbed the small of her back. "You're a survivor, Sam, and too stubborn to let anything happen to Sabrina or the baby."

Her forehead dropped to his chest as she struggled to stem the flow of tears.

"I always seem to fall apart in front of you."

"Don't much care for that, do you?" She felt his lips descend to her hair and allowed herself the joy of being cradled in his arms. "Most people don't look for perfection, Sam, they find it boring. You," he said, and framed her face with his hands, "are never boring."

She sniffed and smiled. "I guess that was a compliment." Giving into impulse, she leaned over and rested her cheek against his. "I don't think you're boring, either."

"Well." He stroked her hair a moment, and his voice was curiously soft. "That's about the nicest thing you've ever said to me.

"Now drink some of that." He pushed her gently away and handed her the brandy.

Obeying, she allowed the warm strength to seep into her veins and relaxed with a sigh. "Bree certainly came through this better than I did." She drank again. Jake straddled a chair, leaning his arms on the back. "When I left her, she was lying there with the baby, looking like she'd just finished having a picnic. Dan looked like he was about to keel over, and I was ready for someone to cart me away. Yet Bree lies there, glowing like a rose."

"Your sister's quite a woman."

"I know." Her eyes dropped to the surface of the table. "She said she has someone to depend on her now. I guess the time's come to stop playing big sister, she doesn't need that anymore."

"So, what will you do now?" His voice was casual.

"I'll stay around a couple of weeks, then I'll go on." She shrugged, seeing only a void.

"To what?"

Her fingers tightened on her glass. "To my work, to my life." She drank, and the brandy was bitter.

"Still set on leaving?" He lifted his own glass, swirling the liquid. Amber danced under the kitchen light. "You haven't seen Wyoming in the autumn."

"No, I haven't," she answered, evading his prior question. "Maybe I'll come back next year." She stared down at her hands, knowing she never would.

"She's hungry!" Dan charged into the kitchen, his grin threatening to split his face. "Just had a baby, and she says she's hungry. Sam, I love you." Plucking her from her chair, Dan tossed her into the air. Her laughter ended on a shriek, as she clutched at him on her journey down. The shriek was strangled as she was smothered by a bear hug. "I swear, if bigamy wasn't against the law, I'd marry you."

"If I was still all in one piece," she managed, turning her face and gulping for air.

"I ask you, Jake." He consulted the other man as his arms threatened to destroy the alignment of Samantha's ribcage. "Have you ever known another like this one?"

"Can't say that I have." She heard the smile in his voice, though it was impossible in her position to see his face. "I'd say Samantha is unique. One of a kind."

Rising, he lifted his brandy and toasted them both.

Chapter 12

"Sam, you're going to spoil her."

"Impossible." Sitting in the front porch rocker with the week-old Jennifer, Samantha smiled at her sister. "She's much too intelligent to be spoiled. Anyway, it's an aunt's privilege."

As she continued to rock, her lips strayed to Jennifer's soft tuft of dark hair. *I won't be able to do this much longer.* She looked to the massive peaks gleaming silver-blue in the afternoon sun. A light breeze stirred the air, bringing the sweet scent of freshly mowed grass. She breathed it in, and the soft scent of Jennifer's talc mingled with it. A sigh escaped.

She had not realized such a small creature could wrap her way around the heart so completely. Another love to leave behind. In just a week, I'll have to say goodbye to all the things that matter; Bree, Dan, Wyoming, and now Jennifer.

Dents and bruises, she thought again, but not the open wound that comes from leaving the man. Arrogant and gentle, demanding and kind, hot tempered and easy; the parts which made up Jake Tanner were complicated and many, but to Samantha, it was a simple equation of love.

Blast you, Jake Tanner, if it weren't for you, I could stay. I belong here. I felt it from the first time I saw the mountains. There's nothing for me in Philadelphia. You've left me without anything to go back to.

"Looks like Lesley's coming to pay a visit," Sabrina observed. Samantha jerked back to the present with a snap.

She watched the late model compact winding down the drive. Ignoring the flare of impossible jealousy, she set her features in casual lines.

"Sabrina, how well you look." Leslie's greeting was obviously tinged by surprise. "It's only been a week, and you look positively..." she hesitated, searching for a word.

"Radiant?" Sabrina suggested and laughed. "I just had a baby, Lesley, not open-heart surgery."

"But to go through all that here, and without a doctor." She turned to Samantha. "I heard from Jake that you were marvelous and handled everything."

Samantha shrugged, uncomfortable at hearing Jake's praise from Lesley's lips. "It was nice of him to say so, but Sabrina did all the work."

"Well, having a baby is not a prospect I look forward to." Lesley shivered delicately. "I certainly intend to put it off as long as possible." Gliding over, she bent her head over the sleeping infant. "She is quite lovely, Sabrina. Very sweet."

"Would you like to hold her?" Samantha offered.

"Oh, no." Lesley stepped back. "I'm afraid I'm not very good with babies."

As she moved, Samantha caught the glint of the large square-cut diamond on her left hand. Lesley followed her gaze, and held out her hand. "You didn't know I was engaged, did you, Sabrina?"

"No." Sabrina cast a quick glance at her sister. "We hadn't heard."

"Well, you have been rather busy." She moved her fingers, enjoying the changing lights. "And we haven't made any formal announcement yet. We're planning a bit of a party for next week. As a matter of fact, I'm just on my way into town to begin shopping for my trousseau. Of course, I'll have to make a trip into New York for some proper clothes, but I'll just have to make do locally for the time being. We've set the wedding for the end of September." She smoothed her perfectly groomed hair with a well-manicured hand. "I could have done with a bit more time, but men have no idea how difficult things are to arrange properly.'' She smiled again. ''Well, I must fly. I have so much to do. I do hope you'll be able to make it to the wedding, Samantha.''

Sabrina glanced again at her sister. ''Sam won't be here in September, Lesley.''

''Oh, too bad.'' The regret in Lesley's voice was mild. Her mind had already run ahead to her wardrobe. She opened the door of the compact and slid behind the wheel. Lifting a slim arm in farewell, she drove away.

Rising, Sabrina took the sleeping Jennifer from her sister's arms and went into the house. When she returned, she sat on the arm of the rocker and laid her hand on Samantha's shoulder.

''I knew it was going to happen,'' Samantha murmured. ''I just didn't want to be here when it did. I didn't think it would hurt this much. Oh, Bree.'' She looked up at her twin with helpless, swimming eyes. ''What am I going to do?''

For the first time in their relationship, their situations were reversed, and Samantha was vulnerable, seeking comfort and advice.

''Sam, you can't go on like this, why don't you talk to him?'' Sabrina stroked the thick fall of her sister's hair. ''Something is wrong here, and the two of you have got to talk things out.''

''No. I won't give him the opportunity to feel sorry for me.''

''Pride can be a very cold companion,'' Sabrina murmured.

Samantha stood up. "I'm going back early, Bree. I can have everything arranged by the day after tomorrow, maybe even tomorrow night."

"Sam, you can't run away from this."

"Just watch me."

"Mom and Dad won't be here for a few more days. They'll be disappointed."

"I'm sorry, I hate to miss them, but I can't handle this." Pausing, she repeated, the admission surprising her, "I *really* can't handle this."

"But Sam." Sabrina joined her at the porch rail. "You should at least talk to Jake. Don't you want to know how he feels? You can't just go flying off without speaking to him, without saying goodbye. Something's not right about all this. I've thought about the two of you; I've seen the way he looks at you."

Shaking her head, Samantha moved toward the door. "No, he hasn't shown his face since the baby was born, and Lesley Marshall has his ring on her finger. A diamond. He has what he wants."

Samantha spent the evening packing, while Shylock watched her in silent accusation from his habitual place in the center of her bed.

Once in bed, she spent most of the night staring at a moon-washed ceiling. When the first pale light of dawn crept into the room she rose. The mauve shadows under her eyes were a sad tribute to the restless hours.

The house slept on, and she deserted it, making her way to the stables. She saddled her mount with quick, deft movements, then galloped over the faint mist of morning.

As the sky lightened, the air came to life with the sweet song of birds. Sadly, she listened to the song of the west, for she knew that the melody would linger forever in her heart. She watched the mountains transformed by the dawn. Ribbons of rose and gold melted into blue until the peaks were no longer silhouettes, but stood proud in the full glory of the sun. She stayed for a last look at the white-faced Herefords grazing on the short, coarse grass. She knew now that her love for this wild, free country was forever bound up with her love for Jake. In saying goodbye to one, she was saying goodbye to the other. Straightening her shoulders, she turned the little mare back to the Lazy L.

When she returned to the house, she greeted her sister with bright chatter, the meaningless words no disguise for sleep-starved eyes. Sabrina made no comment, and shortly, disappeared into the bedroom to tend to the baby.

Alone, Samantha wandered aimlessly from window to window. Tonight, she thought, slipping her hands into the pockets of her jeans, I'll be on a plane. And tomorrow morning, all this will just be a dream.

"Morning, ma'am."

She whirled, nearly upsetting a vase of roses with the movement. Jake leaned against the doorframe, legs crossed at the ankles as if he had been watching for some time.

"What are you doing here?"

He took a few lazy strides into the room. "Well now, I came to fetch you." This information was imparted in an irritatingly slow drawl.

"Fetch me? What are you talking about? I'm not a dog or a maverick calf to be fetched."

"Maverick calf sounds pretty close. You're always running off in the wrong direction." Reaching out, he took her arm. "Come on, we're going for a ride." His voice was pleasant, but the steel was there. She jerked away, angry with his arrogance, wary of his tone.

"I have no intention of going anywhere with you. Why don't you just go away and leave me alone?"

"Now I can't do that, Sam," he returned in a reasonable tone. "We have some unfinished business to attend to. Your time's up."

The fire in her eyes flickered and died. "You can't be serious."

"I'm dead serious."

"What . . . what about Lesley?"

"She's not invited," he returned simply.

"I'm not going with you," she said, somewhere between terror and fury. "You can't make me."

Stopping, he looked down at her from his overpowering height. "Sure I can," he corrected with easy confidence. With a swift movement, he swung her over his shoulder. "See?" He walked effortlessly down the hall. "Nothing to it."

"Let me down!" Furious fists beat against his back. "This is crazy, it's illegal. I'll have you thrown in jail!"

"No kidding? Sam, you're scaring me to death."

He continued easily down the hall, as if he carried an empty sack rather than an irate woman who was thumping against his back. Pausing, he touched the brim of his hat as Sabrina appeared in the bedroom doorway, the baby in her arms.

"Morning, Sabrina." His greeting was genial, and he cocked his head to get a better view of Jennifer. "She's a real beauty."

"Thank you, Jake. We certainly think so." She shifted the baby and smiled. "Are you two going out?"

"Thought we'd go for a little ride," Jake informed her. "We may be gone some time."

"It's a fine day for it, hardly a cloud in the sky."

"Bree." Samantha's voice was desperate. "Don't just stand there, *do* something." She pushed at the hair which hung over her face. "Don't you see what he's doing? He's kidnapping me. Call the police, call Dan." She continued to plead as Jake touched the brim of his hat once more and moved down the hall. "Bree, say something."

"Have a good time," was her sister's surprising response.

Samantha's mouth fell open in dumb astonishment. A stream of imaginative curses was hurled on Jake's unperturbed head as he took the reins of his mount from a grinning cowboy.

"Looks like you got yourself a real handful there, Jake."

"No more than I can handle," he countered, swinging into the saddle with Samantha still held over his shoulder. With a speed which defied his easy-going manner, he had her in front of him in the saddle, spurring the horse into a gallop before she could think of escape.

"You're going to pay for this," Samantha promised, clutching the saddle horn to keep her balance. "You can't just run off with me this way!"

"I didn't see anybody try to stop me," Jake pointed out.

He followed the road for some time without decreasing his pace, then cut across an open field. At a small grove of trees, he reined in, gripping Samantha around the waist when she attempted to wiggle down.

"Now, don't do that, Sam," he warned in a friendly voice. "I'd just have to catch you, and I throw a mean lasso."

He slid from the chestnut, and before her feet could touch the ground, she was back over his shoulder. Without ceremony, she was dumped under the fragile, bending leaves of a willow while he towered over her, grinning with obvious enjoyment.

"You're going to be sorry," she predicted, smoldering with fury. "I'm going to..." The rest of her words slipped back down her throat as he dropped down next to her. "You—you can't do this, Jake. You're not the kind of man who forces himself on a woman."

"Who says?" Pushing her back on the soft grass, he covered her body with his.

Her body betrayed her with instant response. Her skin tingled as his mouth brushed over it. "You're not really going to do this."

"I told you once," his mouth moved to her ear, and his words were warm and soft against it, "not to forget your own words. There are some things you just have to do."

His kiss was long and lingering.

When her mouth was free, she drew in a deep breath and spat out with all her strength, "What kind of man are you to make love to one woman and plan to marry another?"

His eyes lazily narrowed. He propped himself on one elbow, his other arm pinning her down. Lifting his head from his elbow, he undid the top button of her blouse. "Suppose," he continued, moving down to the next button, "you tell me whom I'm supposed to marry."

His fingers trailed a slow line from her throat, down the smooth skin her open blouse revealed, and rested on the next button. The blood began to pound in her ears. His eyes alone held her still as he spread her blouse apart. Slowly, his fingers roamed up the warmth of her skin, moving with casual possession over her. Her eyes clouded with growing need as he explored.

"Tell me who I'm going to marry, Samantha." His body shifted again, molding to hers. His shirt was warm against her naked flesh.

"L—Lesley," she stammered.

"No." His mouth lowered to the curve of her throat, his tongue teasing the vulnerable skin.

She felt the waist of her jeans loosen under his hand. His finger pushed away the material and moved along her hip. With her last claim to lucidity, she pushed against his chest.

"Please stop."

"Now I just can't do that, Sam." His hands teased the curve of her hip, trailing back up to the side of her breast. "I've waited a good long time to get you where I want you."

"I'm not staying... Did you say you weren't marrying Lesley?"

He frowned down in consideration, winding her hair around his finger. "Seems to me I did mention that. I don't know why you're always piling your hair on top of your head when it looks so good spread all over."

"But she was wearing your ring."

"Not mine," Jake corrected, still concentrating on the hair around his fingers. "Your hair's gotten lighter these past few weeks, you haven't been wearing a hat. Les has a diamond, doesn't she? I told you once diamonds don't suit you. They're cold and they don't have much imagination. But that's Les." He shrugged and began to move his mouth over her face again. "It doesn't seem to matter to Jim."

Valiantly, Samantha attempted to follow his words. Her head shook with the effort.

"Les is engaged to Jim Bailey. I'm sure you remember Jim Bailey, you spent enough time with him at the party."

"Yes, but..."

"No buts," he interrupted. "Les likes to have a couple of fish on the line, and when she got it through her head I wasn't in season, she netted Jim without a struggle."

"But I thought..."

"I know what you thought." He cut her off again and smiled. "Running away a few days early, weren't you?"

"I wasn't running. How did you know I was leaving?"

"Sabrina told me."

"Bree?" Samantha whispered. Bree did that?

"Yeah, yesterday. She came to see me while you were packing. I like this spot right here," he stated, planting his lips against the hollow of her throat. "I've had a devil of a time putting things in order since then, so I could take time for a honeymoon. Busy time of year for a cattleman."

"Honeymoon?" Her skin was trembling where his lips continued to taste.

"I've got a good foreman," he continued, as if thinking aloud. "I reckon he can manage things for a while. I could use another day or two. I had a nice long honeymoon in mind, some place quiet." He brought his attention back to her stunned face. "You've never been to Bora Bora have you?"

"Are you talking about getting your ranch in order so you can take time off to marry me?" She attempted to speak slowly and clearly while her emotions whirled like a summer tornado.

"Just being practical," he explained with a bland smile.

"Why you conceited, overbearing... Just what makes you think I'll marry you? You sit back and make all these plans and expect me to run off to Bora Bora with you like a passive little puppy. Of all the chauvinist—"

"How about Antarctica?" he suggested, willing to be reasonable. "Not too many people there either."

"You're crazy. I never said I'd marry you. What makes you think..." Her tirade was cut off effectively as his mouth coaxed her silence. When he let her breathe, her voice had lost its strength. "That's not going to help you. I'm not in love with you."

"Seems to me I recall someone telling me she was a totally honest person." His gaze was disconcertingly direct. He held her chin, preventing her face from turning away. "You want to look at me and tell me that again? You've been fighting me all along, and I think I've just about used up my patience." His lips were teasing hers again, and his hands moved over her with more urgency. "Mmm, but you have a nice body. I can't take much more of this waiting around. Six months is a long time, Sam. I've wanted you from the minute you stood there ordering Dan to have his man tend to the horses."

"Yes, you let me know very early what you wanted." She no longer struggled but lay passive in his arms.

"Gave you something to think about. Of course, you didn't know I wanted you to be my wife, too. It was easy to tell you I wanted you, but a bit difficult to tell you I loved you. Sam, look at me." She shook her head, but the fingers on her chin tightened in authority. "Look at me." She obeyed, her lids opening to reveal eyes veiled with tears. "You stubborn little idiot. Listen carefully, I've never said this to another woman, and I've had to wait too long to say it to you. I love you so much it hurts to think about it. If you don't marry me soon, I'm going to lose my mind." His mouth took hers, spinning the world into nothing. Her arms flew around him as pain evaporated into unspeakable joy. "Samantha." He buried his face in the lushness of her hair. "It's been quite a race."

"I don't understand." She brought his face back to hers, needing to see the truth in his eyes. "Why didn't you tell me before?"

"I didn't think you'd believe that a man had nearly been knocked off his feet by a picture of a girl less than half his age, then had completely lost his balance when he saw the woman she'd become. If you hadn't been so wrapped up in Sabrina those first few minutes, you'd have seen how a man looks when he gets hit by lightning."

"Just like that?" Stunned, she traced the angles of his face to assure herself she was not dreaming.

"Just like that," he agreed, bringing her palm to his lips. "Then after I'd recovered a bit, I knew I had to work around your dedication to Sabrina until you'd figured out there was room in your life for someone else. Then you stood there telling me you were going back home as soon as the baby was born. I nearly strangled you." His fingers tightened on her hand as he brought his eyes back to hers. "How was I supposed to tell you that I loved you, that I wanted to marry you, wanted you to stay in Wyoming? The night of the party, in the kitchen, I made up my mind I wasn't letting you go no matter what I had to do to keep you."

"But I never wanted to leave." She shook her head in brisk denial, as if he should have realized it all along. "It was just that I couldn't bear to see you married to Lesley."

"You know, things might have gotten even more complicated if Sabrina hadn't come by and laid things out for me. She's got a bit more of you in her than I had thought." Laughing, he lifted his face from hers. "She told me to sit down and listen. She'd never seen two people run around in circles so long and get nowhere."

"It's not like Bree to interfere."

"She interfered beautifully. First thing she did was ask me what business I had getting engaged to Lesley. I must have stared at her like she'd lost her mind. After I managed to tell her I was definitely not engaged to Lesley, she let me have it with both barrels. Mixed with the buckshot was the information that you were miserable about going home, and that I was a fool for not seeing it myself. Then she folded her arms, stuck out her chin exactly like someone else has a habit of doing, and asked me what the devil I intended to do about it."

Samantha stared up at him and shook her head in astonishment. "I wish I could have seen that."

He smiled and lowered his mouth. "Just look in the mirror sometime." Flesh met flesh with no barriers, and with a small sound of desperation, he savaged her mouth. The hard lines of his chest pressed into her breasts. "Let me hear you say it, Samantha," he murmured, unable to resist the curve of her neck. "I need to hear you say it."

"I love you." Her mouth searched for his, her arms urging him closer. "I love you. I love you." Her lips found their objective, and her silence told him again.

"I need you, Samantha." His mouth and hands continued to seek, growing wilder, possessive, demanding. "I never knew I could need anyone the way I need you. I want you to myself for a while, no distractions, no complications, just you. We've got six months of loving to make up for. I'm going to keep you fully occupied for a very long time." Lifting his face, he smiled down at her, running his hand through the hair spread over the grass. "A very long time."

She smiled back, running her hands up his chest to circle his neck. "I intend to keep you occupied very well. Your cows are going to get very lonely." Removing his hat, she tossed it carelessly aside, then turned back to him with raised brows. "O.K., cowboy." Her arms lifted to lock around his neck, fingers tangling possessively in his hair. "Start occupying."

"Yes, ma'am." With a polite nod, he lowered his mouth and followed orders.

Silhouette Special Edition

proudly hails

WOMEN OF GLORY

from Lindsay McKenna

Soar with Dana Coulter, Molly Rutledge and Maggie Donovan—
Lindsay McKenna's WOMEN OF GLORY. On land, sea or air, these
three Annapolis grads challenge danger head-on, risking life and limb
for the glory of their country—and for the men they love!

May: NO QUARTER GIVEN (SE #667) Dana Coulter is on the brink
of achieving her lifelong dream of flying—and of meeting the man who
would love to take her to new heights!

June: THE GAUNTLET (SE #673) Molly Rutledge is determined
to excel on her own merit, but Captain Cameron Sinclair is equally
determined to take gentle Molly under his wing....

July: UNDER FIRE (SE #679) Indomitable Maggie never thought
her career—or her heart—would come under fire. But all that changes
when she teams up with Lieutenant Wes Bishop!

SEWG-1

SILHOUETTE·INTIMATE·MOMENTS™

IT'S TIME TO MEET
THE MARSHALLS!

In 1986, bestselling author Kristin James wrote A VERY SPECIAL FAVOR for the Silhouette Intimate Moments line. Hero Adam Marshall quickly became a reader favorite, and ever since then, readers have been asking for the stories of his two brothers, Tag and James. At last your prayers have been answered!

In June, look for Tag's story, SALT OF THE EARTH (IM #385). Then skip a month and look for THE LETTER OF THE LAW (IM #393—August), starring James Marshall. And, as our very special favor to you, we'll be reprinting A VERY SPECIAL FAVOR this September. Look for it in special displays wherever you buy books.

MARSH-1

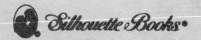
Silhouette Books®